The Metropolis

The Metropolis
UPTON SINCLAIR

ÆGYPAN PRESS

From the 1908 edition.

Upton Sinclair lived from 1878 until 1968.

The Metropolis
A publication of
ÆGYPAN PRESS

www.aegypan.com

Chapter I

"*R*eturn at ten-thirty," the General said to his chauffeur, and then they entered the corridor of the hotel.

Montague gazed about him, and found himself trembling just a little with anticipation. It was not the magnificence of the place. The quiet uptown hotel would have seemed magnificent to him, fresh as he was from the country; but, he did hot see the marblo columns and the gilded carvings — he was thinking of the men he was to meet. It seemed too much to crowd into one day — first the vision of the whirling, seething city, the center of all his hopes of the future; and then, at night, this meeting, overwhelming him with the crowded memories of everything that he held precious in the past.

There were groups of men in faded uniforms standing about in the corridors. General Prentice bowed here and there as they retired and took the elevator to the reception-rooms. In the doorway they passed a stout little man with stubby white moustaches, and the General stopped, exclaiming, "Hello, Major!" Then he added: "Let me introduce Mr. Allan Montague. Montague, this is Major Thorne."

A look of sudden interest flashed across the Major's face. "General Montague's son?" he cried. And then he seized the other's hand in both of his, exclaiming, "My boy! my boy! I'm glad to see you!"

Now Montague was no boy — he was a man of thirty, and rather sedate in his appearance and manner; there was enough in his six feet one to have made two of the round and rubicund little Major. And yet it seemed to him quite proper that the other should address him so. He was back in his boyhood tonight — he was a boy whenever anyone mentioned the name of Major Thorne.

"Perhaps you have heard your father speak of me?" asked the Major, eagerly; and Montague answered, "A thousand times."

He was tempted to add that the vision that rose before him was of a stout gentleman hanging in a grape-vine, while a whole battery of artillery made him their target.

Perhaps it was irreverent, but that was what Montague had always thought of, ever since he had first laughed over the tale his father told. It had happened one January afternoon in the Wilderness, during the terrible battle of Chancellorsville, when Montague's father had been a rising young staff-officer, and it had fallen to his lot to carry to Major Thorne what was surely the most terrifying order that ever a cavalry officer received. It was in the crisis of the conflict, when the Army of the Potomac was reeling before the onslaught of Stonewall Jackson's columns. There was no one to stop them — and yet they must be stopped, for the whole right wing of the army was going. So that cavalry regiment had charged full tilt through the thickets, and into a solid wall of infantry and artillery. The crash of their volley was blinding — and horses wore fairly shot to fragments; and the Major's horse, with its lower jaw torn off, had plunged madly away and left its rider hanging in the aforementioned grape-vine. After he had kicked himself loose, it was to find himself in an arena where pain-maddened horses and frenzied men raced about amid a rain of minie-balls and canister. And in this inferno the gallant Major had captured a horse, and rallied the remains of his shattered command, and held the line until help came — and then helped to hold it, all through the afternoon and the twilight and the night, against charge after charge. — And now to stand and gaze at this stout and red-nosed little personage, and realize that these mighty deeds had been his!

Then, even while Montague was returning his hand-clasp and telling him of his pleasure, the Major's eye caught someone across the room, and he called eagerly, "Colonel Anderson! Colonel Anderson!"

And this was the heroic Jack Anderson! "Parson" Anderson, the men had called him, because he always prayed before everything he did. Prayers at each mess, — a prayer-meeting in the evening, — and then rumor said the Colonel prayed on while his men slept. With his battery of artillery trained to perfection under three years of divine guidance, the gallant Colonel had stood in the line of battle at Cold Harbor — name of frightful memory! — and when the enemy had swarmed out of their entrenchments and swept back the whole line just beyond him, his battery had stood like a cape in a storm-beaten ocean, attacked on two sides at once; and for the half-hour that elapsed before infantry support came up, the Colonel had ridden slowly up and down his line, repeating in calm and godly accents, "Give 'em hell, boys — give 'em hell!" — The Colonel's hand trembled now as he held it out, and his voice was shrill and cracked as he told what pleasure it gave him to meet General Montague's son.

"Why have we never seen you before?" asked Major Thorne. Montague replied that he had spent all his life in Mississippi — his father having married a Southern woman after the war. Once every year the General had come to New York to attend the reunion of the Loyal Legion of the State; but someone had had to stay at home with his mother, Montague explained.

There were perhaps a hundred men in the room, and he was passed about from group to group. Many of them had known his father intimately. It seemed almost uncanny to him to meet them in the body; to find them old and feeble, white-haired and wrinkled. As they lived in the chambers of his memory, they were in their mighty youth-heroes, transfigured and radiant, not subject to the power of time.

Life on the big plantation had been a lonely one, especially for a Southern-born man who had fought in the Union army. General Montague had been a person of quiet tastes, and his greatest pleasure had been to sit with his two boys on his knees and "fight his battles o'er again." He had collected all the literature of the corps which he had commanded — a whole library of it, in which Allan had learned to find his way as soon as he could read. He had literally been brought up on the war — for hours he would lie buried in some big illustrated history, until people came and called him away. He studied maps of campaigns and battlefields, until they became alive with human passion and struggle; he knew the Army of the Potomac by brigade and division, with the names of commanders, and their faces, and their ways — until they lived and spoke, and the bare roll of their names had power to thrill him. — And now here were the men themselves, and all these scenes and memories crowding upon him in tumultuous throngs. No wonder that he was a little dazed, and could hardly find words to answer when he was spoken to.

But then came an incident which called him suddenly back to the world of the present. "There is Judge Ellis," said the General.

Judge Ellis! The fame of his wit and eloquence had reached even far Mississippi — was there any remotest corner of America where men had not heard of the silver tongue of Judge Ellis? "Cultivate him!" Montague's brother Oliver had laughed, when it was mentioned that the Judge would be present — "Cultivate him — he may be useful."

It was not difficult to cultivate one who was as gracious as Judge Ellis. He stood in the doorway, a smooth, perfectly groomed gentleman, conspicuous in the uniformed assembly by his evening dress. The Judge was stout and jovial, and cultivated Dundreary whiskers and a beaming smile. "General Montague's son!" he exclaimed, as he pressed the young man's hands. "Why, why — I'm surprised! Why have we never seen you before?"

Montague explained that he had only been in New York about six hours. "Oh, I see," said the Judge. "And shall you remain long?"

"I have come to stay," was the reply.

"Well, well!" said the other, cordially. "Then we may see more of you. Are you going into business?"

"I am a lawyer," said Montague. "I expect to practice."

The Judge's quick glance had been taking the measure of the tall, handsome man before him, with his raven-black hair and grave features. "You must give us a chance to try your mettle," he said; and then, as others approached to meet him, and he was forced to pass on, he laid a caressing hand on Montague's arm, whispering, with a sly smile, "I mean it."

Montague felt his heart beat a little faster. He had not welcomed his brother's suggestion — there was nothing of the sycophant in him; but he meant to work and to succeed, and he knew what the favor of a man like Judge Ellis would mean to him. For the Judge was the idol of New York's business and political aristocracy, and the doorways of fortune yielded at his touch.

There were rows of chairs in one of the rooms, and here two or three hundred men were gathered. There were stands of battle-flags in the corners, each one of them a scroll of tragic history, to one like Montague, who understood. His eye roamed over them while the secretary was reading minutes of meetings and other routine announcements. Then he began to study the assemblage. There were men with one arm and men with one leg — one tottering old soldier ninety years of age, stone blind, and led about by his friends. The Loyal Legion was an officers' organization, and to that extent aristocratic; but worldly success counted for nothing in it — some of its members were struggling to exist on their pensions, and were as much thought of as a man like General Prentice, who was president of one of the city's largest banks, and a rich man, even in New York's understanding of that term.

The presiding officer introduced "Colonel Robert Gelden, who will read the paper of the evening: 'Recollections of Spottsylvania.'" Montague started at the name — for "Bob" Selden had been one of his father's messmates, and had fought all through the Peninsula Campaign at his side.

He was a tall, hawk-faced man with a grey imperial. The room was still as he arose, and after adjusting his glasses, he began to read his story. He recalled the situation of the Army of the Potomac in the spring of 1846; for three years it had marched and fought, stumbling through defeat after defeat, a mighty weapon, lacking only a man who could wield it. Now at last the man had come — one who would put them into the battle and give them a chance to fight. So they had marched into the Wilderness, and there Lee struck them, and for three days they groped in a blind thicket, fighting hand to hand, amid suffocating smoke. The Colonel read in a quiet, unassuming voice; but one could see that he had hold of his hearers by the light that crossed their features when he told of the army's recoil from the shock, and of the wild joy that ran through the ranks when they took up their march to the left, and realized that this time they were not going back. — So they came to the twelve days' grapple of the Spottsylvania Campaign.

There was still the Wilderness thicket; the enemy's entrenchments, covering about eight miles, lay in the shape of a dome, and at the cupola of it were breastworks of heavy timbers banked with earth, and with a ditch and a tangle of trees in front. The place was the keystone of the Confederate arch, and the name of it was "the Angle" — "Bloody Angle!" Montague heard the man who sat next to him draw in his breath, as if a spasm of pain had shot through him.

At dawn two brigades had charged and captured the place. The enemy returned to the attack, and for twenty hours thereafter the two armies fought, hurling regiment after regiment and brigade after brigade into the trenches. There was a pouring rain, and the smoke hung black about them; they could only see the flashes of the guns, and the faces of the enemy, here and there.

The Colonel described the approach of his regiment. They lay down for a moment in a swamp, and the minie-balls sang like swarming bees, and split the blades of the grass above them. Then they charged, over ground that ran with human blood. In the trenches the bodies of dead and dying men lay three deep, and were trampled out of sight in the mud by the feet of those who fought. They would crouch behind the works, lifting their guns high over their heads, and firing into the throngs on the other side; again and again men sprang upon the breastworks and fired their muskets, and then fell dead. They dragged up cannon, one after another, and blew holes through the logs, and raked the ground with charges of canister.

While the Colonel read, still in his calm, matter-of-fact voice, you might see men leaning forward in their chairs, hands clenched, teeth set. They knew! They knew! Had there ever before been a time in history when breastworks had been charged by artillery? Twenty-four men in the crew of one gun, and only two unhurt! One iron sponge-bucket with thirty-nine bullet holes shot through it! And then blasts of canister sweeping the trenches, and blowing scores of living and dead men to fragments! And into this hell of slaughter new regiments charging, in lines four deep! And squad after squad of the enemy striving to surrender, and shot to pieces by their own comrades as they clambered over the blood-soaked walls! And heavy timbers in the defenses shot to splinters! Huge oak trees — one of them twenty-four inches in diameter — crashing down upon the combatants, gnawed through by rifle-bullets! Since the world began had men ever fought like that?

Then the Colonel told of his own wound in the shoulder, and how, toward dusk, he had crawled away; and how he became lost, and strayed into the enemy's line, and was thrust into a batch of prisoners and marched to the rear. And then of the night that he spent beside a hospital camp in the Wilderness, where hundreds of wounded and dying men lay about on the rain-soaked ground, moaning, screaming, praying to be killed. Again the prisoners were moved, having been ordered to march to the railroad; and on the way the Colonel went blind from suffering and exhaustion, and staggered and fell in the road. You could have heard a pin drop in the room, in the pause between sentences in his story, as he told how the guard argued with him to persuade him to go on. It was their duty to kill him if he refused, but they could not bring themselves to do it. In the end they left the job to one, and he stood and cursed the officer, trying to get up his courage; and finally fired his gun into the air, and went off and left him.

Then he told how an old Negro had found him, and how he lay delirious; and how, at last, the army marched his way. He ended his narrative the simple sentence: "It was not until the siege of Petersburg that I was able to rejoin my Command."

There was a murmur of applause; and then silence. Suddenly, from somewhere in the room, came the sound of singing — "Mine eyes have seen the glory of the coming of the Lord!" The old battle-hymn seemed to strike the very mood of the meeting; the whole throng took it up, and they sang it, stanza by stanza. It was rolling forth like a mighty organ-chant as they came to the fervid closing: —

"He hath sounded forth the trumpet that shall never call retreat; He is sifting out the hearts of men before his judgment seat; Oh! be swift, my soul, to answer Him; be jubilant, my feet, — Our God is marching on!"

There was a pause again; and the presiding officer rose and said that, owing to the presence of a distinguished guest, they would forego one of their rules, and invite Judge Ellis to say a few words. The Judge came forward, and bowed his acknowledgment of their welcome. Then, perhaps feeling a need of relief after the somber recital, the Judge took occasion to apologize for his own temerity in addressing a roomful of warriors; and somehow he managed to make that remind him of a story of an army mule, a very amusing story; and that reminded him of another story, until, when he stopped and sat down, everyone in the room broke into delighted applause.

They went in to dinner. Montague sat by General Prentice, and he, in turn, by the Judge; the latter was reminded of more stories during the dinner, and kept everyone near him laughing. Finally Montague was moved to tell a story himself — about an old Negro down home, who passed himself off for an Indian. The Judge was so good as to consider this an immensely funny story, and asked permission to tell it himself. Several times after that he leaned over and spoke to Montague, who felt a slight twinge of guilt as he recalled his brother's cynical advice, "Cultivate him!" The Judge was so willing to be cultivated, however, that it gave one's conscience little chance.

They went back to the meeting-room again; chairs were shifted, and little groups formed, and cigars and pipes brought out. They moved the precious battle-flags forward, and someone produced a bugle and a couple of drums; then the walls of the place shook, as the whole company burst forth: —

"Bring the good old bugle, boys! we'll sing another song — Sing it with a spirit that will start the world along — Sing it as we used to sing it, fifty thousand strong, — While we were marching through Georgia!"

It was wonderful to witness the fervor with which they went through this rollicking chant — whose spirit we miss because we hear it too often. They were not skilled musicians — they could only sing loud; but the fire leaped into their eyes, and they swayed with the rhythm, and sang! Montague found himself watching the old blind soldier, who sat beating his foot in time, upon his face the look of one who sees visions.

And then he noticed another man, a little, red-faced Irishman, one of the drummers. The very spirit of the drum seemed to have entered into him — into his hands and his feet, his eyes and his head, and his round little body. He played a long roll between the verses, and it seemed as if he must surely be swept away upon the wings of it. Catching Montague's eye, he nodded and smiled; and after that, every once in a while their eyes would meet and exchange a greeting. They sang "The Loyal Legioner" and "The Army Bean" and "John Brown's Body" and "Tramp, tramp, tramp, the boys are marching"; all the while the drum rattled and thundered, and the little drummer laughed and sang, the very incarnation of the carefree spirit of the soldier!

They stopped for a while, and the little man came over and was introduced. Lieutenant O'Day was his name; and after he had left, General Prentice leaned over to Montague and told him a story. "That little man," he said, "began as a drummer-boy in my regiment, and went all through the war in my brigade; and two years ago I met him on the street one cold winter night, as thin as I am, and shivering in a summer overcoat. I took him to dinner with me and watched him eat, and I made up my mind there was something wrong. I made him take me home, and do you know, the man was starving! He had a little tobacco shop, and he'd got into trouble — the trust had taken away his trade. And he had a sick wife, and a daughter clerking at six dollars a week!"

The General went on to tell of his struggle to induce the little man to accept his aid — to accept a loan of a few hundreds of dollars from Prentice, the banker! "I never had anything hurt me so in all my life," he said. "Finally I took him into the bank — and now you can see he has enough to eat!"

They began to sing again, and Montague sat and thought over the story. It seemed to him typical of the thing that made this meeting beautiful to him — of the spirit of brotherhood and service that reigned here. — They sang "We are tenting tonight on the old camp ground"; they sang "Benny Havens, Oh!" and "A Soldier No More"; they sang other songs of tenderness and sorrow, and men felt a trembling in their voices and a mist stealing over their eyes. Upon Montague a spell was falling.

Over these men and their story there hung a mystery — a presence of wonder, that discloses itself but rarely to mortals, and only to those who have dreamed and dared. They had not found it easy to do their duty; they had had their wives and children, their homes and friends and familiar places; and all these they had left to serve the Republic. They had taught themselves a new way of life — they had forged themselves into an iron sword of war. They had marched and fought in dust and heat, in pouring rains and driving, icy blasts; they had become men grim and terrible in spirit-men with limbs of steel, who could march or ride for days and nights, who could lie down and sleep upon the ground in rain-storms and winter snows, who were ready to leap at a word and seize their muskets and rush into the cannon's mouth. They had learned to stare into the face of death, to meet its fiery eyes; to march and eat and sleep, to laugh and play and sing, in its presence — to carry their life in their hands, and toss it about as a juggler tosses a ball. And this for Freedom: for the star-crowned goddess with the flaming eyes, who trod upon the mountaintops and called to them in the shock and fury of the battle; whose trailing robes they followed through the dust and cannon-smoke; for a glimpse of whose shining face they had kept the long night vigils and charged upon the guns in the morning; for a touch of whose shimmering robe they had wasted in prison pens, where famine and loathsome pestilence and raving madness stalked about in the broad daylight.

And now this army of deliverance, with its waving banners and its prancing horses and its rumbling cannon, had marched into the shadow-world. The very ground that it had trod was sacred; and one who fingered the dusty volumes which held the record of its deeds would feel a strange awe come upon him, and thrill with a sudden fear of life — that was so fleeting and so little to be understood. There were boyhood memories in Montague's mind, of hours of consecration, when the vision had descended upon him, and he had sat with face hidden in his hands.

It was for the Republic that these men had suffered; for him and his children — that a government of the people, by the people, for the people, might not perish from the earth. And with the organ-music of the Gettysburg Address echoing within him, the boy laid his soul upon the altar of his country. They had done so much for him — and now, was there anything that he could do? A dozen years had passed since then, and still he knew that deep within him — deeper than all other purposes, than all thoughts of wealth and fame and power — was the purpose that the men who had died for the Republic should find him worthy of their trust.

The singing had stopped, and Judge Ellis was standing before him. The Judge was about to go, and in his caressing voice he said that he would hope to see Montague again. Then, seeing that General Prentice was also standing up, Montague threw off the spell that had gripped him, and shook hands with the little drummer, and with Selden and Anderson and all the others of his dream people. A few minutes later he found himself outside the hotel, drinking deep drafts of the cold November air.

Major Thorne had come out with them; and learning that the General's route lay uptown, he offered to walk with Montague to his hotel.

They set out, and then Montague told the Major about the figure in the grape-vine, and the Major laughed and told how it had felt. There had been more adventures, it seemed; while he was hunting a horse he had come upon two mules loaded with ammunition and entangled with their harness about a tree; he had rushed up to seize them — when a solid shot had struck the tree and exploded the ammunition and blown the mules to fragments. And then there was the story of the charge late in the night, which had recovered the lost ground, and kept Stonewall Jackson busy up to the very hour of his tragic death. And there was the story of Andersonville, and the escape from prison. Montague could have walked the streets all night, exchanging these war-time reminiscences with the Major.

Absorbed in their talk, they came to an avenue given up to the poorer class of people; with elevated trains rattling by overhead, and rows of little shops along it. Montague noticed a dense crowd on one of the corners, land asked what it meant.

"Some sort of a meeting," said the Major.

They came nearer, and saw a torch, with a man standing near it, above the heads of the crowd.

"It looks like a political meeting," said Montague, "but it can't be, now — just after election."

"Probably it's a Socialist," said the Major. "They're at it all the time."

They crossed the avenue, and then they could see plainly. The man was lean and hungry-looking, and he had long arms, which he waved with prodigious violence. He was in a frenzy of excitement, pacing this way and that, and leaning over the throng packed about him. Because of a passing train the two could not hear a sound.

"A Socialist!" exclaimed Montague, wonderingly. "What do they want?"

"I'm not sure," said the other. "They want to overthrow the government."

The train passed, and then the man's words came to them: "They force you to build palaces, and then they put you into tenements! They force you to spin fine raiment, and then they dress you in rags! They force you to build jails, and then they lock you up in them! They force you to make guns, and then they shoot you with them! They own the political parties, and they name the candidates, and trick you into voting for them — and they call it the law! They herd you into armies and send you to shoot your brothers — and they call it order! They take a piece of colored rag and call it the flag and teach you to let yourself be shot — and they call it patriotism! First, last, and all the time, you do the work and they get the benefit — they, the masters and owners, and you — fools — fools — fools!"

The man's voice had mounted to a scream, and he flung his hands into the air and broke into jeering laughter. Then came another train, and Montague could not hear him; but he could see that he was rushing on in the torrent of his denunciation.

Montague stood rooted to the spot; he was shocked to the depths of his being — he could scarcely contain himself as he stood there. He longed to spring forward to beard the man where he stood, to shout him down, to rebuke him before the crowd.

The Major must have seen his agitation, for he took his arm and led him back from the throng, saying: "Come! We can't help it."

"But — but —," he protested, "the police ought to arrest him."

"They do sometimes," said the Major, "but it doesn't do any good."

They walked on, and the sounds of the shrill voice died away. "Tell me," said Montague, in a low voice, "does that go on very often?"

"Around the comer from where I live," said the other, "it goes on every Saturday night."

"And do the people listen?" he asked.

"Sometimes they can't keep the street clear," was the reply.

And again they walked in silence. At last Montague asked, "What does it mean?"

The Major shrugged his shoulders. "Perhaps another civil war," said he.

Chapter II

*A*llan Montague's father had died about five years before. A couple of years later his younger brother, Oliver, had announced his intention of seeking a career in New York. He had no profession, and no definite plans; but his father's friends were men of influence and wealth, and the doors were open to him. So he had turned his share of the estate into cash and departed.

Oliver was a gay and pleasure-loving boy, with all the material of a prodigal son in him; his brother had more than half expected to see him come back in a year or two with empty pockets. But New York had seemed to agree with Oliver. He never told what he was doing — what he wrote was simply that he was managing to keep the wolf from the door. But his letters hinted at expensive ways of life; and at Christmas time, and at Cousin Alice's birthday, he would send home presents which made the family stare.

Montague had always thought of himself as a country lawyer and planter. But two months ago a fire had swept away the family mansion, and then on top of that had come an offer for the land; and with Oliver telegraphing several times a day in his eagerness, they had taken the sudden resolution to settle up their affairs and move to New York.

There were Montague and his mother, and Cousin Alice, who was nineteen, and old "Mammy Lucy," Mrs. Montague's servant. Oliver had met them at Jersey City, radiant with happiness. He looked just as much of a boy as ever, and just as beautiful; excepting that he was a little paler, New York had not changed him at all. There was a man in uniform from the hotel to take charge of their baggage, and a big red touring-car for them; and now they were snugly settled in their apartments, with the younger brother on duty as counselor and guide.

Montague had come to begin life all over again. He had brought his money, and he expected to invest it, and to live upon the income until he had begun to earn something. He had worked hard at his profession, and he meant to work in New York, and to win his way in the end. He knew almost nothing about the city — he faced it with the wide-open eyes of a child.

One began to learn quickly, he found. It was like being swept into a maelstrom: first the hurrying throngs on the ferry-boat, and then the cabmen and the newsboys shouting, and the cars with clanging gongs; then the swift motor, gliding between trucks and carriages and around corners where big policemen shepherded the scurrying populace; and then Fifth Avenue, with its rows of shops and towering hotels; and at last a sudden swing round a corner — and their home.

"I have picked a quiet family place for you," Oliver had said, and that had greatly pleased his brother. But he had stared in dismay when he entered this latest "apartment hotel" — which catered for two or three hundred of the most exclusive of the city's aristocracy — and noted its great arcade, with massive doors of bronze, and its entrance-hall, trimmed with Caen stone and Italian marble, and roofed with a vaulted ceiling painted by modern masters. Men in livery bore their wraps and bowed the way before them; a great bronze elevator shot them to the proper floor; and they went to their rooms down a corridor walled with blood-red marble and paved with carpet soft as a cushion. Here were six rooms of palatial size, with carpets, drapery, and furniture of a splendor quite appalling to Montague.

As soon as the man who bore their wraps had left the room, he turned upon his brother.

"Oliver," he said, "how much are we paying for all this?"

Oliver smiled. "You are not paying anything, old man," he replied. "You're to be my guests for a month or two, until you get your bearings."

"That's very good of you," said the other; "— we'll talk about it later. But meantime, tell me what the apartment costs."

And then Montague encountered his first full charge of New York dynamite. "Six hundred dollars a week," said Oliver.

He started as if his brother had struck him. "Six hundred dollars a week!" he gasped.

"Yes," said the other, quietly.

It was fully a minute before he could find his breath. "Brother," he exclaimed, "you're mad!"

"It is a very good bargain," smiled the other; "I have some influence with them."

Again there was a pause, while Montague groped for words. "Oliver," he exclaimed, "I can't believe you! How could you think that we could pay such a price?"

"I didn't think it," said Oliver; "I told you I expected to pay it myself."

"But how could we let you pay it for us?" cried the other. "Can you fancy that *I* will ever earn enough to pay such a price?"

"Of course you will," said Oliver. "Don't be foolish, Allan — you'll find it's easy enough to make money in New York. Leave it to me, and wait awhile."

But the other was not to be put off. He sat down on the embroidered silk bedspread, and demanded abruptly, "What do you expect my income to be a year?"

"I'm sure I don't know," laughed Oliver; "nobody takes the time to add up his income. You'll make what you need, and something over for good measure. This one thing you'll know for certain — the more you spend, the more you'll be able to make."

And then, seeing that the sober look was not to be expelled from his brother's face, Oliver seated himself and crossed his legs, and proceeded to set forth the paradoxical philosophy of extravagance. His brother had come into a city of millionaires. There was a certain group of people — "the right set," was Oliver's term for them — and among them he would find that money was as free as air. So far as his career was concerned, he would find that there was nothing in all New York so costly as economy. If he did not live like a gentleman, he would find himself excluded from the circle of the elect — and how he would manage to exist then was a problem too difficult for his brother to face.

And so, as quickly as he could, he was to bring himself to a state of mind where things did not surprise him; where he did what others did and paid what others paid, and did it serenely, as if he had done it all his life. He would soon find his place; meantime all he had to do was to put himself into his brother's charge. "You'll find in time that I have the strings in my hands," the latter added. "Just take life easy, and let me introduce you to the right people."

All of which sounded very attractive. "But are you sure," asked

Montague, "that you understand what I'm here for? I don't want to get into the Four Hundred, you know — I want to practice law."

"In the first place," replied Oliver, "don't talk about the Four Hundred — it's vulgar and silly; there's no such thing. In the next place, you're going to live in New York, and you want to know the right people. If you know them, you can practice law, or practice billiards, or practice anything else that you fancy. If you don't know them, you might as well go practice in Dahomey, for all you can accomplish. You might come on here and start in for yourself, and in twenty years you wouldn't get as far as you can get in two weeks, if you'll let me attend to it."

Montague was nearly five years his brother's senior, and at home had taken a semi-paternal attitude toward him. Now, however, the situation seemed to have reversed itself. With a slight smile of amusement, he subsided, and proceeded to put himself into the attitude of a docile student of the mysteries of the Metropolis.

They agreed that they would say nothing about these matters to the others. Mrs. Montague was half blind, and would lead her placid, indoor existence with old Mammy Lucy. As for Alice, she was a woman, and would not trouble herself with economics; if fairy godmothers chose to shower gifts upon her, she would take them.

Alice was built to live in a palace, anyway, Oliver said. He had cried out with delight when he first saw her. She had been sixteen when he left, and tall and thin; now she was nineteen, and with the pale tints of the dawn in her hair and face. In the auto, Oliver had turned and, stared at her, and pronounced the cryptic judgment, "You'll go!"

Just now she was wandering about the rooms, exclaiming with wonder. Everything here was so quiet and so harmonious that at first one's suspicions were lulled. It was simplicity, but of a strange and perplexing kind — simplicity elaborately studied. It was luxury, but grown assured of itself, and gazing down upon itself with aristocratic disdain. And after a while this began to penetrate the vulgarest mind, and to fill it with awe; one cannot remain long in an apartment which is trimmed and furnished in rarest Circassian walnut, and "papered" with hand-embroidered silk cloth, without feeling some excitement — even though there be no one to mention that the furniture has cost eight thousand dollars per room, and that the wall covering has been imported from Paris at a cost of seventy dollars per yard.

Montague also betook himself to gazing about. He noted the great double windows, with sashes of bronze; the bronze fire-proof doors; the bronze electric candles and chandeliers, from which the room was flooded with a soft radiance at the touch of a button; the "duchesse" and "marquise" chairs, with upholstery matching the walls; the huge leather "slumber-couch," with adjustable lamp at its head. When one opened the door of the dressing-room closet, it was automatically filled with light; there was an adjustable three-sided mirror, at which one could study his own figure from every side. There was a little bronze box near the bed, in which one might set his shoes, and with a locked door opening out into the hall, so that the floor-porter could get them without disturbing one. Each of the bathrooms was the size of an ordinary man's parlor, with floor and walls of snow-white marble, and a door composed of an imported plate-glass mirror. There was a great porcelain tub, with glass handles upon the wall by which you could help yourself out of it, and a shower-bath with linen duck curtains, which were changed every day; and a marble slab upon which you might lie to be rubbed by the masseur who would come at the touch of a button.

There was no end to the miracles of this establishment, as Montague found in the course of time. There was no chance that the antique bronze clock on the mantel might go wrong, for it was electrically controlled from the office. You did not open the window and let in the dust, for the room was automatically ventilated, and you turned a switch marked "hot" and "cold." The office would furnish you a guide who would show you the establishment; and you might see your bread being kneaded by electricity, upon an opal glass table, and your eggs being tested by electric light; you might peer into huge refrigerators, ventilated by electric fans, and in which each tiny lamb chop reposed in a separate holder. Upon your own floor was a pantry, provided with hot and cold storage-rooms and an air-tight dumb-waiter; you might have your own private linen and crockery and plate, and your own family butler, if you wished. Your children, however, would not be permitted in the building, even though you were dying — this was a small concession which you made to a host who had invested a million dollars and a half in furniture alone.

A few minutes later the telephone bell rang, and Oliver answered it and said, "Send him up."

"Here's the tailor," ho remarked, as he hung up the receiver.

"Whose tailor?" asked his brother.

"Yours," said he.

"Do I have to have some new clothes?" Montague asked.

"You haven't any clothes at present," was the reply.

Montague was standing in front of the "costumer," as the elaborate mirror was termed. He looked himself over, and then he looked at his brother. Oliver's clothing was a little like the Circassian walnut; at first you thought that it was simple, and even a trifle careless — it was only by degrees you realized that it was original and distinguished, and very expensive.

"Won't your New York friends make allowance for the fact that I am fresh from the country?" asked Montague, quizzically.

"They might," was the reply. "I know a hundred who would lend me money, if I asked them. But I don't ask them."

"Then how soon shall I be able to appear?" asked Montague, with visions of himself locked up in the room for a week or two.

"You are to have three suits tomorrow morning," said Oliver. "Genet has promised."

"Suits made to order?" gasped the other, in perplexity.

"He never heard of any other sort of suits," said Oliver, with grave rebuke in his voice.

M. Genet had the presence of a Russian grand duke, and the manner of a court chamberlain. He brought a subordinate to take Montague's measure, while he himself studied his color-scheme. Montague gathered from the conversation that he was going to a house-party in the country the next morning, and that he would need a dress-suit, a hunting-suit, and a "morning coat." The rest might wait until his return. The two discussed him and his various "points" as they might have discussed a horse; he possessed distinction, he learned, and a great deal could be done with him — with a little skill he might be made into a personality. His French was not in training, but he managed to make out that it was M. Genet's opinion that the husbands of New York would tremble when he made his appearance among them.

When the tailor had left, Alice came in, with her face shining from a cold bathing. "Here you are decking yourselves out!" she cried. "And what about me?"

"Your problem is harder," said Oliver, with a laugh; "but you begin this afternoon. Reggie Mann is going to take you with him, and get you some dresses."

"What!" gasped Alice. "Get me some dresses! A man?"

"Of course," said the other. "Reggie Mann advises half the women in New York about their clothes."

"Who is he? A tailor?" asked the girl.

Oliver was sitting on the edge of the canapé, swinging one leg over the other; and he stopped abruptly and stared, and then sank back, laughing softly to himself. "Oh, dear me!" he said. "Poor Reggie!"

Then, realizing that he would have to begin at the beginning, he proceeded to explain that Reggie Mann was a cotillion leader, the idol of the feminine side of society. He was the special pet and protégé of the great Mrs. de Graffenried, of whom they had surely heard — Mrs. de Graffenried, who was acknowledged to be the mistress of society at Newport, and was destined some day to be mistress in New York. Reggie and Oliver were "thick," and he had stayed in town on purpose to attend to her attiring — having seen her picture, and vowed that he would make a work of art out of her. And then Mrs. Robbie Walling would give her a dance; and all the world would come to fall at her feet.

"You and I are going out to 'Black Forest,' the Wallings' shooting-lodge, tomorrow," Oliver added to his brother. "You'll meet Mrs. Robbie there. You've heard of the Wallings, I hope."

"Yes," said Montague, "I'm not that ignorant."

"All right," said the other, "we're to motor down. I'm going to take you in my racing-car, so you'll have an experience. We'll start early."

"I'll be ready," said Montague; and when his brother replied that he would be at the door at eleven, he made another amused note as to the habits of New Yorkers.

The price which he paid at the hotel included the services of a valet or a maid for each of them, and so when their baggage arrived they had nothing to do. They went to lunch in one of the main dining rooms of the hotel, a room with towering columns of dark-green marble and a maze of palms and flowers. Oliver did the ordering; his brother noticed that the simple meal cost them about fifteen dollars, and he wondered if they were to eat at that rate all the time.

Then Montague mentioned the fact that before leaving home he had received a telegram from General Prentice, asking him to go with him that evening to the meeting of the Loyal Legion. Montague wondered, half amused, if his brother would deem his old clothing fit for such a function. But Oliver replied that it would not matter what he wore there; he would not meet anyone who counted, except Prentice himself. The General and his family were prominent in society, it appeared, and were to be cultivated. But Oliver shrewdly forbore to elaborate upon this, knowing that his brother would be certain to talk about old times, which would be the surest possible method of lodging himself in the good graces of General Prentice.

After luncheon came Reggie Mann, dapper and exquisite, with slender little figure and mincing gait, and the delicate hands and soft voice of a woman. He was dressed for the afternoon parade, and wore a wonderful scarlet orchid in his buttonhole. Montague's hand he shook at his shoulder's height; but when Alice came in he did not shake hands with her. Instead, he stood and gazed, and gazed again, and lifting his hands a little with excess of emotion, exclaimed, "Oh, perfect! perfect!"

"And Ollie, I told you so!" he added, eagerly. "She is tall enough to wear satin! She shall have the pale blue Empire gown — she shall have the pale blue Empire gown if I have to pay for it myself! And oh, what times we shall have with that hair! And the figure — Reval will simply go wild!"

So Reggie prattled on, with his airy grace; he took her hand and studied it, and then turned her about to survey her figure, while Alice blushed and strove to laugh to hide her embarrassment. "My dear Miss Montague," he exclaimed, "I bring all Gotham and lay it at your feet! Ollie, your battle is won! Won without firing a shot! I know the very man for her — his father is dying, and he will have four millions in Transcontinental alone. And he is as handsome as Antinous and as fascinating as Don Juan! Allons! we may as well begin with the trousseau this afternoon!"

Chapter III

Oliver was not rooming with them; he had his own quarters at the club, which he did not wish to leave. But the next morning, about twenty minutes after the hour he had named, he was at the door, and Montague went down.

Oliver's car was an imported French racer. It had only two seats, open in front, with a rumble behind for the mechanic. It was long and low and rakish, a most wicked-looking object; whenever it stopped on the street a crowd gathered to stare at it. Oliver was clad in a black bearskin coat, covering his feet, and with cap and gloves to match; he wore goggles, pushed up over his forehead. A similar costume lay ready in his brother's seat.

The suits of clothing had come, and were borne in his grips by his valet. "We can't carry them with us," said Oliver. "He'll have to take them down by train." And while his brother was buttoning up the coat, he gave the address; then Montague clambered in, and after a quick glance over his shoulder, Oliver pressed a lever and threw over the steering-wheel, and they whirled about and sped down the street.

Sometimes, at home in Mississippi, one would meet automobiling parties, generally to the damage of one's harness and temper. But until the day before, when he had stepped off the ferry, Montague had never ridden in a motorcar. Riding in this one was like traveling in a dream — it slid along without a sound, or the slightest trace of vibration; it shot forward, it darted to right or to left, it slowed up, it stopped, as if of its own will — the driver seemed to do nothing. Such things as car tracks had no effect upon it at all, and serious defects in the pavement caused only the faintest swelling motion; it was only when it leaped ahead like a living thing that one felt the power of it, by the pressure upon his back.

They went at what seemed to Montague a breakneck pace through the city streets, dodging among trucks .and carriages, grazing cars, whirling round corners, taking the wildest of chances. Oliver seemed always to know what the other fellow would do; but the thought that he might do something different kept his companion's heart pounding in a painful way. Once the latter cried out as a man leapt for his life; Oliver laughed, and said, without turning his head, "You'll get used to it by and by."

They went down Fourth Avenue and turned into the Bowery. Elevated trains pounded overhead, and a maze of gin-shops, dime-museums, cheap lodging-houses, and clothing-stores sped past them. Once or twice Oliver's hawklike glance detected a blue uniform ahead, and then they slowed down to a decorous pace, and the other got a chance to observe the miserable population of the neighborhood. It was a cold November day, and an "out of work" time, and wretched outcast men walked with shoulders drawn forward and hands in their pockets.

"Where in the world are we going?" Montague asked.

"To Long Island," said the other. "It's a beastly ride — this part of it — but it's the only way. Some day we'll have an overhead speedway of our own, and we won't have to drive through this mess."

They turned off at the approach to the Williamsburg Bridge, and found the street closed for repairs. They had to make a detour of a block, and they turned with a vicious sweep and plunged into the very heart of the tenement district. Narrow, filthy streets, with huge, canonlike blocks of buildings, covered with rusty iron fire-escapes and decorated with soap-boxes and pails and laundry and babies; narrow stoops, crowded with playing children; grocery-shops, clothing-shops, saloons; and a maze of placards and signs in English and German and Yiddish. Through the throngs Oliver drove, his brows knitted with impatience and his horn honking angrily. "Take it easy," — protested Montague; but the other answered, "Bah!" Children screamed and darted out of the way, and men and women started back, scowling and muttering; when a blockade of wagons and push-carts forced them to stop, the children gathered about and jeered, and a group of hoodlums loafing by a saloon flung ribaldry at them; but Oliver never turned his eyes from the road ahead.

And at last they were out on the bridger. "Slow vehicles keep to the right," ran the sign, and so there was a lane for them to the left. They sped up the slope, the cold air beating upon them like a hurricane. Far below lay the river, with tugs and ferry-boats plowing the wind-beaten grey water, and a city spread out on either bank — a wilderness of roofs, with chimneys sticking up and white jets of steam spouting everywhere. Then they sped down the farther slope, and into Brooklyn.

There was an asphalted avenue, lined with little residences. There was block upon block of them, mile after mile of them — Montague had never, seen so many houses in his life before, and nearly all poured out of the same mold.

Many other automobiles were speeding out by this avenue, and they raced with one another. The one which was passed the most frequently got the dust and smell; and so the universal rule was that when you were behind you watched for a clear track, and then put on speed, and went to the front; but then just when you had struck a comfortable pace, there was a whirring and a puffing at your left, and your rival came stealing past you. If you were ugly, you put on speed yourself, and forced him to fall back, or to run the risk of trouble with vehicles coming the other way. For Oliver there seemed to be but one rule, — pass everything.

They came to the great Ocean Driveway. Here were many automobiles, nearly all going one way, and nearly all racing. There were two which stuck to Oliver and would not be left behind — one, two, three — one, two, three — they passed and repassed. Their dust was blinding, and the continual odor was sickening; and so Oliver set his lips tight, and the little dial on the indicator began to creep ahead, and they whirled away down the drive. "Catch us this time!" he muttered.

A few seconds later Oliver gave a sudden exclamation, as a policeman, concealed behind a bush at the roadside, sprang out and hailed them. The policeman had a motorcycle, and Oliver shouted to the mechanic, "Pull the cord!" His brother turned, alarmed and perplexed, and saw the man reach down to the floor of the car. He saw the policeman leap upon the cycle and start to follow. Then he lost sight of him in the clouds of dust.

For perhaps five minutes they tore on, tense and silent, at a pace that Montague had never equaled in an express train. Vehicles coming the other way would leap into sight, charging straight at them, it seemed, and shooting past a hand's breadth away. Montague had just about made up his mind that one such ride would last him for a lifetime, when he noticed that they were slacking up. "You can let go the cord," said Oliver. "He'll never catch us now."

"What is the cord?" asked the other.

"It's tied to the tag with our number on, in back. It swings it up so it can't be seen."

They were turning off into a country road, and Montague sank back and laughed till the tears ran down his cheeks. "Is that a common trick?" he asked.

"Quite," said the other. "Mrs. Robbie has a trough of mud in their garage, and her driver sprinkles the tag every time before she goes out. You have to do something, you know, or you'd be taken up all the time."

"Have you ever been arrested?"

"I've only been in court once," said Oliver. "I've been stopped a dozen times."

"What did they do the other times — warn you?"

"Warn me?" laughed Oliver. "What they did was to get in with me and ride a block or two, out of sight of the crowd; and then I slipped them a ten-dollar bill and they got out."

To which Montague responded, "Oh, I see!"

They turned into a broad macadamized road, and here were more autos, and more dust, and more racing. Now and then they crossed a trolley or a railroad track, and here was always a warning sign; but Oliver must have had some occult way of knowing that the track was clear, for he never seemed to slow up. Now and then they came to villages, and did reduce speed; but from the pace at which they went through, the villagers could not have suspected it.

And then came another adventure. The road was in repair, and was very bad, and they were picking their way, when suddenly a young man who had been walking on a side path stepped out before them, and drew a red handkerchief from his pocket, and faced them, waving it. Oliver muttered an oath.

"What's the matter?" cried his brother.

"We're arrested!" he exclaimed.

"What!" gasped the other. "Why, we were not going at all."

"I know," said Oliver; "but they've got us all the same."

He must have made up his mind at one glance that the case was hopeless, for he made no attempt to put on speed, but let the young man step aboard as they reached him.

"What is it?" Oliver demanded.

"I have been sent out by the Automobile Association," said the stranger, "to warn you that they have a trap set in the next town. So watch out."

And Oliver gave a gasp, and said, "Oh! Thank you!" The young man stepped off, and they went ahead, and he lay back in his seat and shook with laughter.

"Is that common?" his brother asked, between laughs.

"It happened to me once before," said Oliver. "But I'd forgotten it completely."

They proceeded very slowly; and when they came to the outskirts of the village they went at a funereal pace, while the car throbbed in protest. In front of a country store they saw a group of loungers watching them, and Oliver said, "There's the first part of the trap. They have a telephone, and somewhere beyond is a man with another telephone, and beyond that a man to stretch a rope across the road."

"What would they do with you?" asked the other.

"Haul you up before a justice of the peace, and fine you anywhere from fifty to two hundred and fifty dollars. It's regular highway robbery — there are some places that boast of never levying taxes; they get all their money out of us!"

Oliver pulled out his watch. "We're going to be late to lunch, thanks to these delays," he said. He added that they were to meet at the "Hawk's Nest," which he said was an "automobile joint."

Outside of the town they "hit it up" again; and half an hour later they came to a huge sign, "To the Hawk's Nest," and turned off. They ran up a hill, and came suddenly out of a pine-forest into view of a hostelry, perched upon the edge of a bluff overlooking the Sound. There was a broad yard in front, in which automobiles wheeled and sputtered, and a long shed that was lined with them.

Half a dozen attendants ran to meet them as they drew up at the steps. They all know Oliver, and two fell to brushing his coat, and one got his cap, while the mechanic took the car to the shed. Oliver had a tip for each of them; one of the things that Montague observed was that in New York you had to carry a pocketful of change, and scatter it about wherever you went. They tipped the man who carried their coats and the boy who opened the door. In the washrooms they tipped the boys who filled the basins for them and those who gave them a second brushing.

The piazzas of the inn were crowded with automobiling parties, in all sorts of strange costumes. It seemed to Montague that most of them were flashy people — the men had red faces and the women had loud voices; he saw one in a sky-blue coat with bright scarlet facing. It occurred to him that if these women had not worn such large hats, they would not have needed quite such a supply of the bright-colored veiling which they wound over the hats and tied under their chins, or left to float about in the breeze.

The dining room seemed to have been built in sections, rambling about on the summit of the cliff. The side of it facing the water was all glass, and could be taken down. The ceiling was a maze of streamers and Japanese lanterns, and here and there were orange trees and palms and artificial streams and fountains. Every table was crowded, it seemed; one was half-deafened by the clatter of plates, the voices and laughter, and the uproar of a Negro orchestra of banjos, mandolins, and guitars. Negro waiters flew here and there, and a huge, stout headwaiter, who was pirouetting and strutting, suddenly espied Oliver, and made for him with smiles of welcome.

"Yes, sir — just come in, sir," he said, and led the way down the room, to where, in a corner, a table had been set for sixteen or eighteen people. There was a shout, "Here's Ollie!" — and a pounding of glasses and a chorus of welcome — "Hello, Ollie! You're late, Ollie! What's the matter — car broke down?"

Of the party, about half were men and half women. Montague braced himself for the painful ordeal of being introduced to sixteen people in succession, but this was considerably spared him. He shook hands with Robbie Walling, a tall and rather hollow-chested young man, with slight yellow moustaches; and with Mrs. Robbie, who bade him welcome, and presented him with the freedom of the company.

Then he found himself seated between two young ladies, with a waiter leaning over him to take his order for the drinks. He said, a little hesitatingly, that he would like some whisky, as he was about frozen, upon which the girl on his right, remarked, "You'd better try a champagne cocktail — you'll get your results quicker." She added, to the waiter, "Bring a couple of them, and be quick about it."

"You had a cold ride, no doubt, in that low car," she went on, to Montague. "What made you late?"

"We had some delays," he answered. "Once we thought we were arrested."

"Arrested!" she exclaimed; and others took up the word, crying, "Oh, Ollie! tell us about it!"

Oliver told the tale, and meantime his brother had a chance to look about him. All of the party were young — he judged that he was the oldest person there. They were not of the flashily dressed sort, but no one would have had to look twice to know that there was money in the crowd. They had had their first round of drinks, and started in to enjoy themselves. They were all intimates, calling each other by their first names. Montague noticed that these names always ended in "ie," — there was Robbie and Freddie and Auggie and Clarrie and Bertie and Chappie;

if their names could not be made to end properly, they had nicknames instead.

"Ollie" told how they had distanced the policeman; and Clarrie Mason (one of the younger sons of the once mighty railroad king) told of a similar feat which his car had performed. And then the young lady who sat beside him told how a fat Irishwoman had skipped out of their way as they rounded a corner, and stood and cursed them from the vantage-point of the sidewalk.

The waiter came with the liquor, and Montague thanked his neighbor, Miss Price. Anabel Price was her name, and they called her "Billy"; she was a tall and splendidly formed creature, and he learned in due time that she was a famous athlete. She must have divined that he would feel a little lost in this crowd of intimates, and set to work to make him feel at home — an attempt in which she was not altogether successful.

They were bound for a shooting-lodge, and so she asked him if he were fond of shooting. He replied that he was; in answer to a further question he said that he had hunted chiefly deer and wild turkey. "Ah, then you are a real hunter!" said Miss Price. "I'm afraid you'll scorn our way."

"What do you do?" he inquired.

"Wait and you'll see," replied she; and added, casually, "When you get to be pally with us, you'll conclude we don't furnish."

Montague's jaw dropped just a little. He recovered himself, however, and said that he presumed so, or that he trusted not; afterward, when he had made inquiries and found out what he should have said, he had completely forgotten what he *had* said. — Down in a hotel in Natchez there was an old headwaiter, to whom Montague had once appealed to seat him next to a friend. At the next meal, learning that the request had been granted, he said to the old man, "I'm afraid you have shown me partiality"; to which the reply came, "I always tries to show it as much as I kin." Montague always thought of this whenever he recalled his first encounter with "Billy" Price.

The young lady on the other side of him now remarked that Robbie was ordering another "topsy-turvy lunch." He inquired what sort of a lunch that was; she told him that Robbie called it a "digestion exercise." That was the only remark that Miss de Millo addressed to him during the meal (Miss Gladys de Mille, the banker's daughter, known as "Baby" to her intimates). She was a stout and round-faced girl, who devoted herself strictly to the business of lunching; and Montague noticed at the end that she was breathing rather hard, and that her big round eyes seemed bigger than ever.

Conversation was general about the table, but it was not easy conversation to follow. It consisted mostly of what is known as "joshing," and involved acquaintance with intimate details of personalities and past events. Also, there was a great deal of slang used, which kept a stranger's wits on the jump. However, Montague concluded that all his deficiencies were made up for by his brother, whose sallies were the cause of the loudest laughter. Just now he seemed to the other more like the Oliver he had known of old — for Montague had already noted a change in him. At home there had never been any end to his gaiety and fun, and it was hard to get him to take anything seriously; but now he kept all his jokes for company, and when he was alone he was in deadly earnest. Apparently he was working hard over his pleasures.

Montague could understand how this was possible. Someone, for instance, had worked hard over the ordering of the lunch — to secure the maximum of explosive effect. It began with ice-cream, molded in fancy shapes and then buried in white of egg and baked brown. Then there was a turtle soup, thick and green and greasy; and then — horror of horrors — a great steaming plum-pudding. It was served in a strange phenomenon of a platter, with six long, silver legs; and the waiter set it in front of Robbie Walling and lifted the cover with a sweeping gesture — and then removed it and served it himself. Montague had about made up his mind that this was the end, and begun to fill up on bread-and-butter, when there appeared cold asparagus, served in individual silver holders resembling andirons. Then — appetite now being sufficiently whetted — there came quail, in piping hot little casseroles — ; and then half a grapefruit set in a block of ice and filled with wine; and then little squab ducklings, bursting fat, and an artichoke; and then a café parfait; and then — as if to crown the audacity — huge thick slices of roast beef! Montague had given up long ago — he could keep no track of the deluge of food which poured forth. And between all the courses there were wines of precious brands, tumbled helter-skelter, — sherry and port, champagne and claret and liqueur. Montague watched poor "Baby" de Mille out of the corner of his eye, and pitied her; for it was evident that she could not resist the impulse to eat whatever was put before her, and she was visibly suffering. He wondered whether he might not manage to divert her by conversation, but he lacked the courage to make the attempt.

The meal was over at four o'clock. By that time most of the other parties were far on their way to New York, and the inn was deserted. They possessed themselves of their belongings, and one by one their cars whirled away toward "Black Forest."

Montague had been told that it was a "shooting-lodge." He had a vision of some kind of a rustic shack, and wondered dimly how so many people would be stowed away. When they turned off the main road, and his brother remarked, "Here we are," he was surprised to see a rather large building of granite, with an archway spanning the road. He was still more surprised when they whizzed through and went on.

"Where are we going?" he asked.

"To 'Black Forest,'" said Oliver.

"And what was that we passed?"

"That was the gatekeeper's lodge," was Oliver's reply.

Chapter IV

*T*hey ran for about three miles upon a broad macadamized avenue, laid straight as an arrow's flight through the forest; and then the sound of the sea came to them, and before them was a mighty granite pile, looming grim in the twilight, with a drawbridge and moat, and four great castellated towers. "Black Forest" was built in imitation of a famous old fortress in Provençe — only the fortress had forty small rooms, and its modern prototype had seventy large ones, and now every window was blazing with lights. A man does not let himself be caught twice in such a blunder; and having visited a "shooting-lodge" which had cost three-quarters of a million dollars and was set in a preserve of ten thousand acres, he was prepared for Adirondack "camps" which had cost half a million and Newport "cottages" which had cost a million or two.

Liveried servants took the car, and others opened the door and took their coats. The first thing they saw was a huge, fireplace, a fireplace a dozen feet across, made of great boulders, and with whole sections of a pine tree blazing in it. Underfoot was polished hardwood, with skins of bear and buffalo. The firelight flickered upon shields and battle-axes and broadswords, hung upon the oaken pillars; while between them were tapestries, picturing the Song of Roland and the battle of Roncesvalles. One followed the pillars of the great hall to the vaulted roof, whose glass was glowing blood-red in the western light. A broad stairway ascended to the second floor, which opened upon galleries about the hall.

Montague went to the fire, and stood rubbing his hands before the grateful blaze. "Scotch or Irish, sir?" inquired a lackey, hovering at his side. He had scarcely given his order when the door opened and a second motor load of the party appeared, shivering and rushing for the fire. In a couple of minutes they were all assembled — and roaring with laughter over "Baby" de Mille's account of how her car had run over a dachshund. "Oh, do you know," she cried, "he simply *popped!*"

Half a dozen attendants hovered about, and soon the tables in the hall were covered with trays containing decanters and siphons. By this means everybody in the party was soon warmed up, and then in groups they scattered to amuse themselves.

There was a great hall for indoor tennis, and there were half a dozen squash-courts. Montague knew neither of these games, but he was interested in watching the water polo in the swimming-tank, and in studying the appointments of this part of the building. The tank, with the walls and floor about it, were all of marble; there was a bronze gallery running about it, from which one might gaze into the green depths of the water. There were luxurious dressing-rooms for men and women, with hot and cold needle-baths, steam-rooms with rubbers in attendance and weighing and lifting machines, electric machines for producing "violet rays," and electric air-blasts for the drying of the women's hair.

He watched several games, in which men and women took part; and later on, when the tennis and other players appeared, he joined them in a plunge. Afterward, he entered one of the electric elevators and was escorted to his room, where he found his bag unpacked, and his evening attire laid out upon the bed.

It was about nine when the party went into the dining room, which opened upon a granite terrace and loggia facing the sea. The room was finished in some rare black wood, the name of which he did not know; soft radiance suffused it, and the table was lighted by electric candles set in silver sconces, and veiled by silk shades. It gleamed with its load of crystal and silver, set off by scattered groups of orchids and ferns. The repast of the afternoon had been simply a lunch, it seemed — and now they had an elaborate dinner, prepared by Robbie Waiting's famous ten-thousand-dollar chef. In contrast with the uproar of the inn was the cloistral stillness of this dining room, where the impassive footmen seemed to move on padded slippers, and the courses appeared and vanished as if by magic. Montague did his best to accustom himself to the gowns of the women, which were cut lower than any he had ever seen in his life; but he hesitated every time he turned to speak to the young lady beside him, because he could look so deep down into her bosom, and it was difficult for him to realize that she did not mind it.

The conversation was the same as before, except that it was a little more general, and louder in tone; for the guests had become more intimate, and as Robbie Walling's wines of priceless vintage poured forth, they became a little "high." The young lady who sat on Montague's right was a Miss Vincent, a granddaughter of one of the sugar-kings; she was dark-skinned and slender, and had appeared at a recent lawn fête in the costume of an Indian maiden. The company amused itself by selecting an Indian name for her; all sorts of absurd ones were suggested, depending upon various intimate details of the young lady's personality and habits. Robbie caused a laugh by suggesting "Little Dewdrop" – it appeared that she had once been discovered writing a poem about a dewdrop; someone else suggested "Little Raindrop," and then Ollie brought down the house by exclaiming, "Little Raindrop in the Mud-puddle!" A perfect gale of laughter swept over the company, and it must have been a minute before they could recover their composure; in order to appreciate the humor of the sally it was necessary to know that Miss Vincent had "come a cropper" at the last meet of the Long Island Hunt Club, and been extricated from a slough several feet deep.

This was explained to Montague by the young lady on his left – the one whose half-dressed condition caused his embarrassment. She was only about twenty, with a wealth of golden hair and the bright, innocent face of a child; he had not yet learned her name, for everyone called her "Cherub." Not long after this she made a remark across the table to Baby de Mille, a strange jumble of syllables, which sounded like English, yet was not. Miss de Mille replied, and several joined in, until there was quite a conversation going on. "Cherub" explained to him that "Baby" had invented a secret language, made by transposing letters; and that Ollie and Bertie were crazy to guess the key to it, and could not.

The dinner lasted until late. The wine-glasses continued to be emptied, and to be magically filled again. The laughter was louder, and now and then there were snatches of singing; women lolled about in their chairs – one beautiful boy sat gazing dreamily across the table at Montague, now and then closing his eyes, and opening them more and more reluctantly. The attendants moved about, impassive and silent as ever; no one else seemed to be cognizant of their existence, but Montague could not help noticing them, and wondering what they thought of it all.

When at last the party broke up, it was because the bridge-players wished to get settled for the evening. The others gathered in front of the fireplace, and smoked and chatted. At home, when one planned a day's hunting, he went to bed early and rose before dawn; but here, it seemed, there was game a-plenty, and the hunters had nothing to consider save their own comfort.

The cards were played in the vaulted "gun-room." Montague strolled through it, and his eye ran down the wall, lined with glass cases and filled with every sort of firearm known to the hunter. He recalled, with a twinge of self-abasement, that he had suggested bringing his shotgun along!

He joined a group in one corner, and lounged in the shadows, and studied "Billy" Price, whose conversation had so mystified him. "Billy," whose father was a banker, proved to be a devotee of horses; she was a veritable Amazon, the one passion of whose life was glory. Seeing her sitting in this group, smoking cigarettes, and drinking highballs, and listening impassively to risqué stories, one might easily draw base conclusions about Billy Price. But as a matter of fact she was made of marble; and the men, instead of falling in love with her, made her their confidante, and told her their troubles, and sought her sympathy and advice.

Some of this was explained to Montague by a young lady, who, as the evening wore on, came in and placed herself beside him. "My name is Betty Wyman," she said, "and you and I will have to be friends, because Ollie's my side partner."

Montague had to meet her advances; so had not much time to speculate as to what the term "side partner" might be supposed to convey. Betty was a radiant little creature, dressed in a robe of deep crimson, made of some soft and filmy and complicated material; there was a crimson rose in her hair, and a living glow of crimson in her cheeks. She was bright and quick, like a butterfly, full of strange whims and impulses; mischievous lights gleamed in her eyes and mischievous smiles played about her adorable little cherry lips. Some strange perfume haunted the filmy dress, and completed the bewilderment of the intended victim.

"I have a letter of introduction to a Mr. Wyman in New York," said Montague. "Perhaps he is a relative of yours."

"Is he a railroad president?" asked she; and when he answered in the affirmative, "Is he a railroad king?" she whispered, in a mocking, awe-stricken voice, "Is he rich — oh, rich as Solomon — and is he a terrible man, who eats people alive all the time?"

"Yes," said Montague — "that must be the one."

"Well," said Betty, "he has done me the honor to be my granddaddy; but don't you take any letter of introduction to him."

"Why not?" asked he, perplexed.

"Because he'll eat *you,*" said the girl. "He hates Ollie."

"Dear me," said the other; and the girl asked, "Do you mean that the boy hasn't said a word about me?"

"No," said Montague — "I suppose he left it for you to do."

"Well," said Betty, "it's like a fairy story. Do you ever read fairy stories? In this story there was a princess — oh, the most beautiful princess! Do you understand?"

"Yes," said Montague. "She wore a red rose in her hair."

"And then," said the girl, "there was a young courtier — very handsome and gay; and they fell in love with each other. But the terrible old king — he wanted his daughter to wait a while, until he got through conquering his enemies, so that he might have time to pick out some prince or other, or maybe some ogre who was wasting his lands — do you follow me?"

"Perfectly," said he. "And then did the beautiful princess pine away?"

"Um — no," said Betty, pursing her lips. "But she had to dance terribly hard to keep from thinking about herself." Then she laughed, and exclaimed, "Dear me, we are getting poetical!" And next, looking sober again, "Do you know, I was half afraid to talk to you. Ollie tells me you're terribly serious. Are you?"

"I don't know," said Montague — but she broke in with a laugh, "We were talking about you at dinner last night. They had some whipped cream done up in funny little curlicues, and Ollie said, 'Now, if my brother Allan were here, he'd be thinking about the man who fixed this cream, and how long it took him, and how he might have been reading "The Simple Life."' Is that true?"

"It involves a question of literary criticism" — said Montague.

"I don't want to talk about literature," exclaimed the other. In truth, she wanted nothing save to feel of his armor and find out if there were any weak spots through which he could be teased. Montague was to find in time that the adorable Miss Elizabeth was a very thorny species of rose — she was more like a gay-colored wasp, of predatory temperament.

"Ollie says you want to go down town and work," she went on. "I think you're awfully foolish. Isn't it much nicer to spend your time in an imitation castle like this?"

"Perhaps," said ho, "but I haven't any castle."

"You might get one," answered Betty. "Stay around awhile and let us marry you to a nice girl. They will all throw themselves at your feet, you know, for you have such a delicious melting voice, and you look romantic and exciting." (Montague made a note to inquire whether it was customary in New York to talk about you so frankly to your face.)

Miss Betty was surveying him quizzically meantime. "I don't know," she said. "On second thoughts, maybe you'll frighten the girls. Then it'll be the married women who'll fall in love with you. You'll have to watch out."

"I've already been told that by my tailor," said Montague, with a laugh.

"That would be a still quicker way of making your fortune," said she. "But I don't think you'd fit in the role of a tame cat."

"A *what?*" he exclaimed; and Miss Betty laughed.

"Don't you know what that is? Dear me — how charmingly naïve! But perhaps you'd better get Ollie to explain for you."

That brought the conversation to the subject of slang; and Montague, in a sudden burst of confidence, asked for an interpretation of Miss Price's cryptic utterance. "She said" — he repeated slowly — "that when I got to be pally with her, I'd conclude she didn't furnish."

"Oh, yes," said Miss Wyman. "She just meant that when you knew her, you'd be disappointed. You see, she picks up all the racetrack slang — one can't help it, you know. And last year she took her coach over to England, and so she's got all the English slang. That makes it hard, even for us."

And then Betty sailed in to entertain him with little sketches of other members of the party. A phenomenon that had struck Montague immediately was the extraordinary freedom with which everybody in New York discussed everybody else. As a matter of fact, one seldom discussed anything else; and it made not the least difference, though the person were one of your set, — though he ate your bread and salt, and you ate his, — still you would amuse yourself by pouring forth the most painful and humiliating and terrifying things about him.

There was poor Clarrie Mason: Clarrie, sitting in at bridge, with an expression of feverish eagerness upon his pale face. Clarrie always lost, and it positively broke his heart, though he had ten millions laid by on ice. Clarrie went about all day, bemoaning his brother, who had been kidnapped. Had Montague not heard about it? Well, the newspapers called it a marriage, but it was really a kidnapping. Poor Larry Mason was good-natured and weak in the knees, and he had been carried off by a terrible creature, three times as big as himself, and with a temper like — oh, there were no words for it! She had been an actress; and now she had carried Larry away in her talons, and was building a big castle to keep him in — for he had ten millions too, alas!

And then there was Bertie Stuyvesant, beautiful and winning — the boy who had sat opposite Montague at dinner. Bertie's father had been a coal man, and nobody knew how many millions he had left. Bertie was gay; last week he had invited them to a brook-trout breakfast — in November — and that had been a lark! Somebody had told him that trout never really tasted good unless you caught them yourself, and Bertie had suddenly resolved to catch them for that breakfast. "They have a big preserve up in the Adirondacks," said Betty; "and Bertie ordered his private train, and he and Chappie de Peyster and some others started that night; they drove I don't know how many miles the next day, and caught a pile of trout — and we had them for breakfast the next morning! The best joke of all is that Chappie vows they were so full they couldn't fish, and that the trout were caught with nets! Poor Bertie — somebody'll have to separate him from that decanter now!"

From the hall there came loud laughter, with sounds of scuffling, and cries, "Let me have it!" — "That's Baby de Mille," said Miss Wyman. "She's always wanting to roughhouse it. Robbie was mad the last time she was down here; she got to throwing sofa-cushions, and upset a vase."

"Isn't that supposed to be good form?" asked Montague.

"Not at Robbie's," said she. "Have you had a chance to talk with Robbie yet? You'll like him — he's serious, like you."

"What's he serious about?"

"About spending his money," said Betty. "That's the only thing he has to be serious about."

"Has he got so very much?"

"Thirty or forty millions," she replied; "but then, you see, a lot of it's in the inner companies of his railroad system, and it pays him fabulously. And his wife has money, too — she was a Miss Mason, you know, her father's one of the steel crowd. We've a saying that there are millionaires, and then multi-millionaires, and then Pittsburg millionaires. Anyhow, the two of them spend all their income in entertaining. It's Robbie's fad to play the perfect host — he likes to have lots of people round him. He does put up good times — only he's so very important about it, and he has so many ideas of what is proper! I guess most of his set would rather go to Mrs. Jack Warden's any day; I'd be there tonight, if it hadn't been for Ollie."

"Who's Mrs. Jack Warden?" asked Montague.

"Haven't you ever heard of her?" said Betty. "She used to be Mrs. van Ambridge, and then she got a divorce and married Warden, the big lumber man. She used to give 'boy and girl' parties, in the English fashion; and when we went there we'd do as we please — play tag all over the house, and have pillow-fights, and ransack the closets and get up masquerades! Mrs. Warden's as good-natured as an old cow. You'll meet her sometime — only don't you let her fool you with those soft eyes of hers. You'll find she doesn't mean it; it's just that she likes to have handsome men hanging round her."

At one o'clock a few of Robbie's guests went to bed, Montague among them. He left two tables of bridge fiends sitting immobile, the women with flushed faces and feverish hands, and the men with cigarettes dangling from their lips. There were trays and decanters beside each card-table; and in the hall he passed three youths staggering about in each other's arms and feebly singing snatches of "coon songs." Ollie and Betty had strolled away together to parts unknown.

Montague had entered his name in the order-book to be called at nine o'clock. The man who awakened him brought him coffee and cream upon a silver tray, and asked him if he would have anything stronger. He was privileged to have his breakfast in his room, if he wished; but he went downstairs, trying his best to feel natural in his elaborate hunting costume. No one else had appeared yet, but he found the traces of last night cleared away, and breakfast ready — served in English fashion, with urns of tea and coffee upon the buffet. The grave butler and his satellites were in attendance, ready to take his order for anything else under the sun that he fancied.

Montague preferred to go for a stroll upon the terrace, and to watch the sunlight sparkling upon the sea. The morning was beautiful — everything about the place was so beautiful that he wondered how men and women could live here and not feel the spell of it.

Billy Price came down shortly afterward, clad in a khaki hunting suit, with knee kilts and button-pockets and gun-pads and Cossack cartridge-loops. She joined him in a stroll down the beach, and talked to him about the coming winter season, with its leading personalities and events, — the Horse Show, which opened next week, and the prospects for the opera, and Mrs. de Graffenried's opening entertainment. When they came back it was eleven o'clock, and they found most of the guests assembled, nearly all of them looking a little pale and uncomfortable in the merciless morning light. As the two came in they observed Bertie Stuyvesant standing by the buffet, in the act of gulping down a tumbler of brandy. "Bertie has taken up the 'no breakfast fad,'" said Billy with an ironical smile.

Then began the hunt. The equipment of "Black Forest" included a granite building, steam-heated and elaborately fitted, in which an English expert and his assistants raised imported pheasants — magnificent bronze-colored birds with long, floating black tails. Just before the opening of the season they were dumped by thousands into the covers — fat, and almost tame enough to be fed by hand; and now came the "hunters."

First they drew lots, for they were to hunt in pairs, a man and a woman. Montague drew Miss Vincent — "Little Raindrop in the Mud-puddle." Then Ollie, who was master of ceremonies, placed them in a long line, and gave them the direction; and at a signal they moved through the forest; Following each person were two attendants, to carry the extra guns and reload them; and out in front were men to beat the bushes and scare the birds into flight.

Now Montague's idea of hunting had been to steal through the bayou forests, and match his eyes against those of the wild turkey, and shoot off their heads with a rifle bullet. So, when one of these birds rose in front of him, he fired, and the bird dropped; and he could have done it forever, he judged — only it was stupid slaughter, and it sickened him. However, if the creatures were not shot, they must inevitably perish in the winter snows; and he had heard that Robbie sent the game to the hospitals. Also, the score was being kept, and Miss Vincent, who was something of a shot herself, was watching him with eager excitement, being wild with desire to beat out Billy Price and Chappie de Peyster, who were the champion shots of the company. Baby de Mille, who was on his left, and who could not shoot at all, was blundering along, puffing for breath and eyeing him enviously; and the attendants at his back were trembling with delight and murmuring their applause. So he shot on, as long as the drive lasted, and again on their way back, over a new stretch of the country. Sometimes the birds would rise in pairs, and he would drop them both; and twice when a blundering flock took flight in his direction he seized a second gun and brought down a second pair. When the day's sport came to an end his score was fifteen better than his nearest competitor, and he and his partner had won the day.

They crowded round to congratulate him; first his partner, and then his rivals, and his host and hostess. Montague found that he had suddenly become a person of consequence. Some who had previously taken no notice of him now became aware of his existence; proud society belles condescended to make conversation with him, and Clarrie Mason, who hated de Peyster, made note of a way to annoy him. As for Oliver, he was radiant with delight. "When it came to horses and guns, I knew you'd make good," he whispered.

Leaving the game to be gathered up in carts, they made their way home, and there the two victors received their prizes. The man's consisted of a shaving set in a case of solid gold, set with diamonds. Montague was simply stunned, for the thing could not have cost less than one or two thousand dollars. He could not persuade himself that he had a right to accept of such hospitality, which he could never hope to return. He was to realize in time that Robbie lived for the pleasure of thus humiliating his fellow-men.

After luncheon, the party came to an end. Some set out to return as they had come; and others, who had dinner engagements, went back with their host in his private car, leaving their autos to be returned by the chauffeurs. Montague and his brother were among these; and about dusk, when the swarms of working people were pouring out of the city, they crossed the ferry and took a cab to their hotel.

Chapter V

*T*hey found their apartments looking as if they had been struck by a snowstorm — a storm of red and green and yellow, and all the colors that lie between. All day the wagons of fashionable milliners and costumiers had been stopping at the door, and their contents had found their way to Alice's room. The floors were ankle-deep in tissue paper and tape, and beds and couches and chairs were covered with boxes, in which lay wonderful symphonies of color, half disclosed in their wrappings of gauze. In the midst of it all stood the girl, her eyes shining with excitement.

"Oh, Allan!" she cried, as they entered. "How am I ever to thank you?"

"You're not to thank me," Montague replied. "This is all Oliver's doings."

"Oliver!" exclaimed the girl, and turned to him. "How in the world could you do it?" she cried. "How will you ever get the money to pay for it all?"

"That's my problem," said the man, laughing. "All you have to think about is to look beautiful."

"If I don't," was her reply, "it won't be for lack of clothes. I never saw so many wonderful things in all my life as I've seen today."

"There's quite a show of them," admitted Oliver.

"And Reggie Mann! It was so queer, Allan! I never went shopping with a man before. And he's so — so matter-of-fact. You know, he bought me — everything!"

"That was what he was told to do," said Oliver. "Did you like him?"

"I don't know," said the girl. "He's queer — I never met a man like that before. But he was awfully kind; and the people just turned their stores inside out for us — half a dozen people hurrying about to wait on you at once!"

"You'll get used to such things," said Oliver; and then, stepping toward the bed, "Let's see what you got."

"Most of the things haven't come," said Alice. "The gowns all have to be fitted. — That one is for tonight," she added, as he lifted up a beautiful object made of rose-colored chiffon.

Oliver studied it, and glanced once or twice at the girl. "I guess you can carry it," he said. "What sort of a cloak are you to wear?"

"Oh, the cloak!" cried Alice. "Oliver, I can't believe it's really to belong to me. I didn't know anyone but princesses wore such things."

The cloak was in Mrs. Montague's room, and one of the maids brought it in. It was an opera-wrap of grey brocade, lined with unborn baby lamb — a thing of a gorgeousness that made Montague literally gasp for breath.

"Did you ever see anything like it in your life?" cried Alice. "And Oliver, is it true that I have to have gloves and shoes and stockings — and a hat — to match every gown?"

"Of course." said Oliver. "If you were doing things right, you ought to have a cloak to match each evening gown as well."

"It seems incredible," said the girl. "Can it be right to spend so much money for things to wear?"

But Oliver was not discussing questions of ethics; he was examining sets of tinted crepe de chine lingerie, and hand-woven hose of spun silk. There were boxes upon boxes, and bureau drawers and closet shelves already filled up with hand-embroidered and lace-trimmed creations- chemises and corset-covers, night-robes of "handkerchief linen" lawn, lace handkerchiefs and veils, corsets of French coutil, dressing-jackets of pale-colored silks, and negligees of soft batistes, trimmed with Valen- ciennes lace, or even with fur.

"You must have put in a full day," he said.

"I never looked at so many things in my life," said Alice. "And Mr. Mann never stopped to ask the price of a thing."

"I didn't think to tell him to," said Oliver, laughing.

Then the girl went in to dress — and Oliver faced about to find his brother sitting and staring hard at him.

"Tell me!" Montague exclaimed. "In God's name, what is all this to cost?"

"I don't know," said Oliver, impassively. "I haven't seen the bills. It'll be fifteen or twenty thousand, I guess."

Montague's hands clenched involuntarily, and he sat rigid. "How long will it all last her?" he asked.

"Why," said the other, "when she gets enough, it'll last her until spring, of course — unless she goes South during the winter."

"How much is it going to take to dress her for a year?"

"I suppose thirty or forty thousand," was the reply. "I don't expect to keep count."

Montague sat in silence. "You don't want to shut her up and keep her at home, do you?" inquired his brother, at last.

"Do you mean that other women spend that much on clothes?" he demanded.

"Of course," said Oliver, "hundreds of them. Some spend fifty thousand — I know several who go over a hundred."

"It's monstrous!" Montague exclaimed.

"Fiddlesticks!" was the other's response. "Why, thousands of people live by it — wouldn't know anything else to do."

Montague said nothing to that. "Can you afford to have Alice compete with such women indefinitely?" he asked.

"I have no idea of her doing it indefinitely," was Oliver's reply. "I simply propose to give her a chance. When she's married, her bills will be paid by her husband."

"Oh," said the other, "then this layout is just for her to be exhibited in."

"You may say that," answered Oliver, — "if you want to be foolish. You know perfectly well that parents who launch their daughters in Society don't figure on keeping up the pace all their lifetimes."

"We hadn't thought of marrying Alice off," said Montague.

To which his brother replied that the best physicians left all they could to nature. "Suppose," said he, "that we just introduce her in the right set, and turn her loose and let her enjoy herself — and then cross the next bridge when we come to it?"

Montague sat with knitted brows, pondering.' He was beginning to see a little daylight now. "Oliver," he asked suddenly, "are you sure the stakes in this game aren't too big?"

"How do you mean?" asked the other.

"Will you be able to stay in until the showdown? Until either Alice or myself begins to bring in some returns?"

"Never worry about that," said the other, with a laugh.

"But hadn't you better take me into your confidence?" Montague persisted. "How many weeks can you pay our rent in this place? Have you got the money to pay for all these clothes?"

"I've got it," laughed the other — "but that doesn't say I'm going to pay it."

"Don't you have to pay your bills? Can we do all this upon credit?"

Oliver laughed again. "You go at me like a prosecuting attorney," he said. "I'm afraid you'll have to inquire around and learn some respect for your brother." Then he added, seriously, "You see, Allan, people like Reggie or myself are in position to bring a great deal of custom to trades people, and so they are willing to go out of their way to oblige us. And we have commissions of all sorts coming to us, so it's never any question of cash."

"Oh!" exclaimed the other, opening his eyes, "I see! Is that the way you make money?"

"It's one of the ways we save it," said Oliver. "It comes to the same thing."

"Do people know it?"

"Why, of course. Why not?"

"I don't know," said Montague. "It sounds a little queer."

"Nothing of the kind," said Oliver. "Some of the best people in New York do it. Strangers come to the city, and they want to go to the right places, and they ask me, and I send them. Or take Robbie Walling, who keeps up five or six establishments, and spends several millions a year. He can't see to it all personally — if he did, he'd never do anything else. Why shouldn't he ask a friend to attend to things for him? Or again, a now shop opens, and they want Mrs. Waiting's trade for the sake of the advertising, and they offer her a discount and me a commission. Why shouldn't I get her to try them?"

"It's quite intricate," commented the other. "The stores have more than one price, then?"

"They have as many prices as they have customers," was the answer. "Why shouldn't they? New York is full of raw rich people who value things by what they pay. And why shouldn't they pay high and be happy? That opera-cloak that Alice has — Reval promised it to me for two thousand, and I'll wager you she'd charge some woman from Butte, Montana, thirty-five hundred for one just like it."

Montague got up suddenly. "Stop," he said, waving his hands. "You take all the bloom off the butterfly's wings!"

He asked where they were going that evening, and Oliver said that they were invited to an informal dinner-party at Mrs. Winnie Duval's. Mrs. Winnie was the young widow who had recently married the founder of the great banking-house of Puval and Co. — so Oliver explained; she was a chum of his, and they would meet an interesting set there. She was going to invite her cousin, Charlie Carter — she wanted him to meet Alice. "Mrs. Winnie's always plotting to get Charlie to settle down," said Oliver, with a merry laugh.

He telephoned for his man to bring over his clothes, and he and his brother dressed. Then Alice came in, looking like the goddess of the dawn in the gorgeous rose-colored gown. The color in her cheeks was even brighter than usual; for she was staggered to find how low the gown was cut, and was afraid she was committing a faux pas. "Tell me about it," she stammered. "Mammy Lucy says I'm surely supposed to wear some lace, or a bouquet."

"Mammy Lucy isn't a Paris costumier," said Oliver, much amused. "Dear me — wait until you have seen Mrs. Winnie!"

Mrs. Winnie had kindly sent her limousine car for them, and it stood throbbing in front of the hotel-entrance, its acetylenes streaming far up the street. Mrs. Winnie's home was on Fifth Avenue, fronting the park. It occupied half a block, and had cost two millions to build and furnish. It was known as the "Snow Palace," being all of white marble.

At the curb a man in livery opened the door of the car, and in the vestibule another man in livery bowed the way. Lined up just inside the door was a corps of imposing personages, clad in scarlet waistcoats and velvet knee-breeches, with powdered wigs, and gold buttons, and gold buckles on their patent-leather pumps. These splendid creatures took their wraps, and then presented to Montague and Oliver a bouquet of flowers upon a silver salver, and upon another salver a tiny envelope bearing the name of their partner at this strictly "informal" dinner-party. Then the functionaries stood out of the way and permitted them to view the dazzling splendor of the entrance hall of the Snow Palace. There was a great marble staircase running up from the center of the hall, with a carved marble gallery above, and a marble fireplace below. To decorate this mansion a real palace in the Punjab had been bought outright and plundered; there were mosaics of jade, and wonderful black marble, and rare woods, and strange and perplexing carvings.

The head butler stood at the entrance to the salon, pronouncing their names; and just inside was Mrs. Winnie.

Montague never forgot that first vision of her; she might have been a real princess out of the palace in the Punjab. She was a brunette, rich-colored, full-throated and deep-bosomed, with scarlet lips, and black hair and eyes. She wore a court-gown of cloth of silver, with white kid shoes embroidered with jeweled flowers. All her life she had been collecting large turquoises, and these she had made into a tiara, and a neck ornament spreading over her chest, and a stomacher. Each of these stones was mounted with diamonds, and set upon a slender wire. So as she moved they quivered and shimmered, and the effect was dazzling, barbaric.

She must have seen that Montague was staggered, for she gave him a little extra pressure of the hand, and said, "I'm so glad you came. Ollie has told me all about you." Her voice was soft and melting, not so forbidding as her garb.

Montague ran the gauntlet of the other guests: Charlie Carter, a beautiful, dark-haired boy, having the features of a Greek god, but a sallow and unpleasant complexion; Major "Bob" Venable, a stout little gentleman with a red face and a heavy jowl; Mrs. Frank Landis, a merry-eyed young widow with pink cheeks and auburn hair; Willie Davis, who had been a famous half-back, and was now junior partner in the banking-house; and two young married couples, whose names Montague missed.

The name written on his card was Mrs. Alden. She came in just after him — a matron of about fifty, of vigorous aspect and ample figure, approaching what he had not yet learned to call embonpoint. She wore brocade, as became a grave dowager, and upon her ample bosom there lay an ornament the size of a man's hand, and made wholly out of blazing diamonds — the most imposing affair that Montague had ever laid eyes upon. She gave him her hand to shake, and made no attempt to disguise the fact that she was looking him over in the meantime.

"Madam, dinner is served," said the stately butler; and the glittering procession moved into the dining room — a huge state apartment, finished in some lustrous jet-black wood, and with great panel paintings illustrating the Romaunt de la Rose. The table was covered with a cloth of French embroidery, and gleaming with its load of crystal and gold plate. At either end there were huge candlesticks of solid gold, and in the center a ribbon of orchids and lilies of the valley, matching in color the shades of the candelabra and the daintily painted menu cards.

"You are fortunate in coming to New York late in life," Mrs. Alden was saying to him. "Most of our young men are tired out before they have sense enough to enjoy anything. Take my advice and look about you — don't let that lively brother of yours set the pace for you."

In front of Mrs. Alden there was a decanter of Scotch whisky. "Will you have some?" she asked, as she took it up.

"No, I thank you," said he, and then wondered if perhaps he should not have said yes, as he watched the other select the largest of the half-dozen wine-glasses clustered at her place, and pour herself out a generous libation.

"Have you seen much of the city?" she asked, as she tossed it off — without as much as a quiver of an eyelash.

"No," said he. "They have not given me much time. They took me off to the country — to the Robert Wallings'."

"Ah," said Mrs. Alden; and Montague, struggling to make conversation, inquired, "Do you know Mr. Walling?"

"Quite well," said the other, placidly. "I used to be a Walling myself, you know."

"Oh," said Montague, taken aback; and then added, "Before you were married?"

"No," said Mrs. Alden, more placidly than ever, "before I was divorced."

There was a dead silence, and Montague sat gasping to catch his breath. Then suddenly he heard a faint subdued chuckle, which grew into open laughter; and he stole a glance at Mrs. Alden, and saw that her eyes were twinkling; and then he began to laugh himself. They laughed together, so merrily that others at the table began to look at them in perplexity.

So the ice was broken between them; which filled Montague with a vast relief. But he was still dimly touched with awe — for he realized that this must be the great Mrs. Billy Alden, whose engagement to the Duke of London was now the topic of the whole country. And that huge diamond ornament must be part of Mrs. Alden's million-dollar outfit of jewelry!

The great lady volunteered not to tell on him; and added generously that when he came to dinner with her she would post him concerning the company. "It's awkward for a stranger, I can understand," said she; and continued, grimly: "When people get divorces it sometimes means that they have quarreled — and they don't always make it up afterward, either. And sometimes other people quarrel — almost as bitterly as if they had been married. Many a hostess has had her reputation ruined by riot keeping track of such things."

So Montague made the discovery that the great Mrs. Billy, though. forbidding of aspect, was good-natured when she chose to be, and with a pretty wit. She was a woman with a mind of her own — a hard-fighting character, who had marshaled those about her, and taken her place at the head of the column. She had always counted herself a personage enough to do exactly as she pleased; through the course of the dinner she would take up the decanter of Scotch, and make a pass to help Montague — and then, when he declined, pour out imperturbably what she wanted. "I don't like your brother," she said to him, a little later. "He won't last; but he tells me you're different, so maybe I will like you. Come and see me sometime, and let me tell you what not to do in New York."

Then Montague turned to talk with his hostess, who say on his right.

"Do you play bridge?" asked Mrs. Winnie, in her softest and most gracious tone.

"My brother has given me a book to study from," he answered. "But if he takes me about day and night, I don't know how I'm to manage it."

"Come and let me teach you," said Mrs. Winnie. "I mean it, really," she added. "I've nothing to do — at least that I'm not tired of. Only I don't believe you'd take long to learn all that I know."

"Aren't you a successful player?" he asked sympathetically.

"I don't believe anyone wants me to learn," said Mrs. Winnie. — "They'd rather come and get my money. Isn't that true, Major?"

Major Venable sat on her other hand, and he paused in the act of raising a spoonful of soup to his lips, and laughed, deep down in his throat — a queer little laugh that shook his fat cheeks and neck. "I may say," he said, "that I know several people to whom the status quo is satisfactory."

"Including yourself," said the lady, with a little moue. "The wretched man won sixteen hundred dollars from me last night; and he sat in his club window all afternoon, just to have the pleasure of laughing at me as I went by. I don't believe I'll play at all tonight — I'm going to make myself agreeable to Mr. Montague, and let you win from Virginia Landis for a change."

And then the Major paused again in his attack upon the soup. "My dear Mrs. Winnie," he said, "I can live for much more than one day upon sixteen hundred dollars!"

The Major was a famous club-man and bon vivant, as Montague learned later on. "He's an uncle of Mrs. Bobbie Waiting's," said Mrs. Alden, in his ear. "And incidentally they hate each other like poison."

"That is so that I won't repeat my luckless question again?" asked Montague, with a smile.

"Oh, they meet," said the other. "You wouldn't be supposed to know that. Won't you have any Scotch?"

Montague's thoughts were so much taken up with the people at this repast that he gave little thought to the food. He noticed with surprise that they had real spring lamb — it being the middle of November. But he could not know that the six-weeks-old creatures from which it had come had been raised in cotton-wool and fed on milk with a spoon — and had cost a dollar and a half a pound. A little later, however, there was placed before him a delicately browned sweetbread upon a platter of gold, and then suddenly he began to pay attention. Mrs. Winnie had a coat of arms; he had noticed it upon her auto, and again upon the groat bronze gates of the Snow Palace, and again upon the liveries of her footmen, and yet again upon the decanter of Scotch. And now — incredible and appalling — he observed it branded upon the delicately browned sweetbread!

After that, who would not have watched? There were large dishes of rare fruits upon the table — fruits which had been packed in cotton wool and shipped in cold storage from every corner of the earth. There were peaches which had come from South Africa (they had cost ten dollars apiece). There were bunches of Hamburg grapes, dark purple and bursting fat, which had been grown in a hothouse, wrapped in paper bags. There were nectarines and plums, and pomegranates and persimmons from Japan, and later on, little dishes of plump strawberries — raised in pots. There were quail which had come from Egypt, and a wonderful thing called "crab-flake a la Dewey," cooked in a chafing-dish, and served with mushrooms that had been grown in the tunnels of abandoned mines in Michigan. There was lettuce raised by electric light, and lima beans that had come from Porto Eico, and artichokes brought from France at a cost of one dollar each. — And all these extraordinary viands were washed down by eight or nine varieties of wines, from the cellar of a man who had made collecting them a fad for the last thirty years, who had a vineyard in France for the growing of his own champagne, and kept twenty thousand quarts of claret in storage all the time — and procured his Rhine wine from the cellar of the German Emperor, at a cost of twenty-five dollars a quart!

There were twelve people at dinner, and afterward they made two tables for bridge, leaving Charlie Carter to talk to Alice, and Mrs. Winnie to devote herself to Montague, according to her promise. "Everybody likes to see my house," she said. "Would you?" And she led the way from the dining room into the great conservatory, which formed a central court extending to the roof of the building. She pressed a button, and a soft radiance streamed down from above, in the midst of which Mrs. Winnie stood, with her shimmering jewels a very goddess of the fire.

The conservatory was a place in which he could have spent the evening; it was filled with the most extraordinary varieties of plants. "They were gathered from all over the world," said Mrs. Winnie, seeing that he was staring at them. "My husband employed a connoisseur to hunt them out for him. He did it before we were married — he thought it would make me happy."

In the center of the place there was a fountain, twelve or fourteen feet in height, and set in a basin of purest Carrara marble. By the touch of a button the pool was flooded with submerged lights, and one might see scores of rare and beautiful fish swimming about.

"Isn't it fine!" said Mrs. Winnie, and added eagerly, "Do you know, I come here at night, sometimes when I can't sleep, and sit for hours and gaze. All those living things; with their extraordinary forms — some of them have faces, and look like human beings! And I wonder what they think about, and if life seems as strange to them as it does to me."

She seated herself by the edge of the pool, and gazed in. "These fish were given to me by my cousin, Ned Carter. They call him Buzzie. Have you met him yet? — No, of course not. He's Charlie's brother, and he collects art things — the most unbelievable things. Once, a long time ago, he took a fad for goldfish — some goldfish are very rare and beautiful, you know — one can pay twenty-five and fifty dollars apiece for them. He got all the dealers had, and when he learned that there were some they couldn't get, he took a trip to Japan and China on purpose to get them. You know they raise them there, and some of them are sacred, and not allowed to be sold or taken out of the country. And he had all sorts of carved ivory receptacles for them, that he brought home with him — he had one beautiful marble basin about ten feet long, that had been stolen from the Emperor."

Over Montague's shoulder where he sat, there hung an orchid, a most curious creation, an explosion of scarlet flame. "That is the odonto-glossum," said Mrs. Winnie. "Have you heard of it?"

"Never," said the man.

"Dear me," said the other. "Such is fame!"

"Is it supposed to be famous?" he asked.

"Very," she replied. "There was a lot in the newspapers about it. You see Winton — that's my husband, you know — paid twenty-five thousand dollars to the man who created it; and that made a lot of foolish talk — people come from all over to look at it. I wanted to have it, because its shape is exactly like the coronet on my crest. Do you notice that?"

"Yes," said Montague. "It's curious."

"I'm very proud of my crest," continued Mrs. Winnie. "Of course there are vulgar rich people who have them made to order, and make them ridiculous; but ours is a real one. It's my own — not my husband's; the Duvals are an old French family, but they're not noble. I was a Morris, you know, and our line runs back to the old French ducal house of Mont Morenci. And last summer, when we were motoring, I hunted up one of their châteaux; and see! I brought over this."

Mrs. Winnie pointed to a suit of armor, placed in a passage leading to the billiard-room. "I have had the lights fixed," she added. And she pressed a button, and all illumination vanished, save for a faint red glow just above the man in armor.

"Doesn't he look real?" said she. (He had his visor down, and a battle-axe in his mailed hands.) "I like to imagine that he may have been my twentieth great-grandfather. I come and sit here, and gaze at him and shiver. Think what a terrible time it must have been to live in — when men wore things like that! It couldn't be any worse to be a crab."

"You seem to be fond of strange emotions," said Montague, laughing.

"Maybe I am," said the other. "I like everything that's old and romantic, and makes you forget this stupid society world."

She stood brooding for a moment or two, gazing at the figure. Then she asked, abruptly, "Which do you like best, pictures or swimming?"

"Why," replied the man, laughing and perplexed, "I like them both, at times."

"I wondered which you'd rather see first," explained his escort; "the art gallery or the natatorium. I'm afraid you'll get tired before you've seen everything."

"Suppose we begin with the art-gallery," said he. "There's not much to see in a swimming-pool."

"Ah, but ours is a very special one," said the lady. — "And some day, if you'll be very good, and promise not to tell anyone, I'll let you see my own bath. Perhaps they've told you, I have one in my own apartments, cut out of a block of the most wonderful green marble."

Montague showed the expected amount of astonishment.

"Of course that gave the dreadful newspapers another chance to gossip," said Mrs. Winnie, plaintively. "People found out what I had paid for it. One can't have anything beautiful without that question being asked."

And then followed a silence, while Mrs. Winnie waited for him to ask it. As he forbore to do so, she added, "It was fifty thousand dollars."

They were moving towards the elevator, where a small boy in the wonderful livery of plush and scarlet stood at attention. "Sometimes," she continued, "it seems to me that it is wicked to pay such prices for things. Have you ever thought about it?"

"Occasionally," Montague replied.

"Of course," said she, "it makes work for people; and I suppose they can't be better employed than in making beautiful things. But sometimes, when I think of all the poverty there is, I get unhappy. We have a winter place down South — one of those huge country-houses that look like exposition buildings, and have rooms for a hundred guests; and sometimes I go driving by myself, down to the mill towns, and go through them and talk to the children. I came to know some of them quite well — poor little wretches."

They stepped out of the elevator, and moved toward the art-gallery.

"It used to make me so unhappy," she went on. "I tried to talk to my husband about it, but he wouldn't have it. 'I don't see why you can't be like other people,' he said — he's always repeating that to me. And what could I say?"

"Why not suggest that other people might be like you?" said the man, laughing.

"I wasn't clever enough," said she, regretfully. — "It's very hard for a woman, you know — with no one to understand. Once I went down to a settlement, to see what that was like. Do you know anything about settlements?"

"Nothing at all," said Montague.

"Well, they are people who go to live among the poor, and try to reform them. It takes a terrible lot of courage, I think. I give them money now and then, but I am never sure if it does any good. The trouble with poor people, it seems to me, is that there are so many of them."

"There are, indeed," said Montague, thinking of the vision he had seen from Oliver's racing-car.

Mrs. Winnie had seated herself upon a cushioned seat near the entrance to the darkened gallery. "I haven't been there for some time," she continued. "I've discovered something that I think appeals more to my temperament. I have rather a leaning toward the occult and the mystical, I'm afraid. Did you ever hear of the Babists?"

"No," said Montague.

"Well, that's a religious sect — from Persia, I think — and they are quite the rage. They are priests, you understand, and they give lectures, and teach you all about the immanence of the divine, and about reincarnation, and Karma, and all that. Do you believe any of those things?"

"I can't say that I know about them," said he.

"It is very beautiful and strange," added the other. "It makes you realize what a perplexing thing life is. They teach you how the universe is all one, and the soul is the only reality, and so bodily things don't matter. If I were a Babist, I believe that I could be happy, even if I had to work in a cotton-mill."

Then Mrs. Winnie rose up suddenly. "You'd rather look at the pictures, I know," she said; and she pressed a button, and a soft radiance flooded the great vaulted gallery.

"This is our chief pride in life," she said. "My husband's object has been to get one representative work of each of the great painters of the world. We got their masterpiece whenever we could. Over there in the corner are the old masters — don't you love to look at them?"

Montague would have liked to look at them very much; but he felt that he would rather it were some time when he did not have Mrs. Winnie by his side. Mrs. Winnie must have had to show the gallery quite frequently; and now her mind was still upon the Persian transcendentalists.

"That picture of the saint is a Botticelli," she said. "And do you know, the orange-colored robe always makes me think of the swami. That is my teacher, you know — Swami Babubanana. And he has the most beautiful delicate hands, and great big brown eyes, so soft and gentle — for all the world like those of the gazelles in our place down South!"

Thus Mrs. Winnie, as she roamed from picture to picture, while the souls of the grave old masters looked down upon her in silence.

Chapter VI

Montague had now been officially pronounced complete by his tailor; and Reval had sent home the first of Alice's street gowns, elaborately plain, but fitting her conspicuously, and costing accordingly. So the next morning they were ready to be taken to call upon Mrs. Devon.

Of course Montague had heard of the Devons, but he was not sufficiently initiated to comprehend just what it meant to be asked to call. But when Oliver came in, a little before noon, and proceeded to examine his costume and to put him to rights, and insisted that Alice should have her hair done over, he began to realize that this was a special occasion. Oliver was in quite a state of excitement; and after they had left the hotel, and were driving up the Avenue, he explained to them that their future in Society depended upon the outcome of this visit. Calling upon Mrs. Devon, it seemed, was the American equivalent to being presented at court. For twenty-five years this grand lady had been the undisputed mistress of the Society of the metropolis; and if she liked them, they would be invited to her annual ball, which took place in January, and then forever after their position would be assured. Mrs. Devon's ball was the one great event of the social year; about one

thousand people were asked, while ten thousand disappointed ones
gnashed their teeth in outer darkness.

All of which threw Alice into a state of trepidation.

"Suppose we don't suit her!" she said.

To that the other replied that their way had been made smooth by
Reggie Mann, who was one of Mrs. Devon's favorites.

A century and more ago the founder of the Devon line had come to
America, and invested his savings in land on Manhattan Island. Other
people had toiled and built a city there, and generation after generation
of the Devons had sat by and collected the rents, until now their fortune
amounted to four or five hundred millions of dollars. They were the
richest old family in America, and the most famous; and in Mrs. Devon,
the oldest member of the line, was centered all its social majesty and
dominion. She lived a stately and formal life, precisely like a queen; no
one ever saw her save upon her raised chair of state, and she wore her
jewels even at breakfast. She was the arbiter of social destinies, and the
breakwater against which the floods of new wealth beat in vain. Reggie
Mann told wonderful tales about the contents of her enormous mail —
about wives and daughters of mighty rich men who flung themselves
at her feet and pleaded abjectly for her favor — who laid siege to her
house for months, and intrigued and pulled wires to get near her, and
even bought the favor of her servants! If Reggie might be believed, great
financial wars had been fought, and the stock markets of the world
convulsed more than once, because of these social struggles; and women
of wealth and beauty had offered to sell themselves for the privilege
which was so freely granted to them.

They came to the old family mansion and rang the bell, and the
solemn butler ushered them past the grand staircase and into the front
reception-room to wait. Perhaps five minutes later he came in and rolled
back the doors, and they stood up, and beheld a withered old lady, nearly
eighty years of age, bedecked with diamonds and seated upon a sort of
throne. They approached, and Oliver introduced them, and the old lady
held out a lifeless hand; and then they sat down.

Mrs. Devon asked them a few questions as to how much of New York
they had seen, and how they liked it, and whom they had met; but most
of the time she simply looked them over, and left the making of
conversation to Oliver. As for Montague, he sat, feeling perplexed and
uncomfortable, and wondering, deep down in him, whether it could
really be America in which this was happening.

"You see," Oliver explained to them, when they were seated in their
carriage again, "her mind is failing, and it's really quite difficult for her
to receive."

"I'm glad I don't have to call on her more than once," was Alice's comment. "When do we know the verdict?"

"When you get a card marked 'Mrs. Devon at home,'" said Oliver. And he went on to tell them about the war which had shaken Society long ago, when the mighty dame had asserted her right to be "Mrs. Devon," and the only "Mrs. Devon." He told them also about her wonderful dinner-set of china, which had cost thirty thousand dollars, and was as fragile as a hummingbird's wing. Each piece bore her crest, and she had a china expert to attend to washing and packing it — no common hand was ever allowed to touch it. He told them, also, how Mrs. Devon's housekeeper had wrestled for so long, trying to teach the maids to arrange the furniture in the great reception-rooms precisely as the mistress ordered; until finally a complete set of photographs had been taken, so that the maids might do their work by chart.

Alice went back to the hotel, for Mrs. Robbie Walling was to call and take her home to lunch; and Montague and his brother strolled round to Reggie Mann's apartments, to report upon their visit.

Reggie received them in a pair of pink silk pajamas, decorated with ribbons and bows, and with silk-embroidered slippers, set with pearls — a present from a feminine adorer. Montague noticed, to his dismay, that the little man wore a gold bracelet upon one arm! He explained that he had led a cotillion the night before — or rather this morning; he had got home at five o'clock. He looked quite white and tired, and there were the remains of a breakfast of brandy-and-soda on the table.

"Did you see the old girl?" he asked. "And how does she hold up?"

"She's game," said Oliver.

"I had the devil's own time getting you in," said the other. "It's getting harder every day."

"You'll excuse me," Reggie added, "if I get ready. I have an engagement." And he turned to his dressing-table, which was covered with an array of cosmetics and perfumes, and proceeded, in a matter-of-fact way, to paint his face. Meanwhile his valet was flitting silently here and there, getting ready his afternoon costume; and Montague, in spite of himself, followed the man with his eyes. A haberdasher's shop might have been kept going for quite a while upon the contents of Reggie's dressers. His clothing was kept in a room adjoining the dressing-room; Montague, who was near the door, could see the rosewood wardrobes, each devoted to a separate article of clothing-shirts, for instance, laid upon sliding racks, tier upon tier of them, of every material and color. There was a closet fitted with shelves and equipped like a little shoe store — high shoes and low shoes, black ones, brown ones, and white ones, and each fitted over a last to keep its shape perfect. These shoes were all made to order according to Reggie's designs, and three or four times a year there was a cleaning out, and those which had gone out of fashion became the prey of his "man." There was a safe in one closet, in which Reggie's jewelry was kept.

The dressing-room was furnished like a lady's boudoir, the furniture upholstered with exquisite embroidered silk, and the bed hung with curtains of the same material. There was a huge bunch of roses on the center-table, and the odor of roses hung heavy in the room.

The valet stood at attention with a rack of neckties, from which Reggie critically selected one to match his shirt. "Are you going to take Alice with you down to the Havens's?" he was asking; and he added, "You'll meet Vivie Patton down there — she's had another row at home."

"You don't say so!" exclaimed Oliver.

"Yes," said the other. "Frank waited up all night for her, and he wept and tore his hair and vowed he would kill the Count. Vivie told him to go to hell."

"Good God!" said Oliver. "Who told you that?"

"The faithful Alphomse," said Reggie, nodding toward his valet. "Her maid told him. And Frank vows he'll sue — I half expected to see it in the papers this morning."

"I met Vivie on the street yesterday," said Oliver. "She looked as chipper as ever."

Reggie shrugged his shoulders. "Have you seen this week's paper?" he asked. "They've got another of Ysabel's suppressed poems in." — And then he turned toward Montague to explain that "Ysabel" was the pseudonym of a young débutante who had fallen under the spell of Baudelaire and Wilde, and had published a volume of poems of such furious eroticism that her parents were buying up stray copies at fabulous prices.

Then the conversation turned to the Horse Show, and for quite a while they talked about who was going to wear what. Finally Oliver rose, saying that they would have to get a bite to eat before leaving for the Havens's. "You'll have a good time," said Reggie. "I'd have gone myself, only I promised to stay and help Mrs. de Graffenried design a dinner. So long!"

Montague had heard nothing about the visit to the Havens's; but now, as they strolled down the Avenue, Oliver explained that they were to spend the weekend at Castle Havens. There was quite a party going up this Friday afternoon, and they would find one of the Havens's private cars waiting. They had nothing to do meantime, for their valets would attend to their packing, and Alice and her maid would meet them at the depot.

"Castle Havens is one of the show places of the country," Oliver added. "You'll see the real thing this time." And while they lunched, he went on to entertain his brother with particulars concerning the place and its owners. John had inherited the bulk of the enormous Havens fortune, and he posed as his father's successor in the Steel Trust. Some day someone of the big men would gobble him up; meantime he amused himself fussing over the petty details of administration. Mrs. Havens had taken a fancy to a rural life, and they had built this huge palace in the hills of Connecticut, and she wrote verses in which she pictured herself as a simple shepherdess — and all that sort of stuff. But no one minded that, because the place was grand, and there was always so much to do. They had forty or fifty polo ponies, for instance, and every spring the place was filled with polo men.

At the depot they caught sight of Charlie Carter, in his big red touring-car. "Are you going to the Havens's?" he said. "Tell them we're going to pick up Chauncey on the way."

"That's Chauncey Venable, the Major's nephew," said Oliver, as they strolled to the train. "Poor Chauncey — he's in exile!"

"How do you mean?" asked Montague.

"Why, he daren't come into New York," said the other. "Haven't you read about it in the papers? He lost one or two hundred thousand the other night in a gambling place, and the district attorney's trying to catch him."

"Does he want to put him in jail?" asked Montague.

"Heavens, no!" said Oliver. "Put a Venable in jail? He wants him for a witness against the gambler; and poor Chauncey is flitting about the country hiding with his friends, and wailing because he'll miss the Horse Show."

They boarded the palatial private car, and were introduced to a number of other guests. Among them was Major Venable; and while Oliver buried himself in the new issue of the fantastic-covered society journal, which contained the poem of the erotic "Ysabel," his brother chatted with the Major. The latter had taken quite a fancy to the big handsome stranger, to whom everything in the city was so new and interesting.

"Tell me what you thought of the Snow Palace," said he. "I've an idea that Mrs. Winnie's got quite a crush on you. You'll find her dangerous, my boy — she'll make you pay for your dinners before you get through!"

After the train was under way, the Major got himself surrounded with some apollinaris and Scotch, and then settled back to enjoy himself. "Did you see the 'drunken kid' at the ferry?" he asked. "(That's what our abstemious district attorney terms my precious young heir-appar-

ent.) You'll meet him at the Castle — the Havens are good to him. They
know how it feels, I guess; when John was a youngster his piratical uncle
had to camp in Jersey for six months or so, to escape the strong arm of
the law."

"Don't you know about it?" continued the Major, sipping at his
beverage. "Sic transit gloria mundi! That was when the great Captain
Kidd Havens was piling up the millions which his survivors are spending with such charming insouciance. He was plundering a railroad, and
the original progenitor of the Wallings tried to buy the control away
from him, and Havens issued ten or twenty millions of new stock
overnight, in the face of a court injunction, and got away with most of
his money. It reads like opera bouffe, you know — they had a regular
armed camp across the river for about six months — until Captain Kidd
went up to Albany with half a million dollars' worth of greenbacks in
a satchel, and induced the legislature to legalize the proceedings. That
was just after the war, you know, but I remember it as if it were yesterday.
It seems strange to think that anyone shouldn't know about it."

"I know about Havens in a general way," said Montague.

"Yes," said the Major. "But I know in a particular way, because I've
carried some of that railroad's paper all these years, and it's never paid
any dividends since. It has a tendency to interfere with my appreciation
of John's lavish hospitality."

Montague was reminded of the story of the Roman emperor who
pointed out that money had no smell.

"Maybe not," said the Major. "But all the same, if you were supersti-
tious, you might make out an argument from the Havens fortune. Take
that poor girl who married the Count."

And the Major went on to picture the denouement of that famous
international alliance, which, many years ago, had been the sensation
of two continents. All Society had attended the gorgeous wedding, an
archbishop had performed the ceremony, and the newspapers had
devoted pages to describing the gowns and the jewels and the presents
and all the rest of the magnificence. And the Count was a wretched little
degenerate, who beat and kicked his wife, and flaunted his mistresses in
her face, and wasted fourteen million dollars of her money in a couple
of years. The mind could scarcely follow the orgies of this half-insane
creature — he had spent two hundred thousand dollars on a banquet,
and half as much again for a tortoise-shell wardrobe in which Louis the
Sixteenth had kept his clothes! He had charged a diamond necklace to
his wife, and taken two of the four rows of diamonds out of it before
he presented it to her! He had paid a hundred thousand dollars a year
to a jockey whom the Parisian populace admired, and a fortune for a

palace in Verona, which he had promptly torn down, for the sake of a few painted ceilings. The Major told about one outdoor fête, which he had given upon a sudden whim: ten thousand Venetian lanterns, ten thousand meters of carpet; three thousand gilded chairs, and two or three hundred waiters in fancy costumes; two palaces built in a lake, with sea horses and dolphins, and half a dozen orchestras, and several hundred chorus – girls from the Grand Opera! And in between adventures such as these, he bought a seat in the Chamber of Deputies, and made speeches and fought duels in defense of the Holy Catholic Church – and wrote articles for the yellow journals of America. "And that's the fate of my lost dividends!" growled the Major.

There were several automobiles to meet the party at the depot, and they were whirled through a broad avenue up a valley, and past a little lake, and so to the gates of Castle Havens.

It was a tremendous building, a couple of hundred feet long. One entered into a main hall, perhaps fifty feet wide, with a great fireplace arid staircase of marble and bronze, and furniture of gilded wood and crimson velvet, and a huge painting, covering three of the walls, representing the Conquest of Peru. Each of the rooms was furnished in the style of a different period – one Louis Quatorze, one Louis Quinze, one Marie Antoniette, and so on. There was a drawing room and a regal music-room; a dining room in the Georgian style, and a billiard-room, also in the English fashion, with high wainscoting and open beams in the coiling; and a library, and a morning-room and conservatory. Upstairs in the main suite of rooms was a royal bedstead, which alone was rumored to have cost twenty-five thousand dollars; and you might have some idea of the magnificence of things when you learned that underneath the gilding of the furniture was the rare and precious Circassian walnut.

All this was beautiful. But what brought the guests to Castle Havens was the casino, so the Major had remarked. It was really a private athletic club – with tan-bark hippodrome, having a ring the size of that in Madison Square Garden, and a skylight roof, and thirty or forty arc-lights for night events. There were bowling-alloys, billiard and lounging-rooms, hand-ball, tennis and racket-courts, a completely equipped gymnasium, a shooting-gallery, and a swimming-pool with Turkish and Russian baths. In this casino alone there were rooms for forty guests.

Such was Castle Havens; it had cost three or four millions of dollars, and within the twelve-foot wall which surrounded its grounds lived two world-weary people who dreaded nothing so much as to be alone. There were always guests, and on special occasions there might be three or four score. They went whirling about the country in their autos; they rode and drove; they played games, outdoor and indoor, or gambled, or lounged and chatted, or wandered about at their own sweet will. Coming to one of these places was not different from staying at a great hotel, save that the company was selected, and instead of paying a bill, you gave twenty or thirty dollars to the servants when you left.

It was a great palace of pleasure, in which beautiful and graceful men and women played together in all sorts of beautiful and graceful ways. In the evenings great logs blazed in the fireplace in the hall, and there might be an informal dance — there was always music at hand. Now and then there would be a stately ball, with rich gowns and flashing jewels, and the grounds ablaze with lights, and a full orchestra, and special trains from the city. Or a whole theatrical company would be brought down to give an entertainment in the theater; or a minstrel show, or a troupe of acrobats, or a menagerie of trained animals. Or perhaps there would be a great pianist, or a palmist, or a trance medium. Anyone at all would be welcome who could bring a new thrill — it mattered nothing at all, though the price might be several hundred dollars a minute.

Montague shook hands with his host and hostess, and with a number of others; among them Billy Price who forthwith challenged him, and carried him off to the shooting-gallery. Here he took a rifle, and proceeded to satisfy her as to his skill. This brought him to the notice of Siegfried Harvey, who was a famous cross-country rider and "polo-man." Harvey's father owned a score of copper-mines, and had named him after a race-horse; he was a big broad-shouldered fellow, a favorite of everyone; and next morning, when he found that Montague sat a horse like one who was born to it, he invited him to come out to his place on Long Island, and see some of the fox-hunting.

Then, after he had dressed for dinner, Montague came downstairs, and found Betty Wyman, shining like Aurora in an orange-colored cloud. She introduced him to Mrs. Vivie Patton, who was tall and slender and fascinating, and had told her husband to go to hell. Mrs. Vivie had black eyes that snapped and sparkled, and she was a geyser of animation in a perpetual condition of eruption. Montague wondered if she would have talked with him so gaily had she known what he knew about her domestic entanglements.

The company moved into the dining room, where there was served another of those elaborate and enormously expensive meals which he concluded he was fated to eat for the rest of his life. Only, instead of Mrs. Billy Alden with her Scotch, there was Mrs. Vivie, who drank champagne in terrifying quantities; and afterward there was the inevitable grouping of the bridge fiends.

Among the guests there was a long-haired and wild-looking foreign personage, who was the "lion" of the evening, and sat with half a dozen admiring women about him. Now he was escorted to the music-room, and revealed the fact that he was a violin virtuoso. He played what was called "salon music" — music written especially for ladies and gentlemen to listen to after dinner; and also a strange contrivance called a concerto, put together to enable the player to exhibit within a brief space the utmost possible variety of finger gymnastics. To learn to perform these feats one had to devote his whole lifetime to practicing them, just like any circus acrobat; and so his mind became atrophied, and a naïve and elemental vanity was all that was left to him.

Montague stood for a while staring; and then took to watching the company, who chattered and laughed all through the performance. Afterward, he strolled into the billiard-room, where Billy Price and Chauncey Venable were having an exciting bout; and from there to the smoking-room, where the stout little Major had gotten a group of young bloods about him to play "Klondike." This was a game of deadly hazards, which they played without limit; the players themselves were silent and impassive, but the spectators who gathered about were tense with excitement.

In the morning Charlie Carter carried off Alice and Oliver and Betty in his auto; and Montague spent his time in trying some of Havens's jumping horses. The Horse Show was to open in New York on Monday, and there was an atmosphere of suppressed excitement because of this prospect; Mrs. Caroline Smythe, a charming young widow, strolled about with him and told him all about this Show, and the people who would take part in it.

And in the afternoon Major Venable took him for a stroll and showed him the grounds. He had been told what huge sums had been expended in laying them out; but after all, the figures were nothing compared with an actual view. There were hills and slopes, and endless vistas of green lawns and gardens, dotted with the gleaming white of marble staircases and fountains and statuary. There was a great Italian walk, leading by successive esplanades to an electric fountain with a basin sixty feet across, and a bronze chariot and marble horses. There were sunken gardens, with a fountain brought from the South of France, and Greek peristyles, and seats of marble, and vases and other treasures of art.

And then there were the stables; a huge Renaissance building, with a perfectly equipped theater above. There was a model farm and dairy; a polo-field, and an enclosed riding-ring for the children; and dog-kennels and pigeon-houses, greenhouses and deer-parks — one was prepared for bear-pits and a menagerie. Finally, on their way back, they passed the casino, where musical chimes pealed out the quarter-hours. Montague stopped and gazed up at the tower from which the sounds had come.

The more he gazed, the more he found to gaze at The roof of this building had many gables, in the Queen Anne style; and from the midst of them shot up the tower, which was octagonal and solid, suggestive of the Normans. It was decorated with Christmas-wreaths in white stucco, and a few miscellaneous ornaments like the gilded tassels one sees upon plush curtains. Overtopping all of this was the dome of a Turkish mosque. Rising out of the dome was something that looked like a dove-cot; and out of this rose the slender white steeple of a Methodist country church. On top of that was a statue of Diana.

"What are you looking at?" asked the Major.

"Nothing," said Montague, as he moved on. "Has there ever been any insanity in the Havens family?"

"I don't know," replied the other, puzzled. "They say the old man never could sleep at night, and used to wander about alone in the park. I suppose he had things on his conscience."

They strolled away; and the Major's flood-gates of gossip were opened. There was an old merchant in New York, who had been Havens's private secretary. And Havens was always in terror of assassination, and so whenever they traveled abroad he and the secretary exchanged places. "The old man is big and imposing," said the Major, "and it's funny to hear him tell how he used to receive the visitors and be stared at by the crowds, while Havens, who was little and insignificant, would pretend to make himself useful. And then one day a wild-looking creature came into the Havens office, and began tearing the wrappings off some package that shone like metal — and quick as a flash he and Havens flung themselves down on the floor upon their faces. Then, as nothing happened, they looked up, and saw the puzzled stranger gazing over the railing at them. He had a patent churn, made of copper, which he wanted Havens to market for him!"

Montague could have wished that this party might last for a week or two, instead of only two days. He was interested in the life, and in those who lived it; all whom he met were people prominent in the social world, and some in the business world as well, and one could not have asked a better chance to study them.

Montague was taking his time and feeling his way slowly. But all the time that he was playing and gossiping he never lost from mind his real purpose, which was to find a place for himself in the world of affairs; and he watched for people from whose conversation he could get a view of this aspect of things. So he was interested when Mrs. Smythe remarked that among his fellow-guests was Vandam, an official of one of the great life-insurance companies. "Freddie" Vandam, as the lady called him, was a man of might m the financial world; and Montague said to himself that in meeting him he would really be accomplishing something. Crack shots and polo-players and four-in-hand experts were all very well, but he had his living to earn, and he feared that the problem was going to prove complicated.

So ho was glad when chance brought him and young Vandam together, and Siegfried Harvey introduced them. And then Montague got the biggest shock which New York had given him yet.

It was not what Freddie Vandam said; doubtless he had a right to be interested in the Horse Show, since he was to exhibit many fine horses, and he had no reason to feel called upon to talk about anything more serious to a stranger at a house party. But it was the manner of the man, his whole personality. For Freddie was a man of fashion, with all the exaggerated and farcical mannerisms of the dandy of the comic papers. He wore a conspicuous and foppish costume, and posed with a little cane; he cultivated a waving pompadour, and his silky moustache and beard were carefully trimmed to points, and kept sharp by his active fingers. His conversation was full of French phrases and French opinions; he had been reared abroad, and had a whole-souled contempt for all things American-even dictating his business letters in French, and leaving it for his stenographer to translate them. His shirts were embroidered with violets and perfumed with violets — and there were bunches of violets at his horses' heads, so that he might get the odor as he drove!

There was a cruel saying about Freddie Vandam — that if only he had had a little more brains, he would have been half-witted. And Montague sat, and watched his mannerisms and listened to his inanities, with his mind in a state of bewilderment and dismay. When at last he got up and walked away, it was with a new sense of the complicated nature of the problem that confronted him. Who was there that could give him the key to this mystery — who could interpret to him a world in which a man such as this was in control of four or five hundred millions of trust funds?

Chapter VII

*I*t was quite futile to attempt to induce anyone to talk about serious matters just now — for the coming week all Society belonged to the horse. The parties which went to church on Sunday morning talked about horses on the way, and the crowds that gathered in front of the church door to watch them descend from their automobiles, and to get "points" on their conspicuous costumes — these would read about horses all afternoon in the Sunday papers, and about the gowns which the women would wear at the show.

Some of the party went up on Sunday evening; Montague went with the rest on Monday morning, and had lunch with Mrs. Robbie Walling and Oliver and Alice. They had arrayed him in a frock coat and silk hat and fancy "spats"; and they took him and sat him in the front row of Robbie's box.

There was a great tan-bark arena, in which the horses performed; and then a railing, and a broad promenade for the spectators; and then, raised a few feet above, the boxes in which sat all Society. For the Horse Show had now become a great social function. Last year a visiting foreign prince had seen fit to attend it, and this year "everybody" would come.

Montague was rapidly getting used to things; he observed with a smile how easy it was to take for granted embroidered bed and table linen, and mural paintings, and private cars, and gold plate. At first it had seemed to him strange to be waited upon by a white woman, and by a white man quite unthinkable; but he was becoming accustomed to having silent and expressionless lackeys everywhere about him, attending to his slightest want. So he presumed that if he waited long enough, he might even get used to horses which had their tails cut off to stumps, and their manes to rows of bristles, and which had been taught to lift their feet in strange and eccentric ways, and were driven with burred bits in their mouths to torture them and make them step lively.

There were road-horses, coach-horses, saddle-horses and hunters, polo-ponies, stud-horses — every kind of horse that is used for pleasure, over a hundred different "classes" of them. They were put through their paces about the ring, and there was a committee which judged them, and awarded blue and red ribbons. Apparently their highly artificial kind of excellence was a real thing to the people who took part in the show; for the spectators thrilled with excitement, and applauded the popular victors. There was a whole set of conventions which were generally understood — there was even a new language. You were told that these "turnouts" were "nobby" and "natty"; they were "swagger" and "smart" and "swell."

However, the horse was really a small part of this show; before one had sat out an afternoon he realized that the function was in reality a show of Society. For six or seven hours during the day the broad promenade would be so packed with human beings that one moved about with difficulty; and this throng gazed towards the ring almost never — it stared up into the boxes. All the year round the discontented millions of the middle classes read of the doings of the "smart set"; and here they had a chance to come and see them — alive, and real, and dressed in their showiest costumes. Here was all the grand monde, in numbered boxes, and with their names upon the programs, so that one could get them straight. Ten thousand people from other cities had come to New York on purpose to get a look. Women who lived in boarding-houses and made their own clothes, had come to get hints; all the dressmakers in town were present for the same purpose. . Society report-ers had come, with notebooks in hand; and next morning the imitators of Society all over the United States would read about it, in such fashion as this: "Mrs. Chauncey Venable was becomingly gowned in mauve cloth, made with an Eton jacket trimmed with silk braid, and opening over a chemisette of lace. Her hat was of the same color, draped with a great quantity of mauve and orange tulle, and surmounted with birds of paradise to match. Her furs were silver fox."

The most intelligent of the great metropolitan dailies would print columns of this sort of material; and as for the "yellow" journals, they would have discussions of the costumes by "experts," and half a page of pictures of the most conspicuous of the box-holders. While Montague sat talking with Mrs. Walling, half a dozen cameras were snapped at them; and once a young man with a sketch-book placed himself in front of them and went placidly to work. — Concerning such things the society dame had three different sets of emotions: first, the one which she showed in public, that of bored and contemptuous indifference; second, the one which she expressed to her friends, that of outraged but helpless indignation; and third, the one which she really felt, that of triumphant exultation over her rivals, whose pictures were not published and whose costumes were not described.

It was a great dress parade of society women. One who wished to play a proper part in it would spend at least ten thousand dollars upon her costumes for the week. It was necessary to have a different gown for the afternoon and evening of each day; and some, who were adepts at quick changes and were proud of it, would wear three or four a day, and so need a couple of dozen gowns for the show. And of course there had to be hats and shoes and gloves to match. There would be robes of priceless fur hung carelessly over the balcony to make a setting; and in the evening there would be pyrotechnical displays of jewels. Mrs. Virginia Landis wore a pair of simple pearl earrings, which she told the reporters had cost twenty thousand dollars; and there were two women who displayed four hundred thousand dollars' worth of diamonds — and each of them had hired a detective to hover about in the crowd and keep watch over her!

Nor must one suppose, because the horse was an inconspicuous part of the show, that he was therefore an inexpensive part. One man was to be seen here driving a four-in-hand of black stallions which had cost forty thousand; there were other men who drove only one horse, and had paid forty thousand for that. Half a million was a moderate estimate of the cost of the "string" which some would exhibit. And of course these horses were useless, save for show purposes, and to breed other horses like them. Many of them never went out of their stables except for exercise upon a track; and the cumbrous and enormous; expensive coaches were never by any possibility used elsewhere — when they were taken from place to place they seldom went upon their own wheels.

And there were people here who made their chief occupation in life the winning of blue ribbons at these shows. They kept great country estates especially for the horses, and had private indoor exhibition rings. Robbie Walling and Chauncey Venable were both such people; in the summer of next year another of the Wallings took a string across the water to teach the horse-show game to Society in London. He took twenty or thirty horses, under the charge of an expert manager and a dozen assistants; he sent sixteen different kinds of carriages, and two great coaches, and a ton of harness and other stuff. It required one whole deck of a steamer, and the expedition enabled him to get rid of six hundred thousand dollars.

All through the day, of course, Robbie was down in the ring with his trainers and his competitors, and Montague sat and kept his wife company. There was a steady stream of visitors, who came to congratulate her upon their successes, and to commiserate with Mrs. Chauncey Venable over the sufferings of the un-happy victim of a notoriety-seeking district attorney.

There was just one drawback to the Horse Show, as Montague gathered from the conversation that went on among the callers: it was public, and there was no way to prevent undesirable people from taking part. There were, it appeared, hordes of rich people in New York who were not in Society, and of whose existence Society was haughtily unaware; but these people might enter horses and win prizes, and even rent a box and exhibit their clothes. And they might induce the reporters to mention them — and of course the ignorant populace did not know the difference, and stared at them just as hard as at Mrs. Robbie or Mrs. Winnie. And so for a whole blissful week these people had all the sensations of being in Society! "It won't be very long before that will kill the Horse Show," said Mrs. Vivie Patton, with a snap of her black eyes.

There was Miss Yvette Simpkins, for instance; Society frothed at the mouth when her name was mentioned. Miss Yvette was the niece of a stock-broker who was wealthy, and she thought that she was in Society, and the foolish public thought so, too. Miss Yvette made a specialty of newspaper publicity; you were always seeing her picture, with some new "Worth creation," and the picture would be labeled "Miss Yvette Simpkins, the best-dressed woman in New York," or "Miss Yvette Simpkins, who is known as the best woman whip in Society." It was said that Miss Yvette, who was short and stout, and had a rosy German face, had paid five thousand dollars at one clip for photographs of herself in a new wardrobe; and her pictures were sent to the newspapers in bundles of a dozen at a time. Miss Yvette possessed over a million dollars' worth of diamonds — the finest in the country, according to the newspapers; she had spent a hundred and twenty-six thousand dollars this year upon her clothes, and she gave long interviews, in which she set forth the fact that a woman nowadays could not really be well dressed upon less than a hundred thousand a year. It was Miss Yvette's boast that she had never ridden in a street-car in her life.

Montague always had a soft spot in his heart for the unfortunate Miss Yvette, who labored so hard to be a guiding light; for it chanced to be while she was in the ring, exhibiting her skill in driving tandem, that he met with a fateful encounter. Afterward, when he came to look back upon these early days, it seemed strange to him that he should have gone about this place, so careless and unsuspecting, while the fates were weaving strange destinies about him.

It was on Tuesday afternoon, and he sat in the box of Mrs. Venable, a sister-in-law of the Major. The Major, who was a carefree bachelor, was there himself, and also Betty Wyman, who was making sprightly comments on the passers-by; and there strolled into the box Chappie de

Peyster, accompanied by a young lady.

So many people had stopped and been introduced and then passed on, that Montague merely glanced at her once. He noticed that she was tall and graceful, and caught her name, Miss Hegan.

The turnouts in the ring consisted of one horse harnessed in front of another; and Montague was wondering what conceivable motive could induce a human being to hitch and drive horses in that fashion. The conversation turned upon Miss Yvette, who was in the ring; and Betty remarked upon the airy grace with which she wielded the long whip she carried. "Did you see what the paper said about her this morning?" she asked. "'Miss Simpkins was exquisitely clad in purple velvet,' and so on! She looked for all the world like the Venus at the Hippodrome!"

"Why isn't she in Society?" asked Montague, curiously.

"She!" exclaimed Betty. "Why, she's a travesty!"

There was a moment's pause, preceding a remark by their young lady visitor. "I've an idea," said she, "that the real reason she never got into Society was that she was fond of her old father."

And Montague gave a short glance at the speaker, who was gazing fixedly into the ring. He heard the Major chuckle, and he thought that he heard Betty Wyman give a little sniff. A few moments later the young lady arose, and with some remark to Mrs. Venable about how well her costume became her, she passed on out of the box.

"Who is that?" asked Montague.

"That," the Major answered, "that's Laura Hegan — Jim Hegan's daughter."

"Oh!" said Montague, and caught his breath. Jim Hegan — Napoleon of finance — czar of a gigantic system of railroads, and the power behind the political thrones of many states.

"His only daughter, too," the Major added. "Gad, what a juicy morsel for somebody!"

"Well, she'll make him pay for all he gets, whoever he is!" retorted Betty, vindictively.

"You don't like her?" inquired Montague; and Betty replied promptly, "I do not!"

"Her daddy and Betty's granddaddy are always at swords' points," put in Major Venable.

"I have nothing to do with my granddaddy's quarrels," said the young lady. "I have troubles enough of my own."

"What is the matter with Miss Hegan?" asked Montague, laughing.

"She's an idea she's too good for the world she lives in," said Betty. "When you're with her, you feel as you will before the judgment throne."

"Undoubtedly a disturbing feeling," put in the Major.

"She never hands you anything but you find a pin hidden in it," went on the girl. "All her remarks are meant to be read backward, and my life is too short to straighten out their kinks. I like a person to say what they mean in plain English, and then I can either like them or not."

"Mostly not," said the Major, grimly; and added, "Anyway, she's beautiful."

"Perhaps," said the other. "So is the Jungfrau; but I prefer something more comfortable."

"What's Chappie de Peyster beauing her around for?" asked Mrs. Venable. "Is he a candidate?"

"Maybe his debts are troubling him again," said Mistress Betty. "He must be in a desperate plight. — Did you hear how Jack Audubon proposed to her?"

"Did Jack propose?" exclaimed the Major.

"Of course he did," said the girl. "His brother told me." Then, for Montague's benefit, she explained, "Jack Audubon is the Major's nephew, and he's a bookworm, and spends all his time collecting scarabs."

"What did he say to her?" asked the Major, highly amused.

"Why," said Betty, "he told her he knew she didn't love him; but also she knew that he didn't care anything about her money, and she might like to marry him so that other men would let her alone."

"Gad!" cried the old gentleman, slapping his knee. "A masterpiece!"

"Does she have so many suitors?" asked Montague; and the Major replied, "My dear boy — she'll have a hundred million dollars some day!"

At this point Oliver put in appearance, and Betty got up and went for a stroll with him; then Montague asked for light upon Miss Hegan's remark.

"What she said is perfectly true," replied the Major; "only it riled Betty. There's many a gallant dame cruising the social seas who has stowed her old relatives out of sight in the hold."

"What's the matter with old Simpkins?" asked the other.

"Just a queer boy," was the reply. "He has a big pile, and his one joy in life is the divine Yvette. It is really he who makes her ridiculous — he has a regular press agent for her, a chap he loads up with jewelry and checks whenever he gets her picture into the papers."

The Major paused a moment to greet some acquaintance, and then resumed the conversation. Apparently he could gossip in this intimate fashion about any person whom you named. Old Simpkins had been very poor as a boy, it appeared, and he had never got over the memory of it. Miss Yvette spent fifty thousand at a clip for Paris gowns; but every day her old uncle would save up the lumps of sugar which came with the expensive lunch he had brought to his office. And when he had several pounds he would send them home by messenger!

This conversation gave Montague a new sense of the complicatedness of the world into which he had come. Miss Simpkins was "impossible"; and yet there was — for instance — that Mrs. Landis whom he had met at Mrs. Winnie Duval's. He had met her several times at the show; and he heard the Major and his sister-in-law chuckling over a paragraph in the society journal, to the effect that Mrs. Virginia van Rensselaer Landis had just returned from a successful hunting-trip in the far West. He did not see the humor of this, at least not until they had told him of another paragraph which had appeared some time before: stating that Mrs. Landis had gone to acquire residence in South Dakota, taking with her thirty-five trunks and a poodle; and that "Leanie" Hopkins, the handsome young stock-broker, had taken a six months' vow of poverty, chastity, and obedience.

And yet Mrs. Landis was "in" Society! And moreover, she spent nearly as much upon her clothes as Miss Yvette, and the clothes were quite as conspicuous; and if the papers did not print pages about them, it was not because Mrs. Landis was not perfectly willing. She was painted and made up quite as frankly as any chorus-girl on the stage. She laughed a great deal, and in a high key, and she and her friends told stories which made Montague wish to move out of the way.

Mrs. Landis had for some reason taken a fancy to Alice, and invited her home to lunch with her twice during the show. And after they had got home in the evening, the girl sat upon the bed in her fur-trimmed wrapper, and told Montague and his mother and Mammy Lucy all about her visit.

"I don't believe that woman has a thing to do or to think about in the world except to wear clothes!" she said. "Why, she has adjustable mirrors on ball-bearings, so that she can see every part of her skirts! And she gets all her gowns from Paris, four times a year — she says there are four seasons now, instead of two! I thought that my new clothes amounted to something, but my goodness, when I saw hers!"

Then Alice went on to describe the unpacking of fourteen trunks, which had just come up from the custom-house that day. Mrs. Virginia's couturiere had her photograph and her coloring (represented in actual paints) and a figure made up from exact measurements; and so every one of the garments would fit her perfectly. Each one came stuffed with tissue paper and held in place by a lattice-work of tape; and attached to each gown was a piece of the fabric, from which her shoemaker would make shoes or slippers. There were street-costumes and opera-wraps, robes de chambre and tea-gowns, reception-dresses, and wonderful ball and dinner gowns. Most of these latter were to be embroidered with jewelry before they were worn, and imitation jewels were sewn on, to show how the real ones were to be placed. These garments were made of real lace or Parisian embroidery, and the prices paid for them were almost impossible to credit. Some of them were made of lace so filmy that the women who made them had to sit in damp cellars, because the sunlight would dry the fine threads and they would break; a single yard of the lace represented forty days of labor. There was a pastel "batiste de soie" Pompadour robe, embroidered with cream silk flowers, which had cost one thousand dollars. There was a hat to go with it, which had cost a hundred and twenty-five, and shoes of grey antelope-skin, buckled with mother-of-pearl, which had cost forty. There was a gorgeous and intricate ball-dress of pale green chiffon satin, with orchids embroidered in oxidized silver, and a long court train, studded with diamonds — and this had cost six thousand dollars without the jewels! And there was an auto-coat which had cost three thousand; and an opera-wrap made in Leipzig, of white unborn baby lamb, lined with ermine, which had cost twelve thousand — with a thousand additional for a hat to match! Mrs. Landis thought nothing of paying thirty-five dollars for a lace handker-chief, or sixty dollars for a pair of spun silk hose, or two hundred dollars for a pearl and gold-handled parasol trimmed with cascades of chiffon, and made, like her hats, one for each gown.

"And she insists that these things are worth the money," said Alice. "She says it's not only the material in them, but the ideas. Each costume is a study, like a picture. 'I pay for the creative genius of the artist,' she said to me — 'for his ability to catch my ideas and apply them to my personality — my complexion and hair and eyes. Sometimes I design my own costumes, and so I know what hard work it is!'"

Mrs. Landis came from one of New York's oldest families, and she was wealthy in her own right; she had a palace on Fifth Avenue, and now that she had turned her husband out, she had nothing at all to put in it except her clothes. Alice told about the places in which she kept them — it was like a museum! There was a gown-room, made dust-proof, of polished hardwood, and with tier upon tier of long poles running across, and padded skirt-supporters hanging from them. Everywhere there was order and system — each skirt was numbered, and in a chiffonier-drawer of the same number you would find the waist — and so on with hats and stockings and gloves and shoes and parasols. There was a row of closets, having shelves piled up with dainty lace-trimmed and beribboned lingerie; there were two closets full of hats and three of shoes. "When she went West," said Alice, "one of her maids counted, and found that she had over four hundred pairs! And she actually has a cabinet with a card-catalogue to keep track of them. And all the shelves are lined with perfumed silk sachets, and she has tiny sachets sewed in every skirt and waist; and she has her own private perfume — she gave me some. She calls it Occur de Jeannette, and she says she designed it herself, and had it patented!"

And then Alice went on to describe the maid's work-room, which was also of polished hardwood, and dust-proof, and had a balcony for brushing clothes, and wires upon which to hang them, and hot and cold water, and a big ironing-table and an electric stove. "But there can't be much work to do," laughed the girl, "for she never wears a gown more than two or three times. Just think of paying several thousand dollars for a costume, and giving it to your poor relations after you have worn it only twice! And the worst of it is that Mrs. Landis says it's all nothing unusual; you'll find such arrangements in every home of people who are socially prominent. She says there are women who boast of never appearing twice in the same gown, and there's one dreadful personage in Boston who wears each costume once, and then has it solemnly cremated by her butler!"

"It is wicked to do such things," put in old Mrs. Montague, when she had heard this tale through. "I don't see how people can get any pleasure out of it."

"That's what I said," replied Alice.

"To whom did you say that?" asked Montague. "To Mrs. Landis?"

"No," said Alice, "to a cousin of hers. I was downstairs waiting for her, and this girl came in. And we got to talking about it, and I said that I didn't think I could ever get used to such things."

"What did she say?" asked the other.

"She answered me strangely," said the girl. "She's tall, and very stately, and I was a little bit afraid of her. She said, 'You'll get used to it. Everybody you know will be doing it, and if you try to do differently they'll take offence; and you won't have the courage to do without friends. You'll be meaning every day to stop, but you never will, and you'll go on until you die.'"

"What did you say to that?"

"Nothing," answered Alice. "Just then Mrs. Landis came in, and Miss Hegan went away."

"Miss Hegan?" echoed Montague.

"Yes," said the other. "That's her name — Laura Hegan. Have you met her?"

Chapter VIII

The Horse Show was held in Madison Square Garden, a building occupying a whole city block. It seemed to Montague that during the four days he attended he was introduced to enough people to fill it to the doors. Each one of the exquisite ladies and gentlemen extended to him a delicately gloved hand, and remarked what perfect weather they were having, and asked him how long he had been in New York, and what he thought of it. Then they would talk about the horses, and about the people who were present, and what they had on.

He saw little of his brother, who was squiring the Walling ladies most of the time; and Alice, too, was generally separated from him and taken care of by others. Yet he was never alone — there was always some young matron ready to lead him to her carriage and whisk him away to lunch or dinner.

Many times he wondered why people should be so kind to him, a stranger, and one who could do nothing for them in return. Mrs. Billy Alden undertook to explain it to him, one afternoon, as he sat in her box. There had to be some people to enjoy, it appeared, or there would be no fun in the game. "Everything is new and strange to you," said she, "and you're delicious and refreshing; you make these women think perhaps they oughtn't to be so bored after all! Here's a woman who's bought a great painting; she's told that it's great, but she doesn't understand it herself — all she knows is that it cost her a hundred thousand dollars. And now you come along, and to you it's really a painting — and don't you see how gratifying that is to her?"

"Oliver is always telling me it's bad form to admire," said the man, laughing.

"Yes?" said the other. "Well, don't you let that brother of yours spoil you. There are more than enough of blasé people in town — you be yourself."

He appreciated the compliment, but added, "I'm afraid that when the novelty is worn off, people will be tired of me."

"You'll find your place," said Mrs. Alden — "the people you like and

who like you." And she went on to explain that here he was being passed
about among a number of very different "sets," with different people
and different tastes. Society had become split up in that manner of late
— each set being jealous and contemptuous of all the other sets. Because
of the fact that they overlapped a little at the edges, it was possible for
him to meet here a great many people who never met each other, and
were even unaware of each other's existence.

And Mrs. Alden went on to set forth the difference between these
"sets"; they ran from the most exclusive down to the most "yellow,"
where they shaded off into the disreputable rich — of whom, it seemed,
there were hordes in the city. These included "sporting" and theatrical
and political people, some of whom were very rich indeed; and these
sets in turn shaded off into the criminals and the demimonde — who
might also easily be rich. "Some day," said Mrs. Alden "you should get
my brother to tell you about all these people. He's been in politics, you
know, and he has a racing-stable."

And Mrs. Alden told him about the subtle little differences in the
conventions of these various sets of Society. There was the matter of
women smoking, for instance. All women smoked, nowadays; but some
would do it only in their own apartments, with their women friends;
and some would retire to an out-of-the-way corner to do it; while others
would smoke in their own dining rooms, or wherever the men smoked.
All agreed however, in never smoking "in public" — that is, where they
would be seen by people not of their own set. Such, at any rate, had
always been the rule, though a few daring ones were beginning to defy
even that.

Such rules were very rigid, but they were purely conventional, they
had nothing to do with right or wrong: a fact which Mrs. Alden set
forth with her usual incisiveness. A woman, married or unmarried,
might travel with a man all over Europe, and everyone might know that
she did it, but it would make no difference, so long as she did not do
it in America. There was one young matron whom Montague would
meet, a raging beauty, who regularly got drunk at dinner parties, and
had to be escorted to her carriage by the butler. She moved in the most
exclusive circles, and everyone treated it as a joke. Unpleasant things
like this did not hurt a person unless they got "out" — that is, unless
they became a scandal in the courts or the newspapers. Mrs. Alden
herself had a cousin (whom she cordially hated) who had gotten a
divorce from her husband and married her lover forthwith and had for
this been ostracized by Society. Once when she came to some semi-pub-
lic affair, fifty women had risen at once and left the room! She might
have lived with her lover, both before and after the divorce, and everyone

might have known it, and no one would have cared; but the convenances declared that she should not marry him until a year had elapsed after the divorce.

One thing to which Mrs. Alden could testify, as a result of a lifetime's observation, was the rapid rate at which these conventions, even the most essential of them, were giving way, and being replaced by a general "do as you please." Anyone could see that the power of women like Mrs. Devon, who represented the old regime, and were dignified and austere and exclusive, was yielding before the onslaught of new people, who were bizarre and fantastic and promiscuous and loud. And the younger sets cared no more about anyone — nor about anything under heaven, save to have a good time in their own harum-scarum ways. In the old days one always received a neatly-written or engraved invitation to dinner, worded in impersonal and formal style; but the other day Mrs. Alden had found a message which had been taken from the telephone: "Please come to dinner, but don't come unless you can bring a man, or we'll be thirteen at the table."

And along with this went a perfectly incredible increase in luxury and extravagance. "You are surprised at what you see here today," said she — "but take my word for it, if you were to come back five years later, you'd find all our present standards antiquated, and our present pace-makers sent to the rear. You'd find new hotels and theaters opening, and food and clothing and furniture that cost twice as much as they cost now. Not so long ago a private car was a luxury; now it's as much a necessity as an opera-box or a private ballroom, and people who really count have private trains. I can remember when our girls wore pretty muslin gowns in summer, and sent them to wash; now they wear what they call lingerie gowns, dimity en princesse, with silk embroidery and real lace and ribbons, that cost a thousand dollars apiece and won't wash. Years ago when I gave a dinner, I invited a dozen friends, and my own chef cooked it and my own servants served it. Now I have to pay my steward ten thousand a year, and nothing that I have is good enough. I have to ask forty or fifty people, and I call in a caterer, and he brings everything of his own, and my servants go off and get drunk. You used to get a good dinner for ten dollars a plate, and fifteen was something special; but now you hear of dinners that cost a thousand a plate! And it's not enough to have beautiful flowers on the table — you have to have 'scenery'; there must be a rural landscape for a background, and goldfish in the finger-bowls, and five thousand dollars' worth of Florida orchids on the table, and floral favors of roses that cost a hundred and fifty dollars a dozen. I attended a dinner at the Waldorf last year that had cost fifty thousand dollars; and when I ask those people to see me,

I have to give them as good as I got. The other day I paid a thousand dollars for a tablecloth!"

"Why do you do it?" asked Montague, abruptly.

"God knows," said the other; "I don't. I sometimes wonder myself. I guess it's because I've nothing else to do. It's like the story they tell about my brother — he was losing money in a gambling-place in Saratoga, and someone said to him, 'Davy, why do you go there — don't you know the game is crooked?' 'Of course it's crooked,' said he, 'but, damn it, it's the only game in town!'"

"The pressure is more than anyone can stand," said Mrs. Alden, after a moment's thought. "It's like trying to swim against a current. You have to float, and do what everyone expects you to do — your children and your friends and your servants and your trades people. All the world is in a conspiracy against you."

"It's appalling to me," said the man.

"Yes," said the other, "and there's never any end to it. You think you know it all, but you find you really know very little. Just think of the number of people there are trying to go the pace! They say there are seven thousand millionaires in this country, but I say there are twenty thousand in New York alone — or if they don't own a million, they're spending the income of it, which amounts to the same thing. You can figure that a man who pays ten thousand a year for rent is paying fifty thousand to live; and there's Fifth Avenue — two miles of it, if you count the uptown and downtown parts; and there's Madison Avenue, and half a dozen houses adjoining on every side street; and then there are the hotels and apartment houses, to say nothing of the West Side and Riverside Drive. And you meet these mobs of people in the shops and the hotels and the theaters, and they all want to be better dressed than you. I saw a woman here today that I never saw in my life before, and I heard her say she'd paid two thousand dollars for a lace handkerchief; and it might have been true, for I've been asked to pay ten thousand for a lace shawl at a bargain. It's a common enough thing to see a woman walking on Fifth Avenue with twenty or thirty thousand dollars' worth of furs on her. Fifty thousand is often paid for a coat of sable, and I know of one that cost two hundred thousand. I know women who have a dozen sets of furs — ermine, chinchilla, black fox, baby lamb, and mink and sable; and I know a man whose chauffeur quit him because he wouldn't buy him a ten-thousand-dollar fur coat! And once people used to pack their furs away and take care of them; but now they wear them about the street, or at the seashore, and you can fairly see them fade. Or else their cut goes out of fashion, and so they have to have new ones!"

All that was material for thought. It was all true — there was no question about that. It seemed to be the rule that whenever you questioned a tale of the extravagances of New York, you would hear the next day of something several times more startling. Montague was staggered at the idea of a two-hundred-thousand-dollar fur coat; and yet not long afterward there arrived in the city a titled Englishwoman, who owned a coat worth a million dollars, which hard-headed insurance companies had insured for half a million. It was made of the soft plumage of rare Hawaiian birds, and had taken twenty years to make; each feather was crescent-shaped, and there were wonderful designs in crimson and gold and black. Every day in the casual conversation of your acquaintances you heard of similar incredible things; a tiny antique Persian rug, which could be folded into an overcoat pocket, for ten thousand dollars; a set of five "art fans," each blade painted by a famous artist and costing forty-three thousand dollars; a crystal cup for eighty thousand; an edition deluxe of the works of Dickens for a hundred thousand; a ruby, the size of a pigeon's egg, for three hundred thousand. In some of these great New York palaces there were fountains which cost a hundred dollars a minute to run; and in the harbor there were yachts which cost twenty thousand a month to keep in commission.

And that same day, as it chanced, he learned of a brand-new kind of squandering. He went home to lunch with Mrs. Winnie Duval, and there met Mrs. Caroline Smythe, with whom he had talked at Castle Havens. Mrs. Smythe, whose husband had been a well-known Wall Street plunger, was soft and mushy, and very gushing in manner; and she asked him to come home to dinner with her, adding, "I'll introduce you to my babies."

From what Montague had so far seen, he judged that babies played a very small part in the lives of the women of Society; and so he was interested, and asked, "How many have you?"

"Only two, in town," said Mrs. Smythe. "I've just come up, you see."

"How old are they?" he inquired politely; and when the lady added, "About two years," he asked, "Won't they be in bed by dinner time?"

"Oh my, no!" said Mrs. Smythe. "The dear little lambs wait up for me. I always find them scratching at my chamber door and wagging their little tails."

Then Mrs. Winnie laughed merrily and said, "Why do you fool him?" and went on to inform Montague that Caroline's "babies" were griffons Bruxelloises. Griffons suggested to him vague ideas of dragons and unicorns and gargoyles; but he said nothing more, save to accept the invitation, and that evening he discovered that griffons Bruxelloises were tiny dogs, long-haired, yellow, and fluffy; and that for her two priceless treasures Mrs. Smythe had an expert nurse, to whom she paid a hundred dollars a month, and also a footman, and a special cuisine in which their complicated food was prepared. They had a regular dentist, and a physician, and gold plate to eat from. Mrs. Smythe also owned two long-haired St. Bernards of a very rare breed, and a fierce Great Dane, and a very fat Boston bull pup — the last having been trained to go for an airing all alone in her carriage, with a solemn coachman and footman to drive him.

Montague, deftly keeping the conversation upon the subject of pets, learned that all this was quite common. Many women in Society artificially made themselves barren, because of the inconvenience incidental to pregnancy and motherhood; and instead they lavished their affections upon cats and dogs. Some of these animals had elaborate costumes, rivaling in expensiveness those of their step-mothers. They wore tiny boots, which cost eight dollars a pair — house boots, and street boots lacing up to the knees; they had house-coats, walking-coats, dusters, sweaters, coats lined with ermine, and automobile coats with head and chest-protectors and hoods and goggles — and each coat fitted with a pocket for its tiny handkerchief of fine linen or lace! And they had collars set with rubies and pearls and diamonds — one had a collar that cost ten thousand dollars! Sometimes there would be a coat to match every gown of the owner. There were dog nurseries and resting-rooms, in which they might be left temporarily; and manicure parlors for cats, with a physician in charge. When these pets died, there was an expensive cemetery in Brooklyn especially for their interment; and they would be duly embalmed and buried in plush-lined casket, and would have costly marble monuments. When one of Mrs. Smythe's best loved pugs had fallen ill of congestion of the liver, she had had tan-bark put upon the street in front of her house; and when in spite of this the dog died, she had sent out cards edged in black, inviting her friends to a "memorial service." Also she showed Montague a number of books with very costly bindings, in which were demonstrated the unity, simplicity, and immortality of the souls of cats and dogs.

Apparently the sentimental Mrs. Smythe was willing to talk about these pets all through dinner; and so was her aunt, a thin and angular spinster, who sat on Montague's other side. And he was willing to listen — he wanted to know it all. There were umbrellas for dogs, to be fastened over their backs in wet weather; there were manicure and toilet sets, and silver medicine-chests, and jewel-studded whips. There were sets of engraved visiting-cards; there were wheel-chairs in which invalid cats and dogs might be taken for an airing. There were shows for cats and dogs, with pedigrees and prizes, and nearly as great crowds as the Horse Show;

Mrs. Smythe's St. Bernards were worth seven thousand dollars apiece, and there were bulldogs worth twice that. There was a woman who had come all the way from the Pacific coast to have a specialist perform an operation upon the throat of her Yorkshire terrier! There was another who had built for her dog a tiny Queen Anne cottage, with rooms papered and carpeted and hung with lace curtains! Once a young man of fashion had come to the Waldorf and registered himself and "Miss Elsie Cochrane"; and when the clerk made the usual inquiries as to the relationship of the young lady, it transpired that Miss Elsie was a dog, arrayed in a prim little tea-gown, and requiring a room to herself. And then there was a tale of a cat which had inherited a life-pension from a forty-thousand-dollar estate; it had a two-floor apartment and several attendants, and sat at table and ate shrimps and Italian chestnuts, and had a velvet couch for naps, and a fur-lined basket for sleeping at night!

Four days of horses were enough for Montague, and on Friday morning, when Siegfried Harvey called him up and asked if he and Alice would come out to "The Roost" for the weekend, he accepted gladly. Charlie Carter was going, and volunteered to take them in his car; and so again they crossed the Williamsburg Bridge — "the Jewish Passover," as Charlie called it — and went out on Long Island.

Montague was very anxious to get a "line" on Charlie Carter; for he had not been prepared for the startling promptness with which this young man had fallen at Alice's feet. It was so obvious, that everybody was smiling over it — he was with her every minute that he could arrange it, and he turned up at every place to which she was invited. Both Mrs. Winnie and Oliver were quite evidently complacent, but Montague was by no means the same. Charlie had struck him as a good-natured but rather weak youth, inclined to melancholy; he was never without a cigarette in his fingers, and there had been signs that he was not quite proof against the pitfalls which Society set about him in the shape of decanters and wine-cups: though in a world where the fragrance of spirits was never out of one's nostrils, and where people drank with such perplexing frequency, it was hard to know where to draw a line.

"You won't find my place like Havens's," Siegfried Harvey had said. "It is real country." Montague found it the most attractive of all the homes he had seen so far. It was a big rambling house, all in rustic style, with great hewn logs outside, and rafters within, and a winding oak stairway, and any number of dens and cozy corners, and broad window-seats with mountains of pillows. Everything here was built for comfort — there was a billiard-room and a smoking-room, and a real library with readable bogles and great chairs in which one sank out of sight. There were log fires blazing everywhere, and pictures on the walls that told of sport, and no end of guns and antlers and trophies of all sorts. But you were not to suppose that all this elaborate rusticity would be any excuse for the absence of attendants in livery, and a chef who boasted the cordon bleu, and a dinner-table resplendent with crystal and silver and orchids and ferns. After all, though the host called it a "small" place, he had invited twenty guests, and he had a hunter in his stables for each one of them.

But the most wonderful thing about "The Roost" was the fact that, at a touch of a button, all the walls of the lower rooms vanished into the second story, and there was one huge, log-lighted room, with violins tuning up and calling to one's feet. They set a fast pace here — the dancing lasted until three o'clock, and at dawn again they were dressed and mounted, and following the pink-coated grooms and the hounds across the frost-covered fields.

Montague was half prepared for a tame fox, but this was pared him. There was a real game, it seemed; and soon the pack gave tongue, and away went the hunt. It was the wildest ride that Montague ever had taken — over ditches and streams and innumerable rail-fences, and through thick coverts and densely populated barnyards; but he was in at the death, and Alice was only a few yards behind, to the immense delight of the company. This seemed to Montague the first real life he had met, and he thought to himself that these full-blooded and high-spirited men and women made a "set" into which he would have been glad to fit — save only that he had to earn his living, and they did not.

In the afternoon there was more riding, and walks in the crisp November air; and indoors, bridge and rackets and ping-pong, and a fast and furious game of roulette, with the host as banker. "Do I look much like a professional gambler?" he asked of Montague; and when the other replied that he had not yet met any New York gamblers, young Harvey went on to tell how he had gone to buy this apparatus (the sale of which was forbidden by law) and had been asked by the dealer how "strong" he wanted it!

Then in the evening there was more dancing, and on Sunday another hunt. That night a gambling mood seemed to seize the company — there were two bridge tables, and in another room the most reckless game of poker that Montague had ever sat in. It broke up at three in the morning, and one of the company wrote him a check for sixty-five hundred dollars; but even that could not entirely smooth his conscience, nor reconcile him to the fever that was in his blood.

Most important to him, however, was the fact that during the game he at last got to know Charlie Carter. Charlie did not play, for the reason that he was drunk, and one of the company told him so and refused to play with him; which left poor Charlie nothing to do but get drunker. This he did, and came and hung over the shoulders of the players, and told the company all about himself.

Montague was prepared to allow for the "wild oats" of a youngster with unlimited money, but never in his life had he heard or dreamed of anything like this boy. For half an hour he wandered about the table, and poured out a steady stream of obscenities; his mind was like a swamp, in which dwelt loathsome and hideous serpents which came to the surface at night and showed their flat heads and their slimy coils. In the heavens above or the earth beneath there was nothing sacred to him; there was nothing too revolting to be spewed out. And the company accepted the performance as an old story — the men would laugh, and push the boy away, and say, "Oh, Charlie, go to the devil!"

After it was all over, Montague took one of the company aside and asked him what it meant; to which the man replied: "Good God! Do you mean that nobody has told you about Charlie Carter?"

It appeared that Charlie was one of the "gilded youths" of the Tenderloin, whose exploits had been celebrated in the papers. And after the attendants had bundled him off to bed, several of the men gathered about the fire and sipped hot punch, and rehearsed for Montague's benefit some of his leading exploits.

Charlie was only twenty-three, it seemed; and when he was ten his father had died and left eight or ten millions in trust for him, in the care of a poor, foolish aunt whom he twisted about his ringer. At the age of twelve he was a cigarette fiend, and had the run of the wine-cellar. When he went to a rich private school he took whole trunks full of cigarettes with him, and finally ran away to Europe, to acquire the learning of the brothels of Paris. And then he came home and struck the Tenderloin; and at three o'clock one morning he walked through a plate-glass window, and so the newspapers took him up. That had suddenly opened a new vista in life for Charlie — he became a devotee of fame; everywhere he went he was followed by newspaper reporters and a staring crowd. He carried wads as big round as his arm, and gave away hundred-dollar tips to bootblacks, and lost forty thousand dollars in a game of poker. He gave a fête to the demimonde, with a jeweled Christmas tree in midsummer, and fifty thousand dollars' worth of splendor. But the greatest stroke of all was the announcement that he was going to build a submarine yacht and fill it with chorus-girls! — Now Charlie had sunk out of public attention, and his friends would not see him for days; he would be lying in a "sporting house" literally wallowing in champagne.

And all this, Montague realized, his brother must have known! And

he had said not a word about it — because of the eight or ten millions
which Charlie would have when he was twenty-five!

Chapter IX

*I*n the morning they went home with others of the party by train.
They could not wait for Charlie and his automobile, because Monday
was the opening night of the Opera, and no one could miss that. Here
Society would appear in its most gorgeous raiment, and, there would be
a show of jewelry such as could be seen nowhere else in the world.

General Prentice and his wife had opened their town-house, and had
invited them to dinner and to share their box; and so at about half-past
nine o'clock Montague found himself seated in a great balcony of the
shape of a horseshoe, with several hundred of the richest people in the
city. There was another tier of boxes above, and three galleries above
that, and a thousand or more people seated and standing below him.
Upon the big stage there was an elaborate and showy play, the words of
which were sung to the accompaniment of an orchestra.

Now Montague had never heard an opera, and he was fond of music.
The second act had just begun when he came in, and all through it he
sat quite spellbound, listening to the most ravishing strains that ever he
had heard in his life. He scarcely noticed that Mrs. Prentice was spending
her time studying the occupants of the other boxes through a jeweled
lorgnette, or that Oliver was chattering to her daughter.

But after the act was over, Oliver got him alone outside the box, and
whispered, "For God's sake, Allan, don't make a fool of yourself."

"Why, what's the matter?" asked the other.

"What will people think," exclaimed Oliver, "seeing you sitting there
like a man in a dope dream?"

"Why," laughed the other, "they'll think I'm listening to the music."

To which Oliver responded, "People don't come to the Opera to listen
to the music."

This sounded like a joke, but it was not. To Society the Opera was a great state function, an exhibition of far more exclusiveness and magnificence than the Horse Show; and Society certainly had the right to say, for it owned the opera-house and ran it. The real music-lovers who came, either stood up in the back, or sat in the fifth gallery, close to the ceiling, where the air was foul and hot. How much Society cared about the play was sufficiently indicated by the fact that all of the operas were sung in foreign languages, and sung so carelessly that the few who understood the languages could make but little of the words. Once there was a world-poet who devoted his life to trying to make the Opera an art; and in the battle with Society he all but starved to death. Now, after half a century, his genius had triumphed, and Society consented to sit for hours in darkness and listen to the domestic disputes of German gods and goddesses. But what Society really cared for was a play with beautiful costumes and scenery and dancing, and pretty songs to which one could listen while one talked; the story must be elemental and passionate, so that one could understand it in pantomime — say the tragic love of a beautiful and noble-minded courtesan for a gallant young man of fashion.

Nearly everyone who came to the Opera had a glass, by means of which he could bring each gorgeously-clad society dame close to him, and study her at leisure. There were said to be two hundred million dollars' worth of diamonds in New York, and those that were not in the stores were very apt to be at this show; for here was where they could accomplish the purpose for which they existed — here was where all the world came to stare at them. There were nine prominent Society women, who among them displayed five million dollars' worth of jewels. You would see stomachers which looked like a piece of a coat of mail, and were made wholly of blazing diamonds. You would see emeralds and rubies and diamonds and pearls made in tiaras — that is to say, imitation crowns and coronets — and exhibited with a stout and solemn dowager for a pediment. One of the Wallings had set this fashion, and now everyone of importance wore them. One lady to whom Montague was introduced made a specialty of pearls — two black pearl earrings at forty thousand dollars, a string at three hundred thousand, a brooch of pink pearls at fifty thousand, and two necklaces at a quarter of a million each!

This incessant repetition of the prices of things came to seem very sordid; but Montague found that there was no getting away from it. The people in Society who paid these prices affected to be above all such considerations, to be interested only in the beauty and artistic excellence of the things themselves; but one found that they always talked about the prices which other people had paid, and that somehow other people always knew what they had paid. They took care also to see that the public and the newspapers knew what they had paid, and knew everything else that they were doing. At this Opera, for instance, there was a diagram of the boxes printed upon the program, and a list of all the box-holders, so that anyone could tell who was who. You might see these great dames in their gorgeous robes coming from their carriages, with crowds staring at them and detectives hovering about. And the bosom of each would be throbbing with a wild and wonderful vision of the moment when she would enter her box, and the music would be forgotten, and all eyes would be turned upon her; and she would lay aside her wraps, and flash upon the staring throngs, a vision of dazzling splendor.

Some of these jewels were family treasures, well known to New York for generations; and in such cases it was becoming the fashion to leave the real jewels in the safe-deposit vault, and to wear imitation stones exactly like them. From homes where the jewels were kept, detectives were never absent, and in many cases there were detectives watching the detectives; and yet every once in a while the newspapers would be full of a sensational story of a robbery. Then the unfortunates who chanced to be suspected would be seized by the police and subjected to what was jocularly termed the "third degree," and consisted of tortures as elaborate and cruel as any which the Spanish Inquisition had invented. The advertising value of this kind of thing was found to be so great that famous actresses also had costly jewels, and now and then would have them stolen.

That night, when they had got home, Montague had a talk with his cousin about Charlie Carter. He discovered a peculiar situation. It seemed that Alice already knew that Charlie had been "bad." He was sick and miserable; and her beauty and innocence had touched him and made him ashamed of himself, and ho had hinted darkly at dreadful evils. Thus carefully veiled, and tinged with mystery and romance, Montague could understand how Charlie made an interesting and appealing figure. "He says I'm different from any girl he ever met," said Alice — a remark of such striking originality that her cousin could not keep back his smile.

Alice was not the least bit in love with him, and had no idea of being; and she said that she would accept no invitations, and never go alone with him; but she did not see how she could avoid him when she met him at other people's houses. And to this Montague had to assent.

General Prentice had inquired kindly as to what Montague had seen in New York, and how he was getting along. He added that he had talked about him to Judge Ellis, and that when he was ready to get to work, the Judge would perhaps have some suggestions to make to him. He approved, however, of Montague's plan of getting his bearings first; and said that he would introduce him and put him up at a couple of the leading clubs.

All this remained in Montague's mind; but there was no use trying to think of it at the moment. Thanksgiving was at hand, and in countless country mansions there would be gaieties under way. Bertie Stuyvesant had planned an excursion to his Adirondack camp, and had invited a score or so of young people, including the Montagues. This would be a new feature of the city's life, worth knowing about.

Their expedition began with a theater-party. Bertie had engaged four boxes, and they met there, an hour or so after the performance had begun. This made no difference, however, for the play was like the opera — a number of songs and dances strung together, and with only plot. enough to provide occasion for elaborate scenery and costumes. From the play they were carried to the Grand Central Station, and a little before midnight Bertie's private train set out on its journey.

This train was a completely equipped hotel. There was a baggage compartment and a dining-car and kitchen; and a drawing room and library-car; and a bedroom-car — not with berths, such as the ordinary sleeping-car provides, but with comfortable bedrooms, furnished in white mahogany, and provided with running water and electric light. All these cars were built of steel, and automatically ventilated: and they were furnished in the luxurious fashion of everything with which Bertie Stuyvesant had anything to do. In the library-car there were velvet carpets upon the floor, and furniture of South American mahogany, and paintings upon the walls over which groat artists had labored for years.

Bertie's chef and servants were on board, and a supper was ready in the dining-car, which they ate while watching the Hudson by moonlight. And the next morning they reached their destination, a little station in the mountain wilderness. The train lay upon a switch, and so they had breakfast at their leisure, and then, bundled in furs, came out into the crisp pine-laden air of the woods. There was snow upon the ground, and eight big sleighs waiting; and for nearly three hours they drove in the frosty sunlight, through most beautiful mountain scenery. A good part of the drive was in Bertie's "preserve," and the road was private, as big signs notified one every hundred yards or so.

So at last they reached a lake, winding like a snake among towering hills, and with a huge baronial castle standing out upon the rocky shore. This imitation fortress was the "camp."

Bertie's father had built it, and visited it only half a dozen times in his life. Bertie himself had only been here twice, he said. The deer were so plentiful that in the winter they died in scores. Nevertheless there were thirty game-keepers to guard the ten thousand acres of forest, and prevent anyone's hunting in it. There were many such "preserves" in this Adirondack wilderness, so Montague was told; one man had a whole mountain fenced about with heavy iron railing, and had moose and elk and even wild boar inside. And as for the "camps," there were so many that a new style of architecture had been developed here — to say nothing of those which followed old styles, like this imported Rhine castle. One of Bertie's crowd had a big Swiss chalet; and one of the Wallings had a Japanese palace to which he came every August — a house which had been built from plans drawn in Japan, and by laborers imported especially from Japan. It was full of Japanese ware — furniture, tapestry, and mosaics; and the guides remembered with wonder the strange silent, brown-skinned little men who had labored for days at carving a bit of wood, and had built a tiny pagodalike tea-house with more bits of wood in it than a man could count in a week.

They had a luncheon of fresh venison and partridges and trout, and in the afternoon a hunt. The more active set out to track the deer in the snow; but most prepared to watch the lake-shore, while the game-keepers turned loose the dogs back in the hills. This "hounding" was against the law, but Bertie was his own law here — and at the worst there could simply be a small fine, imposed upon some of the keepers. They drove eight or ten deer to water; and as they fired as many as twenty shots at one deer, they had quite a lively time. Then at dusk they came back, in a fine glow of excitement, and spent the evening before the blazing logs, telling over their adventures.

The party spent two days and a half here, and on the last evening, which was Thanksgiving, they had a wild turkey which Bertie had shot the week before in Virginia, and were entertained by a minstrel show which had been brought up from New York the night before. The next afternoon they drove back to the train.

In the morning, when they reached the city, Alice found a note from Mrs. Winnie Duval, begging her and Montague to come to lunch and attend a private lecture by the Swami Babubanana, who would tell them all about the previous states of their souls. They went — though not without a protest from old Mrs. Montague, who declared it was "worse than Bob Ingersoll."

And then, in the evening, came Mrs. de Graffenried's opening entertainment, which was one of the great events of the social year. In the general rush of things Montague had not had a chance properly to realize it; but Reggie Mann and Mrs. de Graffenried had been working over it for weeks. When the Montagues arrived, they found the Riverside mansion — which was decorated in imitation of an Arabian palace — turned into a jungle of tropical plants.

They had come early at Reggie's request, and he introduced them to Mrs. de Graffenried, a tall and angular lady with a leathern complexion painfully painted; Mrs. de Graffenried was about fifty years of age, but like all the women of Society she was made up for thirty. Just at present there were beads of perspiration upon her forehead; something had gone wrong at the last moment, and so Reggie would have no time to show them the favors, as he had intended.

About a hundred and fifty guests were invited to this entertainment. A supper was served at little tables in the great ballroom, and afterward the guests wandered about the house while the tables were whisked out of the way and the room turned into a play-house. A company from one of the Broadway theaters would be bundled into cabs at the end of the performance, and by midnight they would be ready to repeat the performance at Mrs. do Graffenried's. Montague chanced to be near when this company arrived, and he observed that the guests had crowded up too close, and not left room enough for the actors. So the manager had placed them in a little anteroom, and when Mrs. de Graffenried observed this, she rushed at the man, and swore at him like a dragoon, and ordered the bewildered performers out into the main room.

But this was peering behind the scenes, and he was supposed to be watching the play. The entertainment was another "musical comedy" like the one he had seen a few nights before. On that occasion, however, Bertie Stuyvesant's sister had talked to him the whole time, while now he was let alone, and had a chance to watch the performance.

This was a very popular play; it had had a long run, and the papers told how its author had an income of a couple of hundred thousand dollars a year. And here was an audience of the most rich and influential people in the city; and they laughed and clapped, and made it clear that they were enjoying themselves heartily. And what sort of a play was it?

It was called "The Kaliph of Kamskatka." It had no shred of a plot; the Kaliph had seventeen wives, and there was an American drummer who wanted to sell him another — but then you did not need to remember this, for nothing came of it. There was nothing in the play which could be called a character — there was nothing which could be connected with any real emotion ever felt by human beings. Nor could one say that there was any incident — at least nothing happened because of anything else. Each event was a separate thing, like the spasmodic jerking in the face of an idiot. Of this sort of "action" there was any quantity — at an instant's notice everyone on the stage would fall simultaneously into this condition of idiotic jerking. There was rushing about, shouting, laughing, exclaiming; the stage was in a continual uproar of excitement, which was without any reason or meaning. So it was impossible to think of the actors in their parts; one kept thinking of them as human beings — thinking of the awful tragedy of full-grown men and women being compelled by the pressure of hunger to dress up and paint themselves, and then come out in public and dance, stamp, leap about, wring their hands, make faces, and otherwise be "lively."

The costumes were of two sorts: one fantastic, supposed to represent the East, and the other a kind of reductio ad absurdum of fashionable garb. The leading man wore a "natty" outing-suit, and strutted with a little cane; his stock-in-trade was a jaunty air, a kind of perpetual flourish, and a wink that suggested the cunning of a satyr. The leading lady changed her costume several times in each act; but it invariably contained the elements of bare arms and bosom and back, and a skirt which did not reach her knees, and bright-colored silk stockings, and slippers with heels two inches high. Upon the least provocation she would execute a little pirouette, which would reveal the rest of her legs, surrounded by a mass of lace ruffles. It is the nature of the human mind to seek the end of things; if this woman had worn a suit of tights and nothing else, she would have been as uninteresting as an underwear advertisement in a magazine; but this incessant not-quite-revealing of herself exerted a subtle fascination. At frequent intervals the orchestra would start up a jerky little tune, and the two "stars" would begin to sing in nasal voices some words expressive of passion; then the man would take the woman about the waist and dance and swing her about and bend her backward and gaze into her eyes — actions all vaguely suggestive of the relationship of sex. At the end of the verse a chorus would come gliding on, clad in any sort of costume which admitted of color and the display of legs; the painted women of this chorus were never still for an instant — if they were not actually dancing, they were wriggling their legs, and jerking their bodies from side to side, and nodding their heads, and in all other possible ways being "lively."

But it was not the physical indecency of this show that struck Montague so much as its intellectual content. The dialogue of the piece was what is called "smart"; that is, it was full of a kind of innuendo which implied a secret understanding of evil between the actor and his audience — a sort of countersign which passed between them. After all, it would have been an error to say that there were no ideas in the play — there was one idea upon which all the interest of it was based; and Montague strove to analyze this idea and formulate it to himself. There are certain life principles-one might call them moral axioms — which are the result of the experience of countless ages of the human race, and upon the adherence to which the continuance of the race depends. And here was an audience by whom all these principles were — not questioned, nor yet disputed, nor yet denied — but to whom the denial was the axiom, something which it would be too banal to state flatly, but which it was elegant. and witty to take for granted. In this audience there were elderly people, and married men and women, and young men and maidens; and a perfect gale of laughter swept through it at a story of a married woman whose lover had left her when he got married: —

"She must have been heartbroken," said the leading lady.

"She was desperate," said the leading man, with a grin.

"What did she do?" asked the lady "Go and shoot herself?"

"Worse than that," said the man. "She, went back to her husband and had a baby!"

But to complete your understanding of the significance of this play, you must bring yourself to realize that it was not merely a play, but a kind of a play; it had a name — a "musical comedy" — the meaning of which everyone understood. Hundreds of such plays were written and produced, and "dramatic critics" went to see them and gravely discussed them, and many thousands of people made their livings by traveling over the country and playing them; stately theaters were built for them, and hundreds of thousands of people paid their money every night to see them. And all this no joke and no nightmare — but a thing that really existed. Men and women were doing these things — actual flesh-and-blood human beings.

Montague wondered, in an awestricken sort of way, what kind of human being it could be who had flourished the cane and made the grimaces in that play. Later on, when ho came to know the "Tenderloin," he met this same actor, and he found that he had begun life as a little Irish "mick" who lived in a tenement, and whoso mother stood at the head of the stairway and defended him with a rolling-pin against a policeman who was chasing him. He had discovered that he could make a living by his comical antics; but when he came home and told his mother that he had been offered twenty dollars a week by a show manager, she gave him a licking for lying to her. Now he was making three thousand dollars a week — more than the President of the United States and his Cabinet; but he was not happy, as he confided to Montague, because he did not know how to read, and this was a cause of perpetual humiliation. The secret desire of this little actor's heart was to play Shakespeare; he had "Hamlet" read to him, and pondered how to act it — all the time that he was flourishing his little cane and making his grimaces! He had chanced to be on the stage when a fire had broken out, and five or six hundred victims of greed were roasted to death. The actor had pleaded with the people to keep their seats, but all in vain; and all his life thereafter he went about with this vision of horror in his mind, and haunted by the passionate conviction that he had failed because of his lack of education — that if only he had been a man of culture, he would have been able to think of something to say to hold those terror-stricken people!

At three o'clock in the morning the performance came to an end, and then there were more refreshments; and Mrs. Vivie Patton came and sat by him, and they had a nice comfortable gossip. When Mrs. Vivie once got started at talking about people, her tongue ran on like a windmill.

There was Reggie Mann, meandering about and simpering at people. Reggie was in his glory at Mrs. do Graffenricd's affairs. Reggie had arranged all this — he did the designing and the ordering, and contracted for the shows with the agents. You could bet that ho had got his commission on them, too — though sometimes Mrs. do Graffenricd got the shows to come for nothing, because of the advertising her name would bring. Commissions wore Reggie's specialty — he had begun life as an auto agent. Montague didn't know what that was? An auto agent was a man who was forever begging his friends to use a certain kind of car, so that he might make a living; and Reggie had made about thirty thousand a year in that way. He had come from Boston, where his reputation had been made by the fact that early one morning, as they were driving home from a celebration, he had dared a young society matron to take off her shoes and stockings, and get out and wade in the public fountain; and she had done it, and he had followed her. On the strength of the éclat of this he had been taken up by Mrs. Devon; and one day Mrs. Devon had worn a white gown, and asked him what he thought of it. "It needs but one thing to make it perfect," said Reggie, and taking a red rose, he pinned it upon her corsage. The effect was magical; everyone exclaimed with delight, and so Reggie's reputation as an authority upon dress was made forever. Now he was Mrs. de Graffenried's right-hand man, and they made up their pranks together. Once they had walked down the street in Newport with a big rag doll between them. And Reggie had given a dinner at which the guest of honor had been a monkey — surely Montague had heard of that, for it had been the sensation of the season. It was really the funniest thing imaginable; the monkey wore a suit of broad-cloth with collar and cuffs, and he shook hands with all the guests, and behaved himself exactly like a gentleman — except that he did not get drunk.

And then Mrs. Vivie pointed out the great Mrs. Ridgley-Clieveden, who was sitting with one of her favorites, a grave, black-bearded gentleman who had leaped into fame by inheriting fifty million dollars. "Mrs. R.-C." had taken him up, and ordered his engagement book for him, and he was solemnly playing the part of a social light. He had purchased an old New York mansion, upon the decoration of which three million dollars had been spent; and when he came down to business from Tuxedo, his private train waited all day for him with steam up. Mrs. Vivie told an amusing tale of a woman who had announced her engagement to him, and borrowed large sums of money upon the strength of it, before his denial came out. That had been a source of great delight to Mrs. de Graffenried, who was furiously jealous of "Mrs. R. C."

From the anecdotes that people told, Montague judged that Mrs. de Graffenried must be one of those new leaders of Society, who, as Mrs. Alden said, were inclined to the bizarre and fantastic. Mrs. de Graffenried spent half a million dollars every season to hold the position of leader of the Newport set, and you could always count upon her for new and striking ideas. Once she had given away as cotillion favors tiny globes with goldfish in them; again she had given a dance at which everybody got themselves up as different vegetables. She was fond of going about at Newport and inviting people haphazard to lunch — thirty or forty at a time — and then surprising them with a splendid banquet. Again she would give a big formal dinner, and perplex people by offering them something which they really cared to eat. "You see," explained Mrs. Vivie, "at these dinners we generally get thick green turtle soup, and omelets with some sort of Florida water poured over them, and mushrooms cooked under glass, and real hand-made desserts; but Mrs. de Graffenried dares to have baked ham and sweet potatoes, or even real roast beef. You saw tonight that she had green corn; she must have arranged for that months ahead — we can never get it from Porto Rico until January. And you see this little dish of wild strawberries — they were probably transplanted and raised in a hothouse, and every single one wrapped separately before they were shipped."

All these labors had made Mrs. de Graffenried a tremendous power in the social world. She had a savage tongue, said Mrs. Vivie, and everyone lived in terror of her; but once in a while she met her match. Once she had invited a comic opera star to sing for her guests, and all the men had crowded round this actress, and Mrs. de Graffenried had flown into a passion and tried to drive them away; and the actress, lolling back in her chair, and gazing up idly at Mrs. do Graffenried, had drawled, "Ten years older than God!" Poor Mrs. de Graffenried would carry that saying with her until she died.

Something reminiscent of this came under Montague's notice that same evening. At about four o'clock Mrs. Vivie wished to go home, and asked him to find her escort, the Count St. Elmo de Champignon — the man, by the way, for whom her husband was gunning. Montague roamed all about the house, and finally went downstairs, where a room had been set apart for the theatrical company to partake of refreshments. Mrs. de Graffenriod's secretary was on guard at the door; but some of the boys had got into the room, and were drinking champagne and "making dates" with the chorus-girls. And here was Mrs. de Graffenried herself, pushing them bodily out of the room, a score and more of them — and among them Mrs. Vivie's Count!

Montague delivered his message, and then went upstairs to wait until his own party should be ready to leave. In the smoking-room were a number of men, also waiting; and among them he noticed Major Venable, in conversation with a man whom he did not know. "Come over here," the Major called; and Montague obeyed, at the same time noticing the stranger.

He was a tall, loose-jointed, powerfully built man, a small head and a very striking face: a grim mouth with drooping corners tightly set, and a hawklike nose, and deep-set, peering eyes. "Have you met Mr. Hegan?" said the Major. "Hegan, this is Mr. Allan Montague." Jim Hegan! Montague repressed a stare and took the chair which they offered him. "Have a cigar," said Hegan, holding out his case.

"Mr. Montague has just come to New York," said the Major. "He is a Southerner, too."

"Indeed?" said Hegan, and inquired what State he came from. Montague replied, and added, "I had the pleasure of meeting your daughter last week, at the Horse Show."

That served to start a conversation; for Hegan came from Texas, and when he found that Montague knew about horses — real horses — he warmed to him. Then the Major's party called him away, and the other two were left to carry on the conversation.

It was very easy to chat with Hegan; and yet underneath, in the other's mind, there lurked a vague feeling of trepidation, as he realized that he was chatting with a hundred millions of dollars. Montague was new enough at the game to imagine that there ought to be something strange, some atmosphere of awe and mystery, about a man who was master of a dozen railroads and of the politics of half a dozen States. He was simple and very kindly in his manner, a plain man, interested in plain things. There was about him, as he talked, a trace of timidity, almost of apology, which Montague noticed and wondered at. It was only later, when he had time to think about it, that he realized that Hegan had begun as a farmer's boy in Texas, a "poor white"; and could it be that after all these years an instinct remained in him, so that whenever he met a gentleman of the old South he stood by with a little deference, seeming to beg pardon for his hundred millions of dollars?

And yet there was the power of the man. Even chatting about horses, you felt it; you felt that there was a part of him which did not chat, but which sat behind and watched. And strangest of all, Montague found himself fancying that behind the face that smiled was another face, that did not smile, but that was grim and set. It was a strange face, with its broad, sweeping eyebrows and its drooping mouth; it haunted Montague and made him feel ill at ease.

There came Laura Hegan, who greeted them in her stately way; and Mrs. Hegan, bustling and vivacious, costumed en grande dame. "Come and see me some time," said the man. "You won't be apt to meet me otherwise, for I don't go about much." And so they took their departure; and Montague sat alone and smoked and thought. The face still stayed with him; and now suddenly, in a burst of light, it came to him what it was: the face of a bird of prey — of the great wild, lonely eagle! You have seen it, perhaps, in a menagerie; sitting high up, submitting patiently, biding its time. But all the while the soul of the eagle is far away, ranging the wide spaces, ready for the lightning swoop, and the clutch with the cruel talons!

Chapter X

*T*he next week was a busy one for the Montagues. The Robbie Wallings had come to town and opened their house, and the time drew near for the wonderful débutante dance at which Alice was to be formally presented to Society. And of course Alice must have a new dress for the occasion, and it must be absolutely the most beautiful dress ever known. In an idle moment her cousin figured out that it was to cost her about five dollars a minute to be entertained by the Wallings!

What it would cost the Wallings, one scarcely dared to think. Their ballroom would be turned into a flower-garden; and there would be a supper for a hundred guests, and still another supper after the dance, and costly favors for every figure. The purchasing of these latter had been entrusted to Oliver, and Montague heard with dismay what they were to cost. "Robbie couldn't afford to do anything second-rate," was the younger brother's only reply to his exclamations.

Alice divided her time between the Wallings and her costumiers, and every evening she came home with a new tale of important developments. Alice was new at the game, and could afford to be excited; and Mrs. Robbie liked to see her bright face, and to smile indulgently at her eager inquiries. Mrs. Robbie herself had given her orders to her steward and her florist and her secretary, and went on her way and thought no more about it. That was the way of the great ladies — or, at any rate, it was their pose.

The town-house of the Robbies was a stately palace occupying a block upon Fifth Avenue — one of the half-dozen mansions of the Walling family which were among the show places of the city. It would take a catalogue to list the establishments maintained by the Wallings — there was an estate in North Carolina, and another in the Adirondacks, and others on Long Island and in New Jersey. Also there were several in Newport — one which was almost never occupied, and which Mrs. Billy Alden sarcastically described as "a three-million-dollar castle on a desert."

Montague accompanied Alice once or twice, and had an opportunity to study Mrs. Robbie at home. There were thirty-eight servants in her establishment; it was a little state all in itself, with Mrs. Robbie as queen, and her housekeeper as prime minister, and under them as many different ranks and classes and castes as in a feudal principality. There had to be six separate dining rooms for the various kinds of servants who scorned each other; there were servants' servants and servants of servants' servants. There were only three to whom the mistress was supposed to give orders — the butler, the steward, and the housekeeper; she did not even know the names of many of them, and they were changed so often, that, as she declared, she had to leave it to her detective to distinguish between employees and burglars.

Mrs. Robbie was quite a young woman, but it pleased her to pose as a care-worn matron, weary of the responsibilities of her exalted station. The ignorant looked on and pictured her as living in the lap of ease, endowed with every opportunity: in reality the meanest kitchen-maid was freer — she was quite worn thin with the burdens that fell upon her. The huge machine was forever threatening to fall to pieces, and required the wisdom of Solomon and the patience of Job to keep it running. One paid one's steward a fortune, and yet he robbed right and left, and quarreled with the chef besides. The butler was suspected of getting drunk upon rare and costly vintages, and the new parlor-maid had turned out to be a Sunday reporter in disguise. The man who had come every day for ten years to wind the clocks of the establishment was dead, and the one who took care of the bric-à-brac was sick, and the housekeeper was in a panic over the prospect of having to train another.

And even suppose that you escaped from these things, the real problems of your life had still to be faced. It was not enough to keep alive; you had your career — your duties as a leader of Society. There was the daily mail, with all the pitiful letters from people begging money — actually in one single week there were demands for two million dollars. There were geniuses with patent incubators and stove-lifters, and every time you gave a ball you stirred up swarms of anarchists and cranks. And then there were the letters you really had to answer, and the calls that had to be paid. These latter were so many that people in the same neighborhood had arranged to have the same day at home; thus, if you lived on Madison Avenue you had Thursday; but even then it took a whole afternoon to leave your cards. And then there were invitations to be sent and accepted; and one was always making mistakes and offending somebody — people would become mortal enemies overnight, and expect all the world to know it the next morning. And now there were so many divorces and remarryings, with consequent changing of names; and some men knew about their wives' lovers and didn't care, and some did care, but didn't know — altogether it was like carrying a dozen chess games in your head. And then there was the hairdresser and the manicurist and the masseuse, and the tailor and the bootmaker and the jeweler; and then one absolutely had to glance through a newspaper, and to see one's children now and then.

All this Mrs. Robbie explained at luncheon; it was the rich man's burden, about which common people had no conception whatever. A person with a lot of money was like a barrel of molasses — all the flies in the neighborhood came buzzing about. It was perfectly incredible, the lengths to which people would go to get invited to your house; not only would they write and beg you, they might attack your business interests, and even bribe your friends. And on the other hand, when people thought you needed them, the time you had to get them to come! "Fancy," said Mrs. Robbie, "offering to give a dinner to an English countess, and having her try to charge you for coming!" And incredible as it might seem, some people had actually yielded to her, and the disgusting creature had played the social celebrity for a whole season, and made quite a handsome income out of it. There seemed to be no limit to the abjectness of some of the tuft-hunters in Society.

It was instructive to hear Mrs. Robbie denounce such evils; and yet — alas for human frailty — the next time that Montague called, the great lady was blazing with wrath over the tidings that a new foreign prince was coming to America, and that Mrs. Ridgely-Clieveden had stolen a march upon her and grabbed him. He was to be under her tutelage the entire time, and all the effulgence of his magnificence would be radiated upon that upstart house. Mrs. Robbie revenged herself by saying as many disagreeable things about Mrs. Ridgley-Clieveden as she could think of; winding up with the declaration that if she behaved with this prince as she had with the Russian grand duke, Mrs. Robbie Walling, for one, would cut her dead. And truly the details which Mrs. Robbie cited were calculated to suggest that her rival's hospitality was a reversion to the customs of primitive savagery.

The above is a fair sample of the kind of conversation that one heard whenever one visited any of the Wallings. Perhaps, as Mrs. Robbie said, it may have been their millions that made necessary their attitude toward other people; certain it was, at any rate, that Montague found them all most disagreeable people to know. There was always some tempest in a teapot over the latest machinations of their enemies. And then there was the whole dead mass of people who sponged upon them and toadied to them; and finally the barbarian hordes outside the magic circle of their acquaintance — some specimens of whom came up every day for ridicule. They had big feet and false teeth; they ate mush and molasses; they wore ready-made ties; they said: "Do you wish that I should do it?" Their grandfathers had been butchers and peddlers and other abhorrent things. Montague tried his best to like the Wallings, because of what they were doing for Alice; but after he had sat at their lunch-table and listened to a conversation such as this, he found himself in need of fresh air.

And then he would begin to wonder about his own relation to these people. If they talked about everyone else behind their backs, certainly they must talk about him behind his. And why did they go out of their way to make him at home, and why were they spending their money to launch Alice in Society? In the beginning he had assumed that they did it out of the goodness of their hearts; but now that he had looked into their hearts, he rejected the explanation. It was not their way to shower princely gifts upon strangers; in general, the attitude of all the Wallings toward a stranger was that of the London hooligan — "'Eave a 'arf a brick at 'im!" They considered themselves especially appointed by Providence to protect Society from the vulgar newly rich who poured into the city, seeking for notoriety and recognition. They prided themselves upon this attitude — they called it their "exclusiveness"; and the exclusiveness of the younger generations of Wallings had become a kind of insanity.

Nor could the reason be that Alice was beautiful and attractive. One could have imagined it if Mrs. Robbie had been like — say, Mrs. Winnie Duval. It was easy to think of Mrs. Winnie taking a fancy to a girl, and spending half her fortune upon her. But from a hundred little things that he had seen, Montague had come to realize that the Robbie Wallings, with all their wealth and power and grandeur, were actually quite stingy. While all the world saw them scattering fortunes in their pathway, in reality they were keeping track of every dollar. And Robbie himself was liable to panic fits of economy, in which he went to the most absurd excesses — Montague once heard him haggling over fifty cents with a cabman. Lavish hosts though they both were, it was the literal truth that they never spent money upon anyone but themselves — the end and aim of their every action was the power and prestige of the Robbie Wallings.

"They do it because they are friends of mine," said Oliver, and evidently wished that to satisfy his brother. But it only shifted the problem and set him to watching Robbie and Oliver, and trying to make out the basis of their relationship. There was a very grave question concerned in this. Oliver had come to New York comparatively poor, and now he was rich — or, at any rate, ho lived like a rich man. And his brother, whose scent was growing keener with every day of his stay in New York, had about made up his mind that Oliver got his money from Robbie Walling.

Here, again, the problem would have been simple, if it had been another person than Robbie; Montague would have concluded that his brother was a "hanger-on." There were many great families whose establishments were infested with such parasites. Siegfried Harvey, for instance, was a man who had always half a dozen young chaps hanging about him; good-looking and lively fellows, who hunted and played bridge, and amused the married women while their husbands were at work, and who, if ever they dropped a hint that they were hard up, might be reasonably certain of being offered a check. But if the Robbie Wallings were to write checks, it must be for value received. And what could the value be?

"Ollie" was rather a little god among the ultra-swagger; his taste was a kind of inspiration. And yet his brother noticed that in such questions he always deferred instantly to the Wallings; and surely the Wallings were not people to be persuaded that they needed anyone to guide them in matters of taste. Again, Ollie was the very devil of a wit, and people were heartily afraid of him; and Montague had noticed that he never by any chance made fun of Robbie — that the fetishes of the house of Walling were always treated with respect. So he had wondered if by any chance Robbie was maintaining his brother in princely state for the sake of his ability to make other people uncomfortable. But he realized that the Robbies, in their own view of it, could have no more need of wit than a battleship has need of popguns. Oliver's position, when they were about, was rather that of the man who hardly ever dared to be as clever as he might, because of the restless jealousy of his friend.

It was a mystery; and it made the elder brother very uncomfortable. Alice was young and guileless, and a pleasant person to patronize; but he was a man of the world, and it was his business to protect her. He had always paid his own way through life, and he was very loath to put himself under obligations to people like the Wallings, whom he did not like, and who, he felt instinctively, could not like him.

But of course there was nothing he could do about it. The date for the great festivity was set; and the Wallings were affable and friendly, and Alice all a-tremble with excitement. The evening arrived, and with it came the enemies of the Wallings, dressed in their jewels and fine raiment. They had been asked because they were too important to be skipped, and they had come because the Wallings were too powerful to be ignored. They revenged themselves by consuming many courses of elaborate and costly viands; and they shook hands with Alice and beamed upon her, and then discussed her behind her back as if she were a French doll in a show-case. They decided unanimously that her elder cousin was a "stick," and that the whole family were interlopers and shameless adventurers; but it was understood that since the Robbie Wallings had seen fit to take them up, it would be necessary to invite them about.

At any rate, that was the way it all seemed to Montague, who had been brooding. To Alice it was a splendid festivity, to which exquisite people came to take delight in each other's society. There were gorgeous costumes and sparkling gems; there was a symphony of perfumes, intoxicating the senses, and a golden flood of music streaming by; there were laughing voices and admiring glances, and handsome partners with whom one might dance through the portals of fairyland. — And then, next morning, there were accounts in all the newspapers, with descriptions of one's costume and then some of those present, and even the complete menus of the supper, to assist in preserving the memories of the wonderful occasion.

Now they were really in Society. A reporter called to get Alice's photo for the Sunday supplement; and floods of invitations came — and with them all the cares and perplexities about which Mrs. Robbie had told.

Some of these invitations had to be declined, and one must know whom it was safe to offend. Also, there was a long letter from a destitute widow, and a proposal from a foreign count. Mrs. Robbie's secretary had a list of many hundreds of these professional beggars and blackmailers.

Conspicuous at the dance was Mrs. Winnie, in a glorious electric-blue silk gown. And she shook her fan at Montague, exclaiming, "You wretched man — you promised to come and see me!"

"I've been out of town," Montague protested.

"Well, come to dinner tomorrow night," said Mrs. Winnie. "There'll be some bridge fiends."

"You forget I haven't learned to play," he objected.

"Well, come anyhow," she replied. "We'll teach you. I'm no player myself, and my husband will be there, and he's good-natured; and my brother Dan — he'll have to be whether he likes it or not."

So Montague visited the Snow Palace again, and met Winton Duval, the banker, — a tall, military-looking man of about fifty, with a big grey moustache, and bushy eyebrows, and the head of a lion. His was one of the city's biggest banking-houses, and in alliance with powerful interests in the Street. At present he was going in for mines in Mexico and South America, and so he was very seldom at home. He was a man of most rigid habits — he would come back unexpectedly after a month's trip, and expect to find everything ready for him, both at home and in his office, as if he had just stepped round the corner. Montague observed that he took his menu-card and jotted down his comments upon each dish, and then sent it down to the chef. Other people's dinners he very seldom attended, and when his wife gave her entertainments, he invariably dined at the club.

He pleaded a business engagement for the evening; and as brother Dan did not appear, Montague did not learn any bridge. The other four guests settled down to the game, and Montague and Mrs. Winnie sat and chatted, basking before the fireplace in the great entrance-hall.

"Have you seen Charlie Carter?" was the first question she asked him.

"Not lately," he answered; "I met him at Harvey's."

"I know that," said she. "They tell me he got drunk."

"I'm afraid he did," said Montague.

"Poor boy!" exclaimed Mrs. Winnie. "And Alice saw him! He must be heartbroken!"

Montague said nothing. "You know," she went on, "Charlie really means well. He has honestly an affectionate nature."

She paused; and Montague Said, vaguely, "I suppose so."

"You don't like him," said the other. "I can see that. And I suppose now Alice will have no use for him, either. And I had it all fixed up for her to reform him!"

Montague smiled in spite of himself.

"Oh, I know," said she. "It wouldn't have been easy. But you've no idea what a beautiful boy Charlie used to be, until all the women set to work to ruin him."

"I can imagine it," said Montague; but he did not warm to the subject.

"You're just like my husband," said Mrs. Winnie, sadly. "You have no use at all for anything that's weak or unfortunate."

There was a pause. "And I suppose," she said finally, "you'll be turning into a business man also — with no time for anybody or anything. Have you begun yet?"

— "Not yet," he answered. "I'm still looking round."

"I haven't the least idea about business," she confessed. "How does one begin at it?"

"I can't say I know that myself as yet," said Montague, laughing.

"Would you like to be a protégé of my husband's?" she asked.

The proposition was rather sudden, but he answered, with a smile, "I should have no objections. What would he do with me?"

"I don't know that. But he can do whatever he wants down town. And he'd show you how to make a lot of money if I asked him to." Then Mrs. Winnie added, quickly, "I mean it — he could do it, really."

"I haven't the least doubt of it," responded Montague.

"And what's more," she went on, "you don't want to be shy about taking advantage of the opportunities that come to you. You'll find you won't get along in New York unless you go right in and grab what you can. People will be quick enough to take advantage of you."

"They have all been very kind to me so far," said he. "But when I get ready for business, I'll harden my heart."

Mrs. Winnie sat lost in meditation. "I think business is dreadful," she said. "So much hard work and worry! Why can't men learn to get along without it?"

"There are bills that have to be paid," Montague replied.

"It's our dreadfully extravagant way of life," exclaimed the other. "Sometimes I wish I had never had any money in my life."

"You would soon tire of it," said he. "You would miss this house."

"I should not miss it a bit," said Mrs. Winnie, promptly. "That is really the truth — I don't care for this sort of thing at all. I'd like to live simply, and without so many cares and responsibilities. And some day I'm going to do it, too — I really am. I'm going to get myself a little farm, away off somewhere in the country. And I'm going there to live and raise chickens and vegetables, and have my own flower-gardens, that I can take care of myself. It will all be plain and simple —" and then

Mrs. Winnie stopped short, exclaiming, "You are laughing at me!"

"Not at all!" said Montague. "But I couldn't help thinking about the newspaper reporters —"

"There you are!" said she. "One can never have a beautiful dream, or try to do anything sensible — because of the newspaper reporters!"

If Montague had been meeting Mrs. Winnie Duval for the first time, he would have been impressed by her yearnings for the simple life; he would have thought it an important sign of the times. But alas, he knew by this time that his charming hostess had more flummery about her than anybody else he had encountered — and all of her own devising! Mrs. Winnie smoked her own private brand of cigarettes, and when she offered them to you, there were the arms of the old ducal house of Mont Morenci on the wrappers! And when you got a letter from Mrs. Winnie, you observed a three-cent stamp upon the envelope — for lavender was her color, and two-cent stamps were an atrocious red! So one might feel certain that it Mrs. Winnie ever went in for chicken-raising, the chickens would be especially imported from China or Patagonia, and the chicken-coops would be precise replicas of those in the old Château de Mont Morenci which she had visited in her automobile.

But Mrs. Winnie was beautiful, and quite entertaining to talk to, and so he was respectfully sympathetic while she told him about her pastoral intentions. And then she told him about Mrs. Caroline Smythe, who had called a meeting of her friends at one of the big hotels, and organized a society and founded the "Bide-a-Wee Home" for destitute cats. After that she switched off into psychic research — somebody had taken her to a séance, where grave college professors and ladies in spectacles sat round and waited for ghosts to materialize. It was Mrs. Winnie's first experience at this, and she was as excited as a child who has just found the key to the jam-closet. "I hardly knew whether to laugh or to be afraid," she said. "What would you think?"

"You may have the pleasure of giving me my first impressions of it," said Montague, with a laugh.

"Well," said she, "they had table-tipping — and it was the most uncanny thing to see the table go jumping about the room! And then there were raps — and one can't imagine how strange it was to see people who really believed they were getting messages from ghosts. It positively made my flesh creep. And then this woman — Madame Somebody-or-other — went into a trance — ugh! Afterward I talked with one of the men, and he told me about how his father had appeared to him in the night and told him he had just been drowned at sea. Have you ever heard of such a thing?"

"We have such a tradition in our family," said he.

"Every family seems to have," said Mrs. Winnie. "But, dear me, it made me so uncomfortable — I lay awake all night expecting to see my own father. He had the asthma, you know; and I kept fancying I heard him breathing."

They had risen and were strolling into the conservatory; and she glanced at the man in armor. "I got to fancying that his ghost might come to see me," she said. "I don't think I shall attend anymore séances. My husband was told that I promised them some money, and he was furious — he's afraid it'll get into the papers." And Montague shook with inward laughter, picturing what a time the aristocratic and stately old banker must have, trying to keep his wife out of the papers!

Mrs. Winnie turned on the lights in the fountain, and sat by the edge, gazing at her fish. Montague was half expecting her to inquire whether he thought that they had ghosts; but she spared him this, going off on another line.

"I asked Dr. Parry about it," she said. "Have you met him?"

Dr. Parry was the rector of St. Cecilia's, the fashionable Fifth Avenue church which most of Montague's acquaintances attended. "I haven't been in the city over Sunday yet," he answered. "But Alice has met him."

"You must go with me some time," said she. "But about the ghosts —"

"What did he say?"

"He seemed to be shy of them," laughed Mrs. Winnie. "He said it had a tendency to lead one into dangerous fields. But oh! I forgot — I asked my swami also, and it didn't startle him. They are used to ghosts; they believe that souls keep coming back to earth, you know. I think if it was his ghost, I wouldn't mind seeing it — for he has such beautiful eyes. He gave me a book of Hindu legends — and there was such a sweet story about a young princess who loved in vain, and died of grief; and her soul went into a tigress; and she came in the night-time where her lover lay sleeping by the firelight, and she carried him off into the ghost-world. It was a most creepy thing — I sat out here and read it, and I could imagine the terrible tigress lurking in the shadows, with its stripes shining in the firelight, and its green eyes gleaming. You know that poem — we used to read it in school — 'Tiger, tiger, burning bright!'"

It was not very easy for Montague to imagine a tigress in Mrs. Winnie's conservatory; unless, indeed, one were willing to take the proposition in a metaphorical sense. There are wild creatures which sleep in the heart of man, and which growl now and then, and stir their tawny limbs, and cause one to start and turn cold. Mrs. Winnie wore a dress of filmy softness, trimmed with red flowers which paled beside her own intenser coloring. She had a perfume of her own, with a strange exotic fragrance which touched the chorus of memory as only an odor can.

She leaned towards him, speaking eagerly, with her soft white arms lying upon the basin's rim. So much loveliness could not be gazed at without pain; and a faint trembling passed through Montague, like a breeze across a pool. Perhaps it touched Mrs. Winnie also, for she fell suddenly silent, and her gaze wandered off into the darkness. For a minute or two there was stillness, save for the pulse of the fountain, and the heaving of her bosom keeping time with it.

And then in the morning Oliver inquired, "Where were you, last night?" And when his brother answered, "At Mrs. Winnie's," he smiled and said, "Oh!" Then he added, gravely, "Cultivate Mrs. Winnie — you can't do better at present."

Chapter XI

Montague accepted his friend's invitation to share her pew at St. Cecilia's, and next Sunday morning he and Alice went, and found Mrs. Winnie with her cousin. Poor Charlie had evidently been scrubbed and shined, both physically and morally, and got ready to appeal for "one more chance." While he shook hands with Alice, he was gazing at her with dumb and pleading eyes; he seemed to be profoundly grateful that she did not refuse to enter the pew with him.

A most interesting place was St. Cecilia's. Church-going was another of the customs of men and women which Society had taken up, like the Opera, and made into a state function. Here was a magnificent temple, with carved marble and rare woods, and jewels gleaming decorously in a dim religious light. At the door of this edifice would halt the carriages of Society, and its wives and daughters would alight, rustling with new silk petticoats and starched and perfumed linen, each one a picture, exquisitely gowned and bonneted and gloved, and carrying a demure little prayer-book. Behind them followed the patient men, all in new frock-coats and shiny silk hats; the men of Society were always newly washed and shaved, newly groomed and gloved, but now they seemed to be more so — they were full of the atmosphere of Sunday. Alas for those unregenerate ones, the infidels and the heathen who scoff in outer darkness, and know not the delicious feeling of Sunday — the joy of being washed and starched and perfumed, and made to be clean and comfortable and good, after all the really dreadful wickedness of six days of fashionable life! — And afterward the parade upon the Avenue, with the congregations of several score additional churches, and such a show of stylish costumes that half the city came to see!

Amid this exquisite assemblage at St. Cecilia's, the revolutionary doctrines of the Christian religion produced neither perplexity nor alarm. The chance investigator might have listened in dismay to solemn pronouncements of everlasting damnation, to statements about rich men and the eyes of needles, and the lilies of the field which did not spin. But the congregation of St. Cecilia's understood that these things were to be taken in a quixotic sense; sharing the view of the French marquis that the Almighty would think twice before damning a gentleman like him.

One had heard these phrases ever since childhood, and one accepted them as a matter of course. After all, these doctrines had come from the lips of a divine being, whom it would be presumptuous in a mere mortal to attempt to imitate. Such points one could but leave to those whose business it was to interpret them — the doctors and dignitaries of the church; and when one met them, one's heart was set at rest — for they were not iconoclasts and alarmists, but gentlemen of culture and tact. The bishop who presided in this metropolitan district was a stately personage, who moved in the best Society and belonged to the most exclusive clubs.

The pews in St. Cecilia's were rented, and they were always in great demand; it was one of the customs of those who hung upon the fringe of Society to come every Sunday, and bow and smile, and hope against hope for some chance opening. The stranger who came was dependent upon hospitality; but there were soft-footed and tactful ushers, who would find one a seat, if one were a presentable person. The contingency of an unpresentable person seldom arose, for the proletariat did not swarm at the gates of St. Cecilia's. Out of its liberal income the church maintained a "mission" upon the East Side, where young curates wrestled with the natural depravity of the lower classes — meantime cultivating a soul-stirring tone, and waiting until they should be promoted to a real church. Society was becoming deferential to its religious guides, and would have been quite shocked at the idea that it exerted any pressure upon them; but the young curates were painfully aware of a process of unnatural selection, whereby those whose manner and cut of coat were not pleasing were left a long time in the slums. — On one occasion there had been an amusing blunder; a beautiful new church was built at Newport, and an eloquent young minister was installed, and all Society attended the opening service — and sat and listened in consternation to an arraignment of its own follies and vices! The next Sunday, needless to say, Society was not present; and within half a year the church was stranded, and had to be dismantled and sold!

They had elaborate music at St. Cecilia's, so beautiful that Alice felt uncomfortable, and thought that it was perilously "high." At this Mrs. Winnie laughed, offering to take her to an afternoon service around the corner, where they had a full orchestra, and a harp, and opera music, and incense and genuflections and confessionals. There were people, it seemed, who like to thrill themselves by dallying with the wickedness of "Romanism"; somewhat as a small boy tries to see how near he can walk to the edge of a cliff. The "father" at this church had a jeweled robe with a train so many yards long, and which had cost some incredible number of thousands of dollars; and every now and then he marched in a stately procession through the aisles, so that all the spectators might have a good look at it. There was a fierce controversy about these things in the church, and libraries of pamphlets were written, and intrigues and social wars were fought over them.

But Montague and Alice did not attend this service — they had promised themselves the very plebeian diversion of a ride in the subway; for so far they had not seen this feature of the city. People who lived in Society saw Madison and Fifth Avenues, where their homes were, with the churches and hotels scattered along them; and the shopping district just below, and the theater district at one side, and the park to the north. Unless one went automobiling, that was all of the city one need ever see. When visitors asked about the Aquarium, and the Stock Exchange, and the Museum of Art, and Tammany Hall, and Ellis Island, where the immigrants came, the old New Yorkers would look perplexed, and say: "Dear me, do you really want to see those things? Why, I have been here all my life, and have never seen them!"

For the hordes of sightseers there had been provided a special contrivance, a huge automobile omnibus which seated thirty or forty people, and went from the Battery to Harlem with a young man shouting through a megaphone a description of the sights. The irreverent had nicknamed this the "yap-wagon"; and declared that the company maintained a fake "opium-joint" in Chinatown, and a fake "dive" in the Bowery, and hired tough-looking individuals to sit and be stared at by credulous excursionists from Oklahoma and Kalamazoo. Of course it would never have done for people who had just been passed into

Society to climb upon a "yap-wagon"; but they were permitted to get into the subway, and were whirled with a deafening clatter through a long tunnel of steel and stone. And then they got out and climbed a steep hill like any common mortals, and stood and gazed at Grant's tomb: a huge white marble edifice upon a point overlooking the Hudson. Architecturally it was not a beautiful structure — but one was consoled by reflecting that the hero himself would not have cared about that. It might have been described as a soap-box with a cheese-box on top of it; and these homely and familiar articles were perhaps not altogether out of keeping with the character of the humblest great man who ever lived.

The view up the river was magnificent, quite the finest which the city had to offer; but it was ruined by a hideous gas-tank, placed squarely in the middle of it. And this, again, was not inappropriate — it was typical of all the ways of the city. It was a city which had grown up by accident, with nobody to care about it or to help it; it was huge and ungainly, crude, uncomfortable, and grotesque. There was nowhere in it a beautiful sight upon which a man could rest his eyes, without having them tortured by something ugly near by. At the foot of the slope of the River Drive ran a hideous freight-railroad; and across the river the beautiful Palisades were being blown to pieces to make paving stone — and meantime were covered with advertisements of land-companies. And if there was a beautiful building, there, was sure to be a tobacco advertisement beside it; if there was a beautiful avenue, there were trucks and overworked horses toiling in the harness; if there was a beautiful park, it was filled with wretched, outcast men. Nowhere was any order or system — everything was struggling for itself, and jarring and clashing with everything else; and this broke the spell of power which the Titan city would otherwise have produced. It seemed like a monstrous heap of wasted energies; a mountain in perpetual labor, and producing an endless series of abortions. The men and women in it were wearing themselves out with toil; but there was a spell laid upon them, so that, struggle as they might, they accomplished nothing.

Coming out of the church, Montague had met Judge Ellis; and the Judge had said, "I shall soon have something to talk over with you." So Montague gave him his address, and a day or two later came an invitation to lunch with him at his club.

The Judge's club took up a Fifth Avenue block, and was stately and imposing. It had been formed in the stress of the Civil War days; lean and hungry heroes had come home from battle and gone into business, and those who had succeeded had settled down here to rest. To see them now, dozing in huge leather-cushioned armchairs, you would have had a hard time to guess that they had ever been lean and hungry heroes. They were diplomats and statesmen, bishops and lawyers, great merchants and financiers — the men who had made the city's ruling-class for a century. Everything here was decorous and grave, and the waiters stole about with noiseless feet.

Montague talked with the Judge about New York and what he had seen of it, and the people he had met; and about his father, and the war; and about the recent election and the business outlook. And meantime they ordered luncheon; and when they had got to the cigars, the Judge coughed and said, "And now I have a matter of business to talk over with you."

Montague settled himself to listen. "I have a friend," the Judge explained — "a very good friend, who has asked me to find him a lawyer to undertake an important case. I talked the matter over with General Prentice, and he agreed with me that it would be a good idea to lay the matter before you."

"I am very much obliged to you," said Montague.

"The matter is a delicate one," continued the other. "It has to do with life insurance. Are you familiar with the insurance business?"

"Not at all."

"I had supposed not," said the Judge. "There are some conditions which are not generally known about, but which I may say, to put it mildly, are not altogether satisfactory. My friend is a large policy-holder in several companies, and he is not satisfied with the management of them. The delicacy of the situation, so far as I am concerned, is that the company with which he has the most fault to find is one in which I myself am a director. You understand?"

"Perfectly," said Montague. "What company is it?"

"The Fidelity," replied the other — and his companion thought in a flash of Freddie Vandam, whom he had met at Castle Havens! For the Fidelity was Freddie's company.

"The first thing that I have to ask you," continued the Judge, "is that, whether you care to take the case or not, you will consider my own intervention in the matter absolutely entré nous. My position is simply this: I have protested at the meetings of the directors of the company against what I consider an unwise policy — and my protests have been ignored. And when my friend asked me for advice, I gave it to him; but at the same time I am not in a position to be publicly quoted in connection with the matter. You follow me?"

"Perfectly," said the other. "I will agree to what you ask."

"Very good. Now then, the condition is, in brief, this: the companies are accumulating an enormous surplus, which, under the law, belongs to the policy-holders; but the administrations of the various companies are withholding these dividends, for the sake of the banking-power which these accumulated funds afford to them and their associates. This is, as I hold, a very manifest injustice, and a most dangerous condition of affairs."

"I should say so!" responded Montague. He was amazed at such a statement, coming from such a source. "How could this continue?" he asked.

"It has continued for a long time," the Judge answered.

"But why is it not known?"

"It is perfectly well known to everyone in the insurance business," was the answer. "The matter has never been taken up or published, simply because the interests involved have such enormous and widely extended power that no one has ever dared to attack them,"

Montague sat forward, with his eyes riveted upon the Judge. "Go on," he said.

"The situation is simply this," said the other. "My friend, Mr. Hasbrook, wishes to bring a suit against the Fidelity Company to compel it to pay to him his proper share of its surplus. He wishes the suit pressed, and followed to the court of last resort."

"And do you mean to tell me," asked Montague, "that you would have any difficulty to find a lawyer in New York to undertake such a case?"

"No," said the other, "not exactly that. There are lawyers in New York who would undertake anything. But to find a lawyer of standing who would take it, and withstand all the pressure that would be brought to bear upon him — that might take some time."

"You astonish me, Judge."

"Financial interests in this city are pretty closely tied together, Mr. Montague. Of course there are law firms which are identified with interests opposed to those who control the company. It would be very easy to get them to take the case, but you can see that in that event my friend would be accused of bringing the suit in their interest; whereas he wishes it to appear, as it really is, a suit of an independent person, seeking the rights of the vast body of the policy-holders. For that reason, he wished to find a lawyer who was identified with no interest of any sort, and who was free to give his undivided attention to the issue. So I thought of you."

"I will take the case," said Montague instantly.

"It is my duty to warn you," said the Judge, gravely, "that you will be taking a very serious step. You must be prepared to face powerful, and, I am afraid, unscrupulous enemies. You may find that you have made it impossible for other and very desirable clients to deal with you. You may find your business interests, if you have any, embarrassed — your credit impaired, and so on. You must be prepared to have your character assailed, and your motives impugned in the public press. You may find that social pressure will be brought to bear on you. So it is a step from which most young men who have their careers to make would shrink."

Montague's face had turned a shade paler as he listened. "I am assuming," he said, "that the facts are as you have stated them to me — that an unjust condition exists."

"You may assume that."

"Very well." And Montague clenched his hand, and put it down upon the table. "I will take the case," he said.

For a few moments they sat in silence.

"I will arrange," said the Judge, at last, "for you and Mr. Hasbrook to meet. I must explain to you, as a matter of fairness, that he is a rich man, and will be able to pay you for your services. He is asking a great deal of you, and he should expect to pay for it."

Montague sat in thought. "I have not really had time to get my bearings in New York," he said at last. "I think I had best leave it to you to say what I should charge him."

"If I were in your position," the Judge answered, "I think that I should ask a retaining-fee of fifty thousand dollars. I believe he will expect to pay at least that."

Montague could scarcely repress a start. Fifty thousand dollars! The words made his head whirl round. But then, all of a sudden, he recalled his half-jesting resolve to play the game of business sternly. So he nodded his head gravely, and said, "Very well; I am much obliged to you."

After a pause, he added, "I hope that I may prove able to handle the case to your friend's satisfaction."

"Your ability remains for you to prove," said the Judge. "I have only been in position to assure him of your character."

"He must understand, of course," said Montague, "that I am a stranger, and that it will take me a while to study the situation."

"Of course he knows that. But you will find that Mr. Hasbrook knows a good deal about the law himself. And he has already had a lot of work done. You must understand that it is very easy to get legal advice about such a matter — what is sought is someone to take the conduct of the case."

"I see," said Montague; and the Judge added, with a smile, "Someone to get up on horseback, and draw the fire of the enemy!"

And then the great man was, as usual, reminded of a story; and then of more stories; until at last they rose from the table, and shook hands upon their bargain, and parted.

Fifty thousand dollars! Fifty thousand dollars! It was all Montague could do to keep from exclaiming it aloud on the street. He could hardly believe that it was a reality — if it had been a less-known person than Judge Ellis, he would have suspected that someone must be playing a joke upon him. Fifty thousand dollars was more than many a lawyer made at home in a lifetime; and simply as a retaining-fee in one case! The problem of a living had weighed on his soul ever since the first day in the city, and now suddenly it was solved; all in a few minutes, the way had been swept clear before him. He walked home as if upon air.

And then there was the excitement of telling the family about it. He had an idea that his brother might be alarmed if he were told about the seriousness of the case; and so he simply said that the Judge had brought him a rich client, and that it was an insurance case. Oliver, who knew and cared nothing about law, asked no questions, and contented himself with saying, "I told you how easy it was to make money in New York, if only you knew the right people!" As for Alice, she had known all along that her cousin was a great man, and that clients would come to him as soon as he hung out his sign.

His sign was not out yet, by the way; that was the next thing to be attended to. He must get himself an office at once, and some books, and begin to read up insurance law; and so, bright and early the next morning, he took the subway down town.

And here, for the first time, Montague saw the real New York. All the rest was mere shadow — the rest was where men slept and played, but Jiere was where they fought out the battle of their lives. Here the fierce intensity of it smote him in the face — he saw the cruel waste and ruin of it, the wreckage of the blind, haphazard strife.

It was a city caught in a trap. It was pent in at one end of a narrow little island. It had been no one's business to foresee that it must some day outgrow this space; now men were digging a score of tunnels to set it free, but they had not begun these until the pressure had become unendurable, and now it had reached its climax. In the financial district, land had been sold for as much as four dollars a square inch. Huge blocks of buildings shot up to the sky in a few months — fifteen, twenty, twenty-five stories of them, and with half a dozen stories hewn out of the solid rock beneath; there was to be one building of forty-two stories, six hundred and fifty feet in height. And between them were narrow chasms of streets, where the hurrying crowds overflowed the sidewalks. Yet other streets were filled with trucks and heavy vehicles, with electric cars creeping slowly along, and little swirls and eddies of people darting across here and there.

These huge buildings were like beehives, swarming with life and activity, with scores of elevators shooting through them at bewildering speed. Everywhere was the atmosphere of rush; the spirit of it seized hold of one, and he began to hurry, even though he had no place to go. The man who walked slowly and looked about him was in the way — he was jostled here and there, and people eyed him with suspicion and annoyance.

Elsewhere on the island men did the work of the city; here they did the work of the world. Each room in these endless mazes of buildings was a cell in a mighty brain; the telephone wires were nerves, and by the whole huge organism the thinking and willing of a continent were done. It was a noisy place to the physical ear; but to the ear of the mind it roared with the roaring of a thousand Niagaras. Here was the Stock Exchange, where the scales of trade were held before the eyes of the country. Here was the clearing-house, where hundreds of millions of dollars were exchanged every day. Here were the great banks, the reservoirs into which the streams of the country's wealth were poured. Here were the brains of the great railroad systems, of the telegraph and telephone systems, of mines and mills and factories. Here were the centers of the country's trade; in one place the shipping trade, in another the jewelry trade, the grocery trade, the leather trade. A little farther up town was the clothing district, where one might see the signs of more Hebrews than all Jerusalem had ever held; in yet other districts were the newspaper offices, and the center of the magazine and book-publishing business of the whole country. One might climb to the top of one of the great "sky-scrapers," and gaze down upon a wilderness of houses, with roofs as innumerable as tree-tops, and people looking like tiny insects below. Or one might go out into the harbor late upon a winter afternoon, and see it as a city of a million lights, rising like an incantation from the sea. Round about it was an unbroken ring of docks, with ferry-boats and tugs darting everywhere, and vessels which had come from every port in the world, emptying their cargoes into the huge maw of the Metropolis.

And of all this, nothing had been planned! All lay just as it had fallen, and men bore the confusion and the waste as best they could. Here were huge steel vaults, in which lay many billions of dollars' worth of securities, the control of the finances of the country; and a block or two in one direction were warehouses and gin-mills, and in another direction cheap lodging-houses and sweating-dens. And at a certain hour all this huge machine would come to a halt, and its millions of human units would make a blind rush for their homes. Then at the entrances to bridges and ferries and trams, would be seen sights of madness and terror; throngs of men and women swept hither and thither, pushing and struggling, shouting, cursing — righting, now and then, in sudden panic fear. All decency was forgotten here — people would be mashed into cars like football players in a heap, and guards and policemen would jam the gates tight — or like as not be swept away themselves in the pushing, grunting, writhing mass of human beings. Women would faint and be trampled; men would come out with clothing torn to shreds, and sometimes with broken arms or ribs. And thinking people would gaze at the sight and shudder, wondering — how long a city could hold together, when the masses of its population were thus forced back, day after day, habitually, upon the elemental brute within them.

In this vast business district Montague would have felt utterly lost and helpless, if it had not been for that fifty thousand dollars, and the sense of mastery which it gave him. He sought out General Prentice, and under his guidance selected his suite of rooms, and got his furniture and books in readiness. And a day or two later, by appointment, came Mr. Hasbrook.

He was a wiry, nervous little man, who did not impress one as much of a personality; but he had the insurance situation at his fingers' ends — his grievance had evidently wrought upon him. Certainly, if half of what he alleged were true, it was time that the courts took hold of the affair.

Montague spent the whole day in consultation, going over every aspect of the case, and laying out his course of procedure. And then, at the end, Mr. Hasbrook remarked that it would be necessary for them to make some financial arrangement. And the other set his teeth together, and took a tight grip upon himself, and said, "Considering the importance of the case, and all the circumstances, I think I should have a retainer of fifty thousand dollars."

And the little man never turned a hair! "That will be perfectly satisfactory," he said. "I will attend to it at once." And the other's heart gave a great leap.

And sure enough, the next morning's mail brought the money, in the shape of a cashier's check from one of the big banks. Montague deposited it to his own account, and felt that the city was his!

And so he flung himself into the work. He went to his office every day, and he shut himself up in his own rooms in the evening. Mrs. Winnie was in despair because he would not come and learn bridge, and Mrs. Vivie Patton sought him in vain for a weekend party. He could not exactly say that while the others slept he was toiling upward in the night, for the others did not sleep in the night; but he could say that while they were feasting and dancing, he was delving into insurance law. Oliver argued in vain to make him realize that he could not live forever upon one client; and that it was as important for a lawyer to be a social light as to win his first big case. Montague was so absorbed that he even failed to be thrilled when one morning he opened an invitation envelope, and read the fateful legend: "Mrs. Devon requests the honor of your company" — telling him that he had "passed" on that critical examination morning, and that he was definitely and irrevocably in Society!

Chapter XII

Montague was now a capitalist, and therefore a keeper of the gates of opportunity. It seemed as though the seekers for admission must have had some occult way of finding it out; almost immediately they began to lay siege to him.

About a week after his check arrived, Major Thorne, whom he had met the first evening at the Loyal Legion, called him up and asked to see him; and he came to Montague's room that evening, and after chatting awhile about old times, proceeded to unfold a business proposition. It seemed that the Major had a grandson, a young mechanical engineer, who had been laboring for a couple of years at a very important invention, a device for loading coal upon steamships and weighing it automatically in the process. It was a very complicated problem, needless to say, but it had been solved successfully, and patents had been applied for, and a working model constructed. But it had proved unexpectedly difficult to interest the officials of the great steamship companies in the device. There was no doubt about the practicability of the machine, or the economies it would effect; but the officials raised trivial objections, and caused delays, and offered prices that were ridiculously inadequate. So the young inventor had conceived the idea of organizing a company to manufacture the machines, and rent them upon a royalty. "I didn't know whether you would have any money," said Major Thorne, "– but I thought you might be in touch with others who could be got to look into the matter. There is a fortune in it for those who take it up."

Montague was interested, and he looked over the plans and descriptions which his friend had brought, and said that he would see the working model, and talk the proposition over with others. And so the Major took his departure.

The first person Montague spoke to about it was Oliver, with whom he chanced to be lunching, at the latter's club. This was the "All Night" club, a meeting place of fast young Society men and millionaire Bohemians, who made a practice of going to bed at daylight, and had taken for their motto the words of Tennyson — "For men may come and men may go, but I go on forever." It was not a proper club for his brother to join, Oliver considered; Montague's "game" was the heavy respectable, and the person to put him up was General Prentice. But he was permitted to lunch there with his brother to chaperon him — and also Reggie Mann, who happened in, fresh from talking over the itinerary of the foreign prince with Mrs. Ridgley-Clieveden, and bringing a diverting account of how Mrs. R.-C. had had a fisticuffs with her maid.

Montague mentioned the invention casually, and with no idea that his brother would have an opinion one way or the other. But Oliver had quite a vigorous opinion: "Good God, Allan, you aren't going to let yourself be persuaded into a thing like that!"

"But what do you know about it?" asked the other. "It may be a tremendous thing."

"Of course!" cried Oliver. "But what can you tell about it? You'll be like a child in other people's hands, and they'll be certain to rob you. And why in the world do you want to take risks when you don't have to?"

"I have to put my money somewhere," said Montague.

"His first fee is burning a hole in his pocket!" put in Reggie Mann, with a chuckle. "Turn it over to me, Mr. Montague; and let me spend it in a gorgeous entertainment for Alice; and the prestige of it will bring you more cases than you can handle in a lifetime!"

"He had much better spend it all for soda water than buy a lot of coal chutes with it," said Oliver: "Wait awhile, and let me find you some place to put your money, and you'll see that you don't have to take any risks."

"I had no idea of taking it up until I'd made certain of it," replied the other. "And those whose judgment I took would, of course, go in also."

The younger man thought for a moment. "You are going to dine with

Major Venable tonight, aren't you?" he asked; and when the other answered in the affirmative, he continued, "Very well, then, ask him. The Major's been a capitalist for forty years, and if you can get him to take it up, why, you'll know you're safe."

Major Venable had taken quite a fancy to Montague — perhaps the old gentleman liked to have somebody to gossip with, to whom all his anecdotes were new. He had seconded Montague's name at the "Millionaires'," where he lived, and had asked him there to make the acquaintance of some of the other members. Before Montague parted with his brother, he promised that he would talk the matter over with the Major.

The Millionaires' was the show club of the city, the one which the ineffably rich had set apart for themselves. It was up by the park, in a magnificent white marble palace which had cost a million dollars. Montague felt that he had never really known the Major until he saw him here. The Major was excellent at all times and places, but in this club he became an edition deluxe of himself. He made his headquarters here, keeping his suite of rooms all the year round; and the atmosphere and surroundings of the place seemed to be a part of him.

Montague thought that the Major's face grew redder every day, and the purple veins in it purpler; or was it that the old gentleman's shirt bosom gleamed more brightly in the glare of the lights? The Major met him in the stately entrance hall, fifty feet square and all of Numidian marble, with a ceiling of gold, and a great bronze stairway leading to the gallery above. He apologized for his velvet slippers and for his hobbling walk — he was getting his accursed gout again. But he limped around and introduced his friend to the other millionaires — and then told scandal about them behind their backs.

The Major was the very type of a blue-blooded old aristocrat; he was all noblesse oblige to those within the magic circle of his intimacy — but alas for those outside it! Montague had never heard anyone bully servants as the Major did. "Here you!" he would cry, when something went wrong at the table. "Don't you know any better than to bring me a dish like that? Go and send me somebody who knows how to set a table!" And, strange to say, the servants all acknowledged his perfect right to bully them, and flew with terrified alacrity to do his bidding. Montague noticed that the whole staff of the club leaped into activity whenever the Major appeared; and when he was seated at the table, he led off in this fashion — "Now I want two dry Martinis. And I want them at once — do you understand me? Don't stop to get me any butter plates or finger-bowls — I want two cock-tails, just as quick as you can carry them!"

Dinner was an important event to Major Venable — the most important in life. The younger man humbly declined to make any suggestions,
and sat and watched while his friend did all the ordering. They had
some very small oysters, and an onion soup, and a grouse and asparagus,
with some wine from the Major's own private store, and then a romaine
salad. Concerning each one of these courses, the Major gave special
injunctions, and throughout his conversation he scattered comments
upon them: "This is good thick soup — lots of nourishment in onion
soup. Have the rest of this? — I think the Burgundy is too cold. Sixty-five
is as cold as Burgundy ought ever to be. I don't mind sherry as low as
sixty. — They always cook a bird too much — Robbie Waiting's chef is
the only person I know who never makes a mistake with game."

All this, of course, was between comments upon the assembled
millionaires. There was Hawkins, the corporation lawyer; a shrewd
fellow, cold as a corpse. He was named for an ambassadorship — a very
efficient. man. Used to be old Wyman's confidential adviser and buy
aldermen for him. — And the man at table with him was Harrison,
publisher of the Star; administration newspaper, sound and conserva-
tive. Harrison was training for a cabinet position. He was a nice little
man, and would make a fine splurge in Washington. — And that tall
man coming in was Clarke, the steel magnate; and over there was Adams,
a big lawyer also — prominent reformer — civic righteousness and all
that sort of stuff. Represented the Oil Trust secretly, and went down to
Trenton to argue against some reform measure, and took along fifty
thousand dollars in bills in his valise. "A friend of mine got wind of
what he was doing, and taxed him with it," said the Major, and laughed
gleefully over the great lawyer's reply — "How did I know but I might
have to pay for my own lunch?" — And the fat man with him — that
was Jimmie Featherstone, the chap who had inherited a big estate. "Poor
Jimmie's going all to pieces," the Major declared. "Goes down town to
board meetings now and then — they tell a hair-raising story about him
and old Dan Waterman. He had got up and started a long argument,
when Waterman broke in, 'But at the earlier meeting you argued directly
to the contrary, Mr. Featherstone!' 'Did I?' said Jimmie, looking bewildered. 'I wonder why I did that?' 'Well, Mr. Featherstone, since you ask
me, I'll tell you,' said old Dan — he's savage as a wild boar, you know,
and won't be delayed at meetings. 'The reason is that the last time you
were drunker than you are now. If you would adopt a uniform standard
of intoxication for the directors' meetings of this road, it would expedite
matters considerably.'"

They had got as far as the romaine salad. The waiter came with a bowl
of dressing — and at the sight of it, the old gentleman forgot Jimmie

Featherstone. "Why are you bringing me that stuff?" he cried. "I don't want that! Take it away and get me some vinegar and oil."

The waiter fled in dismay, while the Major went on growling under his breath. Then from behind him came a voice: "What's the matter with you this evening, Venable? You're peevish!"

The Major looked up. "Hello, you old cormorant," said he. "How do you do these days?"

The old cormorant replied that he did very well. He was a pudgy little man, with a pursed-up, wrinkled face. "My friend Mr. Montague – Mr. Symmes," said the Major.

"I am very pleased to meet you, Mr. Montague," said Mr. Symmes, peering over his spectacles.

"And what are you doing with yourself these days?" asked the Major.

The other smiled genially. "Nothing much," said he. "Seducing my friends' wives, as usual."

"And who's the latest?"

"Read the newspapers, and you'll find out," laughed Symmes. "I'm told I'm being shadowed."

He passed on down the room, chuckling to himself; and the Major said, "That's Maltby Symmes. Have you heard of him?"

"No," said Montague.

"He gets into the papers a good deal. He was up in supplementary proceedings the other day – couldn't pay his liquor bill."

"A member of the Millionaires'?" laughed Montague.

"Yes, the papers made quite a joke out of it," said the other. "But you see he's run through a couple of fortunes; the last was his mother's – eleven millions, I believe. He's been a pretty lively old boy in his time."

The vinegar and oil had now arrived, and the Major set to work to dress the salad. This was quite a ceremony, and Montague took it with amused interest. The Major first gathered all the necessary articles together, and looked them all over and grumbled at them. Then he mixed the vinegar and the pepper and salt, a tablespoonful at a time, and poured it over the salad. Then very slowly and carefully the oil had to be poured on, the salad being poked and turned about so that it would be all absorbed. Perhaps it was because he was so busy narrating the escapades of Maltty Symmes that the old gentleman kneaded it about so long; all the time fussing over it like a hen-partridge with her chicks, and interrupting himself every sentence or two: "It was Lenore, the opera star, and he gave her about two hundred thousand dollars' worth of railroad shares. (Really, you know, romaine ought not to be served in a bowl at all, but in a square, flat dish, so that one could keep the ends quite dry.) And when they quarreled, she found the old scamp had fooled her — the shares had never been transferred. (One is not supposed to use a fork at all, you know.) But she sued him, and he settled with her for about half the value. (If this dressing were done properly, there ought not to be any oil in the bottom of the dish at all.)"

This last remark meant that the process had reached its climax — that the long, crisp leaves were receiving their final affectionate overturnings. While the waiter stood at respectful attention, two or three pieces at a time were laid carefully upon the little silver plate intended for Montague. "And now," said the triumphant host, "try it! If it's good, it ought to be neither sweet nor bitter, but just right." — And he watched anxiously while Montague tasted it, saying, "If it's the least bit bitter, say so; and we'll send it out. I've told them about it often enough before."

But it was not bitter, and so the Major proceeded to help himself, after which the waiter whisked the bowl away. "I'm told that salad is the one vegetable we have from the Romans," said the old boy, as he munched at the crisp green leaves. "It's mentioned by Horace, you know. — As I was saying, all this was in Symmes's early days. But since his son's been grown up, he's married another chorus-girl."

After the salad the Major had another cocktail. In the beginning Montague had noticed that his hands shook and his eyes were watery; but now, after these copious libations, he was vigorous, and, if possible, more full of anecdotes than ever. Montague thought that it would be a good time to broach his inquiry, and so when the coffee had been served, he asked, "Have you any objections to talking business after dinner?"

"Not with you," said the Major. "Why? What is it?"

And then Montague told him about his friend's proposition, and described the invention. The other listened attentively to the end; and then, after a pause, Montague asked him, "What do you think of it?"

"The invention's no good," said the Major, promptly.

"How do you know?" asked the other.

"Because, if it had been, the companies would have taken it long ago, without paying him a cent."

"But he has it patented," said Montague.

"Patented hell!" replied the other. "What's a patent to lawyers of concerns of that size? They'd have taken it and had it in use from Maine to Texas; and when he sued, they'd have tied the case up in so many technicalities and quibbles that he couldn't have got to the end of it in ten years — and he'd have been ruined ten times over in the process."

"Is that really done?" asked Montague.

"Done!" exclaimed the Major. "It's done so often you might say it's the only thing that's done. — The people are probably trying to take you in with a fake."

"That couldn't possibly be so," responded the other. "The man is a friend —"

"I've found it an excellent rule never to do business with friends," said the Major, grimly.

"But listen," said Montague; and he argued long enough to convince his companion that that could not be the true explanation. Then the Major sat for a minute or two and pondered; and suddenly he exclaimed, "I have it! I see why they won't touch it!"

"What is it?"

"It's the coal companies! They're giving the steamships short weight, and they don't want the coal weighed truly!"

"But there's no sense in that," said Montague. "It's the steamship companies that won't take the machine."

"Yes," said the Major; "naturally, their officers are sharing the graft." And he laughed heartily at Montague's look of perplexity.

"Do you know anything about the business?" Montague asked.

"Nothing whatever," said the Major. "I am like the German who shut himself up in his inner consciousness and deduced the shape of an elephant from first principles. I know the game of big business from A to Z, and I'm telling you that if the invention is good and the companies won't take it, that's the reason; and I'll lay you a wager that if you were to make an investigation, some such thing as that is what you'd find! Last winter I went South on a steamer, and when we got near port, I saw them dumping a ton or two of good food overboard; and I made inquiries, and learned that one of the officials of the company ran a farm, and furnished the stuff — and the orders were to get rid of so much every trip!"

Montague's jaw had fallen. "What could Major Thorne do against such a combination?" he asked.

"I don't know," said the Major, shrugging his shoulders. "It's a case to take to a lawyer — one who knows the ropes. Hawkins over there would know what to tell you. I should imagine the thing he'd advise would be to call a strike of the men who handle the coal, and tie up the companies and bring them to terms."

"You're joking now!" exclaimed the other.

"Not at all," said the Major, laughing again. "It's done all the time. There's a building trust in this city, and the way it put all its rivals out of business was by having strikes called on their jobs."

"But how could it do that?"

"Easiest thing in the world. A labor leader is a man with a great deal of power, and a very small salary to live on. And even if he won't sell out — there are other ways. I could introduce you to a man right in this

room who had a big strike on at an inconvenient time, and he had the
president of the union trapped in a hotel with a woman, and the poor
fellow gave in and called off the strike."

"I should think the strikers might sometimes get out of hand," said
Montague.

"Sometimes they do," smiled the other. "There is a regular procedure
for that case. Then you hire detectives and start violence, and call out
the militia and put the strike leaders into jail."

Montague could think of nothing to say to that. The program seemed
to be complete.

"You see," the Major continued, earnestly, "I'm advising you as a
friend, and I'm taking the point of view of a man who has money in
his pocket. I've had some there always, but I've had to work hard to
keep it there. All my life I've been surrounded by people who wanted
to do me good; and the way they wanted to do it was to exchange my
real money for pieces of paper which they'd had printed with fancy
scroll-work and eagles and flags. Of course, if you want to look at the
thing from the other side, why, then the invention is most ingenious,
and trade is booming just now, and this is a great country, and merit is
all you need in it – and everything else is just as it ought to be. It makes
ahl the difference in the world, you know, whether a man is buying a
horse or selling him!"

Montague had observed with perplexity that such incendiary talk as
this was one of the characteristics of people in these lofty altitudes. It
was one of the liberties accorded to their station. Editors and bishops
and statesmen and all the rest of their retainers had to believe in the
respectabilities, even in the privacy of their clubs – the people's ears
were getting terribly sharp these days! But among the real giants of
business you might have thought yourself in a society of revolutionists;
they would tear up the mountain tops and hurl them at each other.
When one of these old warhorses once got started, he would tell tales
of deviltry to appall the soul of the hardiest muck-rake man. It was
always the other fellow, of course; but then, if you pinned your man
down, and if he thought that he could trust you – he would acknowledge
that he had sometimes fought the enemy with the enemy's own weapons!

But of course one must understand that all this radicalism was for
conversational purposes only. The Major, for instance, never had the
slightest idea of doing anything about all the evils of which he told;
when it came to action, he proposed to do just what he had done all
his life – to sit tight on his own little pile. And the Millionaires' was
an excellent place to learn to do it!

"See that old money-bags over there in the corner," said the Major.

"He's a man you want to fix in your mind – old Henry S. Grimes. Have you heard of him?"

"Vaguely," said the other.

"He's Laura Hegan's uncle. She'll have his money also some day – but Lord, how he does hold on to it meantime! It's quite tragic, if you come to know him – he's frightened at his own shadow. He goes in for slum tenements, and I guess he evicts more people in a month than you could crowd into this building!"

Montague looked at the solitary figure at the table, a man with a wizened-up little face like a weasel's, and a big napkin tied around his neck. "That's so as to save his shirt-front for tomorrow," the Major explained. "He's really only about sixty, but you'd think he was eighty. Three times every day he sits here and eats a bowl of graham crackers and milk, and then goes out and sits rigid in an armchair for an hour. That's the regimen his doctors have put him on – angels and ministers of grace defend us!"

The old gentleman paused, and a chuckle shook his scarlet jowls. "Only think!" he said – "they tried to do that to me! But no, sir – when Bob Venable has to eat graham crackers and milk, he'll put in arsenic instead of sugar! That's the way with many a one of these rich fellows, though – you picture him living in Capuan luxury, when, as a matter of fact, he's a man with a torpid liver and a weak stomach, who is put to bed at ten o'clock with a hot-water bag and a flannel nightcap!"

The two had got up and were strolling toward the smoking-room; when suddenly at one side a door opened, and a group of men came out. At the head of them was an extraordinary figure, a big powerful body with a grim face. "Hello!" said the Major. "All the big bugs are here tonight. There must be a governors' meeting."

"Who is that?" asked his companion; and he answered, "That? Why, that's Dan Waterman."

Dan Waterman! Montague stared harder than ever, and now he identified the face with the pictures he had seen. Waterman, the Colossus of finance, the Croesus of copper and gold! How many trusts had Waterman organized! And how many puns had been made upon that name of his!

"Who are the other men?" Montague asked.

"Oh, they're just little millionaires," was the reply.

The "little millionaires" were following as a kind of bodyguard; one of them, who was short and pudgy, was half running, to keep up with Waterman's heavy stride. When they came to the coat-room, they crowded the attendants away, and one helped the great man on with his coat, and another held his hat, and another his stick, and two others tried to talk to him. And Waterman stolidly buttoned his coat, and then seized his hat and stick, and without a word to anyone, bolted through the door.

It was one of the funniest sights that Montague had ever seen in his life, and he laughed all the way into the smoking-room. And, when Major Venable had settled himself in a big chair and bitten off the end of a cigar and lighted it, what floodgates of reminiscence were opened!

For Dan Waterman was one of the Major's own generation, and he knew all his life and his habits. Just as Montague had seen him there, so he had been always; swift, imperious, terrible, trampling over all opposition; the most powerful men in the city quailed before the glare of his eyes. In the old days Wall Street had reeled in the shock of the conflicts between him and his most powerful rival.

And the Major went on to tell about Waterman's rival, and his life. He had been the city's traction-king, old Wyman had been made by him. He was the prince among political financiers; he had ruled the Democratic party in state and nation. He would give a quarter of a million at a time to the boss of Tammany Hall, and spend a million in a single campaign; on "dough-day," when the district leaders came to get the election funds, there would be a table forty feet long completely covered with hundred-dollar bills. He would have been the richest man in America, save that he spent his money as fast as he got it. He had had the most famous racing-stable in America; and a house on Fifth Avenue that was said to be the finest Italian palace in the world. Over three millions had been spent in decorating it; all the ceilings had been brought intact from palaces abroad, which he had bought and demolished! The Major told a story to show how such a man lost all sense of the value of money; he had once been sitting at lunch with him, when the editor of one of his newspapers had come in and remarked, "I told you we would need eight thousand dollars, and the check you send is for ten." "I know it," was the smiling answer — "but somehow I thought eight seemed harder to write than ten!"

"Old Waterman's quite a spender, too, when it comes to that," the Major went on. "He told me once that it cost him five thousand dollars a day for his ordinary expenses. And that doesn't include a million-dollar yacht, nor even the expenses of it.

"And think of another man I know of who spent a million dollars for a granite pier, so that he could land and see his mistress! — It's a fact, as sure as God made me! She was a well-known society woman, but she was poor, and he didn't dare to make her rich for fear of the scandal. So she had to live in a miserable fifty-thousand-dollar villa; and when other people's children would sneer at her children because they lived in a fifty-thousand-dollar villa, the answer would be, 'But you haven't got any pier!' And if you don't believe that —"

But here suddenly the Major turned, and observed a boy who had brought him some cigars, and who was now standing near by, pretending to straighten out some newspapers upon the table. "Here, sir!" cried the Major, "what do you mean — listening to what I'm saying! Out of the room with you now, you rascal!"

Chapter XIII

*A*nother weekend came, and with it an invitation from the Lester Todds to visit them at their country place in New Jersey. Montague was buried in his books, but his brother routed him out with strenuous protests. His case be damned — was he going to ruin his career for one case? At all hazards, he must meet people — "people who counted." And the Todds were such, a big money crowd, and a power in the insurance world; if Montague were going to be an insurance lawyer, he could not possibly decline their invitation. Freddie Vandam would be a guest — and Montague smiled at the tidings that Betty Wyman would be there also. He had observed that his brother's weekend visits always happened at places where Betty was, and where Betty's granddaddy was not.

So Montague's man packed his grips, and Alice's maid her trunks; and they rode with a private-car party to a remote Jersey suburb, and were whirled in an auto up a broad shell road to a palace upon the top of a mountain. Here lived the haughty Lester Todds, and scattered about on the neighboring hills, a set of the ultra-wealthy who had withdrawn to this seclusion. They were exceedingly "classy"; they affected to regard all the Society of the city with scorn, and had their own all-the-year-round diversions — an open-air horse show in summer, and in the fall fox-hunting in fancy uniforms.

The Lester Todds themselves were ardent pursuers of all varieties of game, and in various clubs and private preserves they followed the seasons, from Florida and North Carolina to Ontario, with occasional

side trips to Norway, and New Brunswick, and British Columbia. Here
at home they had a whole mountain of virgin forest, carefully preserved;
and in the Renaissance palace at the summit-which they carelessly
referred to as a "lodge" — you would find such articles de vertu as a
ten-thousand-dollar table with a set of two-thousand-dollar chairs, and
quite ordinary-looking rugs at ten and twenty thousand dollars each. —
All these prices you might ascertain without any difficulty at all, because
there were many newspaper articles describing the house to be read in
an album in the hall. On Saturday afternoons Mrs. Todd welcomed the
neighbors in a pastel grey reception-gown, the front of which contained
a peacock embroidered in silk, with jewels in every feather, and a
diamond solitaire for an eye; and in the evening there was a dance, and
she appeared in a gown with several hundred diamonds sewn upon it,
and received her guests upon a rug set with jewels to match.

All together, Montague judged this the "fastest" set he had yet
encountered; they ate more and drank more and intrigued more openly.
He had been slowly acquiring the special lingo of Society, but these
people had so much more slang that he felt all lost again. A young lady
who was gossiping to him about those present remarked that a certain
youth was a "spasm"; and then, seeing the look of perplexity upon his
face, she laughed, "I don't believe you know what I mean!" Montague
replied that he had ventured to infer that she did not like him.

And then there was Mrs. Harper, who came from Chicago by way of
London. Ten years ago Mrs. Harper had overwhelmed New York with
the millions brought from her great department-store; and had then
moved on, sighing for new worlds to conquer. When she had left
Chicago, her grammar had been unexceptionable; but since she had
been in England, she said "you ain't" and dropped all her g's; and when
Montague brought down a bird at long range, she exclaimed, conde-
scendingly, "Why, you're quite a dab at it!" He sat in the front seat of
an automobile, and heard the great lady behind him referring to the
sturdy Jersey farmers, whose ancestors had fought the British and
Hessians all over the state, as "your peasantry."

It was an extraordinary privilege to have Mrs. Harper for a guest; "at
home" she moved about in state recalling that of Queen Victoria, with
flags and bunting on the way, and crowds of school children cheering.
She kept up half a dozen establishments, and had a hundred thousand
acres of game preserves in Scotland. She made a specialty of collecting
jewels which had belonged to the romantic and picturesque queens of
history. She appeared at the dance in a breastplate of diamonds covering
the entire front of her bodice, so that she was literally clothed in light;
and with her was her English friend, Mrs. Percy, who had accompanied

her in her triumph through the courts and camps of Europe, and displayed a famous lorgnette-chain, containing one specimen of every rare and beautiful jewel known. Mrs. Percy wore a gown of cloth of gold tissue, covered with a fortune in Venetian lace, and made a tremendous sensation — until the rumor spread that it was a rehash of the costume which Mrs. Harper had worn at the Duchess of London's ball. The Chicago lady herself never by any chance appeared in the same costume twice.

Alice had a grand time at the Todds'; all the men fell in love with her — one in particular, a young chap named Fayette, quite threw himself at her feet. He was wealthy, but unfortunately he had made his money by eloping with a rich girl (who was one of the present party), and so, from a practical point of view, his attentions were not desirable for Alice.

Montague was left with the task of finding these things out for himself, for his brother devoted himself exclusively to Betty Wyman. The way these two disappeared between meals was a jest of the whole company; so that when they were on their way home, Montague felt called upon to make paternal inquiries.

"We're as much engaged as we dare to be," Oliver answered him.

"And when do you expect to marry her?"

"God knows," said he, "I don't. The old man wouldn't give her a cent."

"And you couldn't support her?"

"I? Good heavens, Allan — do you suppose Betty would consent to be poor?"

"Have you asked her?" inquired Montague.

"I don't want to ask her, thank you! I've not the least desire to live in a hovel with a girl who's been brought up in a palace."

"Then what do you expect to do?"

"Well, Betty has a rich aunt in a lunatic asylum. And then I'm making money, you know — and the old boy will have to relent in the end. And we're having a very good time in the meanwhile, you know."

"You can't be very much in love," said Montague — to which his brother replied cheerfully that they were as much in love as they felt like being.

This was on the train Monday morning. Oliver observed that his brother relapsed into a brown study, and remarked, "I suppose you're going back now to bury yourself in your books. You've got to give me one evening this week for a dinner that's important."

"Where's that?" asked the other.

"Oh, it's a long story," said Oliver. "I'll explain it to you some time. But first we must have an understanding about next week, also — I suppose you've not overlooked the fact that it's Christmas week. And you won't be permitted to do any work then."

"But that's impossible!" exclaimed the other.

"Nothing else is possible," said Oliver, firmly. "I've made an engagement for you with the Eldridge Devons up the Hudson —"

"For the whole week?"

"The whole week. And it'll be the most important thing you've done. Mrs. Winnie's going to take us all in her car, and you will make no end of indispensable acquaintances."

"Oliver, I don't see how in the world I can do it!" the other protested in dismay, and went on for several minutes arguing and explaining what he had to do. But Oliver contented himself with the assurance that where there's a will, there's a way. One could not refuse an invitation to spend Christmas with the Eldridge Devons!

And sure enough, there was a way. Mr. Hasbrook had mentioned to him that he had had considerable work done upon the case, and would have the papers sent round. And when Montague reached his office that morning, he found them there. There was a package of several thousand pages; and upon examining them, he found to his utter consternation that they contained a complete bill of complaint, with all the necessary references and citations, and a preliminary draft of a brief — in short, a complete and thoroughgoing preparation of his case. There could not have been less than ten or fifteen thousand dollars' worth of work in the papers; and Montague sat quite aghast, turning over the neatly typewritten sheets. He could indeed afford to attend Christmas house parties, if all his clients were to treat him like this!

He felt a little piqued about it — for he had noted some of these points for himself, and felt a little proud about them. Apparently he was to be nothing but a figure-head in the case! And he turned to the phone and called up Mr. Hasbrook, and asked him what he expected him to do with these papers. There was the whole case here; and was he simply to take them as they stood?

No one could have replied more considerately than did Mr. Hasbrook. The papers were for Montague's benefit — he would do exactly as he pleased with them. He might use them as they stood, or reject them altogether, or make them the basis for his own work — anything that appealed to his judgment would be satisfactory. And so Montague turned about and wrote an acceptance to the formal invitation which had come from the Eldridge Devons.

Later on in the day Oliver called up, and said that he was to go out to dinner the following evening, and that he would call for him at eight. "It's with the Jack Evanses," Oliver added. "Do you know them?"

Montague had heard the name, as that of the president of a chain of Western railroads. "Do you mean him?" he asked.

"Yes," said the other. "They're a rum crowd, but there's money in it. I'll call early and explain it to you."

But it was explained sooner than that. During the next afternoon Montague had a caller — none other than Mrs. Winnie Duval. Someone had left Mrs. Winnie some more money, it appeared; and there was a lot of red tape attached to it, which she wanted the new lawyer to attend to. Also, she said, she hoped that he would charge her a lot of money by way of encouraging himself. It was a mere bagatelle of a hundred thousand or so, from some forgotten aunt in the West.

The business was soon disposed of, and then Mrs. Winnie asked Montague if he had anyplace to go to for dinner that evening: which was the occasion of his mentioning the Jack Evanses. "O dear me!" said Mrs. Winnie, with a laugh. "Is Ollie going to take you there? What a funny time you'll have!"

"Do you know them?" asked the other.

"Heavens, no!" was the answer. "Nobody knows them; but everybody knows about them. My husband meets old Evans in business, of course, and thinks he's a good sort. But the family — dear me!"

"How much of it is there?"

"Why, there's the old lady, and two grown daughters and a son. The son's a fine chap, they say — the old man took him in hand and put him at work in the shops. But I suppose he thought that daughters were too much of a proposition for him, and so he sent them to a fancy school — and, I tell you, they're the most highly polished human specimens that ever you encountered!"

It sounded entertaining. "But what does Oliver want with them?" asked Montague, wonderingly.

"It isn't that he wants them — they want him. They're cumbers, you know — perfectly frantic. They've come to town to get into Society."

"Then you mean that they pay Oliver?" asked Montague.

"I don't know that," said the other, with a laugh. "You'll have to ask Ollie. They've a number of the little brothers of the rich hanging round them, picking up whatever plunder's in sight."

A look of pain crossed Montague's face; and she saw it, and put out her hand with a sudden gesture. "Oh!" she exclaimed, "I've offended you!"

"No," said he, "it's not that exactly — I wouldn't be offended. But I'm worried about my brother."

"How do you mean?"

"He gets a lot of money somehow, and I don't know what it means."

The woman sat for a few moments in silence, watching him. "Didn't he have any when he came here?" she asked.

"Not very much," said he.

"Because," she went on, "if he didn't, he certainly managed it very cleverly — we all thought he had."

Again there was a pause; then suddenly Mrs. Winnie said: "Do you know, you feel differently about money from the way we do in New York. Do you realize it?"

"I'm not sure," said he. "How do you mean?"

"You look at it in an old-fashioned sort of way — a person has to earn it — it's a sign of something he's done. It came to me just now, all in a flash — we don't feel that way about money. We haven't any of us earned ours; we've just got it. And it never occurs to us to expect other people to earn it — all we want to know is if they have it."

Montague did not tell his companion how very profound a remark he considered that; he was afraid it would not be delicate to agree with her. He had heard a story of a Negro occupant of the "mourners' bench," who was voluble in confession of his sins, but took exception to the fervor with which the congregation said "Amen!"

"The Evanses used to be a lot funnier than they are now," continued Mrs. Winnie, after a while. "When they came here last year, they were really frightful. They had an English chap for social secretary — a younger son of some broken-down old family. My brother knew a man who had been one of their intimates in the West, and he said it was perfectly excruciating — this fellow used to sit at the table and give orders to the whole crowd: 'Your ice-cream fork should be at your right hand, Miss Mary. — One never asks for more soup, Master Robert. — And Miss Anna, always move your soup-spoon from you — that's better!'"

"I fancy I shall feel sorry for them," said Montague.

"Oh, you needn't," said the other, promptly. "They'll get what they want."

"Do you think so?"

"Why, certainly they will. They've got the money; and they've been abroad — they're learning the game. And they'll keep at it until they succeed — what else is there for them to do? And then my husband says that old Evans is making himself a power here in the East; so that pretty soon they won't dare offend him."

"Does that count?" asked the man.

"Well, I guess it counts!" laughed Mrs. Winnie. "It has of late." And she went on to tell him of the Society leader who had dared to offend the daughters of a great magnate, and how the magnate had retaliated by turning the woman's husband out of his high office. That was often the way in the business world; the struggles were supposed to be affairs of men, but oftener than not the moving power was a woman's intrigue. You would see a great upheaval in Wall Street, and it would be two of the big men quarreling over a mistress; you would see some man rush suddenly into a high office – and that would be because his wife had sold herself to advance him.

Mrs. Winnie took him up town in her auto, and he dressed for dinner; and then came Oliver, and his brother asked, "Are you trying to put the Evanses into Society?"

"Who's been telling you about them?" asked the other.

"Mrs. Winnie," said Montague.

"What did she tell you?"

Montague went over her recital, which his brother apparently found satisfactory. "It's not as serious as that," he said, answering the earlier question. "I help them a little now and then."

"What do you do?"

"Oh, advise them, mostly – tell them where to go and what to wear. When they first came to New York, they were dressed like parakeets, you know. And" – here Oliver broke into a laugh – "I refrain from making jokes about them. And when I hear other people abusing them, I point out that they are sure to land in the end, and will be dangerous enemies. I've got one or two wedges started for them."

"And do they pay you for doing it?"

"You'd call it paying me, I suppose," replied the other. "The old man carries a few shares of stock for me now and then."

"Carries a few shares?" echoed Montague, and Oliver explained the procedure. This was one of the customs which had grown up in a community where people did not have to earn their money. The recipient of the favor put up nothing and took no risks; but the other person was supposed to buy some stock for him, and then, when the stock went up, he would send a check for the "profits." Many a man who would have resented a direct offer of money, would assent pleasantly when a powerful friend offered to "carry a hundred shares for him." This was the way one offered a tip in the big world; it was useful in the case of newspaper men, whose good opinion of a stock was desired, or of politicians and legislators, whose votes might help its fortunes. When one expected to get into Society, one must be prepared to strew such tips about him.

"Of course," added Oliver, "what the family would really like me to do is to get the Robbie Wallings to take them up. I suppose I could get round half a million of them if I could manage that."

To all of which Montague replied, "I see."

A great light had dawned upon him. So that was the way it was managed! That was why one paid thirty thousand a year for one's apartments, and thirty thousand more for a girl's clothes! No wonder it was better to spend Christmas week at the Eldridge Devons than to labor at one's law books!

"One more question," Montague went on. "Why are you introducing me to them?"

"Well," his brother answered, "it won't hurt you; you'll find it amusing. You see, they'd heard I had a brother; and they asked me to bring you. I couldn't keep you hidden forever, could I?"

All this was while they were driving up town. The Evanses' place was on Riverside Drive; and when Montague got out of the cab and saw it looming up in the semi-darkness, he emitted an exclamation of wonder. It was as big as a jail!

"Oh, yes, they've got room enough," said Oliver, with a laugh. "I put this deal through for them — it's the old Lamson palace, you know."

They had the room; and likewise they had all the trappings of snobbery — Montague took that fact in at a glance. There were knee-breeches and scarlet facings and gold braid — marble balconies and fireplaces and fountains — French masters and real Flemish tapestry. The staircase of their palace was a winding one, and there was a white velvet carpet which had been specially woven for it, and had to be changed frequently; at the top of it was a white cashmere rug which had a pedigree of six centuries — and so on.

And then came the family: this tall, raw-boned, gigantic man, with weather-tanned face and straggling grey moustache — this was Jack Evans; and Mrs. Evans, short and pudgy, but with a kindly face, and not too many diamonds; and the Misses Evans, — stately and slender and perfectly arrayed. "Why, they're all right!" was the thought that came to Montague.

They were all right until they opened their mouths. When they spoke, you discovered that Evans was a miner, and that his wife had been cook on a ranch; also that Anne and Mary had harsh voices, and that they never by any chance said or did anything natural.

They were escorted into the stately dining room — Henri II., with a historic mantel taken from the palace of Fontainebleau, and four great allegorical paintings of Morning, Evening, Noon, and Midnight upon the walls. There were no other guests — the table, set for six, seemed like a toy in the vast apartment. And in a sudden flash — with a start of almost terror — Montague realized what it must mean not to be in Society. To have all this splendor, and nobody to share it! To have Henri II. dining rooms and Louis XVI. parlors and Louis XIV. libraries — and see them all empty! To have no one to drive with or talk with, no one to visit or play cards with — to go to the theater and the opera and have no one to speak to! Worse than that, to be stared at and smiled at! To live in this huge palace, and know that all the horde of servants, underneath their cringing deference, were sneering at you! To face that — to live in the presence of it day after day! And then, outside of your home, the ever widening circles of ridicule and contempt — Society, with all its hangers-on and parasites, its imitators and admirers!

And someone had defied all that — someone had taken up the sword and gone forth to beat down that opposition! Montague looked at this little family of four, and wondered which of them was the driving force in this most desperate emprise!

He arrived at it by a process of elimination. It could not be Evans himself. One saw that the old man was quite hopeless socially; nothing could change his big hairy hands or his lean scrawny neck, or his irresistible impulse to slide down in his chair and cross his long legs in front of him. The face and the talk of Jack Evans brought irresistibly to mind the mountain trail and the prospector's pack-mule, the smoke of campfires and the odor of bacon and beans. Seventeen long years the man had tramped in deserts and mountain wildernesses, and Nature had graven her impress deep into his body and soul.

He was very shy at this dinner; but Montague came to know him well in the course of time. And after he had come to realize that Montague was not one of the grafters, he opened up his heart. Evans had held on to his mine when he had found it, and he had downed the rivals who had tried to take it away from him, and he had bought the railroads who had tried to crush him — and now he had come to Wall Street to fight the men who had tried to ruin his railroads. But through it all, he had kept the heart of a woman, and the sight of real distress was unbearable to him. He was the sort of man to keep a roll of ten-thousand-dollar bills in his pistol pocket, and to give one away if he thought he could do it without offence. And, on the other hand, men told how once when he had seen a porter insult a woman passenger on his line, he jumped up and pulled the bell-cord, and had the man put out on the roadside at midnight, thirty miles from the nearest town!

No, it was the women folks, he said to Montague, with his grim laugh. It didn't trouble him at all to be called a "noovoo rich"; and when he felt like dancing a shakedown, he could take a run out to God's country. But the women folks had got the bee in their bonnet. The old man added sadly that one of the disadvantages of striking it rich was that it left the women folks with nothing to do.

Nor was it Mrs. Evans, either. "Sarey," as she was called by the head of the house, sat next to Montague at dinner; and he discovered that with the very least encouragement, the good lady was willing to become homelike and comfortable. Montague gave the occasion, because he was a stranger, and volunteered the opinion that New York was a shamelessly extravagant place, and hard to get along in; and Mrs. Evans took up the subject and revealed herself as a good-natured and kindly personage, who had wistful yearnings for mush and molasses, and flap-jacks, and bread fried in bacon-grease, and similar sensible things, while her chef was compelling her to eat pâté de foie gras in aspic, and milk-fed guinea-chicks, and biscuits glacees Tortoni. Of course she did not say that at dinner, — she made a game effort to play her part, — with the result of at least one diverting experience for Montague.

Mrs. Evans was telling him what a dreadful place she considered the city for young men; and how she feared to bring her boy here. "The men here have no morals at all," said she, and added earnestly, "I've come to the conclusion that Eastern men are naturally amphibious!"

Then, as Montague knitted his brows and looked perplexed, she added, "Don't you think so?" And he replied, with as little delay as possible, that he had never really thought of it before.

It was not until a couple of hours later that the light dawned upon him, in the course of a conversation with Miss Anne. "We met Lady Stonebridge at luncheon today," said that young person. "Do you know her?"

"No," said Montague, who had never heard of her.

"I think those aristocratic English women use the most abominable slang," continued Anne. "Have you noticed it?"

"Yes, I have," he said.

"And so utterly cynical! Do you know, Lady Stonebridge quite shocked mother — she told her she didn't believe in marriage at all, and that she thought all men were naturally polygamous!"

Later on, Montague came to know "Mrs. Sarey"; and one afternoon, sitting in her Petit Trianon drawing room, he asked her abruptly, "Why in the world do you want to get into Society?" And the poor lady caught her breath, and tried to be indignant; and then, seeing that he was in earnest, and that she was cornered, broke down and confessed. "It isn't me," she said, "it's the gals." (For along with the surrender went a reversion to natural speech.) "It's Mary, and more particularly Anne."

They talked it over confidentially — which was a great relief to Mrs. Sarey's soul, for she was cruelly lonely. So far as she was concerned, it was not because she wanted Society, but because Society didn't want her. She flashed up in sudden anger, and clenched her fists, declaring that Jack Evans was as good a man as walked the streets of New York — and they would acknowledge it before he got through with them, too! After that she intended to settle down at home and be comfortable, and mend her husband's socks.

She went on to tell him what a hard road was the path of glory. There were hundreds of people ready to know them — but oh, such a riffraff! They might fill up their home with the hangers-on and the yellow, but no, they could wait. They had learned a lot since they set out. One very aristocratic lady had invited them to dinner, and their hopes had been high — but alas, while they were sitting by the fireplace, someone admired a thirty-thousand-dollar emerald ring which Mrs. Evans had on her finger, and she had taken it off and passed it about among the company, and somewhere it had vanished completely! And another person had invited Mary to a bridge-party, and though she had played hardly at all, her hostess had quietly informed her that she had lost a thousand dollars. And the great Lady Stonebridge had actually sent for her and told her that she could introduce her in some of the very best circles, if only she was willing to lose always! Mrs. Evans had possessed a very homely Irish name before she was married; and Lady Stonebridge had got five thousand dollars from her to use some great influence she possessed in the Royal College of Heralds, and prove that she was descended directly from the noble old family of Magennis, who had been the lords of Iveagh, way back in the fourteenth century. And now Oliver had told them that this imposing charter would not help them in the least!

In the process of elimination, there were the Misses Evans left. Montague's friends made many jests when they heard that he had met them — asking him if he meant to settle down. Major Venable went so far as to assure him that there was not the least doubt that either of the girls would take him in a second. Montague laughed, and answered that Mary was not so bad — she had a sweet face and was good-natured; but also, she was two years younger than Anne; and he could not get over the thought that two more years might make another Anne of her.

For it was Anne who was the driving force of the family! Anne who had planned the great campaign, and selected the Lamson palace, and pried the family loose from the primeval rocks of Nevada! She was cold as an iceberg, tireless, pitiless to others as to herself; for seventeen years her father had wandered and dug among the mountains; and for seventeen years, if need be, she would dig beneath the walls of the fortress of Society!

After Montague had had his heart to heart talk with the mother, Miss Anne Evans became very haughty toward him; whereby he knew that the old lady had told about it, and that the daughter resented his presumption. But to Oliver she laid bare her soul, and Oliver would come and tell his brother about it: how she plotted and planned and studied, and brought new schemes to him every week. She had some of the real people bought over to secret sympathy with her; if there was some especial favor which she asked for, she would set to work with the good-natured old man, and the person would have some important money service done him. She had the people of Society all marked — she was learning all their weaknesses, and the underground passages of their lives, and working patiently to find the key to her problem — some one family which was socially impregnable, but whose finances were in such a shape that they would receive the proposition to take up the Evanses, and definitely put them in. Montague used to look back upon all this with wonder and amusement — from those days in the not far distant future, when the papers had cable descriptions of the gowns of the Duchess of Arden, née Evans, who was the bright particular star of the London social season!

Chapter XIV

Montague had written a reluctant letter to Major Thorne, telling him that he had been unable to interest anyone in his proposition, and that he was not in position to undertake it himself. Then, according to his brother's injunction, he left his money in the bank, and waited. There would be "something doing" soon, said Oliver.

And as they drove home from the Evanses', Oliver served notice upon him that this event might be expected any day. He was very mysterious about it, and would answer none of his brother's questions — except to say that it had nothing to do with the people they had just visited.

"I suppose," Montague remarked, "you have not failed to realize that Evans might play you false."

And the other laughed, echoing the words, "Might do it!" Then he went on to tell the tale of the great railroad builder of the West, whose daughter had been married, with elaborate festivities; and some of the young men present, thinking to find him in a sentimental mood, had asked him for his views about the market. He advised them to buy the stock of his road; and they formed a pool and bought, and as fast as they bought, he sold — until the little venture cost the boys a total of seven million and a half!

"No, no," Oliver added. "I have never put up a dollar for anything of Evans's, and I never shall. — They are simply a side issue, anyway," he added carelessly.

A couple of mornings later, while Montague was at breakfast, his brother called him up and said that he was coming round, and would go down town with him. Montague knew at once that that meant something serious, for he had never before known his brother to be awake so early.

They took a cab; and then Oliver explained. The moment had arrived — the time to take the plunge, and come up with a fortune. He could not tell much about it, for it was a matter upon which he stood pledged to absolute secrecy. There were but four people in the country who knew about it. It was the chance of a lifetime — and in four or five hours it would be gone. Three times before it had come to Oliver, and each time he had multiplied his capital several times; that he had not made millions was simply because he did not have enough money. His brother must take his word for this and simply put himself into his hands.

"What is it you want me to do?" asked Montague, gravely.

"I want you to take every dollar you have, or that you can lay your hands on this morning, and turn it over to me to buy stocks with."

"To buy on margin, you mean?"

"Of course I mean that," said Oliver. Then, as he saw his brother frown, he added, "Understand me, I have absolutely certain information as to how a certain stock will behave today."

"The best judges of a stock often make mistakes in such matters," said Montague.

"It is not a question of any person's judgment," was the reply. "It is a question of knowledge. The stock is to be *made* to behave so."

"But how can you know that the person who intends to make it behave may not be lying to you?"

"My information does not come from that person, but from a person who has no such interest — who, on the contrary, is in on the deal with me, and gains only as I gain."

"Then, in other words," said Montague, "your information is stolen?"

"Everything in Wall Street is stolen," was Oliver's concise reply.

There was a long silence, while the cab rolled swiftly on its way.

"Well?" Oliver asked at last.

"I can imagine," said Montague, "how a man might intend to move a certain stock, and think that he had the power, and yet find that he was mistaken. There are so many forces, so many chances to be considered — it seems to me you must be taking a risk."

Oliver laughed. "You talk like a child," was his reply. "Suppose that I were in absolute control of a corporation, and that I chose to run it for purposes of market manipulation, don't you think I might come pretty near knowing what its stock was going to do?"

"Yes," said Montague, slowly, "if such a thing as that were conceivable."

"If it were conceivable!" laughed his brother. "And now suppose that I had a confidential man — a secretary, we'll say — and I paid him twenty thousand a year, and he saw chances to make a hundred thousand in an hour — don't you think he might conceivably try it?"

"Yes," said Montague, "he might. But where do you come in?"

"Well, if the man were going to do anything worth while, he'd need capital, would he not? And he'd hardly dare to look for any money in the Street, where a thousand eyes would be watching him. What more natural than to look out for some person who is in Society and has the ear of private parties with plenty of cash?"

And Montague sat in deep thought. "I see," he said slowly; "I see!" Then, fixing his eyes upon Oliver, he exclaimed, earnestly, "One thing more!"

"Don't ask me anymore," protested the other. "I told you I was pledged —"

"You must tell me this," said Montague. "Does Bobbie Walling know about it?"

"He does not," was the reply. But Montague had known his brother long and intimately, and he could read things in his eyes. He knew that that was a lie. He had solved the mystery at last!

Montague knew that he had come to a parting of the ways. He did not like this kind of thing — he had not come to New York to be a stock-gambler. But what a difficult thing it would be to say so; and how unfair it was to be confronted with such an issue, and compelled to decide in a few minutes in a cab!

He had put himself in his brother's hands, and now he was under obligations to him, which he could not pay off. Oliver had paid all his expenses; he was doing everything for him. He had made all his difficulties his own, and all in frankness and perfect trust — upon the assumption that his brother would play the game with him. And now, at the critical moment, he was to face about, and say; "I do not like the game. I do not approve of your life!" Such a painful thing it is to have a higher moral code than one's friends!

If he refused, he saw that he would have to face a complete break; he could not go on living in the world to which he had been introduced. Fifty thousand had seemed an enormous fee, yet even a week or two had sufficed for it to come to seem inadequate. He would have to have many such fees, if they were to go on living at their present rate; and if Alice were to have a social career, and entertain her friends. And to ask Alice to give up now, and retire, would be even harder than to face his brother here in the cab.

Then came the temptation. Life was a battle, and this was the way it was being fought. If he rejected the opportunity, others would seize it; in fact, by refusing, he would be handing it to them. This great man, whoever he might be, who was manipulating stocks for his own convenience — could anyone in his senses reject a chance to wrench from him some part of his spoils? Montague saw the impulse of refusal dying away within him.

"Well?" asked his brother, finally.

"Oliver," said the other, "don't you think that I ought to know more about it, so that I can judge?"

"You could not judge, even if I told you all," said Oliver. "It would take you a long time to become familiar with the circumstances, as I am. You must take my word; I know it is certain and safe."

Then suddenly he unbuttoned his coat, and took out some papers, and handed his brother a telegram. It was dated Chicago, and read, "Guest is expected immediately. — HENRY." "That means, 'Buy Transcontinental this morning,'" said Oliver.

"I see," said the other. "Then the man is in Chicago?"

"No," was the reply. "That is his wife. He wires to her."

"— How much money have you?" asked Oliver, after a pause.

"I've most of the fifty thousand," the other answered, "and about thirty thousand we brought with us."

"How much can you put your hands on?"

"Why, I could get all of it; but part of the money is mother's, and I would not touch that."

The younger man was about to remonstrate, but Montague stopped him, "I will put up the fifty thousand I have earned," he said. "I dare not risk anymore."

Oliver shrugged his shoulders. "As you please," he said. "You may never have another such chance in your life."

He dropped the subject, or at least he probably tried to. Within a few minutes, however, he was back at it again, with the result that by the time they reached the banking-district, Montague had agreed to draw sixty thousand.

They stopped at his bank. "It isn't open yet, —" said Oliver, "but the paying teller will oblige you. Tell him you want it before the Exchange opens."

Montague went in and got his money, in six new, crisp, ten-thousand-dollar bills. He buttoned them up in his inmost pocket, wondering a little, incidentally, at the magnificence of the place, and at the swift routine manner in which the clerk took in and paid out such sums as this. Then they drove to Oliver's bank, and he drew a hundred and twenty thousand; and then he paid off the cab, and they strolled down Broadway into Wall Street. It lacked a quarter of an hour of the time of the opening of the Exchange; and a stream of prosperous-looking men were pouring in from all the cars and ferries to their offices.

"Where are your brokers?" Montague inquired.

"I don't have any brokers — at least not for a matter such as this," said Oliver. And he stopped in front of one of the big buildings. "In there," he said, "are the offices of Hammond and Streeter — second floor to your left. Go there and ask for a member of the firm, and introduce yourself under an assumed name —"

"What!" gasped Montague.

"Of course, man — you would not dream of giving your own name! What difference will that make?"

"I never thought of doing such a thing," said the other.

"Well, think of it now."

But Montague shook his head. "I would not do that," he said.

Oliver shrugged his shoulders. "All right," he said; "tell him you don't care to give your name. They're a little shady — they'll take your money."

"Suppose they won't?" asked the other.

"Then wait outside for me, and I'll take you somewhere else."

"What shall I buy?"

"Ten thousand shares of Transcontinental Common at the opening price; and tell them to buy on the scale up, and to raise the stop; also to take your orders to sell over the 'phone. Then wait there until I come for you."

Montague set his teeth together and obeyed orders. Inside the door marked Hammond and Streeter a pleasant-faced young man advanced to meet him, and led him to a grey-haired and affable gentleman, Mr. Streeter. And Montague introduced himself as a stranger in town, from the South, and wishing to buy some stock. Mr. Streeter led him into an inner office and seated himself at a desk and drew some papers in front of him. "Your name, please?" he asked.

"I don't care to give my name," replied the other. And Mr. Streeter put down his pen.

"Not give your name?" he said.

"No," said Montague quietly.

"Why?" — said Mr. Streeter — "I don't understand —"

"I am a stranger in town," said Montague, "and not accustomed to dealing in stocks. I should prefer to remain unknown."

The man eyed him sharply. "Where do you come from?" he asked.

"From Mississippi," was the reply.

"And have you a residence in New York?"

"At a hotel," said Montague.

"You have to give some name," said the other.

"Any will do," said Montague. "John Smith, if you like."

"We never do anything like this," said the broker.

"We require that our customers be introduced. There are rules of the Exchange — there are rules —"

"I am sorry," said Montague; "this would be a cash transaction."

"How many shares do you want to buy?"

"Ten thousand," was the reply.

Mr. Streeter became more serious. "That is a large order," he said. Montague said nothing.

"What do you wish to buy?" was the next question.

"Transcontinental Common," he replied.

"Well," said the other, after another pause — "we will try to accommodate you. But you will have to consider it — er —"

"Strictly confidential," said Montague.

So Mr. Streeter made out the papers, and Montague, looking them over, discovered that they called for one hundred thousand dollars.

"That is a mistake," he said. "I have only sixty thousand."

"Oh," said the other, "we shall certainly have to charge you a ten percent, margin."

Montague was not prepared for this contingency; but he did some mental arithmetic. "What is the present price of the stock?" he asked.

"Fifty-nine and five-eighths," was the reply.

"Then sixty thousand dollars is more than ten percent, of the market price," said Montague.

"Yes," said Mr. Streeter. "But in dealing with a stranger we shall certainly have to put a 'stop loss' order at four points above, and that would leave you only two points of safety — surely not enough."

"I see," said Montague — and he had a sudden appalling realization of the wild game which his brother had planned for him.

"Whereas," Mr. Streeter continued, persuasively, "if you put up ten percent, you will have six points."

"Very well," said the other promptly. "Then please buy me six thousand shares."

So they closed the deal, and the papers were signed, and Mr. Streeter took the six new, crisp ten-thousand-dollar bills.

Then he escorted him to the outer office, remarking pleasantly on the way, "I hope you're well advised. We're inclined to be bearish upon Transcontinental ourselves — the situation looks rather squally."

These words were not worth the breath it took to say them; but Montague was not aware of this, and felt a painful start within. But he answered, carelessly, that one must take his chance, and sat down in one of the customer's chairs. Hammond and Streeter's was like a little lecture-hall, with rows of seats and a big blackboard in front, with the initials of the most important stocks in columns, and yesterday's closing prices above, on little green cards. At one side was a ticker, with two attendants awaiting the opening click.

In the seats were twenty or thirty men, old and young; most of them regular habitués, victims of the fever of the Street. Montague watched them, catching snatches of their whispered conversation, with its intricate and disagreeable slang. He felt intensely humiliated and uncomfortable — for he had got the fever of the Street into his own veins, and he could not conquer it. There were nasty shivers running up and down his spine, and his hands were cold.

He stared at the little figures, fascinated; they stood for some vast and tremendous force outside, which could not be controlled or even comprehended, — some merciless, annihilating force, like the lightning or the tornado. And he had put himself at the mercy of it; it might do its will with him! "Tr. C. 59 ⅝" read the little pasteboard; and he had only six points of safety. If at any time in the day that figure should be changed to read "53 ⅝" — then every dollar of Montague's sixty thousand would be gone forever! The great fee that he had worked so hard for and rejoiced so greatly over — that would be all gone, and a slice out of his inheritance besides!

A boy put into his hand a little four-page paper — one of the countless news-sheets which different houses and interests distributed free for advertising or other purposes; and a heading "Transcontinental" caught his eye, among the paragraphs in the Day's Events. He read: "The directors' meeting of the Transcontinental R.R. will be held at noon. It is confidently predicted that the quarterly dividend will be passed, as it has been for the last three quarters. There is great dissatisfaction among the stock-holders. The stock has been decidedly weak, with no apparent inside support; it fell off three points just before closing yesterday, upon the news of further proceedings by Western state officials, and widely credited rumors of dissensions among the directors, with renewed opposition to the control of the Hopkins interests."

Ten o'clock came and went, and the ticker began its long journey. There was intense activity in Transcontinental, many thousands of shares changing hands, and the price swaying back and forth. When Oliver came in, in half an hour, it stood at 59 $\frac{3}{8}$.

"That's all right," said he. "Our time will not come till afternoon."

"But suppose we are wiped out before afternoon?" said the other.

"That is impossible," answered Oliver. "There will be big buying all the morning."

They sat for a while, nervous and restless. Then, by way of breaking the monotony, Oliver suggested that his brother might like to see the "Street." They went around the corner to Broad Street. Here at the head stood the Sub-treasury building, with all the gold of the government inside, and a Gatling gun in the tower. The public did not know it was there, but the financial men knew it, and it seemed as if they had huddled all their offices and banks and safe-deposit vaults under its shelter. Here, far underground, were hidden the two hundred millions of securities of the Oil Trust — in a huge six-hundred-ton steel vault, with a door so delicately poised that a finger could swing it on its hinges. And opposite to this was the white Grecian building of the Stock Exchange. Down the street were throngs of men within a roped arena, pushing, shouting, jostling; this was "the curb," where one could buy or sell small blocks of stock, and all the wildcat mining and oil stocks which were not listed by the Exchange. Rain or shine, these men were always here; and in the windows of the neighboring buildings stood others shouting quotations to them through megaphones, or signaling in deaf and dumb language. Some of these brokers wore colored hats, so that they could be distinguished; some had offices far off, where men sat all day with strong glasses trained upon them. Everywhere was the atmosphere of speculation — the restless, feverish eyes; the quick, nervous gestures; the haggard, care-worn faces. For in this game every man was pitted against every other man; and the dice were loaded so that nine out of every ten were doomed in advance to ruin and defeat. They procured passes to the visitors' gallery of the Exchange. From here one looked down into a room one or two hundred feet square, its floor covered with a snowstorm of torn pieces of paper, and its air a Babel of shouts and cries. Here were gathered perhaps two thousand men and boys; some were lounging and talking, but most were crowded about the various trading-posts, pushing, climbing over each other, leaping up, waving their hands and calling aloud. A "seat" in this exchange was worth about ninety-five thousand dollars, and so no one of these men was poor; but yet they came, day after day, to play their parts in this sordid arena, "seeking in sorrow for each other's joy": inventing a thousand petty tricks to outwit and deceive each other; rejoicing in a thousand petty triumphs; and spending their lives, like the waves upon the shore, a very symbol of human futility. Now and then a sudden impulse would seize them, and they would become like howling demons, surging about one spot, shrieking, gasping, clawing each other's clothing to pieces; and the spectator shuddered, seeing them as the victims of some strange and dreadful enchantment, which bound them to struggle and torment each other until they were worn out and grey.

But one felt these things only dimly, when he had put all his fortune into Transcontinental Common. For then he had sold his own soul to the enchanter, and the spell was upon him, and he hoped and feared and agonized with the struggling throng. Montague had no need to ask which was his "post"; for a mob of a hundred men were packed about it, with little whirls and eddies here and there on the outside. "Something doing today all right," said a man in his ear.

It was interesting to watch; but there was one difficulty — there were no quotations provided for the spectators. So the sight of this activity merely set them on edge with anxiety — something must be happening to their stock! Even Oliver was visibly nervous — after all, in the surest cases, the game was a dangerous one; there might be a big failure, or an assassination, or an earthquake! They rushed out and made for the nearest broker's office, where a glance at the board showed them Transcontinental at 60. They drew a long breath, and sat down again to wait.

That was about half-past eleven. At a quarter to twelve the stock went up an eighth, and then a quarter, and then another eighth. The two gripped their hands in excitement. Had the time come?

Apparently it had. A minute later the stock leaped to 61, on large buying. Then it went three-eighths more. A buzz of excitement ran through the office, and the old-timers sat up in their seats. The stock went another quarter.

Montague heard a man behind him say to his neighbor, "What does it mean?"

"God knows," was the answer; but Oliver whispered in his brother's ear, "I know what it means. The insiders are buying."

Somebody was buying, and buying furiously. The ticker seemed to set all other business aside and give its attention to the trading in Transcontinental. It was like a base-ball game, when one side begins to pile up runs, and the man in the coacher's box chants exultantly, and the dullest spectator is stirred – since no man can be indifferent to success. And as the stock went higher and higher, a little wave of excitement mounted with it, a murmur running through the room, and a thrill passing from person to person. Some watched, wondering if it would last, and if they had not better take on a little; then another point would be scored, and they would wish they had done it, and hesitate whether to do it now. But to others, like the Montagues, who "had some," it was victory, glorious and thrilling; their pulses leaped faster with every new change of the figures; and between times they reckoned up their gains, and hung between hope and dread for the new gains which were on the way, but not yet in sight.

There was little lull, and the boys who tended the board had a chance to rest. The stock was above 66; at which price, owing to the device of "pyramiding." Montague was on "velvet," to use the picturesque phrase of the Street. His earnings amounted to sixty thousand dollars, and even if the stock were to fall and he were to be sold out, he would lose nothing.

He wished to sell and realize his profits; but his brother gripped him fast by the arm. "No! no!" he said. "It hasn't really come yet!"

Some went out to lunch – to a restaurant where they could have a telephone on their table, so as to keep in touch with events. But the Montagues had no care about eating; they sat picturing the directors in session, and speculating upon a score of various eventualities. Things might yet go wrong, and all their profits would vanish like early snowflakes – and all their capital with them. Oliver shook like a leaf, but he would not stir. "Stay game!" he whispered.

He took out his watch, and glanced at it. It was after two o'clock. "It may go over till tomorrow!" he muttered. – But then suddenly came the storm.

The ticker recorded a rise in the price of Transcontinental of a point and a half, upon a purchase of five thousand shares; and then half a point for two thousand more. After that it never stopped. It went a point at a time; it went ten points in about fifteen minutes. And Babel broke loose in the office, and in several thousand other offices in the street, and spread to others all over the world. Montague had got up, and was moving here and there, because the tension was unendurable; and at the door of an inner office he heard someone at the telephone exclaiming, "For the love of God, can't you find out what's the matter?" – A moment later a man rushed in, breathless and wild-eyed, and his voice rang through the office, "The directors have declared a quarterly dividend of three percent, and an extra dividend of two!"

And Oliver caught his brother by the arm and started for the door with him. "Get to your broker's," he said. "And if the stock has stopped moving, sell; and sell in any case before the close." And then he dashed away to his own headquarters.

At about half after three o'clock, Oliver came into Hammond and Streeter's, breathless, and with his hair and clothing disheveled. He was half beside himself with exultation; and Montague was scarcely less wrought up — in fact he felt quite limp after the strain he had been through.

"What price did you get?" his brother inquired; and he answered, "An average of 78 $\frac{3}{8}$." There had been another sharp rise at the end, and he had sold all his stock without checking the advance.

"I got five-eighths," said Oliver. "O ye gods!"

There were some unhappy "shorts" in the office; Mr. Streeter was one of them. It was bitterness and gall to them to see the radiant faces of the two lucky ones; but the two did not even see this. They went out, half dancing, and had a drink or two to steady their nerves.

They would not actually get their money until the morrow; but Montague figured a profit of a trifle under a quarter of a million for himself. Of this about twenty thousand would go to make up the share of his unknown informant; the balance he considered would be an ample reward for his six hours' work that day.

His brother had won more than twice as much. But as they drove up home, talking over it in awe-stricken whispers, and pledging themselves to absolute secrecy, Oliver suddenly clenched his fist and struck his knee.

"By God!" ho exclaimed. "If I hadn't been a fool and tried to save an extra margin, I could have had a million!"

Chapter XV

*A*fter such a victory one felt in a mood for Christmas festivities, — for music and dancing and all beautiful and happy things.

Such a thing, for instance, as Mrs. Winnie, when she came to meet him; clad in her best automobile coat, a thing of purest snowy ermine, so truly gorgeous that wherever she went, people turned and stared and caught their breath. Mrs. Winnie was a picture of joyful health, with a glow in her rich complexion, and a sparkle in her black eyes.

She sat in her big touring-car — in which one could afford to wear ermine. It was a little private self-moving hotel; in the limousine were seats for six persons, with revolving easy chairs, and berths for sleeping, and a writing-desk and a wash-stand, and a beautiful electric chandelier to light it at night. Its trimmings were of South American mahogany, and its upholstering of Spanish and Morocco leathers; it had a telephone with which one spoke to the driver; an ice-box and a lunch hamper — in fact, one might have spent an hour discovering new gimcracks in this magic automobile. It had been made especially for Mrs. Winnie a couple of years ago, and the newspapers said it had cost thirty thousand dollars; it had then been quite a novelty, but now "everybody" was getting them. In this car one might sit at ease, and laugh and chat, and travel at the rate of an express train; and with never a jar or a quiver, nor the faintest sound of any sort.

The streets of the city sped by them as if by enchantment. They went through the park, and out Riverside Drive, and up the river-road which runs out of Broadway all the way to Albany. It was a macadamized avenue, lined with beautiful and stately homes. As one went farther yet, he came to the great country estates — a whole district of hundreds of square miles given up to them. There were forests and lakes and streams; there were gardens and greenhouses filled with rare plants and flowers, and parks with deer browsing, and peacocks and lyre-birds strutting about. The road wound in and out among hills, the surfaces of which would be one unbroken lawn; and upon the highest points stood palaces of every conceivable style and shape.

One might find these great domains anywhere around the city, at a distance of from thirty to sixty miles; there were two or three hundred of them, and incredible were the sums of money which had been spent upon their decoration. One saw an artificial lake of ten thousand acres, made upon land which had cost several hundred dollars an acre; one saw gardens with ten thousand rose-bushes, and a quarter of a million dollars' worth of lilies from Japan; there was one estate in which had been planted a million dollars' worth of rare trees, imported from all over the world. Some rich men, who had nothing else to amuse them, would make their estates over and over again, changing the view about their homes as one changes the scenery in a play. Over in New Jersey the Hegans were building a castle upon a mountaintop, and had built a special railroad simply to carry the materials. Here, also, was the estate of the tobacco king, upon which three million dollars had been spent before the plans of the mansion had even been drawn; there were artificial lakes and streams, and fantastic bridges and statuary, and scores of little model plantations and estates, according to the whim of the owner. And here in the Pocantico Hills was the estate of the oil king, about four square miles, with thirty miles of model driveways; many car-loads of rare plants had been imported for its gardens, and it took six hundred men to keep it in order. There was a golf course, a little miniature Alps, upon which the richest man in the world pursued his lost health, with armed guards and detectives patrolling the dace all day, and a tower with a search-light, whereby at night he could flood the grounds with light by pressing a button.

In one of these places lived the heir of the great house of Devon. His cousin dwelt in Europe, saying that America was not a fit place for a gentleman to live in. Each of them owned a hundred million dollars' worth of New York real estate, and drew their tribute of rents from the toil of the swarming millions of the city. And always, according to the policy of the family, they bought new real estate. They were directors of the great railroads tributary to the city, and in touch with the political machines, and in every other way in position to know what was under way: if a new subway were built to set the swarming millions free, the millions would find the land all taken up, and apartment-houses newly built for them — and the Devons were the owners. They had a score of the city's greatest hotels — and also slum tenements, and brothels and dives in the Tenderloin. They did not even have to know what they owned; they did not have to know anything, or do anything — they lived in their palaces, at home or abroad, and in their offices in the city the great rent-gathering machine ground on.

Eldridge Devon's occupation was playing with his country-place and his automobiles. He had recently sold all his horses, and turned his stables into a garage equipped with a score or so of cars; he was always getting a new one, and discussing its merits. As to Hudson Cliff, the estate, he had conceived the brilliant idea of establishing a gentleman's country-place which should be self-supporting — that is to say, which should furnish the luxuries and necessities of its owner's table for no more than it would have cost to buy them. Considering the prices usually paid, this was no astonishing feat, but Devon took a child's delight in it; he showed Montague his greenhouses, filled with rare flowers and fruits, and his model dairy, with marble stables and nickel plumbing, and attendants in white uniforms and rubber gloves. He was a short and very stout gentleman with red cheeks, and his conversation was not brilliant.

To Hudson Cliff came many of Montague's earlier acquaintances, and others whom he had not met before. They amused themselves in all the ways with which he had become familiar at house-parties; likewise on Christmas Eve there were festivities for the children, and on Christmas night a costume ball, very beautiful and stately. Many came from New York to attend this, and others from the neighborhood; and in returning calls, Montague saw others of these hill-top mansions.

Also, and most important of all, they played bridge — as they had played at every function which he had attended so far. Here Mrs. Winnie, who had rather taken him up, and threatened to supplant Oliver as his social guide and chaperon, insisted that no more excuses would be accepted; and so for two mornings he sat with her in one of the sun-parlors, and diligently put his mind upon the game. As he proved an apt pupil, he was then advised that he might take a trial plunge.

And so Montague came into touch with a new social phenomenon; perhaps on the whole the most significant and soul-disturbing phenomenon which Society had exhibited to him. He had just had the experience of getting a great deal of money without earning it, and was fresh from the disagreeable memories of it — the trembling and suspense, the burning lustful greed, the terrible nerve-devouring excitement. He had hoped that he would not soon have to go through such an experience again — and here was the prospect of an endless dalliance with it!

For that was the meaning of bridge; it was a penalty which people were paying for getting their money without earning it. The disease got into their blood, and they could no longer live without the excitement of gain and the hope of gain. So after their labors were over, when they were supposed to be resting and enjoying themselves, they would get together and torment themselves with an imitation struggle, mimicking the grim and dreadful gamble of business. Down in the Street, Oliver had pointed out to his brother a celebrated "plunger," who had sometimes won six or eight millions in a single day; and that man would play at stocks all morning, and "play the ponies" in the afternoon, and then spend the evening in a millionaires' gambling-house. And so it was with the bridge fiends.

It was a social plague; it had run through all Society, high and low. It had destroyed conversation and all good-fellowship — it would end by destroying even common decency, and turning the best people into vulgar gamblers. — Thus spoke Mrs. Billy Alden, who was one of the guests; and Montague thought that Mrs. Billy ought to know, for she herself was playing all the time.

Mrs. Billy did not like Mrs. Winnie Duval; and the beginning of the conversation was her inquiry why he let that woman corrupt him. Then the good lady went on to tell him what bridge had come to be; how people played it on the trains all the way from New York to San Francisco; how they had tables in their autos, and played while they were touring over the world. "Once," said she, "I took a party to see the America's Cup races off Sandy Hook; and when we got back to the pier, someone called, 'Who won?' And the answer was, 'Mrs. Billy's ahead, but we're going on this evening.' I took a party of friends through the Mediterranean and up the Nile, and we passed Venice and Cairo and the Pyramids and the Suez Canal, and they never once looked up — they were playing bridge. And you think I'm joking, but I mean just literally what I say. I know a man who was traveling from New York to Philadelphia, and got into a game with some strangers, and rode all the way to Palm Beach to finish it!"

Montague heard later of a well-known Society leader who was totally incapacitated that winter, from too much bridge at Newport; and she was passing the winter at Hot Springs and Palm Beach — and playing bridge there. They played it even in sanitariums, to which they had been driven by nervous breakdown. It was an occupation so exhausting to the physique of women that physicians came to know the symptoms of it, and before they diagnosed a case, they would ask, "Do you play bridge?" It had destroyed the last remnants of the Sabbath — it was a universal custom to have card-parties on that day.

It was a very expensive game, as they played it in Society; one might easily win or lose several thousand dollars in an evening, and there were many who could not afford this. If one did not play, he would be dropped from the lists of those invited; and when one entered a game, etiquette required him to stay in until it was finished. So one heard of young girls who had pawned their family plate, or who had sold their honor, to pay their bills at the game; and all Society knew of one youth who had robbed his hostess of her jewels and pawned them, and then taken her the tickets — telling her that her guests had robbed him. There were women received in the best Society, who lived as adventuresses pure and simple, upon their skill at the game; hostesses would invite rich guests and fleece them. Montague never forgot the sense of amazement and dismay with which he listened while first Mrs. Winnie and then his brother warned him that he must avoid playing with a certain aristocratic dame whom he met in this most aristocratic household — because she was such a notorious cheater!

"My dear fellow," laughed his brother, when he protested, "we have a phrase 'to cheat at cards like a woman.'" And then Oliver went on to tell him of his own first experience at cards in Society, when he had played poker with several charming young débutantes; they would call their hands and take the money without showing their cards, and he had been too gallant to ask to see them. But later he learned that this was a regular practice, and so he never played poker with women. And Oliver pointed out one of these girls to his brother — sitting, as beautiful as a picture and as cold as marble, with a half-smoked cigarette on the edge of the table, and whisky and soda and glasses of cracked ice beside her. Later on, as he chanced to be reading a newspaper, his brother leaned over his shoulder and pointed out another of the symptoms of the craze — an advertisement headed, "Your luck will change." It gave notice that at Rosenstein's Parlors, just off Fifth Avenue, one might borrow money upon expensive gowns and furs!

All during the ten days of this house-party, Mrs. Winnie devoted herself to seeing that Montague had a good time; Mrs. Winnie sat beside him at table — he found that somehow a convention had been established which assigned him to Mrs. Winnie as a matter of course. Nobody said anything to him about it, but knowing how relentlessly the affairs of other people were probed and analyzed, he began to feel exceedingly uncomfortable.

There came a time when he felt quite smothered by Mrs. Winnie; and immediately after lunch one day he broke away and went for a long walk by himself. This was the occasion of his meeting with an adventure.

An inch or two of snow had fallen, and lay gleaming in the sunlight. The air was keen, and he drank deep drafts of it, and went striding away over the hills for an hour or so. There was a gale blowing, and as he came over the summits it would strike him, and he would see the river white with foam. And then down in the valleys again all would be still.

Here, in a thickly wooded place, Montague's attention was arrested suddenly by a peculiar sound, a heavy thud, which seemed to shake the earth. It suggested a distant explosion, and he stopped for a moment and then went on, gazing ahead. He passed a turn, and then he saw a great tree which had fallen directly across the road.

He went on, thinking that this was what he had heard. But as he came nearer, he saw his mistake. Beyond the tree lay something else, and he began to run toward it. It was two wheels of an automobile, sticking up into the air.

He sprang upon the tree-trunk, and in one glance he saw the whole story. A big touring-car had swept round the sharp turn, and swerved to avoid the unexpected obstruction, and so turned a somersault into the ditch.

Montague gave a thrill of horror, for there was the form of a man pinned beneath the body of the car. He sprang toward it, but a second glance made him stop — he saw that blood had gushed from the man's mouth and soaked the snow all about. His chest was visibly crushed flat, and his eyes were dreadful, half-started from their sockets.

For a moment Montague stood staring, as if turned to stone. Then from the other side of the car came a moan, and he ran toward the sound. A second man lay in the ditch, moving feebly. Montague sprang to help him.

The man wore a heavy bearskin coat. Montague lifted him, and saw that he was a very elderly person, with a cut across his forehead, and a face as white as chalk. The other helped him to a position with his back against the bank, and he opened his eyes and groaned.

Montague knelt beside him, watching his breathing. He had a sense of utter helplessness — there was nothing he could think of to do, save to unbutton the man's coat and keep wiping the blood from his face.

"Some whisky," the stranger moaned. Montague answered that he had none; but the other replied that there was some in the car.

The slope of the bank was such that Montague could crawl under, and find the compartment with the bottle in it. The old man drank some, and a little color came back to his face. As the other watched him, it came to him that this face was familiar; but he could not place it.

"How many were there with you?" Montague asked; and the man answered, "Only one."

Montague went over and made certain that the other man — who was obviously the chauffeur — was dead. Then he hurried down the road, and dragged some brush out into the middle of it, where it could be seen from a distance by any other automobile that came along; after which he went back to the stranger, and bound his handkerchief about his forehead to stop the bleeding from the cut.

The old man's lips were tightly set, as if he were suffering great pain. "I'm done for!" he moaned, again and again.

"Where are you hurt?" Montague asked.

"I don't know," he gasped. "But it's finished me! I know it — it's the last straw."

Then he closed his eyes and lay back. "Can't you get a doctor?" he asked.

"There are no houses very near," said Montague. "But I can run —"

"No, no!" the other interrupted, anxiously. "Don't leave me! Some-one will come. — Oh, that fool of a chauffeur — why couldn't he go slow when I told him? That's always the way with them — they're always trying to show off."

"The man is dead," said Montague, quietly.

The other started upon his elbow. "Dead!" ho gasped.

"Yes," said Montague. "He's under the car."

The old man's eyes had started wild with fright; and he caught Montague by the arm. "Dead!" he said. "O my God — and it might have been me!"

There was a moment's pause. The stranger caught his breath, and whispered again: "I'm done for! I can't stand it! it's too much!"

Montague had noticed when he lifted the man that he was very frail and slight of build. Now he could feel that the hand that held his arm was trembling violently. It occurred to him that perhaps the man was not really hurt, but that his nerves had been upset by the shock.

And he felt certain of this a moment later, when the stranger suddenly leaned forward, clutching him with redoubled intensity, and staring at him with wide, horror-stricken eyes.

"Do you know what it means to be afraid of death?" he panted. "Do you know what it means to be afraid of death?"

Then, without waiting for a reply, he rushed on — "No, no! You can't! you can't! I don't believe any man knows it as I do! Think of it — for ten years I've never known a minute when I wasn't afraid of death! It follows me around — it won't let me be! It leaps out at me in places, like this! And when I escape it, I can hear it laughing at me — for it knows I can't get away!"

The old man caught his breath with a choking sob. He was clinging to Montague like a frightened child, and staring with a wild, hunted look upon his face. Montague sat transfixed.

"Yes," the other rushed on, "that's the truth, as God hears me! And it's the first time I've ever spoken it in my life! I have to hide it — because men would laugh at me — they pretend they're not afraid! But I lie awake all night, and it's like a fiend that sits by my bedside! I lie and listen to my own heart — I feel it beating, and I think how weak it is, and what thin walls it has, and what a wretched, helpless thing it is to have your life depend on that! — You don't know what that is, I suppose."

Montague shook his head.

"You're young, you see," said the other. "You have health — everybody has health, except me! And everybody hates me — I haven't got a friend in the world!"

Montague was quite taken aback by the suddenness of this outburst. He tried to stop it, for he felt almost indecent in listening — it was not fair to take a man off his guard like this. But the stranger could not be stopped — he was completely unstrung, and his voice grew louder and louder.

"It's every word of it true," he exclaimed wildly. "And I can't stand it anymore. I can't stand anything anymore. I was young and strong once — I could take care of myself; and I said: I'll make money, I'll be master of other men! But I was a fool — I forgot my health. And now all the money on earth can't do me any good! I'd give ten million dollars today for a body like any other man's — and this — this is what I have!"

He struck his hands against his bosom. "Look at it!" he cried, hysterically. "This is what I've got to live in! It won't digest any food, and I can't keep it warm — there's nothing right with it! How would you like to lie awake at night and say to yourself that your teeth were decaying and you couldn't help it — your hair was falling out, and nobody could stop it? You're old and worn out — falling to pieces; and everybody hates you — everybody's waiting for you to die, so that they can get you out of the way. The doctors come, and they're all humbugs! They shake their heads and use long words — they know they can't do you any good, but they want their big fees! And all they do is to frighten you worse, and make you sicker than ever!"

There was nothing that Montague could do save to sit and listen to this outburst of wretchedness. His attempts to soothe the old man only had the effect of exciting him more.

"Why does it all have to fall on me?" he moaned. "I want to be like other people — I want to live! And instead, I'm like a man with a pack of hungry wolves prowling round him — that's what it's like! It's like Nature — hungry and cruel and savage! You think you know what life is; it seems so beautiful and gentle and pleasant — that's when you're on top! But now I'm down, and I *know* what it is — it's a thing like a nightmare, that reaches out for you to clutch you and crush you! And you can't get away from it — you're helpless as a rat in a corner — you're damned — you're damned!" The miserable man's voice broke in a cry of despair, and he sank down in a heap in front of Montague, shaking and sobbing. The other was trembling slightly, and stricken with awe.

There was a long silence, and then the stranger lifted his tear-stained face, and Montague helped to support him. "Have a little more of the whisky," said he.

"No," the other answered feebly, "I'd better not."

"— My doctors won't let me have whisky," he added, after a while. "That's my liver. I've so many don'ts, you know, that it takes a notebook to keep track of them. And all of them together do me no good! Think of it — I have to live on graham crackers and milk — actually, not a thing has passed my lips for two years but graham crackers and milk."

And then suddenly, with a start, it came to Montague where he had seen this wrinkled old face before. It was Laura Hegan's uncle, whom the Major had pointed out to him in the dining room of the Millionaires' Club! Old Henry S. Grimes, who was really only sixty, but looked eighty; and who owned slum tenements, and evicted more people in a month than could be crowded into the club-house!

Montague gave no sign, but sat holding the man in his arms. A little trickle of blood came from under the handkerchief and ran down his cheek; Montague felt him tremble as he touched this with his ringer.

"Is it much of a cut?" he asked.

"Not much," said Montague; "two or three stitches, perhaps."

"Send for my family physician," the other added. "If I should faint, or anything, you'll find his name in my card-case. What's that?"

There was the sound of voices down the road. "Hello!" Montague shouted; and a moment later two men in automobile costume came running toward him. They stopped, staring in dismay at the sight which confronted them.

At Montague's suggestion they made haste to find a log by means of which they lifted the auto sufficiently to drag out the body of the chauffeur. Montague saw that it was quite cold.

He went back to old Grimes. "Where do you wish to go?" he asked.

The other hesitated. "I was bound for the Harrisons' —" he said.

"The Leslie Harrisons?" asked Montague. (They were people he had met at the Devons'.)

The other noticed his look of recognition. "Do you know them?" he asked.

"I do," said Montague.

"It isn't far," said the old man. "Perhaps I had best go there." — And then he hesitated for a moment; and catching Montague by the arm, and pulling him toward him, whispered, "Tell me — you-you won't tell —"

Montague, comprehending what he meant, answered, "It will be between us." At the same time he felt a new thrill of revulsion for this most miserable old creature.

They lifted him into the car; and because they delayed long enough to lay a blanket over the body of the chauffeur, he asked peevishly why they did not start. During the ten or fifteen minutes' trip he sat clinging to Montague, shuddering with fright every time they rounded a turn in the road.

They reached the Harrisons' place; and the footman who opened the door was startled out of his studied impassivity by the sight of a big bundle of bearskin in Montague's arms. "Send for Mrs. Harrison," said Montague, and laid the bundle upon a divan in the hall. "Get a doctor as quickly as you can," he added to a second attendant.

Mrs. Harrison came. "It's Mr. Grimes," said Montague; and then he heard a frightened exclamation, and turned and saw Laura Hegan, in a walking costume, fresh from the cold outside.

"What is it?" she cried. And he told her, as quickly as he could, and she ran to help the old man. Montague stood by, and later carried him upstairs, and waited below until the doctor came.

It was only when he set out for home again that he found time to think about Laura Hegan, and how beautiful she had looked in her furs. He wondered if it would always be his fate to meet her under circumstances which left her no time to be aware of his own existence.

At home he told about his adventure, and found himself quite a hero for the rest of the day. He was obliged to give interviews to several newspaper reporters, and to refuse to let one of them take his picture. Everyone at the Devons' seemed to know old Harry Grimes, and Montague thought to himself that if the comments of this particular group of people were a fair sample, the poor wretch was right in saying that he had not a friend in the world.

When he came downstairs the next morning, he found elaborate accounts of the accident in the papers, and learned that Grimes had nothing worse than a scalp wound and a severe shock. Even so, he felt it was incumbent upon him to pay a visit of inquiry, and rode over shortly before lunch.

Laura Hegan came down to see him, wearing a morning gown of white. She confirmed the good news of the papers, and said that her uncle was resting quietly. (She did not say that his physician had come post-haste, with two nurses, and taken up his residence in the house, and that the poor old millionaire was denied even his graham crackers and milk). Instead she said that he had mentioned Montague's kindness particularly, and asked her to thank him. Montague was cynical enough to doubt this.

It was the first time that he had ever had any occasion to talk with Miss Hegan. He noticed her gentle and caressing voice, with the least touch of the South in it; and he was glad to find that it was possible for her to talk without breaking the spell of her serene and noble beauty. Montague stayed as long as he had any right to stay.

And all the way as he rode home he was thinking about Laura Hegan. Here for the first time was a woman whom he felt he should like to know; a woman with reserve and dignity, and some ideas in her life. And it was impossible for him to know her — because she was rich!

There was no dodging this fact — Montague did not even try. He had met women with fortunes already, and he knew how they felt about themselves, and how the rest of the world felt about them. They might wish in their hearts to be something else besides the keepers of a treasure-chest, but their wishes were futile; the money went with them, and they had to defend it against all comers. Montague recalled one heiress after another — débutantes, some of them, exquisite and delicate as butterflies — but under the surface as hard as chain-armor. All their lives they had been trained to think of themselves as representing money, and of everyone who came near them as adventurers seeking money. In every word they uttered, in every glance and motion, one might read this meaning. And then he thought of Laura Hegan, with the fortune she would inherit; and he pictured what her life must be — the toadies and parasites and flatterers who would lay siege to her — the scheming mammas and the affectionate sisters and cousins who would plot to gain her confidence! For a man who was poor, and who meant to keep his self-respect, was there any possible conclusion except that she was entirely unknowable to him?

Chapter XVI

Montague came back to the city, and dug into his books again; while Alice gave her spare hours to watching the progress of the new gown in which she was to uphold the honor of the family at Mrs. Devon's opening ball. The great event was due in the next week and Society was as much excited about it as a family of children before Christmas. All whom Montague met were invited and all were going unless they happened to be in mourning. Their gossip was all of the disappointed ones, and their bitterness and heartburning.

Mrs. Devon's mansion was thrown open early on the eventful evening, but few would come until midnight. It was the fashion to attend the Opera first, and previous to that half a dozen people would give big dinners. He was a fortunate person who did not hear from his liver after this occasion; for at one o'clock came Mrs. Devon's massive supper, and then again at four o'clock another supper. To prepare these repasts a dozen extra chefs had been imported into the Devon establishment for a week — for it was part of the great lady's pride to permit no outside caterer to prepare anything for her guests.

Montague had never been able to get over his wonder at the social phenomenon known as Mrs. Devon. He came and took his chances in the jostling throngs; and except that he got into casual conversation with one of the numerous detectives whom he took for a guest he came off fairly well. But all the time that he was being passed about and introduced and danced with, he was looking about him and wondering. The grand staircase and the hall and parlors had been turned into tropical gardens, with palms and trailing vines, and azaleas and roses, and great vases of scarlet poinsettia, with hundreds of lights glowing through them. (It was said that this ball had exhausted the flower supply of the country as far south as Atlanta.) And then in the reception room one came upon the little old lady, standing' beneath a bower of orchids. She was clad in a robe of royal purple trimmed with silver, and girdled about with an armor-plate of gems. If one might credit the papers, the diamonds that were worn at one of these balls were valued at twenty million dollars.

The stranger was quite overwhelmed by all the splendor. There was a cotillion danced by two hundred gorgeously clad women and their partners — a scene so gay that one could only think of it as happening in a fairy legend, or some old romance of knighthood. Four sets of favors were given during this function, and jewels and objects of art were showered forth as if from a magician's wand. Mrs. Devon herself soon disappeared, but the riot of music and merry-making went on until near morning, and during all this time the halls and rooms of the great mansion were so crowded that one could scarcely move about.

Then one went home, and realized that all this splendor, and the human effort which it represented, had been for nothing but a memory! Nor would he get the full meaning of it if he failed to realize that it was simply one of thousands — a pattern which everyone there would strive to follow in some function of his own. It was a signal bell, which told the world that the "season" was open. It loosed the floodgates of extravagance, and the torrent of dissipation poured forth. From then on there would be a continuous round of gaieties; one might have three banquets every single night — for a dinner and two suppers was now the custom, at entertainments! And filling the rest of one's day were receptions and teas and musicales — a person might take his choice among a score of opportunities, and never leave the circle he met at Mrs. Devon's. Nor was this counting the tens of thousands of aspirants and imitators all over the city; nor in a host of other cities, each with thousands of women who had nothing to do save to ape the ways of the Metropolis. The mind could not realize the volume of this deluge of destruction — it was a thing which stunned the senses, and thundered in one's ears like Niagara.

The meaning of it all did not stop with the people who poured it forth; its effects were to be traced through the whole country. There were hordes of tradesmen and manufacturers who supplied what Society bought, and whose study it was to induce people to buy as much as possible. And so they devised what were called "fashions" — little eccentricities of cut and material, which made everything go out of date quickly. There had once been two seasons, but now there were four; and through window displays and millions of advertisements the public was lured into the trap. The "yellow" journals would give whole pages to describing "What the 400 are wearing"; there were magazines with many millions of readers, which existed for nothing save to propagate these ideas. And everywhere, in all classes of Society, men and women were starving their minds and hearts, and straining their energies to follow this phantom of fashion; the masses were kept poor because of it, and the youth and hope of the world was betrayed by it. In country villages poor farmers' wives were trimming their bonnets over to be "stylish"; and servant-girls in the cities were wearing imitation sealskins, and shop-clerks and seamstresses selling themselves into brothels for the sake of ribbons and gilt jewelry.

It was the instinct of decoration, perverted by the money-lust. In the Metropolis the sole test of excellence was money, and the possession of money was the proof of power; and every natural desire of men and women had been tainted by this influence. The love of beauty, the impulse to hospitality, the joys of music and dancing and love — all these things had become simply means to the demonstration of money-power! The men were busy making more money — but their idle women had nothing in life save this mad race in display. So it had come about that the woman who could consume wealth most conspicuously — who was the most effective instrument for the destroying of the labor and the lives of other people — this was the woman who was most applauded and most noticed.

The most appalling fact about Society was this utter blind material-ism. Such expectations as Montague had brought with him had been derived from the literature of Europe; in a grand monde such as this, he expected to meet diplomats and statesmen, scientists and explorers, philosophers and poets and painters. But one never heard anything about such people in Society. It was a mark of eccentricity to be interested in intellectual affairs, and one might go about for weeks and not meet a person with an idea. When these people read, it was a sugar-candy novel, and when they went to the play, it was a musical comedy. The one single intellectual product which it could point to as its own, was a rancid scandal-sheet, used mainly as a moans of blackmail. Now and then some aspiring young matron of the "elite" would try to set up a salon after the fashion of the continent, and would gather a few feeble wits about her for a time. But for the most part the intellectual workers of the city held themselves severely aloof; and Society was loft a little clique of people whose fortunes had become historic in a decade or two, and who got together in each other's palaces and gorged themselves, and gambled and gossiped about each other, and wove about their personalities a veil of awful and exclusive majesty.

Montague found himself thinking that perhaps it was not they who were to blame. It was not they who had set up wealth as the end and goal of things — it was the whole community, of which they were a part. It was not their fault that they had been left with power and nothing to use it for; it was not their fault that their sons and daughters found themselves stranded in the world, deprived of all necessity, and of the possibility of doing anything useful.

The most pitiful aspect of the whole thing to Montague was this "second generation" who were coming upon the scene, with their lives all poisoned in advance. No wrong which they could do to the world would ever equal the wrong which the world had done them, in permitting them to have money which they had not earned. They were cut off forever from reality, and from the possibility of understanding life; they had big, healthy bodies, and they craved experience — and they had absolutely nothing to do. That was the real meaning of all this orgy of dissipation — this "social whirl" as it was called; it was the frantic chase of some new thrill, some excitement that would stir the senses of people who had nothing in the world to interest them. That was why they were building palaces, and flinging largesses of banquets and balls, and tearing about the country in automobiles, and traveling over the earth in steam yachts and private trains.

— And first and last, the lesson of their efforts was, that the chase was futile; the jaded nerves would not thrill. The most conspicuous fact about Society was its unutterable and agonizing boredom; of its great solemn functions the shop-girl would read with greedy envy, but the women who attended them would be half asleep behind their jeweled fans. It was typified to Montague by Mrs. Billy Alderi's yachting party on the Nile; yawning in the face of the Sphinx, and playing bridge beneath the shadow of the pyramids — and counting the crocodiles and proposing to jump in by way of "changing the pain!"

People attended these ceaseless rounds of entertainments, simply because they dreaded to be left alone. They wandered from place to place, following like a herd of sheep whatever leader would inaugurate a new diversion. One could have filled a volume with the list of their "fads." There were new ones every week — if Society did not invent them, the yellow journals invented them. There was a woman who had her teeth filled with diamonds; and another who was driving a pair of zebras. One heard of monkey dinners and pajama dinners at Newport, of horseback dinners and vegetable dances in New York. One heard of fashion-albums and autograph-fans and talking crows and rare orchids and reindeer meat; of bracelets for men and ankle rings for women; of "vanity-boxes" at ten and twenty thousand dollars each; of weird and repulsive pets, chameleons and lizards and king-snakes — there was one young woman who wore a cat-snake as a necklace. One would take to slumming and another to sniffing brandy through the nose; one had a table-cover made of woven roses, and another was wearing perfumed flannel at sixteen dollars a yard; one had inaugurated ice-skating in August, and another had started a class for the study of Plato. Some were giving tennis tournaments in bathing-suits, and playing leap-frog after dinner; others had got dispensations from the Pope, so that they might have private chapels and confessors; and yet others were giving "progressive dinners," moving from one restaurant to another — a cocktail and blue-points at Sherry's, a soup and Madeira at Delmonico's, some terrapin with amontillado at the Waldorf — and so on.

One of the consequences of the furious pace was that people's health broke down very quickly; and there were all sorts of bizarre ways of restoring it. One person would be eating nothing but spinach, and another would be living on grass. One would chew a mouthful of soup thirty-two times; another would eat every two hours, and another only once a week. Some went out in the early morning and walked barefooted in the grass, and others went hopping about the floor on their hands and knees to take off fat. There were "rest cures" and "water cures," "new thought" and "metaphysical healing" and "Christian Science"; there was an automatic horse, which one might ride indoors, with a register showing the distance traveled. Montague met one man who had an electric machine, which cost thirty thousand dollars, and which took hold of his arms and feet and exercised him while he waited. Ho met a woman who told him she was riding an electric camel!

Everywhere one went there were new people, spending their money in new and incredible ways. Here was a man who had bought a chapel and turned it into a theater, and hired professional actors, and persuaded his friends to come and see him act Shakespeare. Hero was a woman who costumed herself after figures in famous paintings, with arrange-

ments of roses and cherry leaves, and wreaths of ivy and laurel — and
with costumes for her pet dogs to match! Hero was a man who paid six
dollars a day for a carnation four inches across; and a girl who wore a
hat trimmed with fresh morning-glories, and a ball costume with swarms
of real butterflies tied with silk threads; and another with a hat made
of woven silver, with ostrich plumes forty inches long made entirely of
silvei films. Here was a man who hired a military company to drill all
day long to prepare a floor for dancing; and another who put up a
building at a cost of thirty thousand dollars to give a débutante dance
for his daughter, and then had it torn down the day after. Here was a
man who bred rattlesnakes and turned them loose by thousands, and
had driven everybody away from the North Carolina estate of one of
the Wallings. Here was a man who was building himself a yacht with a
model dairy and bakery on board, and a French laundry and a brass
band. Here was a million-dollar racing-yacht with auto-boats on it and
a platoon of marksmen, and some Chinese laundrymen, and two
physicians for its half-insane occupant. Here was a man who had bought
a Rhine castle for three-quarters of a million, and spent as much in
restoring it, and filled it with servants dressed in fourteenth-century
costumes. Here was a five-million-dollar art collection hidden away
where nobody ever saw it!

One saw the meaning of this madness most clearly in the young men
of Society. Some were killing themselves and other people in automobile
races at a hundred and twenty miles an hour. Some went in for auto-
boats, mere shells of things, shaped like a knife-blade, that tore through
the water at forty miles an hour. Some would hire professional pugilists
to knock them out; others would get up dog-fights and bear-fights, and
boxing matches with kangaroos. Montague was taken to the home of
one young man who had given his life to hunting wild game in every
corner of the globe, and would travel round the world for a new species
to add to his museum of trophies. He had heard that Baron Rothschild
had offered a thousand pounds for a "bongo," a huge grass-eating
animal, which no white man had ever seen; and he had taken a year's
trip into the interior, with a train of a hundred and thirty natives, and
had brought out the heads of forty different species, including a bongo
— which the Baron did not get! He met another who had helped to
organize a balloon club, and two twenty-four-hour trips in the clouds.
(This, by the way, was the latest sport — at Tuxedo they had races between
balloons and automobiles; and Montague met one young lady who
boasted that she had been up five times.) There was another young
millionaire who sat and patiently taught Sunday School, in the presence
of a host of reporters; there was another who set up a chain of newspa-

pers all over the country and made war upon his class. There were others who went in for settlement work and Russian revolutionists — there were even some who called themselves Socialists! Montague thought that this was the strangest fad of all; and when he met one of these young men at an afternoon tea, he gazed at him with wonder and perplexity — thinking of the man he had heard ranting on the street-corner.

This was the "second generation." Appalling as it was to think of, there was a third growing up, and getting ready to take the stage. And with wealth accumulating faster than ever, who could guess what they might do? There were still in Society a few men and women who had earned their money, and had some idea of the toil and suffering that it stood for; but when the third generation had taken possession, these would all be dead or forgotten, and there would no longer be any link to connect them with reality!

In the light of this thought one was moved to watch the children of the rich. Some of these had inherited scores of millions of dollars while they were still in the cradle; now and then one of them would be presented with a million-dollar house for a birthday gift. When such a baby was born, the newspapers would give pages to describing its layette, with baby dresses at a hundred dollars each, and lace handkerchiefs at five dollars, and dressing-sets with tiny gold brushes and powder-boxes; one might see a picture of the precious object in a "Moses basket," covered with rare and wonderful Valenciennes lace.

This child would grow up in an atmosphere of luxury and self-indulgence; it would be bullying the servants at the age of six, and talking scandal and smoking cigarettes at twelve. It would be petted and admired and stared at, and paraded about in state, dressed up like a French doll; it would drink in snobbery and hatefulness with the very air it breathed. One might meet in these great houses little tots not yet in their teens whose talk was all of the cost of things, and of the inferiority of their neighbors. There was nothing in the world too good for them. — They had little miniature automobiles to ride about the country in, and blooded Arabian ponies, and doll-houses in real Louis Seize, with jeweled rugs and miniature electric lights. At Mrs. Caroline Smythe's, Montague was introduced to a pale and anemic-looking youth of thirteen, who dined in solemn state alone when the rest of the family was away, and insisted upon having all the footmen in attendance; and his unfortunate aunt brought a storm about her ears by forbidding the butler to take champagne upstairs into the nursery before lunch.

A little remark stayed in Montague's mind as expressing the attitude of Society toward such matters. Major Venable had chanced to remark jestingly that children were coming to understand so much nowadays that it was necessary for the ladies to be careful. To which Mrs. Vivie Patton answered, with a sudden access of seriousness: "I don't know — do you find that children have any morals? Mine haven't."

And then the fascinating Mrs. Vivie went on to tell the truth about her own children. They were natural-born savages, and that was all there was to it. They did as they pleased, and no one could stop them. The Major replied that nowadays all the world was doing as it pleased, and no one seemed to be able to stop it; and with that jest the conversation was turned to other matters. But Montague sat in silence, thinking about it — wondering what would happen to the world when it had fallen under the sway of this generation of spoiled children, and had adopted altogether the religion of doing as one pleased.

In the beginning people had simply done as they pleased spontaneously, and without thinking about it; but now, Montague discovered, the custom had spread to such an extent that it was developing a philosophy. There was springing up a new cult, whose devotees were planning to make over the world upon the plan of doing as one pleased. Because its members were wealthy, and able to command the talent of the world, the cult was developing an art, with a highly perfected technique, and a literature which was subtle and exquisite and alluring. Europe had had such a literature for a century, and England for a generation or two. And now America was having it, too!

Montague had an amusing insight into this one day, when Mrs. Vivie invited him to one of her "artistic evenings." Mrs. Vivie was in touch with a special set which went in for intellectual things, and included some amateur Bohemians and men of "genius." "Don't you come if you'll be shocked," she had said to him — "for Strathcona will be there."

Montague deemed himself able to stand a good deal by this time. He went, and found Mrs. Vivie and her Count (Mr. Vivie had apparently not been invited) and also the young poet of Diabolism, whose work was just then the talk of the town. He was a tall, slender youth with a white face and melancholy black eyes, and black locks falling in cascades about his ears; he sat in an Oriental corner, with a manuscript copied in tiny handwriting upon delicately scented "art paper," and tied with passionate purple ribbons. A young girl clad in white sat by his side and held a candle, while he read from this manuscript his unprinted (because unprintable) verses.

And between the readings the young poet talked. He talked about himself and his work — apparently. that was what he had come to talk about. His words flowed like a swift stream, limpid, sparkling, incessant; leaping from place to place — here, there, quick as the play of light upon the water. Montague labored to follow the speaker's ideas, until he found his mind in a whirl and gave it up. Afterward, when he thought it over, he laughed at himself; for Strathcona's ideas were not serious things, having relationship to truth — they were epigrams put together to dazzle the hearer, studies in paradox, with as much relation to life as fireworks. He took the sum-total of the moral experience of the human race, and turned it upside down and jumbled it about, and used it as bits of glass in a kaleidoscope. And the hearers would gasp, and whisper, "Diabolical!"

The motto of this "school" of poets was that there was neither good nor evil, but that all things were "interesting." After listening to Strathcona for half an hour, one felt like hiding his head, and denying that he had ever thought of having any virtue; in a world where all things were uncertain, it was presumptuous even to pretend to know what virtue was. One could only be what one was; and did not that mean that one must do as one pleased?

You could feel a shudder run through the company at his audacity. And the worst of it was that you could not dismiss it with a laugh; for the boy was really a poet — he had fire and passion, the gift of melodious ecstasy. He was only twenty, and in his brief meteor flight he had run the gamut of all experience; he had familiarized himself with all human achievement — past, present, and future. There was nothing anyone could mention that he did not perfectly comprehend: the raptures of the saints, the consecration of the martyrs — yes, he had known them; likewise he had touched the depths of depravity, he had been lost in the innermost passages of the caverns of hell. And all this had been interesting — in its time; now he was sighing for new worlds of experience — say for unrequited love, which should drive him to madness.

It was at this point that Montague dropped out of the race, and took to studying from the outside the mechanism of this young poet's conversation. Strathcona flouted the idea of a moral sense; but in reality he was quite dependent upon it — his recipe for making epigrams was to take what other people's moral sense made them respect, and identify it with something which their moral sense made them abhor. Thus, for instance, the tale which he told about one of the members of his set, who was a relative of a bishop. The great man had occasion to rebuke him for his profligate ways, declaring in the course of his lecture that he was living off the reputation of his father; to which the boy made the crushing rejoinder: "It may be bad to live off the reputation of one's father, but it's better than living off the reputation of God." — This was very subtle and it was necessary to ponder it. God was dead; and the worthy bishop did not know it! But let him take a new God, who had no reputation, and go out into the world and make a living out of him!

Then Strathcona discussed literature. He paid his tribute to the "Fleurs de Mal" and the "Songs before Sunrise"; but most, he said, he owed to "the divine Oscar." This English poet of many poses and some vices the law had seized and flung into jail; and since the law is a thing so brutal and wicked that whoever is touched by it is made thereby a martyr and a hero, there had grown up quite a cult about the memory of "Oscar." All up-to-date poets imitated his style and his attitude to life; and so the most revolting of vices had the cloak of romance flung about them — were given long Greek and Latin names, and discussed with parade of learning as revivals of Hellenic ideals. The young men in Strathcona's set referred to each other as their "lovers"; and if one showed any perplexity over this, he was regarded, not with contempt — for it was not aesthetic to feel contempt — but with a slight lifting of the eyebrows, intended to annihilate.

One must not forget, of course, that these young people were poets, and to that extent were protected from their own doctrines. They were interested, not in life, but in making pretty verses about life; there were some among them who lived as cheerful ascetics in garret rooms, and gave melodious expression to devilish emotions. But, on the other hand, for every poet, there were thousands who were not poets, but people to whom life was real. And these lived out the creed, and wrecked their lives; and with the aid of the poet's magic, the glamour of melody and the fire divine, they wrecked the lives with which they came into contact. The new generation of boys and girls were deriving their spiritual sustenance from the poetry of Baudelaire and Wilde; and rushing with the hot impulsiveness of youth into the dreadful traps which the traders in vice prepared for them. One's heart bled to see them, pink-cheeked and bright-eyed, pursuing the hem of the Muse's robe in brothels and dens of infamy!

Chapter XVII

*T*he social mill ground on for another month. Montague withdrew himself as much as his brother would let him; but Alice, was on the go all night and half the day. Oliver had sold his racing automobile to a friend — he was a man of family now, he said, and his wild days were over. He had got, instead, a limousine car for Alice; though she declared she had no need of it — if ever she was going to anyplace, Charlie Carter always begged her to use his. Charlie's siege was as persistent as ever, as Montague noticed with annoyance.

The great law case was going forward. After weeks of study and investigation, Montague felt that he had the matter well in hand; and he had taken Mr. Hasbrook's memoranda as a basis for a new work of his own, much more substantial. Bit by bit; as he dug into the subject, he had discovered a state of affairs in the Fidelity Company, and, indeed, in the whole insurance business and its allied realms of banking and finance, which shocked him profoundly. It was impossible for him to imagine how such conditions could exist and remain unknown to the public — more especially as everyone in Wall Street with whom he talked seemed to know about them and to take them for granted.

His client's papers had provided him with references to the books; Montague had taken this dry material and made of it a protest which had the breath of life in it. It was a thing at which he toiled with deadly earnestness; it was not merely a struggle of one man to get a few thousand dollars, it was an appeal in behalf of millions of helpless people whose trust had been betrayed. It was the first step in a long campaign, which the young lawyer meant should force a great evil into the light of day.

He went over his bill of complaint with Mr. Hasbrook, and he was glad to see that the work he had done made its impression upon him. In fact, his client was a little afraid that some of his arguments might be too radical in tone — from the strictly legal point of view, he made haste to explain. But Montague reassured him upon this point.

And then came the day when the great ship was ready for launching. The news must have spread quickly, for a few hours after the papers in the suit had been filed, Montague received a call from a newspaper reporter, who told him of the excitement in financial circles, where the thing had fallen like a bomb. Montague explained the purpose of the suit, and gave the reporter a number of facts which he felt certain would attract attention to the matter. When he picked up the paper the next morning, however, he was surprised to find that only a few lines had been given to the case, and that his interview had been replaced by one with an unnamed official of the Fidelity, to the effect that the attack upon the company was obviously for black-mailing purposes.

That was the only ripple which Montague's work produced upon the surface of the pool; but there was a great commotion among the fish at the bottom, about which he was soon to learn.

That evening, while he was hard at work in his study, he received a telephone call from his brother. "I'm coming round to see you," said Oliver. "Wait for me."

"All right," said the other, and added, "I thought you were dining at the Waitings'."

"I'm there now," was the answer. "I'm leaving."

"What is the matter?" Montague asked.

"There's hell to pay," was the reply — and then silence.

When Oliver appeared, a few minutes later, he did not even stop to set down his hat, but exclaimed, "Allan, what in heaven's name have you been doing?"

"What do you mean?" asked the other.

"Why, that suit!"

"What about it?"

"Good God, man!" cried Oliver. "Do you mean that you really don't know what you've done?"

Montague was staring at him. "I'm afraid I don't," said he.

"Why, you're turning the world upside down!" exclaimed the other. "Everybody you know is crazy about it."

"Everybody I know!" echoed Montague. "What have they to do with it?"

"Why, you've stabbed them in the back!" half shouted Oliver. "I could hardly believe my ears when they told me. Robbie Walling is simply wild — I never had such a time in my life."

"I don't understand yet," said Montague, more and more amazed. "What has he to do with it?"

"Why, man," cried Oliver, "his brother's a director in the Fidelity! And his own interests — and all the other companies! You've struck at the whole insurance business!"

Montague caught his breath. "Oh, I see!" he said.

"How could you think of such a thing?" cried the other, wildly. "You promised to consult me about things —"

"I told you when I took this case," put in Montague, quickly.

"I know," said his brother. "But you didn't explain — and what did I know about it? I thought I could leave it to your common sense not to mix up in a thing like this."

"I'm very sorry," said Montague, gravely. "I had no idea of any such result."

"That's what I told Robbie," said Oliver. "Good God, what a time I had!"

He took his hat and coat and laid them on the bed, and sat down and began to tell about it. "I made him realize the disadvantage you were under," he said, "being a stranger and not knowing the ground. I believe he had an idea that you tried to get his confidence on purpose to attack him. It was Mrs. Robbie, I guess — you know her fortune is all in that quarter."

Oliver wiped the perspiration from his forehead. "My!" he said. — "And fancy what old Wyman must be saying about this! And what a time poor Betty must be having! And then Freddie Vandam — the air will be blue for half a mile round his place! I must send him a wire and explain that it was a mistake, and that we're getting out of it."

And he got up, to suit the action to the word. But halfway to the desk he heard his brother say, "Wait."

He turned, and saw Montague, quite pale. "I suppose by 'getting out of it,'" said the latter, "you mean dropping the case."

"Of course," was the answer.

"Well, then," he continued, very gravely, — "I can see that it's going to be hard, and I'm sorry. But you might as well understand me at the very beginning — I will never drop this case."

Oliver's jaw fell limp. "Allan!" he gasped.

There was a silence; and then the storm broke. Oliver knew his brother well enough to realize just how thoroughly he meant what he said; and so he got the full force of the shock all at once. He raved and swore and wrung his hands, and declaimed at his brother, saying that he had betrayed him, that he was ruining him — dumping himself and the whole family into the ditch. They would be jeered at and insulted — they would be blacklisted and thrown out of Society. Alice's career would be cut short — every door would be closed to her. His own career would die before it was born; he would never get into the clubs — he would be a pariah — he would be bankrupted and penniless. Again and again Oliver went over the situation, naming person after person who would be outraged, and describing what that person would do; there were the

Wallings and the Venables and the Havens, the Vandams and the Todds and the Wymans — they were all one regiment, and Montague had flung a bomb into the center of them!

It was very terrible to him to see his brother's rage and despair; but he had seen his way clear through this matter, and he knew that there was no turning back for him. "It is painful to learn that all one's acquaintances are thieves," he said. "But that does not change my opinion of stealing."

"But my God!" cried Oliver; "did you come to New York to preach sermons?"

To which the other answered, "I came to practice law. And the lawyer who will not fight injustice is a traitor to his profession."

Oliver threw up his hands in despair. What could one say to a sentiment such as that?

— But then again he came to the charge, pointing out to his brother the position in which he had placed himself with the Wallings. He had accepted their hospitality; they had taken him and Alice in, and done everything in the world for them — things for which no money could ever repay them. And now he had struck them!

But the only effect of that was to make Montague regret that he had ever had anything to do with the Wallings. If they expected to use their friendship to tie his hands in such a matter, they were people he would have left alone.

"But do you realize that it's not merely yourself you're ruining?" cried Oliver. "Do you know what you're doing to Alice?"

"That is harder yet for me," the other replied. "But I am sure that Alice would not ask me to stop."

Montague was firmly set in his own mind; but it seemed to be quite impossible for his brother to realize that this was the case. He would give up; but then, going back into his own mind, and facing the thought of this person and that, and the impossibility of the situation which would arise, he would return to the attack with new anguish in his voice. He implored and scolded, and even wept; and then he would get himself together again, and come and sit in front of his brother and try to reason with him.

And so it was that in the small hours of the morning, Montague, pale and nervous, but quite unshaken, was sitting and listening while his brother unfolded before him a picture of the Metropolis as he had come to see it. It was a city ruled by mighty forces — money-forces; great families and fortunes, which had held their sway for generations, and regarded the place, with all its swarming millions, as their birthright. They possessed it utterly — they held it in the hollow of their hands.

Railroads and telegraphs and telephones — banks and insurance and trust companies — all these they owned; and the political machines and the legislatures, the courts and the newspapers, the churches and the colleges. And their rule was for plunder; all the streams of profit ran into their coffers. The stranger who came to their city succeeded as he helped them in their purposes, and failed if they could not use him. A great editor or bishop was a man who taught their doctrines; a great statesman was a man who made the laws for them; a great lawyer was one who helped them to outwit the public. Any man who dared to oppose them, they would cast out and trample on, they would slander and ridicule and ruin.

And Oliver came down to particulars — he named these powerful men, one after one, and showed what they could do. If his brother would only be a man of the world, and see the thing! Look at all the successful lawyers! Oliver named them, one after one — shrewd devisers of corporation trickery, with incomes of hundreds of thousands a year. He could not name the men who had refused to play the game — for no one had ever heard of them. But it was so evident what would happen in this case! His friends would cast him off; his own client would get his price — whatever it was — and then leave him in the lurch, and laugh at him! "If you can't make up your mind to play the game," cried Oliver, frantically, "at least you can give it up! There are plenty of other ways of getting a living — if you'll let me, I'll take care of you myself, rather than have you disgrace me. Tell me — will you do that? Will you quit altogether?"

And Montague suddenly leaped to his feet, and brought his fist down upon the desk with a bang. "No!" he cried; "by God, no!"

"Let me make you understand me once for all," he rushed on. "You've shown me New York as you see it. I don't believe it's the truth — I don't believe it for one single moment! But let me tell you this, I shall stay here and find out — and if it is true, it won't stop me! I shall stay here and defy those people! I shall stay and fight them till the day I die! They may ruin me, — I'll go and live in a garret if I have to, — but as sure as there's a God that made me, I'll never stop till I've opened the eyes of the people to what they're doing!"

Montague towered over his brother, white-hot and terrible. Oliver shrank from him — he never had seen such a burst of wrath from him before. "Do you understand me now?" Montague cried; and he answered, in a despairing voice, "Yes, yes."

"I see it's all up," he added weakly. "You and I can't pull together."

"No," exclaimed the other, passionately, "we can't. And we might as well give up trying. You have chosen to be a time-server and a lick-spittle, and I don't choose it! Do you think I've learned nothing in the time I've been here? Why, man, you used to be daring and clever — and now you never draw a breath without wondering if these rich snobs will like the way you do it! And you want Alice to sell herself to them — you want me to sell my career to them!"

There was a long pause. Oliver had turned very pale. And then suddenly his brother caught himself together, and said: "I'm sorry. I didn't mean to quarrel, but you've goaded me too much. I'm grateful for what you have tried to do for me, and I'll pay you back as soon as I can. But I can't go on with this game. I'll quit, and you can disown me to your friends — tell them that I've run amuck, and to forget they ever knew me. They'll hardly blame you for it — they know you too well for that. And as for Alice, I'll talk it out with her tomorrow, and let her decide for herself — if she wants to be a Society queen, she can put herself in your hands, and I'll get out of her way. On the other hand, if she approves of what I'm doing, why we'll both quit, and you won't have to bother with either of us."

That was the basis upon which they parted for the night; but like most resolutions taken at white heat, it was not followed literally. It was very hard for Montague to have to confront Alice with such a choice; and as for Oliver, when he went home and thought it over, he began to discover gleams of hope. He might make it clear to everyone that he was not responsible for his brother's business vagaries, and take his chances upon that basis. After all, there were wheels within wheels in Society; and if the Robbie Waitings chose to break with him — why, they had plenty of enemies. There might even be interests which would be benefited by Allan's course, and would take him up.

Montague had resolved to write and break every engagement which he had made, and to sever his connection with Society at one stroke. But the next day his brother came again, with compromises and new protestations. There was no use going to the other extreme: he, Oliver, would have it out with the Wallings, and they might all go on their way as if nothing had happened.

— So Montague made his debut in the role of knight-errant. He went with many qualms and misgivings, uncertain how each new person would take it. The next evening he was promised for a theater-party with Siegfried Harvey; and they had supper in a private room at Delmonico's, and there came Mrs. Winnie, resplendent as an apple tree in early April — and murmuring with bated breath, "Oh, you dreadful man, what have you been doing?"

"Have I been poaching on *your* preserves?" he asked promptly.

"No, not mine," she said, "but —" and then she hesitated.

"On Mr. Duval's?" he asked.

"No," she said, "not his — but everybody else's! He was telling me about it today — there's a most dreadful uproar. He wanted me to try to find out what you were up to, and who was behind it."

Montague listened, wonderingly. Did Mrs. Winnie mean to imply that her husband had asked her to try to worm his business secrets out of him? That was what she seemed to imply. "I told him I never talked business with my friends," she said. "He can ask you himself, if he chooses. But what *does* it all mean, anyhow?"

Montague smiled at the naïve inconsistency.

"It means nothing," said he, "except that I am trying to get justice for a client."

"But can you afford to make so many powerful enemies?" she asked.

"I've taken my chances on that," he replied.

Mrs. Winnie answered nothing, but looked at him with wondering admiration in her eyes. "You arc different from the men about you," she remarked, after a while — and her tone gave Montague to understand that there was one person who meant to stand by him.

But Mrs. Winnie Duval was not all Society. Montague was amused to notice with what suddenness the stream of invitations slacked up; it was necessary for Alice to give her calling list many revisions. Freddie Vandam had promised to invite them to his place on Long Island, and of course that invitation would never come; likewise they would never again see the palace of the Lester Todds, upon the Jersey mountaintop.

Oliver put in the next few days in calling upon people to explain his embarrassing situation. He washed his hands of his brother's affairs, he said; and his friends might do the same, if they saw fit. With the Robbie Waitings he had a stormy half hour, about which he thought it best to say little to the rest of the family. Robbie did not break with him utterly, because of their Wall Street Alliance; but Mrs. Robbie's feeling was so bitter, he said, that it would be best if Alice saw nothing of her for a while. He had a long talk with Alice, and explained the situation. The girl was utterly dumbfounded, for she was deeply grateful to Mrs. Robbie, and fond of her as well; and she could not believe that a friend could be so cruelly unjust to her.

The upshot of the whole situation was a very painful episode. A few days later Alice met Mrs. Robbie at a reception; and she took the lady aside, and tried to tell her how distressed and helpless she was. And the result was that Mrs. Robbie flew into a passion and railed at her, declaring in the presence of several people that she had sponged upon her and abused her hospitality! And so poor Alice came home, weeping and half hysterical.

All of which, of course, was like oil upon a fire; the heavens were lighted up with the conflagration. The next development was a paragraph in Society's scandal-sheet — telling with infinite gusto how a certain ultra-fashionable matron had taken up a family of stranded waifs from a far State, and introduced them into the best circles, and even gone so far as to give a magnificent dance in their honor; and how the discovery had been made that the head of the family had been secretly preparing an attack upon their business interests; and of the tearing of hair and gnashing of teeth which had followed — and the violent quarrel in a public place. The paragraph concluded with the prediction that the strangers would find themselves the center of a merry social war.

Oliver was the first to show them this paper. But lest by any chance they should miss it, half a dozen unknown friends were good enough to mail them copies, carefully marked. — And then came Reggie Mann, who as freelance and gossip-gatherer sat on the fence and watched the fun; Reggie wore a thin veil of sympathy over his naked glee, and brought them the latest reports from all portions of the battleground. Thus they were able to know exactly what everybody was saying about them — who was amused and who was outraged, and who proposed to drop them and who to take them up.

Montague listened for a while, but then he got tired of it, and went for a walk to escape it — but only to run into another trap. It was dark, and he was strolling down the Avenue, when out of a brilliantly lighted jewelry shop came Mrs. Billy Alden to her carriage. And she hailed him with an exclamation.

"You man," she cried, "what have you been doing?"

He tried to laugh it off and escape, but she took him by the arm, commanding, "Get in here and tell me about it."

So he found himself moving with the slow stream of vehicles on the Avenue, and with Mrs. Billy gazing at him quizzically and asking him if he did not feel like a hippopotamus in a frog-pond.

He replied to her raillery by asking her under which flag she stood. But there was little need to ask that, for anyone who was fighting a Walling became ipso facto a friend of Mrs. Billy's. She told Montague that if he felt his social position was imperiled, all he had to do was to come to her. She would gird on her armor and take the field.

"But tell me how you came to do it," she said.

He answered that there was very little to tell. He had taken up a case which was obviously just, but having no idea what a storm it would raise.

Then he noticed that his companion was looking at him sharply. "Do you really mean that's all there is to it?" she asked.

"Of course I do," said he, perplexed.

"Do you know," was her unexpected response, "I hardly know what to make of you. I'm afraid to trust you, on account of your brother."

Montague was embarrassed. "I don't know what you mean," he said.

"Everybody thinks there's some trickery in that suit," she answered.

"Oh," said Montague, "I see. Well, they will find out. If it will help you any to know it, I've been having no end of scenes with my brother."

"I'll believe you," said Mrs. Billy, genially. "But it seems strange that a man could have been so blind to a situation! I feel quite ashamed because I didn't help you myself!"

The carriage had stopped at Mrs. Billy's home, and she asked him to dinner. "There'll be nobody but my brother," she said, — "we're resting this evening. And I can make up to you for my negligence!"

Montague had no engagement, and so he went in, and saw Mrs. Billy's mansion, which was decorated in imitation of a Doge's palace, and met Mr. "Davy" Alden, a mild-mannered little gentleman who obeyed orders promptly. They had a comfortable dinner of half-a-dozen courses, and then retired to the drawing room, where Mrs. Billy sank into a huge easy chair, with a decanter of whisky and some cracked ice in readiness beside it. Then from a tray she selected a thick black cigar, and placidly bit off the end and lighted it, and then settled back at her ease, and proceeded to tell Montague about New York, and about the great families who ruled it, and where and how they had got their money, and who were their allies and who their enemies, and what particular skeletons were hidden in each of their closets.

It was worth coming a long way to listen to Mrs. Billy tête-à-tête; her thoughts were vigorous, and her imagery was picturesque. She spoke of old Dan Waterman, and described him as a wild boar rooting chestnuts. He was all right, she said, if you didn't come under his tree. And Montague asked, "Which is his tree?" and she answered, "Anyone he happens to be under at the time."

And then she came to the Waitings. Mrs. Billy had been in on the inside of that family, and there was nothing she didn't know about it; and she brought the members up, one by one, and dissected them, and exhibited them for Montague's benefit. They were typical bourgeois people, she said. They were burghers. They had never shown the least capacity for refinement — they ate and drank, and jostled other people out of the way. The old ones had been boors, and the new ones were cads.

And Mrs. Billy sat and puffed at her cigar. "Do you know the history of the family?" she asked. "The founder was a rough old ferryman. He fought his rivals so well that in the end he owned all the boats; and then someone discovered the idea of buying legislatures and building rail-roads, and he went into that. It was a time when they simply grabbed things — if you ever look into it, you'll find they're making fortunes today out of privileges that the old man simply sat down on and held. There's a bridge at Albany, for instance, to which they haven't the slightest right; my brother knows about it — they've given themselves a contract with their railroad by which they're paid for every passenger, and their profit every year is greater than the cost of the bridge. The son was the head of the family when I came in; and I found that he had it all arranged to leave thirty million dollars to one of his sons, and only ten million to my husband. I set to work to change that, I can tell you. I used to go around to see him, and scratch his back and tickle him and make him feel good. Of course the family went wild — my, how they hated me! They set old Ellis to work to keep me off — have you met Judge Ellis?"

"I have," said Montague.

"Well, there's a pussy-footed old hypocrite for you," said Mrs. Billy. "In those days he was Waiting's business lackey — used to pass the money to the legislators and keep the wheels of the machine greased. One of the first things I said to the old man was that I didn't ask him to entertain my butler, and he mustn't ask me to entertain his valet — and so I forbid Ellis to enter my house. And when I found that he was trying to get between the old man and me, I flew into a rage and boxed his ears and chased him out of the room!"

Mrs. Billy paused, and laughed heartily over the recollection. "Of course that tickled the old man to death," she continued. "The Wallings never could make out how I managed to get round him as I did; but it was simply because I was honest with him. They'd come sniveling round, pretending they were anxious about his health; while I wanted his money, and I told him so."

The valiant lady turned to the decanter. "Have some Scotch?" she asked, and poured some for herself, and then went on with her story. "When I first came to New York," she said, "the rich people's houses were all alike — all dreary brownstone fronts, sandwiched in on one or two city lots. I vowed that I would have a house with some room all around it — and that was the beginning of those palaces that all New York walks by and stares at. You can hardly believe it now — those houses were a scandal! But the sensation tickled the old man. I remember one day we walked up the Avenue to see how they were coming on; and he pointed with his big stick to the second floor, and asked, 'What's that?' I answered, 'It's a safe I'm building into the house.' (That was a new thing, too, in those days.) — 'I'm going to keep my money in that,' I said. 'Bah!' he growled, 'when you're done with this house, you won't have any money left.' — 'I'm planning to make you fill it for me,' I answered; and do you know, he chuckled all the way home over it!"

Mrs. Billy sat laughing softly to herself. "We had great old battles in those days," she said. "Among other things, I had to put the Waitings into Society. They were sneaking round on the outside when I came — licking people's boots and expecting to be kicked. I said to myself, I'll put an end to that — we'll have a showdown! So I gave a ball that made the whole country sit up and gasp — it wouldn't be noticed particularly nowadays, but then people had never dreamed of anything so gorgeous. And I made out a list of all the people I wanted to know in New York, and I said to myself: 'If you come, you're a friend, and if you don't come, you're an enemy.' And they all came, let me tell you! And there was never any question about the Waitings being in Society after that."

Mrs. Billy halted; and Montague remarked, with a smile, that doubtless she was sorry now that she had done it.

"Oh, no," she answered, with a shrug of her shoulders. "I find that all I have to do is to be patient — I hate people, and think I'd like to poison them, but if I only wait long enough, something happens to them much worse than I ever dreamed of. You'll be revenged on the Robbies some day."

"I don't want any revenge," Montague answered. "I've no quarrel with them — I simply wish I hadn't accepted their hospitality. I didn't know they were such little people. It seems hard to believe it."

Mrs. Billy laughed cynically. "What could you expect?" she said. "They know there's nothing to them but their money. When that's gone, they're gone — they could never make anymore."

The lady gave a chuckle, and added: "Those words make me think of Davy's experience when he wanted to go to Congress! Tell him about it, Davy."

But Mr. Alden did not warm to the subject; he left the tale to his sister.

"He was a Democrat, you know," said she, "and he went to the boss and told him he'd like to go to Congress. The answer was that it would cost him forty thousand dollars, and he kicked at the price. Others didn't have to put up such sums, he said — why should he? And the old man growled at him, 'The rest have other things to give. One can deliver the letter-carriers, another is paid for by a corporation. But what can you do? What is there to you but your money?' — So Davy paid the money — didn't you, Davy?" And Davy grinned sheepishly.

"Even so," she went on, "he came off better than poor Devon. They got fifty thousand out of him, and sold him out, and he never got to

Congress after all! That was just before he concluded that America wasn't
a fit place for a gentleman to live in."

— And so Mrs. Billy got started on the Devons! And after that came
the Havens and the Wymans and the Todds — it was midnight before
she got through with them all.

Chapter XVIII

*T*he newspapers said nothing more about the Hasbrook suit; but in
financial circles Montague had attained considerable notoriety because
of it. And this was the means of bringing him a number of new cases.

But alas, there were no more fifty-thousand-dollar clients! The first
caller was a destitute widow with a deed which would have entitled her
to the greater part of a large city in Pennsylvania — only unfortunately
the deed was about eighty years old. And then there was a poor old man
who had been hurt in a street-car accident and had been tricked into
signing away his rights; and an indignant citizen who proposed to bring
a hundred suits against the traction trust for transfers refused. All were
contingency cases, with the chances of success exceedingly remote. And
Montague noticed that the people had come to him as a last resort,
having apparently heard of him as a man of altruistic temper.

There was one case which interested him particularly, because it
seemed to fit in so ominously with the grim prognosis of his brother.
He received a call from an elderly gentleman, of very evident refinement
and dignity of manner, who proceeded to unfold to him a most amazing
story. Five or six years ago he had invented a storage-battery, which was
the most efficient known. He had organized a company with three
million dollars' capital to manufacture it, himself taking a third interest
for his patents, and becoming president of the company. Not long
afterward had come a proposal from a group of men who wished to
organize a company to manufacture automobiles; they proposed to
form an alliance which would give them the exclusive use of the battery.

But these men were not people with whom the inventor cared to deal — they were traction and gas magnates widely known for their unscrupulous methods. And so he had declined their offer, and set to work instead to organize an automobile company himself. He had just got under way when he discovered that his rivals had set to work to take his invention away from him. A friend who owned another third share in his company had hypothecated his stock to help form the new company; and now came a call from the bank for more collateral, and he was obliged to sell out. And at the next stockholders' meeting it developed that their rivals had bought it, and likewise more stock in the open market; and they proceeded to take possession of the company, ousting the former president — and then making a contract with their automobile company to furnish the storage-battery at a price which left no profit for the manufacturers! And so for two years the inventor had not received a dollar of dividends upon his million dollars' worth of paper; and to cap the climax, the company had refused to sell the battery to his automobile company, and so that had gone into bankruptcy, and his friend was ruined also!

Montague went into the case very carefully, and found that the story was true. What interested him particularly in it was the fact that he had met a couple of these financial highwaymen in social life; he had come to know the son and heir of one of them quite well, at Siegfried Harvey's. This gilded youth was engaged to be married in a very few days, and the papers had it that the father-in-law had presented the bride with a check for a million dollars. Montague could not but wonder if it was the million that had been taken from his client!

There was to be a "bachelor dinner" at the Millionaires' on the night before the wedding, to which he and Oliver had been invited. As he was thinking of taking up his case, he went to his brother, saying that he wished to decline; but Oliver had been getting back his courage day by day, and declared that it was more important than ever now that he should hold his ground, and face his enemies — for Alice's sake, if not for his own. And so Montague went to the dinner, and saw deeper yet into the history of the stolen millions.

It was a very beautiful affair, in the beginning. There was a large private dining room, elaborately decorated, with a string orchestra concealed in a bower of plants. But there were cocktails even on the side-board at the doorway; and by the time the guests had got to the coffee, everyone was hilariously drunk. After each toast they would hurl their glasses over their shoulders. The purpose of a "bachelor dinner," it appeared, was a farewell to the old days and the boon companions; so there were sentimental and comic songs which had been composed for the occasion, and were received with whirlwinds of laughter.

By listening closely and reading between the lines, one might get quite a history of the young host's adventurous career. There was a house up on the West Side; and there was a yacht, with, orgies in every part of the world. There was the summer night in Newport harbor, when someone had hit upon the dazzling scheme of freezing twenty-dollar gold pieces in tiny blocks of ice, to be dropped down the girls' backs! And there was a banquet in a studio in New York, when a huge pie had been brought on, from which a half-nude girl had emerged, with a flock of canary birds about her! Then there was a damsel who had been wont to dance upon the tops of supper tables, clad in diaphanous costume; and who had got drunk after a theater-party, and set out to smash up a Broadway restaurant. There was a cousin from Chicago, a wild lad, who made a specialty of this diversion, and whose mistresses were bathed in champagne. — Apparently there were numberless places in the city where such orgies were carried on continually; there were private clubs, and artists' "studios" — there were several allusions to a high tower, which Montague did not comprehend. Many such matters, however, were explained to him by an elderly gentleman who sat on his right, and who seemed to stay sober, no matter how much he drank. Incidentally he gravely advised Montague to meet one of the young host's mistresses, who was a "stunning" girl, and was in the market.

Toward morning the festivities changed to a series of wrestling-bouts; the young men stripped off their clothing and tore the table to pieces, and piled it out of the way in a corner, smashing most of the crockery in the process. Between the matches, champagne would be opened by knocking off the heads of the bottles; and this went on until four o'clock in the morning, when many of the guests were lying in heaps upon the floor.

Montague rode home in a cab with the elderly gentleman who had sat next to him; and on the way he asked if such affairs as this were common. And his companion, who was a "steel man" from the West, replied by telling him of some which he had witnessed at home. At Siegfried Harvey's theater-party Montague had seen a popular actress in a musical comedy, which was then the most successful play running in New York. The house was sold out weeks ahead, and after the matinee you might observe the street in front of the stage-entrance blocked by people waiting to see the woman come out. She was lithe and supple, like a panther, and wore close-fitting gowns to reveal her form. It seemed that her play must have been built with one purpose in mind, to see how much lewdness could be put upon a stage without interference by the police. — And now his companion told him how this woman had been invited to sing at a banquet given by the magnates of a mighty Trust, and had gone after midnight to the most exclusive club in the town, and sung her popular ditty, "Won't you come and play with me?" The merry magnates had taken the invitation literally — with the result that the actress had escaped from the room with half her clothing torn off her. And a little while later an official of this trust had wished to get rid of his wife and marry a chorus-girl; and when public clamor had forced the directors to ask him to resign, he had replied by threatening to tell about this banquet!

The next day — or rather, to be precise, that same morning — Montague and Alice attended the gorgeous wedding. It was declared by the newspapers to be the most "important" social event of the week; and it took half a dozen policemen to hold back the crowds which filled the street. The ceremony took place at St. Cecilia's, with the stately bishop officiating, in his purple and scarlet robes. Inside the doors were all the elect, exquisitely groomed and gowned, and such a medley of delicious perfumes as not all the vales in Arcady could equal. The groom had been polished and scrubbed, and looked very handsome, though somewhat pale; and Montague could not but smile as he observed the best man, looking so very solemn, and recollected the drunken wrestler of a few hours before, staggering about in a pale blue undershirt ripped up the back.

The Montagues knew by this time whom they were to avoid. They were graciously taken under the wing of Mrs. Eldridge Devon — whose real estate was not affected by insurance suits; and the next morning they had the satisfaction of seeing their names in the list of those present — and even a couple of lines about Alice's costume. (Alice was always referred to as "Miss Montague"; it was very pleasant to be the "Miss Montague," and to think of all the other would-be Miss Montagues in the city, who were thereby haughtily rebuked!) In the "yellow" papers there were also accounts of the trousseau of the bride, and of the wonderful gifts which she had received, and of the long honeymoon which she was to spend in the Mediterranean upon her husband's yacht. Montague found himself wondering if the ghosts of its former occupants would not haunt her, and whether she would have been as happy, had she known as much as he knew.

He found food for a good deal of thought in the memory of this banquet. Among the things which he had gathered from the songs was a hint that Oliver, also, had some secrets, which he had not seen fit to tell his brother. The keeping of young girls was apparently one of the established customs of the "little brothers of the rich" — and, for that matter, of many of the big brothers, also. A little later Montague had a curious glimpse into the life of this "half-world." He had occasion one evening to call up a certain financier whom he had come to know quite well — a man of family and a member of the church. There were some important papers to be signed and sent off by a steamer; and the great man's secretary said that he would try to find him. A minute or two later he called up Montague and asked him if he would be good enough to go to an address uptown. It was a house not far from Riverside Drive; and Montague went there and found his acquaintance, with several other prominent men of affairs whom he knew, conversing in a drawing room with one of the most charming ladies he had ever met. She was exquisite to look at, and one of the few people in New York whom he had found worth listening to. He spent such an enjoyable evening, that when he was leaving, he remarked to the lady that he would like his cousin Alice to meet her; and then he noticed that she flushed slightly, and was embarrassed. Later on he learned to his dismay that the charming and beautiful lady did not go into Society.

Nor was this at all rare; on the contrary, if one took the trouble to make inquiries, he would find that such establishments were everywhere taken for granted. Montague talked about it with Major Venable; and out of his gossip storehouse the old gentleman drew forth a string of anecdotes that made one's hair stand on end. There was one all-powerful magnate, who had a passion for the wife of a great physician; and he had given a million dollars or so to build a hospital, and had provided that it should be the finest in the world, and that this physician should go abroad for three years to study the institutions of Europe! No conventions counted with this old man — if he saw a woman whom he wanted, he would ask for her; and women in Society felt that it was an honor to be his mistress. Not long after this a man who voiced the anguish of a mighty nation was turned out of several hotels in New York because he was not married according to the laws of South Dakota; but this other man would take a woman to any hotel in the city, and no one would dare oppose him!

And there was another, a great traction king, who kept mistresses in Chicago and Paris and London, as well as in New York; he had one just around the corner from his palatial home, and had an underground passage leading to it. And the Major told with glee how he had shown this to a friend, and the latter had remarked, "I'm too stout to get through there." — "I know it," replied the other, "else I shouldn't have told you!"

And so it went. One of the richest men in New York was a sexual degenerate, with half a dozen women on his hands all the time; he would send them checks, and they would use these to blackmail him. This man's young wife had been shut up in a closet for twenty-four hours by her mother to compel her to marry him. – And then there was the charming tale of how he had gone away upon a mission of state, and had written long messages full of tender protestations, and given them to a newspaper correspondent to cable home "to his wife." The correspondent had thought it such a touching example of conjugal devotion that he told about it at a dinner-party when he came back; and he was struck by the sudden silence that fell. "The messages had been sent to a code address!" chuckled the Major. "And everyone at the table knew who had got them!"

A few days after this, Montague received a telephone message from Siegfried Harvey, who said that he wanted to see him about a matter of business. He asked him to lunch at the Noonday Club; and Montague went – though not without a qualm. For it was in the Fidelity Building, the enemy's bailiwick: a magnificent structure with halls of white marble, and a lavish display of bronze. It occurred to Montague that somewhere in this structure people were at work preparing an answer to his charges; he wondered what they were saying.

The two had lunch, talking meanwhile about the coming events in Society, and about politics and wars; and when the coffee was served and they were alone in the room, Harvey settled his big frame back in his chair, and began: –

"In the first place," he said, "I must explain that I've something to say that is devilish hard to get into. I'm so much afraid of your jumping to a wrong conclusion in the middle of it – I'd like you to agree to listen for a minute or two before you think at all."

"All right," said Montague, with a smile. "Fire away."

And at once the other became grave. "You've taken a case against this company," he said. "And Ollie has talked enough to me to make me understand that you've done a plucky thing, and that you must be everlastingly sick of hearing from cowardly people who want you to drop it. I'd be very sorry to be classed with them, for even a moment; and you must understand at the outset that I haven't a particle of interest in the company, and that it wouldn't matter to me if I had. I don't try to use my friends in business, and I don't let money count with me in my social life. I made up my mind to take the risk of speaking to you about this case, simply because I happen to know one or two things about it that I thought you didn't know. And if that's so, you are at a great disadvantage; but in any case, please understand that I have no motive but friendship, and so if I am butting in, excuse me."

When Siegfried Harvey talked, he looked straight at one with his clear blue eyes, and there was no doubting his honesty. "I am very much obliged to you," said Montague. "Pray tell me what you have to say."

"All right," said the other. "It can be done very quickly. You have taken a case which involves a great many sacrifices upon your part. And I wondered if it had ever occurred to you to ask whether you might not be taken advantage of?"

"How do you mean?" asked Montague.

"Do you know the people who are behind you?" inquired the other. "Do you know them well enough to be sure what are their motives in the case?"

Montague hesitated, and thought. "No," he said, "I couldn't say that I do."

"Then it's just as I thought," replied Harvey. "I've been watching you — you are an honest man, and you're putting yourself to no end of trouble from the best of motives. And unless I'm mistaken, you're being used by men who are not honest, and whom you wouldn't work with if you knew their purposes."

"What purposes could they have?"

"There are several possibilities. In the first place, it might be a 'strike' suit — somebody who is hoping to be bought off for a big price. That is what nearly everyone thinks is the case. But I don't; I think it's more likely someone within the company who is trying to put the administration in a hole."

"Who could that be?" exclaimed Montague, amazed.

"I don't know that. I'm not familiar enough with the situation in the Fidelity — it's changing all the time. I simply know that there are factions struggling for the control of it, and hating each other furiously, and ready to do anything in the world to cripple each other. You know that their forty millions of surplus gives an enormous power; I'd rather be able to swing forty millions in the Street than to have ten millions in my own right. And so the giants are fighting for the control of those companies; and you can't tell who's in and who's out — you can never know the real meaning of anything that happens in the struggle. All that you can be sure of is that the game is crooked from end to end, and that nothing that happens in it is what it pretends to be."

Montague listened, half dazed, and feeling as if the ground he stood on were caving beneath his feet.

"What do you know about those who brought you this case?" asked his companion, suddenly.

"Not much," he said weakly.

Harvey hesitated a moment. "Understand me, please," he said. "I've no wish to pry into your affairs, and if you don't care to say anymore, I'll understand it perfectly. But I've heard it said that the man who started the thing was Ellis."

Montague, in his turn, hesitated; then he said, "That is correct — between you and me."

"Very good," said Harvey, "and that is what made me suspicious. Do you know anything about Ellis?"

"I didn't," said the other. "I've heard a little since."

"I can fancy so," said Harvey. "And I can tell you that Ellis is mixed up in life-insurance matters in all sorts of dubious ways. It seems to me that you have reason to be most careful where you follow him."

Montague sat with his hands clenched and his brows knitted. His friend's talk had been like a flash of lightning; it revealed huge menacing forms in the darkness about him. All the structure of his hopes seemed to be tottering; his case, that he had worked so hard over — his fifty thousand dollars that he had been so proud of! Could it be that he had been tricked, and had made a fool of himself?

"How in the world am I to know?" he cried.

"That is more than I can tell," said his friend. "And for that matter, I'm not sure that you could do anything now. All that I could do was to warn you what sort of ground you were treading on, so that you could watch out for yourself in future."

Montague thanked him heartily for that service; and then he went back to his office, and spent the rest of the day pondering the matter.

What he had heard had made a vast change in things. Before it everything had seemed simple; and now nothing was clear. He was overwhelmed with a sense of the utter futility of his efforts; he was trying to build a house upon quicksands. There was nowhere a solid spot upon which he could set his foot. There was nowhere any truth — there were only contending powers who used the phrases of truth for their own purposes! And now he saw himself as the world saw him, — a party to a piece of trickery, — a knave like all the rest. He felt that he had been tripped up at the first step in his career.

The conclusion of the whole matter was that he took an afternoon train for Albany; and the next morning he talked the matter out with the Judge. Montague had realized the need of going slowly, for, after all, he had no definite ground for suspicion; and so, very tactfully and cautiously he explained, that it had come to his ears that many people believed there were interested parties behind the suit of Mr. Hasbrook; and that this had made him uncomfortable, as he knew nothing whatever about his client. He had come to ask the Judge's advice in the matter.

No one could have taken the thing more graciously than did the great man; he was all kindness and tact. In the first place, he said, he had warned him in advance that enemies would attack him and slander him, and that all kinds of subtle means would be used to influence him. And he must understand that these rumors were part of such a campaign; it made no difference how good a friend had brought them to him — how could he know who had brought them to that friend?

The Judge ventured to hope that nothing that anyone might say could influence him to believe that he, the Judge, would have advised him to do anything improper.

"No," said Montague, "but can you assure me that there are no interested parties behind Mr. Hasbrook?"

"Interested parties?" asked the other.

"I mean people connected with the Fidelity or other insurance companies."

"Why, no," said the Judge; "I certainly couldn't assure you of that."

Montague looked surprised. "You mean you don't know?"

"I mean," was the answer, "that I wouldn't feel at liberty to tell, even if I did know."

And Montague stared at him; he had not been prepared for this frankness.

"It never occurred to me," the other continued, "that that was a matter which could make any difference to you."

"Why —" began Montague.

"Pray understand me, Mr. Montague," said the Judge. "It seemed to me that this was obviously a just case, and it seemed so to you. And the only other matter that I thought you had a right to be assured of was that it was seriously meant. Of that I felt assured. It did not seem to me of any importance that there might be interested individuals behind Mr. Hasbrook. Let us suppose, for instance, that there were some parties who had been offended by the administration of the Fidelity, and were anxious to punish it. Could a lawyer be justified in refusing to take a just case, simply because he knew of such private motives? Or, let us assume an extreme case — a factional fight within the company, as you say has been suggested to you. Well, that would be a case of thieves falling out; and is there any reason why the public should not reap the advantage of such a situation? The men inside the company are the ones who would know first what is going on; and if you saw a chance to use such an advantage in a just fight — would you not do it?"

So the Judge went on, gracious and plausible — and so subtly and exquisitely corrupting! Underneath his smoothly flowing sentences Montague could feel the presence of one fundamental thought; it was unuttered and even unhinted, but it pervaded the Judge's discourse as a mood pervades a melody. The young lawyer had got a big fee, and he had a nice easy case; and as a man of the world, he could not really wish to pry into it too closely. He had heard gossip, and felt that his reputation required him to be disturbed; but he had come, simply to be smoothed down the back and made at ease, and enabled to keep his fee without losing his good opinion of himself.

Montague quit, because he concluded that it was not worth while to try to make himself understood. After all, he was in the case now, and there was nothing to be gained by a breach. Two things he felt that he had made certain by the interview — first, that his client was a "dummy," and that it was really a case of thieves falling out; and second, that he had no guarantee that he might not be left in the lurch at any moment — except the touching confidence of the Judge in some parties unknown.

Chapter XIX

Montague came home with his mind made up that there was nothing he could do except to be more careful next time. For this mistake he would have to pay the price.

He had still to learn what the full price was. The day after his return there came a caller — Mr. John C. Burton, read his card. He proved to be a canvassing agent for the company which published the scandal-sheet of Society. They were preparing a deluxe account of the prominent families of New York; a very sumptuous affair, with a highly exclusive set of subscribers, at the rate of fifteen hundred dollars per set. Would Mr. Montague by any chance care to have his family included?

And Mr. Montague explained politely that he was a comparative stranger in New York, and would not belong properly in such a volume. But the agent was not satisfied with this. There might be reasons for his subscribing, even so; there might be special cases; Mr. Montague, as a stranger, might not realize the important nature of the offer; after he had consulted his friends, he might change his mind — and so on. As Montague listened to this series of broad hints, and took in the meaning of them, the color mounted, to his cheeks — until at last he rose abruptly and bid the man good afternoon.

But then as he sat alone, his anger died away, and there was left only discomfort and uneasiness. And three or four days later he bought another issue of the paper, and sure enough, there was a new paragraph!

He stood on the street-corner reading it. The social war was raging hotly, it said; and added that Mrs. de Graffenried was threatening to take up the cause of the strangers. Then it went on to picture a certain exquisite young man of fashion who was rushing about among his friends to apologize for his brother's indiscretions. Also, it said, there was a brilliant social queen, wife of a great banker, who had taken up the cudgels. — And then came three sentences more, which made the blood leap like flame into Montague's cheeks:

"There have not been lacking comments upon her suspicious ardor. It has been noticed that since the advent of the romantic-looking Southerner, this restless lady's interest in the Babists and the trance mediums has waned; and now Society is watching for the denouement of a most interesting situation."

To Montague these words came like a blow in the face. He went on down the street, half dazed. It seemed to him the blackest shame that New York had yet shown him. He clenched his fists as he walked, whispering to himself, "The scoundrels!"

He realized instantly that he was helpless. Down home one would have thrashed the editor of such a paper; but here he was in the wolves' own country, and he could do nothing. He went back to his office, and sat down at the desk.

"My dear Mrs. Winnie," he wrote. "I have just read the enclosed paragraph, and I cannot tell you how profoundly pained I am that your kindness to us should have made you the victim of such an outrage. I am quite helpless in the matter, except to enable you to avoid any further annoyance. Please believe me when I say that we shall all of us understand perfectly if you think that we had best not meet again at present; and that this will make no difference whatever in our feelings."

This letter Montague sent by a messenger; and then he went home. Perhaps ten minutes after he arrived, the telephone bell rang — and there was Mrs. Winnie.

"Your note has come," she said. "Have you an. engagement this evening?"

"No," he answered.

"Well," she said, "will you come to dinner?"

"Mrs. Winnie —" he protested.

"Please come," she said. "Please!"

"I hate to have you —" he began.

"I wish you to come!" she said, a third time.

So he answered, "Very well."

He went; and when he entered the house, the butler led him to the elevator, saying, "Mrs. Duval says will you please come upstairs, sir." And there Mrs. Winnie met him, with flushed cheeks and eager countenance.

She was even lovelier than usual, in a soft cream-colored gown, and a crimson rose in her bosom. "I'm all alone tonight," she said, "so we'll dine in my apartments. We'd be lost in that big room downstairs."

She led him into her drawing room, where great armfuls of new roses scattered their perfume. There was a table set for two, and two big chairs before the fire which blazed in the hearth. Montague noticed that her hand trembled a little, as she motioned him to one of them; he could read her excitement in her whole aspect. She was flinging down the gauntlet to her enemies!

"Let us eat first and talk afterward," she said, hurriedly. "We'll be happy for a while, anyway."

And she went on to be happy, in her nervous and eager way. She talked about the new opera which was to be given, and about Mrs. de Graffenried's new entertainment, and about Mrs. Ridgley-Clieveden's ball; also about the hospital for crippled children which she wanted to build, and about Mrs. Vivie Patton's rumored divorce. And, meantime, the sphinxlike attendants moved here and there, and the dinner came and went. They took their coffee in the big chairs by the fire; and the table was swept clear, and the servants vanished, closing the doors behind them.

Then Montague set his cup aside, and sat gazing somberly into the fire. And Mrs. Winnie watched him. There was a long silence.

Suddenly he heard her voice. "Do you find it so easy to give up our friendship?" she asked.

"I didn't think about it's being easy or hard," he answered. "I simply thought of protecting you."

"And do you think that my friends are nothing to me?" she demanded. "Have I so very many as that?" And she clenched her hands with a sudden passionate gesture. "Do you think that I will let those wretches frighten me into doing what they want? I'll not give in to them — not for anything that Lelia can do!"

A look of perplexity crossed Montague's face. "Lelia?" he asked.

"Mrs. Robbie Walling!" she cried. "Don't you suppose that she is responsible for that paragraph?"

Montague started.

"That's the way they fight their battles!" cried Mrs. Winnie. "They pay money to those scoundrels to be protected. And then they send nasty gossip about people they wish to injure."

"You don't mean that!" exclaimed the man.

"Of course I do," cried she. "I know that it's true! I know that Robbie Walling paid fifteen thousand dollars for some trumpery volumes that they got out! And how do you suppose the paper gets its gossip?"

"I didn't know," said Montague. "But I never dreamed —"

"Why," exclaimed Mrs. Winnie, "their mail is full of blue and gold monogram stationery! I've known guests to sit down and write gossip about their hostesses in their own homes. Oh, you've no idea of people's vileness!"

"I had some idea," said Montague, after a pause. — "That was why I wished to protect you."

"I don't wish to be protected!" she cried, vehemently. "I'll not give them the satisfaction. They wish to make me give you up, and I'll not do it, for anything they can say!"

Montague sat with knitted brows, gazing into the fire. "When I read that paragraph," he said slowly. "I could not bear to think of the unhappiness it might cause you. I thought of how much it might disturb your husband —"

"My husband!" echoed Mrs. Winnie.

There was a hard tone in her voice, as she went on. "He will fix it up with them," she said, — "that's his way. There will be nothing more published, you can feel sure of that."

Montague sat in silence. That was not the reply he had expected, and it rather disconcerted him.

"If that were all —" he said, with hesitation. "But I could not know. I thought that the paragraph might disturb him for another reason — that it might be a cause of unhappiness between you and him —"

There was a pause. "You don't understand," said Mrs. Winnie, at last.

Without turning his head he could see her hands, as they lay upon her knees. She was moving them nervously. "You don't understand," she repeated.

When she began to' speak again, it was in a low, trembling voice. "I must tell you," she said; "I have felt sure that you did not know."

There was another pause. She hesitated, and her hands trembled; then suddenly she hurried on. — "I wanted you to know. I do not love my husband. I am not bound to him. He has nothing to say in my affairs."

Montague sat rigid, turned to stone. He was half dazed by the words. He could feel Mrs. Winnie's gaze fixed upon him; and he could feel the hot flush that spread over her throat and cheeks.

"It — it was not fair for you not to know," she whispered. And her voice died away, and there was again a silence. Montague was dumb.

"Why don't you say something?" she panted, at last; and he caught the note of anguish in her voice. Then he turned and stared at her, and saw her tightly clenched hands, and the quivering of her lips.

He was shocked quite beyond speech. And he saw her bosom heaving quickly, and saw the tears start into her eyes. Suddenly she sank down, and covered her face with her hands and broke into frantic sobbing.

"Mrs. Winnie!" he cried; and started to his feet.

Her outburst continued. He saw that she was shuddering violently. "Then you don't love me!" she wailed.

He stood trembling and utterly bewildered. "I'm so sorry!" he whispered. "Oh, Mrs. Winnie — I had no idea —"

"I know it! I know it!" she cried. "It's my fault! I was a fool! I knew it all the time. But I hoped — I thought you might, if you knew —"

And then again her tears choked her; she was convulsed with pain and grief.

Montague stood watching her, helpless with distress. She caught hold of the arm of the chair, convulsively, and he put his hand upon hers.

"Mrs. Winnie —" he began.

But she jerked her hand away and hid it. "No, no!" she cried, in terror. "Don't touch me!"

And suddenly she looked up at him, stretching out her arms. "Don't you understand that I love you?" she exclaimed. "You despise me for it, I know — but I can't help it. I will tell you, even so! It's the only satisfaction I can have. I have always loved you! And I thought — I thought it was only that you didn't understand. I was ready to brave all the world — I didn't care who knew it, or what anybody said. I thought we could be happy — I thought I could be free at last. Oh, you've no idea how unhappy I am — and how lonely — and how I longed to escape! And I believed that you — that you might —"

And then the tears gushed into Mrs. Winnie's eyes again, and her voice became the voice of a little child.

"Don't you think that you might come to love me?" she wailed.

Her voice shook Montague, so that he trembled to the depths of him. But his face only became the more grave.

"You despise me because I told you!" she exclaimed.

"No, no, Mrs. Winnie," he said. "I could not possibly do that —"

"Then — then why —" she whispered. — "Would it be so hard to love me?"

"It would be very easy," he said, "but I dare not let myself."

She looked at him piteously. "You are so cold — so merciless!" she cried.

He answered nothing, and she sat trembling. "Have you ever loved a woman?" she asked.

There was a long pause. He sat in the chair again. "Listen, Mrs. Winnie" — he began at last.

"Don't call me that!" she exclaimed. "Call me Evelyn — please."

"Very well," he said — "Evelyn. I did not intend to make you unhappy — if I had had any idea, I should never have seen you again. I will tell you — what I have never told anybody before. Then you will understand."

He sat for a few moments, in a somber reverie.

"Once," he said, "when I was young, I loved a woman — a quadroon girl. That was in New Orleans; it is a custom we have there. They have a world of their own, and we take care of them, and of the children; and everyone knows about it. I was very young, only about eighteen; and she was even younger. But I found out then what women are, and what love means to them. I saw how they could suffer. And then she died in childbirth — the child died, too."

Montague's voice was very low; and Mrs. Winnie sat with her hands clasped, and her eyes riveted upon his face. "I saw her die," he said. "And that was all. I have never forgotten it. I made up my mind then that I had done wrong; and that never again while I lived would I offer my love to a woman, unless I could devote all my life to her. So you see, I am afraid of love. I do not wish to suffer so much, or to make others suffer. And when anyone speaks to me as you did, it brings it all back to me — it makes me shrink up and wither."

He paused, and the other caught her breath.

"Understand me," she said, her voice trembling. "I would not ask any pledges of you. I would pay whatever price there was to pay — I am not afraid to suffer."

"I do not wish you to suffer," he said. "I do not wish to take advantage of any woman."

"But I have nothing in the world that I value!" she cried. "I would go away — I would give up everything, to be with a man like you. I have no ties — no duties —"

He interrupted her. "You have your husband —" he said.

And she cried out in sudden fury — "My husband!"

"Has no one ever told you about my husband?" she asked, after a pause.

"No one," he said.

"Well, ask them!" she exclaimed. "Meantime, take my word for it — I owe nothing to my husband."

Montague sat staring into the fire. "But consider my own case," he said. "*I have duties — my mother and my cousin —*"

"Oh, don't say anymore!" cried the woman, with a break in her voice. "Say that you don't love me — that is all there is to say! And you will never respect me again! I have been a fool — I have ruined everything! I have flung away your friendship, that I might have kept!"

"No," he said.

But she rushed on, vehemently — "At least, I have been honest — give me credit for that! That is how all my troubles come — I say what is in my mind, and I pay the price for my blunders. It is not as if I were cold and calculating — so don't despise me altogether."

"I couldn't despise you," said Montague. "I am simply pained, because I have made you unhappy. And I did not mean to."

Mrs. Winnie sat staring ahead of her in a somber reverie. "Don't think anymore about it," she said, bitterly. "I will get over it. I am not worth troubling about. Don't you suppose I know how you feel about this world that I live in? And I'm part of it — I beat my wings, and try to get out, but I can't. I'm in it, and I'll stay in till I die; I might as well give up. I thought that I could steal a little joy — you have no idea how hungry I am for a little joy! You have no idea how lonely I am! And how empty my life is! You talk about your fear of making me unhappy; it's a grim jest — but I'll give you permission, if you can! I'll ask nothing — no promises, no sacrifices! I'll take all the risks, and pay all the penalties!"

She smiled through her tears, a sardonic smile. He was watching her, and she turned again, and their eyes met; again he saw the blood mount from her throat to her cheeks. At the same time came the old stirring of the wild beasts within him. He knew that the less time he spent in sympathizing with Mrs. Winnie, the better for both of them.

He had started to rise, and words of farewell were on his lips; when suddenly there came a knock upon the door.

Mrs. Winnie sprang to her feet. "Who is that?" she cried.

And the door opened, and Mr. Duval entered.

"Good evening," he said pleasantly, and came toward her.

Mrs. Winnie flushed angrily, and stared at him. "Why do you come here unannounced?" she cried.

"I apologize," he said — "but I found this in my mail —"

And Montague, in the act of rising to greet him, saw that he had the offensive clipping in his hand. Then he saw Duval give a start, and realized that the man had not been aware of his presence in the room.

Duval gazed from Montague to his wife, and noticed for the first time her tears, and her agitation. "I beg pardon," he said. "I am evidently trespassing."

"You most certainly are," responded Mrs. Winnie.

He made a move to withdraw; but before he could take a step, she had brushed past him and left the room, slamming the door behind her.

And Duval stared after her, and then he stared at Montague, and laughed. "Well! well! well!" he said.

Then, checking his amusement, he added, "Good evening, sir."

"Good evening," said Montague.

He was trembling slightly, and Duval noticed it; he smiled genially. "This is the sort of material out of which scenes are made," said he. "But I beg you not to be embarrassed — we won't have any scenes."

Montague could think of nothing to say to that.

"I owe Evelyn an apology," the other continued. "It was entirely an accident — this clipping, you see. I do not intrude, as a rule. You may make yourself at home in future."

Montague flushed scarlet at the words.

"Mr. Duval," he said, "I have to assure you that you are mistaken —"

The other stared at him. "Oh, come, come!" he said, laughing. "Let us talk as men of the world."

"I say that you are mistaken," said Montague again.

The other shrugged his shoulders. "Very well," he said genially. "As you please. I simply wish to make matters clear to you, that's all. I wish you joy with Evelyn. I say nothing about her — you love her. Suffice it that I've had her, and I'm tired of her; the field is yours. But keep her out of mischief, and don't let her make a fool of herself in public, if you can help it. And don't let her spend too much money — she costs me a million a year already. — Good evening, Mr. Montague."

And he went out. Montague, who stood like a statue, could hear him chuckling all the way down the hall.

At last Montague himself started to leave. But he heard Mrs. Winnie coming back, and he waited for her. She came in and shut the door, and turned toward him.

"What did he say?" she asked.

"He — was very pleasant," said Montague.

And she smiled grimly. "I went out on purpose," she said. "I wanted you to see him — to see what sort of a man he is, and how much 'duty' I owe him! You saw, I guess."

"Yes, I saw," said he.

Then again he started to go. But she took him by the arm. "Come and talk to me," she said. "Please!"

And she led him back to the fire. "Listen," she said. "He will not come here again. He is going away tonight — I thought he had gone already. And he does not return for a month or two. There will be no one to disturb us again."

She came close to him and gazed up into his face. She had wiped her tears away, and her happy look had come back to her; she was lovelier than ever.

"I took you by surprise," she said, smiling. "You didn't know what to make of it. And I was ashamed — I thought you would hate me. But I'm not going to be unhappy anymore — I don't care at all. I'm glad that I spoke!"

And Mrs. Winnie put up her hands and took him by the lapels of his coat. "I know that you love me," she said; "I saw it in your eyes just now, before he came in: It is simply that you won't let yourself go. You have so many doubts and so many fears. But you will see that I am right; you will learn to love me. You won't be able to help it — I shall be so kind and good! Only don't go away —"

Mrs. Winnie was so close to him that her breath touched his cheek. "Promise me, dear," she whispered — "promise me that you won't stop seeing me — that you will learn to love me. I can't do without you!"

Montague was trembling in every nerve; he felt like a man caught in a net. Mrs. Winnie had had everything she ever wanted in her life; and now she wanted him! It was impossible for her to face any other thought.

"Listen," he began gently.

But she saw the look of resistance in his eyes, and she cried "No no — don't! I cannot do without you! Think! I love you! What more can I say to you? I cannot believe that you don't care for me — you *have* been fond of me — I have seen it in your face. Yet you're afraid of me — why? Look at me — am I not beautiful to look at I And is a woman's love such a little thing — can you fling it away and trample upon it so easily? Why do you wish to go? Don't you understand — no one knows we are here — no one cares! You can come here whenever you wish — this is my place — mine! And no one will think anything about it. They all do it. There is nothing to be afraid of!"

She put her arms about him, and clung to him so that he could feel the beating of her heart upon his bosom. "Oh, don't leave me here alone tonight!" she cried.

To Montague it was like the ringing of an alarm-bell deep within his soul. "I must go," he said.

She flung back her head and stared at him, and he saw the terror and anguish in her eyes. "No, no!" she cried, "don't say that to me! I can't bear it — oh, see what I have done! Look at me! Have mercy on me!"

"Mrs. Winnie," he said, "you must have mercy on *me!*"

But he only felt her clasp him more tightly. He took her by the wrists, and with quiet force he broke her hold upon him; her hands fell to her sides, and she stared at him, aghast.

"I must go," he said, again.

And he started toward the door. She followed him dumbly with her eyes.

"Good-bye," he said. He knew that there was no use of anymore words; his sympathy had been like oil upon flames. He saw her move, and as he opened the door, she flung herself down in a chair and burst into frantic weeping. He shut the door softly and went away.

He found his way down the stairs, and got his hat and coat, and went out, unseen by anyone. He walked down the Avenue — and there suddenly was the giant bulk of St. Cecilia's lifting itself into the sky. He stopped and looked at it — it seemed a great tumultuous surge of emotion. And for the first time in his life it seemed to him that he understood why men had put together that towering heap of stone!

Then he went on home.

He found Alice dressing for a ball, and Oliver waiting for her. He went to his room, and took off his coat; and Oliver came up to him, and with a sudden gesture reached over to his shoulder, and held up a trophy.

He drew it out carefully, and measured the length of it, smiling mischievously in the meanwhile. Then he held it up to the light, to see the color of it.

"A black one!" he cried. "Coal black!" And he looked at his brother, with a merry twinkle in his eyes. "Oh, Allan!" he chuckled.

Montague said nothing.

Chapter XX

*I*t was about a week from the beginning of Lent, when there would be a lull in the city's gaieties, and Society would shift the scene of its activities to the country clubs, and to California and Hot Springs and Palm Beach. Mrs. Caroline. Smythe invited Alice to join her in an expedition to the last-named place; but Montague interposed, because he saw that Alice had been made pale and nervous by three months of night-and-day festivities. Also, a trip to Florida would necessitate ten or fifteen thousand dollars' worth of new clothes; and these would not do for the summer, it appeared — they would be faded and passé by that time.

So Alice settled back to rest; but she was too popular to be let alone — a few days later came another invitation, this time from General Prentice and his family. They were planning a railroad trip — to be gone for a month; they would have a private train, and twenty five people in the party, and would take in California and Mexico — "swinging round the circle," as it was called. Alice was wild to go, and Montague gave his consent. Afterward he learned to his dismay that Charlie Carter was one of those invited, and he would have liked to have Alice withdraw; but she did not wish to, and he could not make up his mind to insist.

These train trips were the very latest diversion of the well-to-do; a year ago no one had heard of them, and now fifty parties were leaving New York every month. You might see a dozen of such hotel-trains at once at Palm Beach; there were some people who lived on board all the time, having special tracks built for them in pleasant locations wherever they stopped. One man had built a huge automobile railroad car, shaped like a ram, and having accommodation for sixty people. The Prentice train had four cars, one of them a "library car," finished in St. Iago mahogany, and provided with a pipe-organ. Also there were bathrooms and a barber-shop, and a baggage car with two autos on board for exploring purposes.

Since the episode of Mrs. Winnie, Oliver had apparently concluded that his brother was one of the initiated. Not long afterward he permitted him to a glimpse into that side of his life which had been hinted at in the songs at the bachelors' dinner.

Oliver had planned to take Betty Wyman to the theater; but Betty's grandfather had come home from the West unexpectedly, and so Oliver came round and took his brother instead.

"I was going to play a joke on her," he said. "We'll go to see one of my old flames."

It was a translation of a French farce, in which the marital infidelities of two young couples were the occasion of many mishaps. One of the characters was a waiting-maid, who was in love with a handsome young soldier, and was pursued by the husband of one of the couples. It was a minor part, but the young Jewish girl who played it had so many pretty graces and such a merry laugh that she made it quite conspicuous. When the act was over, Oliver asked him whose acting he liked best, and he named her.

"Come and be introduced to her," Oliver said.

He opened a door near their box. "How do you do, Mr. Wilson," he said, nodding to a man in evening dress, who stood near by. Then he turned toward the dressing-rooms, and went down a corridor, and knocked upon one of the doors. A voice called, "Come in," and he opened the door; and there was a tiny room, with odds and ends of clothing scattered about, and the girl, clad in corsets and underskirt, sitting before a mirror. "Hello, Rosalie," said he.

And she dropped her powder-puff, and sprang up with a cry — "Ollie!" 'In a moment more she had her arms about his neck.

"Oh, you wretched man," she cried. "Why don't you come to see me anymore? Didn't you get my letters?"

"I got some," said he. "But I've been busy. This is my brother, Mr. Allan Montague."

The other nodded to Montague, and said, "How do you do?" — but without letting go of Oliver. "Why don't you come to see me?" she exclaimed.

"There, there, now!" said Oliver, laughing good-naturedly. "I brought my brother along so that you'd have to behave yourself."

"I don't care about your brother!" exclaimed the girl, without even giving him another glance. Then she held Oliver at arm's length, and gazed into his face. "How can you be so cruel to me?" she asked.

"I told you I was busy," said he, cheerfully. "And I gave you fair warning, didn't I? How's Toodles?"

"Oh, Toodles is in raptures," said Rosalie. "She's got a new fellow." And then, her manner changing to one of merriment, she added: "Oh, Ollie! He gave her a diamond brooch! And she looks like a countess — she's hoping for a chance to wear it in a part!"

"You've seen Toodles," said Oliver, to his brother "She's in 'The Kaliph of Kamskatka.'."

"They're going on the road next week," said Rosalie. "And then I'll be all alone." She added, in a pleading voice: "Do, Ollie, be a good boy and take us out tonight. Think how long it's been since I've seen you! Why, I've been so good I don't know myself in the looking-glass. Please, Ollie!"

"All right," said he, "maybe I will."

"I'm not going to let you get away from me," she cried. "I'll come right over the footlights after you!"

"You'd better get dressed," said Oliver. "You'll be late."

He pushed aside a tray with some glasses on it, and seated himself upon a trunk; and Montague stood in a corner and watched Rosalie, while she powdered and painted herself, and put on an airy summer dress, and poured out a flood of gossip about "Toodles" and "Flossie" and "Grace" and some others. A few minutes later came a stentorian voice in the hallway: "Second act!" There were more embraces, and then Ollie brushed the powder from his coat, and went away laughing.

Montague stood for a few moments in the wings, watching the scene-shifters putting the final touches to the new set, and the various characters taking their positions. Then they went out to their seats. "Isn't she a jewel?" asked Oliver.

"She's very pretty," the other admitted.

"She came right out of the slums," said Oliver — "over on Rivington Street. That don't happen very often."

"How did you come to know her?" asked his brother.

"Oh, I picked her out. She was in a chorus, then. I got her first speaking part."

"Did you?" said the other, in surprise. "How did you do that?"

"Oh, a little money," was the reply. "Money will do most anything. And I was in love with her — that's how I got her."

Montague said nothing, but sat in thought.

"We'll take her out to supper and make her happy," added Oliver, as the curtain started up. "She's lonesome, I guess. You see, I promised Betty I'd reform."

All through that scene and the next one Rosalie acted for them; she was so full of verve and merriment that there was quite a stir in the audience, and she got several rounds of applause. Then, when the play was over, she extricated herself from the arms of the handsome young soldier, and fled to her dressing-room, and when Oliver and Montague arrived, she was half ready for the street.

They went up Broadway, and from a group of people coming out of another stage-entrance a young girl came to join them — an airy little creature with the face of a doll-baby, and a big hat with a purple feather on top. This was "Toodles" — otherwise known as Helen Gwynne; and she took Montague's arm, and they fell in behind Oliver and his companion.

Montague wondered what one said to a chorus-girl on the way to supper. Afterward his brother told him that Toodles had been the wife of a real-estate agent in a little town in Oklahoma, and had run away from respectability and boredom with a traveling theatrical company. Now she was tripping her part in the musical comedy which Montague had seen at Mrs. Lane's; and incidentally swearing devotion to a handsome young "wine-agent." She confided to Montague that she hoped the latter might see her that evening — he needed to be made jealous.

"The Great White Way" was the name which people had given to this part of Broadway; and at the head of it stood a huge hotel with flaming lights, and gorgeous marble and bronze, and famous paintings upon the walls and ceilings inside. At this hour every one of its many dining rooms was thronged with supper-parties, and the place rang with laughter and the rattle of dishes, and the strains of several orchestras which toiled heroically in the midst of the uproar. Here they found a table, and while Oliver was ordering frozen poached eggs and quails in aspic, Montague sat and gazed about him at the revelry, and listened to the prattle of the little ex-seamstress from Rivington Street.

His brother had "got her," he said, by buying a speaking part in a play for her; and Montague recalled the orgies of which he had heard at the bachelors' dinner, and divined that here he was at the source of the stream from which they were fed. At the table next to them was a young Hebrew, whom Toodles pointed out as the son and heir of a great clothing manufacturer. He was "keeping" several girls, said she; and the queenly creature who was his vis-à-vis was one of the chorus in "The Maids of Mandalay." And a little way farther down the room was a boy with the face of an angel and the air of a prince of the blood — he had inherited a million and run away from school, and was making a name for himself in the Tenderloin. The pretty little girl all in green who was with him was Violet Pane, who was the artist's model in a new play that had made a hit. She had had a full-page picture of herself in the Sunday supplement of the "sporting paper" which was read here — so Rosalie remarked.

"Why don't you ever do that for me?" she added, to Oliver.

"Perhaps I will," said he, with a laugh. "What does it cost?"

And when he learned that the honor could be purchased for only fifteen hundred dollars, he said, "I'll do it, if you'll be good." And from that time on the last trace of worriment vanished from the face and the conversation of Rosalie.

As the champagne cocktails disappeared, she and Oliver became confidential. Then Montague turned to Toodles, to learn more about how the "second generation" was preying upon the women of the stage.

"A chorus-girl got from ten to twenty dollars a week," said Toodles; and that was hardly enough to pay for her clothes. Her work was very uncertain — she would spend weeks at rehearsal, and then if the play failed, she would get nothing. It was a dog's life; and the keys of freedom and opportunity were in the keeping of rich men, who haunted the theaters and laid siege to the girls. They would send in notes to them, or fling bouquets to them, with cards, or perhaps money, hidden in them. There were millionaire artists and bohemians who kept a standing order for seats in the front rows at opening performances; they had accounts with florists and liverymen and confectioners, and gave carte blanche to scores of girls who lent themselves to their purposes. Sometimes they were in league with the managers, and a girl who held back would find her chances imperiled; sometimes these men would even finance shows to give a chance to some favorite.

Afterward Toodles turned to listen to Oliver and his companion; and Montague sat back and gazed about the room. Next to him was a long table with a dozen, people at it; and he watched the buckets of champagne and the endless succession of fantastic-looking dishes of food, and the revelers, with their flushed faces and feverish eyes and loud laughter. Above all the tumult was the voice of the orchestra, calling, calling, like the storm wind upon the mountains; the music was wild and chaotic, and produced an indescribable sense of pain and confusion. When one realized that this same thing was going on in thousands of places in this district it seemed that here was a flood of dissipation that out-rivaled even that of Society.

It was said that the hotels of New York, placed end to end, would reach all the way to London; and they took care of a couple of hundred thousand people a day — a horde which had come from all over the world in search of pleasure and excitement. There were sight-seers and "country customers" from forty-five states; ranchers from Texas, and lumber kings from Maine, and mining men from Nevada. At home they had reputations, and perhaps families to consider; but once plunged into the whirlpool of the Tenderloin, they were hidden from all the world. They came with their pockets full of money; and hotels and restaurants, gambling-places and pool-rooms and brothels — all were lying in wait for them! So eager had the competition become that there was a tailoring establishment and a bank that were never closed the year round, except on Sunday.

Everywhere about one's feet the nets of vice were spread. The head waiter in one's hotel was a "steerer" for a "dive," and the house detective was "touting" for a gambling-place. The handsome woman who smiled at one in "Peacock Alley" was a "Madame"; the pleasant-faced young man who spoke to one at the bar was on the look-out for customers for a brokerage-house next door. Three times in a single day in another of these great caravanserais Montague was offered "short change"; and so his eyes were opened to a new kind of plundering. He was struck by the number of attendants in livery who swarmed about him, and to whom he gave tips for their services. He did not notice that the boys in the wash-rooms and coat-rooms could not speak a word of English; he could not know that they were searched every night, and had everything taken from them, and that the Greek who hired them had paid fifteen thousand dollars a year to the hotel for the privilege.

So far had the specialization in evil proceeded that there were places of prostitution which did a telephone-business exclusively, and would send a woman in a cab to any address; and there were high-class assignation-houses, which furnished exquisite apartments and the services of maids and valets. And in this world of vice the modern doctrine of the equality of the sexes was fully recognized; there were gambling-houses and pool-rooms and opium-joints for women, and drinking-places which catered especially for them. In the "orange room" of one of the big hotels, you might see rich women of every rank and type, fingering the dainty leather-bound and gold-embossed wine cards. In this room alone were sold over ten thousand drinks every day; and the hotel paid a rental of a minion a year to the Devon estate. Not far away the Devons also owned dives-dives, where, in the early hours of the morning, you might see richly-gowned white women drinking.

In this seething caldron of graft there were many strange ways of making money, and many strange and incredible types of human beings to be met. Once, in "Society," Montague had pointed out to him a woman who had been a "tattooed lady" in a circus; there was another who had been a confederate of gamblers upon the ocean steamships, and another who had washed dishes in a mining-camp. There was one of these great hotels whose proprietor had been a successful burglar; and a department-store whose owner had begun life as a "fence." In any crowd of these revelers you might have such strange creatures pointed out to you; a multimillionaire who sold rotten jam to the people; another who had invented opium soothing-syrup for babies; a convivial old gentleman who disbursed the "yellow dog fund" of several railroads; a handsome chauffeur who had run away with an heiress. Once a great scientist had invented a new kind of underwear, and had endeavored to make it a gift to humanity; and here was a man who had seized upon it and made millions out of it! Here was a "trance medium," who had got a fortune out of an imbecile old manufacturer; here was a great newspaper proprietor, who published advertisements of assignations at a dollar a line; here was a cigar manufacturer, whose smug face was upon every billboard — he had begun as a tin manufacturer, and to avoid the duty, he had had his raw material cast in the form of statues, and brought them in as works of art!

And terrible and vile as were the sources from which the fortunes had been derived, they were no viler nor more terrible than the purposes for which they had been spent. Mrs. Vivie Patton had hinted to Montague of a "Decameron Club," whose members gathered in each others' homes and vied in the telling of obscene stories; Strathcona had told him about another set of exquisite ladies and gentlemen who gave elaborate entertainments, in which they dressed in the costumes of bygone periods, and imitated famous characters in history, and the vices and orgies of courts and camps. One heard of "Cleopatra nights" on board of yachts at Newport. There was a certain Wall Street "plunger," who had begun life as a mining man in the West; and when his customers came in town, he would hire a trolley-car, and take a load of champagne and half a dozen prostitutes, and spend the night careering about the country. This man was now quartered in one of the great hotels in New York; and in his apartments he would have prize fights and chicken fights; and bloodthirsty exhibitions called "purring matches," in which men tried to bark each other's shins; or perhaps a "battle royal," with a diamond scarf-pin dangling from the ceiling, and half a dozen Negroes in a free-for-all fight for the prize.

No picture of the ways of the Metropolis would be complete which did not force upon the reluctant reader some realization of the extent to which new and hideous incitements to vice were spreading. To say that among the leisured classes such practices were raging like a pestilence would be no exaggeration. Ten years ago they were regarded with aversion by even the professionally vicious; but now the commonest prostitute accepted them as part of her fate. And there was no height to which they had not reached — ministers of state were enslaved by them; great fortunes and public events were controlled by them. In Washington there had been an ambassador whose natural daughter taught them in the houses of the great, until the scandal forced the minister's recall. Some of these practices were terrible in their effects, completely wrecking the victim in a short time; and physicians who studied their symptoms would be horrified to see them appearing in the homes of their friends.

And from New York, the center of the wealth and culture of the country, these vices spread to every corner of it. Theatrical companies and traveling salesmen carried them; visiting merchants and sightseers acquired them. Pack-peddlers sold vile pictures and books — the manufacturing or importing of which was now quite an industry; one might read catalogues printed abroad in English, the contents of which would make one's flesh creep. There were cheap weeklies, costing ten cents a year, which were thrust into area-windows for servant-girls; there were yellow-covered French novels of unbelievable depravity for the mistress of the house. It was a curious commentary upon the morals of Society that upon the trains running to a certain suburban community frequented by the ultra-fashionable, the newsboys did a thriving business in such literature; and when the pastor of the fashionable church eloped with a Society girl, the bishop publicly laid the blame to the morals of his parishioners!

The theory was that there were two worlds, and that they were kept rigidly separate. There were two sets of women; one to be toyed with and flung aside, and the other to be protected and esteemed. Such things as prostitutes and kept women might exist, but people of refinement did not talk about them, and were not concerned with them. But Montague was familiar with the saying, that if you follow the chain of the slave, you will find the other end about the wrist of the master; and he discovered that the Tenderloin was wreaking its vengeance upon Fifth Avenue. It was not merely that the men of wealth were carrying to their wives and children the diseases of vice; they were carrying also the manners and the ideals.

Montague had been amazed by the things he had found in New York Society; the smoking and drinking and gambling of women, their hard and cynical views of life, their continual telling of coarse stories. And here, in this underworld, he had come upon the fountain head of the corruption. It was something which came to him in a sudden flash of intuition; — the barriers between the two worlds were breaking down!

He could picture the process in a hundred different forms. There was Betty Wyman. His brother had meant to take her to the theater, to let her see Rosalie, by way of a joke! So, of course, Betty knew of his escapades, and of those of his set; she and her girl friends were whispering and jesting about them. Hero sat Oliver, smiling and cynical, toying with Rosalie as a cat might toy with a mouse; and tomorrow he would be with Betty — and could anyone doubt any longer whence Betty had derived her attitude towards life? And the habits of mind that Oliver had taught her as a girl she would not forget as a wife; he might be anxious to keep her to himself, but there would be others whose interest was different.

And Montague recalled other things that he had seen or heard in. Society, that he could put his finger upon, as having come out of this underworld. The more he thought of the explanation, the more it seemed to explain. This "Society," which had perplexed him — now he could describe it: its manners and ideals of life were those which he would have expected to find in the "fast" side of stage life.

It was, of course, the women who made Society, and gave it its tone; and the women of Society were actresses. They were actresses in their love of notoriety and display; in their taste in clothes and jewels, their fondness for cigarettes and champagne. They made up like actresses;

they talked and thought like actresses. The only obvious difference was that the women of the stage were carefully selected — were at least up to a certain standard of physical excellence; whereas the women of Society were not selected at all, and some were lean, and some were stout, and some were painfully homely.

Montague recalled cases where the two sets had met as at some of the private entertainments. It was getting to be the fashion to hobnob with the stage people on such occasions; and he recalled how naturally the younger people took to this. Only the older women held aloof; looking down upon the women of the stage from an ineffable height, as belonging to a lower caste — because they were obliged to work for their livings. But it seemed to Montague, as he sat and talked with this poor chorus-girl, who had sold herself for a little pleasure, that it was easier to pardon her than the woman who had been born to luxury, and scorned those who produced her wealth.

But most of all, one's sympathies went out to a person who was not to be met in either of these sets; to the girl who had not sold herself, but was struggling for a living in the midst of this ravening corruption. There were thousands of self-respecting women, even on the stage; Toodles herself had been among them, she told Montague. "I kept straight for a long time," she said, laughing cheerfully — "and on ten dollars a week! I used to go out on the road, and then they paid me sixteen; and think of trying to live on one-night stands — to board yourself and stop at hotels and dress for the theater — on sixteen a week, and no job half the year! And all that time — do you know Cyril Chambers, the famous church painter?"

"I've heard of him," said Montague.

"Well, I was with a show here on Broadway the next winter; and every night for six months he sent me a bunch of orchids that couldn't have cost less than seventy-five dollars! And he told me he'd open accounts for me in all the stores I chose, if I'd spend the next summer in Europe with him. He said I could take my mother or my sister with me — and I was so green in those days, I thought that must mean he didn't intend anything wrong!"

Toodles smiled at the memory. "Did you go?" asked the man.

"No," she answered. "I stayed here with a roof-garden show that failed. And I went to my old manager for a job, and he said to me, 'I can only pay you ten a week. But why are you so foolish?' 'How do you mean?' I asked; and he answered, 'Why don't you get a rich sweetheart? Then I could pay you sixty.' That's what a girl hears on the stage!"

"I don't understand," said Montague, perplexed. "Did he mean he could get money out of the man?"

"Not directly," said Toodles; "but tickets — and advertising. Why, men will hire front-row seats for a whole season, if they're interested in a girl in the show. And they'll take all their friends to see her, and she'll be talked about — she'll be somebody, instead of just nobody, as I was."

"Then it actually helps her on the stage!" said Montague.

"Helps her!" exclaimed Toodles. "My God! I've known a girl who'd been abroad with a tip-top swell — and had the gowns and the jewels to prove it — to come home and get into the front row of a chorus at a hundred dollars a week."

Toodles was cheerful and all unaware; and that only made the tragedy of it all one shade more black to Montague. He sat lost in somber reverie, forgetting his companions, and the blare and glare of the place.

In the center of this dining room was a great cone-shaped stand, containing a display of food; and as they strolled out, Montague stopped to look at it. There were platters garnished with flowers and herbs, and containing roast turkeys and baked hams, jellied meats and game in aspic, puddings and tarts and frosted cakes — every kind of food-fantasticality imaginable. One might have spent an hour in studying it, and from top to bottom he would have found nothing simple, nothing natural. The turkeys had paper curls and rosettes stuck over them; the hams were covered with a white gelatin, the devilled crabs with a yellow mayonnaise — and all painted over in pink and green and black with landscapes and marine views — with "ships and shoes and sealing-wax and cabbages and kings." The jellied meats and the puddings were in the shape of fruits and flowers; and there were elaborate works of art in pink and white confectionery — a barn-yard, for instance, with horses and cows, and a pump, and a dairymaid — and one or two alligators.

And all this was changed every day! Each morning you might see a procession of a score of waiters bearing aloft a new supply. Montague remembered Betty Wyman's remark at their first interview, apropos of the whipped cream made into little curlicues; how his brother had said, "If Allan were here, he'd be thinking about the man who fixed that cream, and how long it took him, and how he might have been reading 'The Simple Life'!"

He thought of that now; he stood here and gazed, and wondered about all the slaves of the lamp who served in this huge temple of luxury. He looked at the waiters — pale, hollow-chested, harried-looking men: he imagined the hordes of servants of yet lower kinds, who never emerged into the light of day; the men who washed the dishes, the men who carried the garbage, the men who shoveled the coal into the furnaces, and made the heat and light and power. Pent up in dim cellars, many stories underground, and bound forever to the service of sensuality – how terrible must be their fate, how unimaginable their corruption! And they were foreigners; they had come here seeking liberty. And the masters of the new country had seized them and pent them here!

From this as a starting-point his thought went on, to the hordes of toilers in every part of the world, whose fate it was to create the things which these blind revelers destroyed; the women and children in countless mills and sweatshops, who spun the cloth, and cut and sewed it; the girls who made the artificial flowers, who rolled the cigarettes, who gathered the grapes from the vines; the miners who dug the coal and the precious metals out of the earth; the men who watched in ten thousand signal-towers and engines, who fought the elements from the decks of ten thousand ships – to bring all these things here to be destroyed. Step by step, as the flood of extravagance rose, and the energies of the men were turned to the creation of futility and corruption – so, step by step, increased the misery and degradation of all these slaves of Mammon. And who could imagine what they would think about it – if ever they came to think?

– And then, in a sudden flash, there came back to Montague that speech he had heard upon the street-corner, the first evening he had been in New York! He could hear again the pounding of the elevated trains, and the shrill voice of the orator; he could see his haggard and hungry face, and the dense crowd gazing up at him. And there came to him the words of Major Thorne:

"It means another civil war!"

Chapter XXI

Alice had been gone for a couple of weeks, and the day was drawing near when the Hasbrook case came up for trial. The Saturday before that being the date of the Micareme dance of the Long Island Hunt Club, Siegfried Harvey was to have a house-party for the weekend, and Montague accepted his invitation. He had been working hard, putting the finishing touches to his brief, and he thought that a rest would be good for him.

He and his brother went down upon Friday afternoon, and the first person he met was Betty Wyman, whom he had not seen for quite a while. Betty had much to say, and said it. As Montague had not been seen with Mrs. Winnie since the episode in her house, people had begun to notice the break, and there was no end of gossip; and Mistress Betty wanted to know all about it, and how things stood between them.

But he would not tell her, and so she saucily refused to tell him what she had heard. All the while they talked she was eyeing him quizzically, and it was evident that she took the worst for granted; also that he had become a much more interesting person to her because of it. Montague had the strangest sensations when he was talking with Betty Wyman; she was delicious and appealing, almost irresistible; and yet her views of life were so old! "I told you you wouldn't do for a tame cat!" she said to him.

Then she went on to talk to him about his case, and to tease him about the disturbance he had made.

"You know," she said, "Ollie and I were in terror — we thought that grandfather would be furious, and that we'd be ruined. But somehow, it didn't work out that way. Don't you say anything about it, but I've had a sort of a fancy that he must be on your side of the fence."

"I'd be glad to know it," said Montague, with a laugh — "I've been trying for a long time to find out who is on my side of the fence."

"He was talking about it the other day," said Betty, "and I heard him tell a man that he'd read your argument, and thought it was good."

"I'm glad to hear that," said Montague.

"So was I," replied she. "And I said to him afterward, 'I suppose you don't know that Allan Montague is my Ollie's brother.' And he did you the honor to say that he hadn't supposed any member of Ollie's family could have as much sense!"

Betty was staying with an aunt near by, and she went back before dinner. In the automobile which came for her was old Wyman himself, on his way home from the city; and as a snowstorm had begun, he came in and stood by the fire while his car was exchanged for a closed one from Harvey's stables. Montague did not meet him, but stood and watched him from the shadows — a mite of a man, with a keen and eager face, full of wrinkles. It was hard to realize that this little body held one of the great driving minds of the country. He was an intensely nervous and irritable man, bitter and implacable — by all odds the most hated and feared man in Wall Street. He was swift, imperious, savage as a hornet. "Directors at meetings that I attend vote first and discuss afterward," was one of his sayings that Montague had heard quoted. Watching him here by the fireside, rubbing his hands and chatting pleasantly, Montague had a sudden sense of being behind the scenes, of being admitted to a privilege denied to ordinary mortals — the beholding of royalty in everyday attire!

After dinner that evening Montague had a chat in the smoking-room with his host; and he brought up the subject of the Hasbrook case, and told about his trip to Washington, and his interview with Judge Ellis.

Harvey also had something to communicate. "I had a talk with Freddie Vandam about it," said he.

"What did he say?" asked Montague.

"Well," replied the other, with a laugh, "he's indignant, needless to say. You know, Freddie was brought up by his father to regard the Fidelity as his property, in a way. He always refers to it as 'my company.' And he's very high and mighty about it — it's a personal affront if anyone attacks it. But it was evident to me that he doesn't know who's behind this case."

"Did he know about Ellis?" asked Montague.

"Yes," said the other, "he had found out that much. It was he who told me that originally. He says that Ellis has been sponging off the company for years — he has a big salary that he never earns, and has borrowed something like a quarter of a million dollars on worthless securities."

Montague gave a gasp.

"Yes," laughed Harvey. "But after all, that's a little matter. The trouble with Freddie Vandam is that that sort of thing is all he sees; and so he'll never be able to make out the mystery. He knows that this clique or that in the company is plotting to get some advantage, or to use him for their purposes — but he never realizes how the big men are pulling the wires behind the scenes. Some day they'll throw him overboard altogether, and then he'll realize how they've played with him. That's what this Hasbrook case means, you know — they simply want to frighten him with a threat of getting the company's affairs into the courts and the newspapers."

Montague sat for a while in deep thought.

"What would you think would be Wyman's relation to the matter?" he asked, at last.

"I wouldn't know," said Harvey. "He's supposed to be Freddie's backer — but what can you tell in such a tangle?"

"It is certainly a mess," said Montague.

"There's no bottom to it," said the other. "Absolutely — it would take your breath away! Just listen to what Vandain told me today!"

And then Harvey named one of the directors of the Fidelity who was well known as a philanthropist. Having heard that the wife of one of his junior partners had met with an accident in childbirth, and that the doctor had told her husband that if she ever had another child, she would die, this man had asked, "Why don't you have her life insured?" The other replied that he had tried, and the companies had refused her. "I'll fix it for you," said he; and so they put in another application, and the director came to Freddie Vandam and had the policy put through "by executive order." Seven months later the woman died, and the Fidelity had paid her husband in full — a hundred thousand or two!

"That's what's going on in the insurance world!" said Siegfried Harvey.

And that was the story which Montague took with him to add to his enjoyment of the festivities at the country club. It was a very gorgeous affair; but perhaps the somberness of his thoughts was to blame; the flowers and music and beautiful gowns failed entirely in their appeal, and he saw only the gluttony and drunkenness — more of it than ever before, it seemed to him.

Then, too, he had an unpleasant experience. He met Laura Hegan; and presuming upon her cordial reception of his visit, he went up and spoke to her pleasantly. And she greeted him with frigid politeness; she was so brief in her remarks and turned away so abruptly as almost to snub him. He went away quite bewildered. But later on he recalled the gossip about himself and Mrs. Winnie, and he guessed that that was the explanation of Miss Hegar's action.

The episode threw a shadow over his whole visit. On Sunday he went out into the country and tramped through a snowstorm by himself, filled with a sense of disgust for all the past, and of foreboding for the future. He hated this money-world, in which all that was worst in human beings was brought to the surface; he hated it, and wished that he had never set foot within its bounds. It was only by tramping until he was too tired to feel anything that he was able to master himself.

— And then, toward dark, he came back, and found a telegram which had been forwarded from New York.

"Meet me at the Penna depot, Jersey City, at nine tonight. Alice."

This message, of course, drove all other thoughts from his mind. He had no time even to tell Oliver about it — he had to jump into an automobile and rush to catch the next train for the city. And all through the long, cold ride in ferry-boats and cabs he pondered this mystery. Alice's party had not been expected for two weeks yet; and only two days before there had come a letter from Los Angeles, saying that they would probably be a week over time. And here she was home again!

He found there was an express from the West due at the hour named; apparently, therefore, Alice had not come in the Prentice's train at all. The express was half an hour late, and so he paced up and down the platform, controlling his impatience as best he could. And finally the long train pulled in, and he saw Alice coming down the platform. She was alone!

"What does it mean?" were the first words he said to her.

"It's a long story," she answered. "I wanted to come home.";

"You mean you've come all the way from the coast by yourself!" he gasped.

"Yes," she said, "all the way."

"What in the world —" he began.

"I can't tell you here, Allan," she said. "Wait till we get to some quiet place."

"But," he persisted. "The Prentice? They let you come home alone?"

"They didn't know it," she said. "I ran away."

He was more bewildered than ever. But as he started to ask more questions, she laid a hand upon his arm. "Please wait, Allan," she said. "It upsets me to talk about it. It was Charlie Carter."

And so the light broke. He caught his breath and gasped, "Oh!"

He said not another word until they had crossed the ferry and settled themselves in a cab, and started. "Now," he said, "tell me."

Alice began. "I was very much upset," she said. "But you must understand, Allan, that I've had nearly a week to think it over, and I don't mind it now. So I want you please not to get excited about it; it wasn't poor Charlie's fault — he can't help himself. It was my mistake. I ought to have taken your advice and had nothing to do with him."

"Go on," said he; and Alice told her story.

The party had gone sight-seeing, and she had had a headache and had stayed in the car. And Charlie Carter had come and begun making love to her. "He had asked me to marry him already — that was at the beginning of the trip," she said. "And I told him no. After that he would never let me alone. And this time he went on in a terrible way — he flung himself down on his knees, and wept, and said he couldn't live without me. And nothing I could say did any good. At last he — he caught hold of me — and he wouldn't let me go. I was furious with him, and frightened. I had to threaten to call for help before he would stop. And so — you see how it was."

"I see," said Montague, gravely. "Go on."

"Well, after that I made up my mind that I couldn't stay anywhere where I had to see him. And I knew he would never go away without a scene. If I had asked Mrs. Prentice to send him away, there would have been a scandal, and it would have spoiled everybody's trip. So I went out, and found there was a train for the East in a little while, and I packed up my things, and left a note for Mrs. Prentice. I told her a story — I said I'd had a telegram that your mother was ill, and that I didn't want to spoil their good time, and had gone by myself. That was the best thing I could think of. I wasn't afraid to travel, so long as I was sure that Charlie couldn't catch up with me."

Montague said nothing; he sat with his hands gripped tightly.

"It seemed like a desperate thing to do," said Alice, nervously. "But you see, I was upset and unhappy. I didn't seem to like the party anymore — I wanted to be home. Do you understand?"

"Yes," said Montague, "I understand. And I'm glad you are here."

They reached home, and Montague called up Harvey's and told his brother what had happened. He could hear Oliver gasp with astonishment. "That's a pretty how-do-you-do!" he said, when he had got his breath back; and then he added, with a laugh, "I suppose that settles poor Charlie's chances."

"I'm glad you've come to that conclusion," said the other, as he hung up the receiver.

This episode gave Montague quite a shock. But he had little time to think about it — the next morning at eleven o'clock his case was to come up for trial, and so all his thoughts were called away. This case had been the one real interest of his life for the last three months; it was his purpose, the thing for the sake of which he endured everything else that repelled him. And he had trained himself as an athlete for a great race; he was in form, and ready for the effort of his life. He went down town that morning with every fiber of him, body and mind, alert and eager; and he went into his office, and in his mail was a letter from Mr. Hasbrook. He opened it hastily and read a message, brief and direct and decisive as a sword-thrust:

"I beg to inform you that I have received a satisfactory proposition from the Fidelity Company. I have settled with them, and wish to withdraw the suit. Thanking you for your services, I remain, sincerely."

To Montague the thing came like a thunderbolt. He sat utterly dumbfounded — his hands went limp, and the letter fell upon the desk in front of him.

And at last, when he did move, he picked up the telephone, and told his secretary to call up Mr. Hasbrook. Then he sat waiting; and when the bell rang, picked up the receiver, expecting to hear Mr. Hasbrook's voice, and to demand an explanation. But he heard, instead, the voice of his own secretary: "Central says the number's been discontinued, sir."

And he hung up the receiver, and sat motionless again. The dummy had disappeared!

To Montague this incident meant a change in the prospect of his whole life. It was the collapse of all his hopes. He had nothing more to work for, nothing more to think about; the bottom had fallen out of his career!

He was burning with a sense of outrage. He had been tricked and made a fool of; he had been used and flung aside. And now there was nothing he could do — he was utterly helpless. What affected him most was his sense of the overwhelming magnitude of the powers which had made him their puppet; of the utter futility of the efforts that he or any other man could make against them. They were like elemental, cosmic forces; they held all the world in their grip, and a common man was as much at their mercy as a bit of chaff in a tempest.

All day long he sat in his office, brooding and nursing his wrath. He had moods when he wished to drop everything, to shake the dust of the city from his feet, and go back home and recollect what it was to be a gentleman. And then again he had righting moods, when he wished to devote all his life to punishing the men who had made use of him. He would get hold of some other policy-holder in the Fidelity, one whom he could trust; he would take the case without pay, and carry it through to the end! He would force the newspapers to talk about it — he would force the people to heed what he said!

And then, toward evening, he went homo, bitter and sore. And there was his brother sitting in his study, waiting for him.

"Hello," he said, and took off his coat, preparing his mind for one more ignominy — the telling of his misfortune to Oliver, and listening to his inevitable, "I told you so."

But Oliver himself had something to communicate something that would not bear keeping. He broke out at once — "Tell me, Allan! What in the world has happened between you and Mrs. Winnie?"

"What do you mean?" asked Montague, sharply.

"Why," said Oliver, "everybody is talking about some kind of a quarrel."

"There has been no quarrel," said Montague.

"Well, what is it, then?"

"It's nothing."

"It must be something!" exclaimed Oliver. "What do all the stories mean?"

"What stories?"

"About you two. I met Mrs. Vivie Patton just now, and she swore me to secrecy, and told me that Mrs. Winnie had told someone that you had made love to her so outrageously that she had to ask you to leave the house."

Montague shrunk as from a blow. "Oh!" he gasped.

"That's what she said," said he.

"It's a lie!" he cried.

"That's what I told Mrs. Vivie," said the other; "it doesn't sound like you —"

Montague had flushed scarlet. "I don't mean that!" he cried. "I mean that Mrs. Winnie never said any such thing."

"Oh," said Oliver, and he shrugged his shoulders. "Maybe not," he added. "But I know she's furious with you about something — everybody's talking about it. She tells people that she'll never speak to you again. And what I want to know is, why is it that you have to do things to make enemies of everybody you know?"

Montague said nothing; he was trembling with anger.

"What in the world did you do to her?" began the other. "Can't you trust me — -"

And suddenly Montague sprang to his feet. "Oh, Oliver," he exclaimed, "let me alone! Go away!"

And he went into the next room and slammed the door, and began pacing back and forth like a caged animal.

It was a lie! It was a lie! Mrs. Winnie had never said such a thing! He would never believe it — it was a nasty piece of backstairs gossip!

But then a new burst of rage swept over him What did it matter Whether it was true or not — whether anything was true or not? What did it matter if anybody had done all the hideous and loathsome things that everybody else said they had done? It was what everybody was saying! It was what everybody believed — what everybody was interested in! It was the measure of a whole society — their ideals and their standards! It was the way they spent their time, repeating nasty scandals about each other; living in an atmosphere of suspicion and cynicism, with endless whispering and leering, and gossip of low intrigue.

A flood of rage surged up within him, and swept him, away — rage against the world into which he had come, and against himself for the part he had played in it. Everything seemed to have come to a head at once; and he hated everything — hated the people he had met, and the things they did, and the things they had tempted him to do. He hated the way he had got his money, and the way he had spent it. He hated the idleness and wastefulness, the drunkenness and debauchery, the meanness and the snobbishness.

And suddenly he turned and flung open the door of the room where Oliver still sat. And he stood in the doorway, exclaiming, "Oliver, I'm done with it!"

Oliver stared at him. "What do you mean?" he asked.

"I mean," cried his brother, "that I've had all I can stand of 'Society!' And I'm going to quit. You can go on — but I don't intend to take another step with you! I've had enough — and I think Alice has had enough, also. We'll take ourselves off your hands — we'll get out!"

"What are you going to do?" gasped Oliver.

"I'm going to give up these expensive apartments — give them up tomorrow, when our week is up. And I'm going to stop squandering money for things I don't want. I'm going to stop accepting invitations, and meeting people I don't like and don't want to know. I've tried your game — I've tried it hard, and I don't like it; and I'm going to get out before it's too late. I'm going to find some decent and simple place to live in; and I'm going down town to find out if there isn't some way in New York for a man to earn an honest living!"

THE END

Printed in the United States
127428LV00002B/94-159/A